BETWEEN TWO EVILS

LYNNE STEVIE

Nick and Chris

Stay sweet and keep reading!

.

ACKNOWLEDGEMENTS:

I want to say a big thank you to Traci Hohenstein for her support and advice. Plus, thanks for making me take chances and come out of my shell from time to time. Thanks to T.J. Loveless and Jacqueline M. Rhoades for reading and helping with the really rough draft. Your advice was awesome. It was amazing to work with Sherri Butler Photography on the cover, plus a special thanks goes out to Stephanie Getts for allowing me to use your image as my cover model. A big shout out to all my friends in the Indie Marketing Group. I couldn't ask for a better group of writers to be friends with. Your support and advice is always appreciated. Kay Keppler, editor extraordinaire, please, please don't ever retire. I love your no nonsense approach and I wouldn't want to release a novel without your feedback!

I'm extremely grateful to my family. Mom, Dad, Sophia, Chris, Nick and everyone who encourages me to be just who I am. They are my proof readers (that's you mom) and my cheerleaders (that's you too mom!). I love you all. Lastly and most importantly, I must thank my husband Chris for always believing in me, putting up with my craziness and for bringing me tea and cookies.

Other Titles by Lynne Stevie

ANGELS KISS a Dark Angels Novel

BETWEEN
TWO EVILS

"Covetousness is the greatest of monsters, as well as the root of all evil."

William Penn

BETWEEN TWO EVILS

PROLOGUE

Mountains of Wallachia, Romania 1829

The relentless wind caused the thick animal hides to pound against the old wooden frames of the bender tents creating a sound like thunder crashing against the mountainside. However, what kept every member of the Roma clan of gypsies awake wasn't the thunder of the hides, but the screams of the young girl in labor.

The gypsies had huddled their small caravan in a deep shelf of the rough mountain face when the girl went into labor on the journey between camps. The worn bender tent the young girl called home was joined with others to create an area large enough for the midwives to attend her as she fought to give birth.

"Mother," Nya whispered through sweat and tears.

"Yes, child." Inez held her daughter's delicate hand as the midwives shook their heads and whispered in low tones. For two days Inez had listened to the midwives talk about the babe and watched as her daughter suffered. The child she labored with was killing her, and yet Nya wouldn't let them remove it.

"Protect him." Panting through the pain, her beautiful daughter, at only fourteen, was but a child herself. Nevertheless, in this unforgiving land, her daughter's wisdom and sorrow had long ago surpassed her age. Nya's exquisite face, now twisted in agony, and her magical abilities, least of which was knowing the sex of the babe before it was born, were what got her in this situation in the first place.

"Child." Inez shook her head and brushed the dark locks of hair from Nya's sweat-stained face. She remembered the day eight months ago when her only daughter crawled home torn and beaten. Nya had been out gathering herbs for the medicines and spells Inez sold to the others of their tribe and to the Boyars, the rich land owners of Romania. She begged Nya to tell her who'd attacked her. Together they had the power to destroy any living creature who dared to hurt them. But it was no living creature who'd brutalized her beautiful daughter—and soon that vile being would

1

have an heir.

"Please let me save you," Inez begged.

"No!" Nya's strangled scream echoed through the thin walls of the caravan. "Leave us." she yelled at the women who had turned toward the mattress in the corner where Nya was laid out.

"Nya, please, it's killin' you!" Inez tried again to get her daughter to see reason.

"Leave us!" Nya screamed again through her agony. Inez shook her head and watched as the women went out into the night.

"Mother, you must protect him!"

"Why would I protect this…evil?" Sickened, Inez walked to the opening of the caravan. The midwives were crying to the tribe elders, and the men were arming themselves with their knives and short swords. Inez turned away from the horde.

"Nya, the elders know of its wickedness just as I do." Inez knelt by her beautiful daughter and grabbed her hand. "They'll not let it live. Let me save you."

"I've seen him." Nya's eyes were glassy with the coming of her death. "His name is Zev." Her voice was feather light. "He will be powerful and…" Nya ran her other hand over her grossly distended belly. "…there is evil in him."

Nya pulled her mother forward, surprising her with her strength.

"Mother, listen to me," Nya whispered. "He'll save our blood line. Please, take him to the Prince, I beg you."

"Nya, sweet child, Alexandru II won't care about a Roma child. We're peasants and drifters. The Prince…"

"No!" Nya shook her head. "*The Prince*, Mother."

Inez gasped and tried to pull her hand away. "No, Nya, no!"

"Our family has served him well for hundreds of years. Zev will be invaluable to him."

Nya squeezed Inez's hand and waited until she looked into her eyes before continuing.

"Tell the Prince…tell him that one day Zev will take the Prince's heart after a great battle, yet the Prince will be relieved to release it to him." Nya took a deep breath.

"Momma, do you understand? The Prince will be comforted to release his heart to Zev for protection."

"Nya, that makes no sense. Shh…." Inez dampened a cloth for

2

her daughter's feverish face.

"Mother, promise me. I have seen it. You must protect him. You and I are the last of our people. Zev will be more powerful than both of us, and he will increase the Gana."

"Hush. Don't speak her name." Inez lowered her head and searched the room to be sure they were still alone. The Gana was their name for Dina. The Queen of the witches, or czarownica, as the Roma people called them. If anyone in the tribe heard Nya speak of witchcraft, the elders could kill them both.

"Promise me!"

A scream broke from Nya's body before Inez could answer. It was as if the girl had been holding it and she simply could not contain it any longer. The midwives rushed back and began pulling the babe out of Inez's now-silent daughter. The boy came feet first, and the seasoned midwife's hands shook as if this were her first birthing rather than her hundredth. Inez watched her daughter exhale her last breath as the thing was finally ripped free.

"Nya…" She placed her head next to her daughter's and wept. "My Nya…" But the girl was still. Her long, raven hair framed her sweat-covered face, and her beautiful hazel eyes were frozen in death.

He came into the world with a roar instead of a wail. His thunderous cry echoed off the rock walls surrounding their camp. He had dark, curly ringlets, ten little toes, and ten little fingers. The child looked perfect. But as the midwife wiped his face with a thin, clean cloth, she saw his black eyes.

It was a monster. The prophecy said that an evil born of a czarownica would destroy their clan. Minneura knew what she had to do. Turning her back on Inez and her dead daughter, she placed the cloth over the babe's mouth and nose. The boy struggled with unnatural rage, and the black of his eyes expanded until she could see no whites at all.

The old midwife might have succeeded in killing the infant if she had not been drawn back to his dark eyes. Once her gazed stopped on them she was enthralled. She released her hold on the infant's face and turned to face Inez and the elders who had gathered to view the birth. Minneura's eyes were as black as the infant's, and tears of blood ran down her wrinkled cheeks. She held the child up to the crowd.

3

"I am Zev, the son of Ravana and descendant of Gana." Minneura's mouth was moving, but it was the deep voice of a man that the elders heard.

The gathered crowd hissed and shrank back at the mention of the names. The old midwife wrapped the cloth around the infant and tucked the baby up against her chest. She winced as she gently patted his back.

"I have waited for this time to be reborn and I will not be denied," she continued in the same deep tone. The old woman swayed soothingly and continued to pat the child on the back. She looked down lovingly at the boy as if he were her own child.

Inez pushed away from her daughter's deathbed. Hunched over from the grief that lay hot in her stomach, she approached the midwife. The elders separated to let her pass. She knew what had to be done. No matter what she'd promised her daughter or what her daughter had foreseen of the future, this evil must not be allowed to grow. They all knew of the prophecy. The baby must be destroyed before it killed the whole tribe.

"Minneura, give it to me." Inez held her arms out for the bundle.

Inez took a step back when the midwife raised her head, her eyes as dull as the soot of a long-dead fire. She forced herself to reach for the babe again. The old midwife wouldn't release it. When she tugged, Minneura moved with the bundle.

Inez stared at her and watched as Minneura's eyes went back to the washed-out blue she'd been born with. As soon as the color returned, the midwife released her hold on the babe and pushed the child away. The rounded bodice of her blouse showed why she'd winced. A trickle of blood from a small wound oozed down between her breasts. The woman backed away and then collapsed. She touched the spot on her chest and then stared at her bloody fingers in confusion.

"Minneura." Inez started toward the old woman and then stopped when the bundle in her arms moved. Out of habit she'd tucked the thing against her body. Disgusted with herself, she pulled it away and moved toward the waiting elders, glancing down for just a moment.

Inez froze as did everyone in the room.

The babe was smiling up at her and cooing softly. Inez could see her daughter Nya in the child, mixed with the wild power of nature and the earth. His dark ringlets caressed his rosy cheeks and fell around his large eyes that softened to a hazel color as she watched. They looked so much like Nya's—the brown of rich mountain soil surrounding a ring of green as welcoming as the tall grass that grows in the spring. Inez was captivated by the child until she noticed his smile. His mouth was full of perfect tiny teeth still bloody from his feeding.

She shivered. The enchantment broken, she moved again toward the elders.

"*Protect me as you promised.*" The voice she heard was not evil, but childlike and compelling.

"Did you hear him?" Inez stopped and looked to the others huddled around her daughter's dead body. Every one of them shook their heads and backed away from her as much as possible in the cramped space. She looked back down at the tiny baby when he grabbed a lock of her hair and tangled it in his chubby fingers.

Inez raised her eyes to the gathered crowd and saw them clearly for the first time. It wasn't just the child they were afraid of. She could feel their hatred and fear as their eyes bore down on her as well.

She'd often wondered about her fellow Roma's attitude toward her and her daughter, especially when Nya came of age and no man stepped forward to wed her. As beautiful as she was, she should have had many suitors, but she'd had none. Inez had fooled herself into believing it was because Nya had no dowry to offer a husband, as the girls with fathers had. The truth was painful, but she understood now. Their link to the Gana, their lineage to powerful magic, had driven suitors away from her beautiful daughter. As the knot of anguish grew in her stomach, a fierce anger began to heat her blood.

A breeze swept through the caravan of tents, gently moving Inez's skirts and the child's ringlets. The baby gurgled happily at the sensation. Inez's gaze fell upon her daughter. None of her fellow midwives had moved to cover her battered body.

"Give it to us," Rankin, the leader of the tribe, called to her. "You know what must be done."

As he approached, the gentle breeze picked up. The gust carried the whispers of the men and women outside to her ears.

Whispers of immortal witches and fire, whispers of panic and the perversion of all magic.

Inez looked up at Rankin and he stopped his approach. "You're sickened by the power we hold, and yet you've used us for generations," she said. "We've aided your tribe, but we've never been a part of it." Outside, the horses stomped and pulled at their bindings, and the dogs barked as the gusts turned into a fierce wind. The voices of the tribe members rose as they tried to calm the animals.

Stupid humans. They should listen to the animals. They always know when a storm's ah comin'. Inez smiled down at the boy in her arms.

"You are a part of us, Inez. That's why we must kill this evil to save us all." Rankin reached to take the baby as the first of the caravan's hides blew off.

Inez clutched the child and looked up into the large man's face.

"Your hatred and fear 'ill kill you long before this child reaches his first birthday." Inez held the child tighter and called upon the earth for power. Mother earth answered her call, and lightning struck outside the caravan.

"You'll leave us now, I must attend to my daughter and my grandchild."

"Look what it did to Minneura. It bit her and ate her blood!" Rankin yelled above the howl of the wind. "It is treacherous and needs to be destroyed. Give it to us!"

Inez looked down at the child and saw her daughter's eyes reflected in the tiny face. It was true the boy had bitten the old woman and obviously would need blood to survive, but the child also had the goodness of its mother. She held him tighter.

"Zev is both good and evil," she said. "What man or woman doesn't have the power of both inside? It is what we choose to do that defines what we are."

Inez stepped forward, forcing Rankin to move back.

"Now, leave me. You and the rest would be safer in the village. You should pack up and go there now."

Another lightning strike lit up the darkness, and screams echoed outside the caravan. The women pulled the men outside to help the others secure the animals and pack up the camp. Inez was tired to her soul, but she had work to do. She'd prepare her daughter for her return to mother earth, and then she'd do as her daughter wished and take Zev to The Prince for protection.

The wind in the caravan was no more than a slight breeze, but the intensity of her anger and the storm outside was rising. The tempest would be enough to make the tribe flee, but she didn't fool herself into thinking they would leave her and the baby alive for long. If she stayed, they would return to kill them in their sleep.

So tonight she would not sleep. Tonight, she and the babe must escape.

Of course, she would never reveal her daughter's prophecy to The Prince. He would never save the child or her if he knew. But with her talents, and the power she felt growing inside the baby, they could be of service to him.

That was the key to their safety. That was how they'd gain protection from Vlad Dracula, The Prince of Darkness.

LYNNE STEVIE

CHAPTER ONE

Present Day Romania

Trembling Hands

"Thank you all for a lovely evening." Lavanya addressed her eight guests assembled in the formal parlor as the fire crackled in the twelve-foot-wide stone fireplace. "I'm excited for the weekend and happy all of you could visit my family home, Poenari Castle, here in Romania. I know you've traveled many nights to be here, and I'm sure you're anxious to get settled in."

Lavanya stepped away from the warmth of the fire and threw open the huge double doors leading to the hall.

"Your rooms are ready. Alex will guide you, and your servants are waiting to help you prepare for your daytime rest." Lavanya held her hand out and Alex appeared at the door, ready to lead the way. Several of the men helped the ladies to their feet as they all prepared to head below the castle to their rooms. Formal "good days" were heard as they all made their way to the grand staircase. Lavanya winked at Tru, her American friend, as she left arm-in-arm with the tall, dark, and handsome Naasir.

Lovely... One couple had made a connection, only three to go.

Smiling she thanked the servants as they filed into the parlor and began cleaning and preparing for the next evening's events. Despite her ease with her guests, she was in desperate need of a nightcap. Lavanya didn't normally entertain at Poenari Castle—in fact, she hadn't been here in almost twenty years—and her return to her father's home was making her anxious. But these couples were special, and the castle was the most convenient location for the attendees.

Lavanya's tense shoulders relaxed as she entered her suite. She loved her rooms in the castle. The wall sconces and oriental paper lanterns were dimmed now as the night ended, and the blood-red candles in the candelabras cast a warm glow on the deep green walls. The deep green color always made her feel as if she were in the rain forest, and it perfectly matched a forest green Burberry dress that she adored.

"Decorate using the colors you look good in, right?" she murmured, quoting Sergio, her decorator. The candlelight's glow against the mirrors and silver threw off sparks like rain drops falling through the moonlight. Even the dark, polished stone floor shone like the Black Sea at midnight.

A sad smile tilted the corners of her mouth a fraction. She missed Sergio as if he'd passed away only last week, not more than fifteen years ago.

Lavanya went into her dressing room, carefully removed her gown, and draped it over her vanity chair. Then she slipped on a heavy silk robe and sat at her 1940s mirrored vanity to take off her makeup. A light rap on the door alerted her to Chloe's arrival, forcing her back into the here and now.

"Come in, Chloe."

Lavanya scooped out a dollop of cold cream from the beautiful antique jar and smiled in earnest at the frivolity that came with wealth. Her assistant regularly refilled the antique glass jar and discarded the newer plastic container the cream came in now. Still smiling she smoothed it onto her face, enjoying the contrast between her dark red nails and the white paste that matched her complexion. Her skin was the color of fresh milk and as cold and smooth as the black stone floors under her feet. Set against the white background of her skin and cold cream, her deep violet eyes were shocking even to her. Immortality amped up everyone's natural attributes; however, since she was born into this life, her appearance and strengths were more pronounced than someone who was "revamped," or turned into a vampire. Of course, she'd received good genes from her mother, a stunning movie star, arguably one of the most beautiful women of all time. Plus, her father was the king of the undead—Vlad III, Dracula himself.

She knew little about her parents. She couldn't claim the talented actress as her mother, even though she'd passed on now, because the humans didn't know about vampires. The rift between the vampire world and the human world was wide. Vampires were still in the dark, so to speak. Her mother had been forced to give her up at birth for her own protection as much as the need to keep the existence of vampires a secret.

"Mistress Lavanya," Chloe's soft voice whispered from the master suite.

"Chloe, please place the tray by the bed. I'm almost finished in here."

No matter how hard Lavanya tried, she couldn't break Chloe from using the formal title. Although Lavanya couldn't see Chloe, her personal maid, she knew she'd be carrying a huge silver tray with her daily absinthe cocktail. Lavanya's mouth watered as the earthy herbal scent of the cocktail reached her. Absinthe was an indulgence she adored. She loved to drip the ice-cold water over the sugar cube and watch the spirit froth up in the glass. Anticipation made her work the paste into her skin more quickly.

Removing the last of the cold cream with a tissue, she absently checked her new polish, Bastille My Heart by Opi. It had been perfect tonight with the silver gown, and it still looked good. She reached next for her lotion and then applied the Le Mer body crème to her hands and feet. In this cold, drafty castle, staying hydrated was a full-time job.

The chime of a crystal decanter and the crinkle of paper alerted Lavanya that Chloe had brought the household reports as well as her nightcap. Eight immortals and their entourages were visiting the castle this weekend, and several would no doubt make special requests. As hostess, she must make every attempt to fulfill their needs. She had confidence in the staff here at the castle, and she'd done some background work on the individuals to anticipate their needs. However, reviewing the daily activities and attending to any problems right away was always a good idea.

Ready for her cocktail, she rose and passed through the double doors that separated her dressing room from her bedroom. Chloe looked up and smiled at her. Lavanya noticed a slight shake in the maid's hands as she adjusted the silk coverlet on the iron bed, but she dismissed it as nerves caused by the full house at the moment. Then she glanced toward the balcony.

The moon was almost full, and the doors framed it perfectly. The wilderness looked fierce even from this distance. Her father's castle fortress sat on a mountain peak just east of the Arefu commune and the people he loved. It was extremely remote, and she could never get used to the quietness of the nights here.

Born of both vampire and human, Lavanya had the best of

both worlds. She could move freely through the human world when most vampires were still forced to keep to the shadows. Although her skin burned easily if exposed for long periods, the sun wouldn't kill her. Because of that, her rooms were at the top of the castle with a wide expanse of balcony looking out over the jagged mountains and the Arges River valley. Best of all with her vampire enhanced eyesight she was able to take in all the beauty even from this distance with only the moon to light the sky. For better or worse, she was an anomaly; she'd never met another who was born into this life. No one really knew how her mother managed to carry her to full term. But here she was.

A shiver went through Lavanya, and of course Chloe noticed.

"Mistress."

"Chloe, start a fire for me, please." *Damned old castle*. Even though it was technically summer here in Romania, it was cold.

"I'm freezing in this drafty place, and a fire would feel lovely. Besides, I think I'll sit for a while and go over the reports before retiring."

"Yes, Mistress." Chloe nodded, went to the sitting area, and lit the fire. Watching Chloe prepare the room for her reminded Lavanya of the night she'd decided to move out of the castle and start her own life.

Her father had been fast asleep in his hidden crypt when she ventured into her parents' wing of the castle those many years ago. Renfield, her father's servant, had warned her not to go there, but he was away and she was desperate to know more about her mother, who had been dead for years.

Vlad obviously had loved and doted on his wife. As per his instructions, their rooms had been kept exactly as they were when her mother, Eva Maria, died. All her pictures still hung on the walls and even her jewelry was still on her dressing table where she'd taken it off the night before she died. Diamonds of all shapes and sizes—and one of the biggest rubies Lavanya had ever seen— sat as if her mother were just down the hall and would be back at any moment. Her slippers still sat on her side of the big iron bed, ready for her to slip on and go about her evening.

She'd spent only a few moments running her fingers through the clothing and smelling her mother's perfume before she'd burst into tears. Lavanya couldn't understand why her father hadn't given her mother the gift of immortality and yet kept all her belongings as if she were coming back. One of the maids found her and helped her back to her suite. That night she decided to leave the castle and start her own life. She couldn't live in the past. With her father and mother both gone she had nothing to tie her to the castle or the land. She chose America and the city of Miami as her new home for its warmth and color.

Just then a chill ran up her back, as if the castle knew she didn't like it and was playing with her. She pulled her dressing gown tighter. Lavanya refused to allow this place to spook her—she wasn't a child having a bad dream. Although, by vampire standards, she was still a child.

Lavanya took a seat on her favorite silver velvet chaise and gracefully bundled her long, soft beige, silk dressing gown under her legs. Of course, as soon as her bottom hit the cushioned seat, her little Chihuahua, Buttercup, made her presence known by jumping into her lap.

"Hello, my sweet."

Lavanya nuzzled Buttercup's neck and rubbed her soft fur. At three and one-half pounds, the dog was a tiny creature, but her size was of little importance. She had the heart of a warrior. Her fur might be graying, but she regularly chased the wolf hounds that guarded the property out of the house. The bit of gray fur at the nape of Buttercup's neck reminded Lavanya that her own body seemed to be stuck at around twenty-five, although she was over seventy five in human years.

Buttercup spread out on Lavanya's chest and stretched for a moment. But before long she shivered and circled until Lavanya placed a large fur throw around her and then over her head to create a nest.

Having the little dog with her helped to alleviate her homesickness. She missed her friends, her home, and her city. Although her full name was Lavanya Draculesti, most of her human friends knew her as Anya Ulesti. She easily portrayed an eccentric art house, trust fund baby, who enjoyed driving around in a 1939 Chrysler New Yorker. She really did love art deco and her Chrysler New Yorker, but not because she liked vintage cars. She liked them because that's what she grew up with in the 1940s and 1950s. For now, she could get away with the charade, but soon it

13

would be time to reinvent herself again if she wanted to maintain some connection to the human world. Even as she savored every new technology, she was finding it hard to give up the style and culture of her youth.

Tonight she missed the oppressive heat of Miami and the sounds of the eccentric people who populated its streets. The wonderful art deco revival and passion of the Latin people made the city colorful and vibrant to every sense. If only she could hear the cutting sound of the palm trees waving in the ocean breeze, she'd feel better.

"Okay, enough of this boo-hoo crap," she told herself. She'd be home in a few weeks and nothing could be gained by feeling sorry for herself now. She'd come back here, into her father's territory, for the party she was hosting. Her father sparked such controversy, and yet the people of his homeland were deathly loyal to him—even to this day. Although it was difficult sometimes, she was glad to be his daughter. And besides, business was business, and his name alone guaranteed that their kind—new and old— would flock to see his castle and her.

She wondered for the thousandth time what her father would think about how she spent her time and the career she'd chosen. He'd been asleep for so long she could no longer even guess what he would say about Count on Love, the world's only vampire dating service. But the business was her creation, and its success her biggest joy.

Lavanya had known there was a need for an undead matchmaking service, but she'd had no idea how many immortals would come out of the coffin to use it. Most vampires were solitary creatures, and immortality gave them a vast amount of time to cultivate some seriously eccentric behaviors. Neither attribute made it easy for a vampire to meet a mate, hence the reason for the party tonight.

She'd had eight clients that needed to get acquainted, and her father's castle was the most central location with a plentiful and willing supply of food. Vampires didn't need to eat every day, but they tended to get ill-tempered if unfed for too long. Willing donors were a must. Plus, a weekend in the mountains would help the couples get to know each other away from their own territories, which was crucial. Because the castle was neutral ground, no one would worry about protecting their own turf. They could relax and learn about each other, physically and intellectually.

If the body language she'd observed tonight could be believed, she'd just made four more successful match-mate connections. Her accountant would be extremely happy, but she felt exhausted.

The matching part was easy for her. She knew within the first few moments of meeting someone what type of mate they should have. It was a gift that she'd managed to capitalize on. Her father was psychic and could control others through his thoughts, but her talent lay more in knowing what others secretly desired. The hard part was putting on the professional persona of Lavanya Draculesti, the only born vampire and descendant of the original Vlad III Tepes—The Impaler.

The slight tinkling of the silver spoon hitting the glass brought Lavanya's attention back to Chloe as she constructed Lavanya's cocktail. Lavanya watched the young woman's hand shake slightly as she tried to balance the sugar cube on the small spoon.

"Chloe, is something wrong?"

"Mistress, no ma'am, there's no problem." Her hand steadied.

Although Lavanya could see the strain of containing the tremor on the young woman's face, she decided a change of subject might ease Chloe. "Are the couples retiring for the day?"

"Yes, ma'am, their servants are tucking them in now." She fidgeted with the silver pitcher on the mirrored night table, busying herself by rearranging things.

Lavanya flipped through her nightly report. As the fire sparked to life, the room took on the glow of polished silver. The crystal chandelier blazed with a rainbow of color, and the iron bed, with its tufted headboard of gray silk surrounding a cameo-shaped mirror, beckoned her to sleep. The shirred silver fabric on the canopy above the huge king-size bed looked thick and cozy. Funny, as Lavanya looked on her design now, she could see how it resembled the opulent pillowy finish of the inside of a modern coffin. That had not been her intention, but that's exactly what it looked like to her now.

She turned her attention back to the reports from the staff. No trouble so far, for which she was thankful. She'd been a little worried at first that the guest's servants wouldn't get along. Luckily, they seemed to have gotten situated and were adapting to the schedule quite nicely.

A small, devious smile lit her face as she wondered how many of the servants would couple this weekend. As long as their activities didn't interfere with her clients' ability to relax and get to know the mate she chose for them, she didn't mind. The servants could have some fun, too.

It was fascinating to see the servants and confidants the vampires chose. Servants held a place of authority in the vampire world because they were a vampires' main connection with the human world. Most vampires chose a personal servant very carefully, not only for their discretion—because a vampire's indiscretions could be complex and dangerous—but for their opinions, as well. In return for loyal service, vampires prolonged their servants' lives and aided them—and their families— monetarily. Lavanya hoped that each servant liked the mate she chose for their master or mistress.

Lavanya had confidence in her choices for mates in all four cases, but she was worried about one couple in particular. Raziya Afolayan was a gorgeous African woman with a beautiful head of dark caramel curls that framed a sweet smile. Raz's warm smile and her compact stature were a perfect fit for Uki Akiyama, the Asian beauty. Because Uki was only four feet nine inches, finding a mate for her who wouldn't make her feel inferior in size was difficult. And Lavanya didn't want Uki to be dwarfed or feel overpowered by a mate.

But size was not Lavanya's biggest concern for the couple. Neither of the women had specifically asked for a same sex partner. On the up side, neither had said that they wouldn't consider another woman. When she'd met Uki in Tokyo and felt her quiet strength, Lavanya just knew that Raz would be perfect for her.

Of course, she'd discussed this with both women before this weekend. Uki had been hesitant at first, but after corresponding with Raz for several months, she agreed to come and meet Raz. Raz herself couldn't be happier, because in her youth she had dabbled in lesbian relationships.

Lavanya shivered again and pulled the fur throw closer, dragging her thoughts back to the report in front of her. Chloe noticed the shiver as she brought the absinthe to Lavanya. She sat the small glass and saucer down beside the chaise and then knelt in front of her mistress.

"You're chilled because you've not eaten in days." Chloe tilted her head, exposing the long line of her neck and the large artery that pulsed with life.

The smell of Chloe's skin was intoxicating, salty and sweet, as she offered herself up as dinner. Lavanya hated using humans as food, but there was no way around it. Vampires needed fresh human blood to sustain them. No blood bank or animal substitute would do. She'd tried everything, hoping that her unique genetic makeup would allow her some way out of the feedings, but in this way she was just like any other vampire. Lavanya held the craving at bay and tilted Chloe's head back upright so she could face her.

"How long has your family served my father?" Lavanya liked Chloe and she could never understand the willingness of some to be used so easily.

"Mistress, you misunderstand. It is your father the Count who has taken care of my family for generations. It is my honor to serve you now." Placing her hand over Lavanya's where it rested on her chin, she tilted again to give her a place to attack.

Lavanya's mind raced with need and her lips quivered. As her fangs descended, Buttercup jumped to the floor and scooted under the bed.

Once her fangs came out, Lavanya couldn't stop. She pulled Chloe to her and growled as she tore into her neck. Her teeth punctured the vein, and the spurt of blood as it hit the back of her throat was hot and thick. At the first taste, Lavanya became animalistic. She moaned as she bit; her mouth opened wider, and her nails became stronger. They dug into Chloe's arms as she held her and greedily drank. It had been too long since she'd fed.

Lavanya clouded the woman's mind so she wouldn't feel the pain as she let the warm, thick syrup of life fill her stomach. She could feel her body energizing and refueling, restoring the sweetness of youth. Fine lines filled out, and her complexion smoothed to alabaster. She vibrated with energy as the blood strengthened her.

She wanted more of the decadent syrup. She wanted to drain the fountain completely. But she needed to be careful not to harm Chloe. That thought circled around behind the need. She relaxed her grip on the servant and filled her mind with a nice memory of sleep on a down-filled bed.

She wanted more, a lot more, but she forced her fangs to retract and licked over the wound—not the tiny pin pricks that humans like to imagine, but a gaping ragged bite as if an animal had gotten ahold of Chloe's neck. Her saliva would help heal the wound. In a matter of hours it would look like a human love mark, and by morning it would be just a little tan spot.

Please don't let me have taken too much. She pushed Chloe back, but continued to lick the wound clean and stop the bleeding. Slowly she allowed her to wake from the dream she'd given her.

"Chloe, are you feeling okay?" Lavanya gave Chloe's wound one last lash with her tongue and pulled back to look into her eyes.

"Yes," Chloe said with half-hooded eyes and a dreamy smile. She was still under her influence, so Lavanya decided to ask her a few more questions.

"Why were your hands shaking when you brought me my evening drink?"

"I'm frightened, Mistress."

"Why would you be frightened?" Lavanya brought Chloe closer and settled her on the chaise next to her. Out of the corner of her eye she noticed Buttercup coming out from her hiding place, now that Lavanya's fangs had retracted.

"Gram Helgaleena dreamt of a beast. She said it would come on the blue moon. Oh, but she told me not to bother you with it." The girl looked terrified.

"You're never a bother, dear." Lavanya stroked Chloe's hair, soothing her.

"Gram made me promise to stay close to you this week, Mistress."

"Of course, I will always protect you and your family, you know that. But then all who dwell here would protect you. Why did she want you to stay with me in particular?"

"She said, like your father, only you would be able to control this beast." Chloe seemed to wilt in Lavanya's arms. "I'm sorry. I'm very tired, Mistress."

"Of course you are, Chloe. I want you to wake now, and I don't want you to worry about any beast. Your grandmother is just superstitious. Go now and have some orange juice. Then retire to your chamber. You will wake tomorrow afternoon and be refreshed." Lavanya pulled Chloe's shirt collar back up and helped her to her feet.

Chloe seemed to stumble a little, but she woke. "Yes, Mistress. Is there anything else you desire?" She straightened, and as she adjusted her collar, her fingers played over the bite mark. She pretended not to notice.

"Chloe, I'm wonderful. Thank you for everything." Lavanya sat back to read her reports, and Buttercup chose that moment to take her seat next to her in the nest of fur. She gave the dog a little nuzzle, and Buttercup settled in.

"Thank you, Mistress. I'll see you next evening." Chloe nodded slightly and hurried from the room

Lavanya felt exhilarated as she went through the reports, but her mind was stuck on what Chloe had told her. With the sweet power of fresh human blood flowing through her, she wondered: *What kind of beast could be worse than us?*

LYNNE STEVIE

CHAPTER TWO

A Deal Must Be Fulfilled

"For Doomhammer! Your time has come!" The image on the screen screamed as the preview for Rage of the Firelands began. Modern technology wasn't really Zev's thing, but he was addicted to World of Warcraft.

WoW, beer, and junk food, how could his night get any better? He opened the huge bag of chips and twisted off the cap to his Klinskoye Svetloe beer. Shoving a handful of the salty chips into his mouth and wiping the crumbs on his jeans, he reached for the bag of peanut M&Ms next. He popped a couple in his mouth and sat the bag down next to his new Black Mamba gaming PC with the 23-inch 3D screen. Just being here in the tiny cabin again listening to the purr of the generator outside and the crackle of the fire helped sooth his restlessness.

"Yes!" Zev said as he picked up the wireless keyboard and signed on to the RP-PVP server. He rubbed his hands together and flexed his fingers as he prepared to battle.

And then the computer died and the lights went out.

"Shit!" Zev roared. The power failure plunged the small room into darkness. He picked up the keyboard, ready to hurl it into the rustic log wall, when he remembered it was brand new.

He set the keyboard back down and knocked over his beer, which spilled all over the floor.

"Damn it!" *Time to get the lights back on.*

Guided by the flickering light of the fire, Zev easily moved through the small cabin to the front door. The new generator was still roaring along, breaking up the silence of the frigid mountain. Zev stepped out into the icy wind to check it anyway. His shoulder-length dark hair, still damp from a shower, immediately froze in the cold, but the chill didn't bother Zev. He stomped across the porch and down around the cabin to the new Kipor generator. Snow had fallen steadily while he'd gotten settled today, and now a thick, white blanket covered the top of the new equipment. He brushed it off and checked all the connections. The generator seemed to be running perfectly.

So it wasn't the generator. Frustrated, he stomped through the deepening snow back to the front of the cabin. The wind whipped his hair, and heavy snowflakes swirled around him. He dusted the covered porch with new snow as he stamped it off his shoes and shook it out of his hair and off his body. When he stepped into the cabin, Zev had to close the door hard to keep out the voracious wind and flurries.

Great, now the fire's gone out. The fire had been roaring before he'd gone outside, but now not even the ashes glowed. The cabin was pitch black. Zev's brow furrowed. He made it inside only a few steps before he was stopped as if he'd been swept up by a huge ocean wave. The invisible tsunami jerked him off his feet, then rolled and beat him against the old wood floor. The force of it crushed him. He struggled to push it off or get out from under the weight of it, but it held every inch of his heavily muscled, six-foot-five frame pinned to the floor. And now—he felt the biting cold stinging his nose and face.

He couldn't breathe with the pressure on his chest, and his lungs burned as he tried to pull in air. He opened his mouth to shout, but he didn't have enough air in his lungs to make a sound.

The force pressing in on him was merciless and evil. As his lungs collapsed and his strength diminished, he felt his hair float around his face. The sensation reminded him again of a cold ocean wave and the way its dark blue water could lift you up or crush you under its force.

Zev tried to stay calm and locate who controlled this power, but all he could see was a dense black fog, like a black hole in space, swirling on the edges. He had excellent night vision, but this darkness seemed not just to block the light, but devour it. He feared that the assault would steal his vision and suffocate him, but he knew this mountain wilderness better than anywhere else on earth, and he tried to draw strength from the elements around him as his grandmother had taught him. Magic was her creed and she had passed on her knowledge and gifts to him. But the blackness that surrounded him cut off more than air to his lungs. The weight of it was total, and all he had to keep him company was the howl that begged to be freed from his chest.

"It is time to repay your debt to me." The cold, black weight whispered.

Shit. Zev knew from that one sentence that his time had come. Almost two hundred years ago, he'd received a favor. Now death had come to collect payment for it.

LYNNE STEVIE

CHAPTER THREE

Treasures

Lavanya shuffled into the kitchen nook still half asleep and shielding her eyes from the late day sun streaming in through the large windows. "Good afternoon, Renfield." Her raspy voice reminding her how tired she was. She hadn't slept well. Instead of resting she'd been running from imaginary beasts in her dreams. As she took her seat she could feel the cold all the way to her bones.

"Good day, dear."

After a long sigh she poured herself a steaming cup of coffee and reached for a large homemade cinnamon roll. She licked the sticky sugar off her fingers, but couldn't quite garner her usual enthusiasm for her favorite food. Instead she bundled her robe covered legs under her, cradled her coffee and looked out at the green covered mountains. Maybe the sun streaming in would warm her up some.

"Lavanya." She jumped a little in her seat.

"Yes."

"What's bothering you? You seem positively out of sorts this afternoon." He raised a brow over his newspaper. "You haven't touched your cinnamon roll—which, by the way, has no nutritional value at all."

He did so enjoy disparaging her food choices and scowling at her over his paper. She'd always hated that look. His salt-and-pepper hair gave him a parental appearance, and with his reading glasses lowered, he could look directly into her soul. Well, at least it always seemed like he could.

"Funny you should ask. Something Chloe said last night has been bothering me." She paused to take a bite of her cinnamon roll and make him wait. He was always telling her *it's the small pleasures in life that make it worth living.* And sweets were one of her small pleasures. She enjoyed eating and drinking human food, although it would never sustain her totally. She could eat meat and vegetables, but why force those on herself when it was the sweets she enjoyed?

Renfield frowned as he waited for her to continue.

"Helgaleena is frightening Chloe with stories of a beast—something to fear that only I or my father can control, and it's coming on the blue moon." Lavanya looked up to gauge his reaction, but as usual, behind his wire rim glasses his face was unreadable. "Do you have any idea what that might mean?"

"You know as well as I do that Helgaleena puts too much faith in her dreams, and she's always dreamed of monsters. Even as a child she was frightened of her own shadow." He pulled his paper back up and covered his face as he answered.

Lavanya reached over and pulled his paper down to get a look at his face. "Yes, I know Helgaleena well, she's practically my sister." Lavanya grew up with Chloe's grandmother Helgaleena. Velka, Helgaleena's mother, was the only mother she'd ever known. Because of her vampire tendencies she didn't spend much time with her real mother, but Velka understood and accepted Lavanya as she was. "I also know that her dreams have a way of coming true in strange ways. I don't have the time to go to the village before my guests wake for the evening, or I'd go ask her myself. Any ideas?"

He shrugged. "Your father is a master at controlling all manner of beasts and humans alike. I have no idea which one Helgaleena is referring too. It sounds like she just had a bad dream. Our Helgaleena is very superstitious and always enjoyed causing trouble for you, if I recall. Maybe it's just that." He poured some cream into his coffee. "Have you been to visit her since you arrived?"

"No...I haven't had time. With all the guests arriving and preparing for the hunt, the concert, and all the other activities for the weekend I just forgot." Lavanya realized that she felt a little guilty about not visiting yet.

"Well, I suggest you visit. She may just be trying to get your attention." He took a slow sip of his coffee.

"You could be right. We were very competitive and even combative as children. Maybe she's mad that I haven't visited." Lavanya picked at the sweet cinnamon confection on her plate again. She so enjoyed how the sugar melted on her tongue, even her fangs descended a little to taste the sweet crunchy goodness of the icing.

"I'll make plans to see her tomorrow afternoon." Seeing Helgaleena again would be good for her. Plus, it would put her overactive imagination to rest.

"So, how's the mating game going?" Renfield smiled over his coffee cup, changing the subject and obviously enjoying the little jab at her career. He never took her job seriously. He'd assumed she was just doing this for a hobby until she'd added some hefty figures to their wealth and the accountant brought it to his attention. Even though he didn't think of Count on Love as just a hobby anymore, he still enjoyed teasing her about it.

"Wonderfully, thank you very much. All the couples arrived last night, and they had a lovely time getting acquainted. Everyone had a 'bite to eat.' Thank you by the way, for arranging the extra donors from the village." She gave him a small nod and he bowed his head.

"My pleasure."

"I really have no doubts except for Raz and Uki. I know they'd be happy together. I just have to make Uki get over her hang-up about the whole lesbian thing."

He choked on his coffee. "Lavanya, you know I don't like it when you speak of such things—and at the table, no less."

She stifled a laugh. "I live to surprise you, Renfield." Then she followed that up with a big bite of cinnamon roll just to seal the deal. He huffed and pulled his paper back up to hide.

"Lesbian," she whispered just for the fun of hearing him clear his throat again. *Small pleasures*, she thought and smiled.

"When are you going to make a love match for yourself?"

With one question he managed to change her mood from happy to annoyed.

"Why do you continue ask me that?" He'd harped on this subject for the last fifty years. "I'm happy with my life."

And she was. She found companionship when she wanted and enjoyed having a man in her bed at times, but who could she find to span the worlds that she lived in? Vampires were stuck in the night and couldn't enjoy the sunlight like she could, and humans were stuck believing she couldn't exist. If her father's relationships had taught her anything, it was that mixing with humans didn't work in the long run.

"Just curious, dear." He continued to hide behind his paper.

"When you find someone who's at home in our supernatural world and the human world, strong and sexy, truthful and…. You get the picture." Suddenly her cinnamon roll didn't hold the same draw as it had before the conversation started.

"As fun as this has been, I need to get ready for my clients. They'll be waking soon." She patted her lips on the lovely embroidered napkin and stood, dusting the crumbs from her dressing gown. "I have a hunt planned for this evening and I need to make sure everything is in place. Are you coming tonight? Everyone would love to meet you."

"Ah, my dear. I don't think I'm up for a hunt."

"Renfield, we'll just be riding the Kabardin horses around the countryside, looking for some *treasures* that I've hidden. The horses need the exercise, and everyone will enjoy their beauty and grace on the rocky mountain trails."

"Treasures?" He shot her a sharp look.

"Yes, but don't worry." She shouldn't shock him, but she just couldn't resist. "I had George get four of our human donors, so there's no problem. He's to hide them in an hour or so around the mountain range. Each couple will be given the humans' scent and instructed to hunt." She said it with huge eyes, catching a glimpse of his startled face. This was way too much fun.

"Lavanya. I'm surprised at you." He folded his paper and placed it roughly next to his coffee, his spine stiff in his chair.

Lavanya had to hold her side as she laughed. "Renfield, you know me better than that. The treasures aren't human. They're the newest golden iPhones that aren't available in stores yet. The first team to return with their *healthy* human in tow will win the prizes. Really, do you think I'm that callous?" She finished with a smile and dramatic twirl of her full-length gown as she swept out of the room. He really was too much fun to play with.

"Lavanya." His voice caught her at the doorway. "I spoke to George earlier and gave him some ideas about hiding places. A hint of a grin picked at the edges of his lips as he pulled the paper back in front of his face.

"Thanks." She stifled a growl when she heard his laugh. He'd known all along about the game she'd planned. It was impossible to fool him. He seemed to *always* know everything. "Lesbian."

"Lavan..." As he pulled the paper away from his face to scold her about her language, she childishly stuck her tongue out.

Lavanya was rewarded with an eye roll and a strenuous newspaper shaking. Not bad. That was about as ruffled as he ever got. With a small smile, she turned on her satin slipper and left. The sun wouldn't set until six here in the mountains of Făgăraş, but she needed to be ready for her guests. Plus, it seemed she needed to plan a trip into Arefu for a visit with Helgaleena.

LYNNE STEVIE

messengers he gambled with his own life and refused the assignment. Vlad's rage was legendary, but Zev was done being manipulated and used. It had been risky to deny Vlad, but protecting this woman, Lavanya, seemed curiously important to the blood sucker. He and Vlad both knew that Zev was the only one with the special skills and strengths to assure the job got done right. So he'd bet his life for his freedom.

Finally, after more than one hundred years, he'd found something the bastard wanted more than the magical servants Zev and Inez had become. In the end Vlad agreed to break the spells that bound Zev and Inez to him in exchange for this one last job.

"Inez," he yelled, grabbing a threadbare towel and wrapping it around his waist as he exited the small bath. "I need you to…"

The bed and room were clean, all the blood was gone. Even the old quilt looked the same as it had yesterday. He took a deep breath and let his animal senses take over. *Hmm, nothing.* The smell of death was masked by the scent of cardamom and the woodsy smell of a fresh fire. Inez had burnt off the blood and bodies without damaging any of his personal items in the cottage.

He looked at her in awe. Her frail body was a beautiful disguise. She could be anyone's grandmother, with long gray hair, arthritis-ravaged hands, and liver-spotted skin. No one would suspect she was well over four hundred years old, and even Zev still marveled at the incredible power that lay within her.

"You outdid yourself, you crafty little czarownica." He crossed the room to where she sat in the rocker sewing and placed a gentle kiss on her wrinkled cheek. "We're going to be free of Vlad. Just one last job and we'll never have to see another blood sucker again."

"Humm, so you say." Inez continued to rock and sew as if what he'd told her didn't matter.

"One last job old woman and its done."

"I'm not so sure Wilkie, but that's another story and we've no time for stories. You go on now, get to it. I'll be close. If you need me, I'll know." Inez went back to sewing.

He didn't take time to argue with her. The sooner he figured out who was threatening the woman, Lavanya, the sooner he could kill them and then be free of all the vampires.

33

LYNNE STEVIE

CHAPTER FIVE

Family Ties

Lavanya entered her suite, still worried about Helgaleena's dream. Renfield was usually right about everything. *But...*

Buttercup rushed out from under the bed to greet her. Lavanya scooped her up and nuzzled the dog's soft fur. The little spitfire could always warm and relax her.

"Beast on the Blue Moon," she whispered to the tiny dog. "Silly, isn't it?"

She wished she had as uncomplicated a relationship with Helgaleena as she did with Buttercup. Helgaleena was family. Hell, Lavanya had thought they'd always be close, but eventually they grew apart. Helgaleena had had a family and aged as Lavanya stayed the same, never growing old or having children. She'd hoped children might be possible since she'd experienced a menstrual cycle during her very brief puberty phase, but it had happened only once and that was more than sixty years ago.

Lavanya wasn't bitter, *she wasn't*. Her relationship with Helgaleena had always been exasperating, like a hangnail that kept getting caught on things. She hoped the visit tomorrow would set everything right. In the meantime, she needed to focus on tonight's hunt.

"Chloe," Lavanya called out as she sat the tiny Chihuahua on her bed. She could hear her maid shuffling things about in the dressing room.

"Yes, Mistress." Holding Lavanya's formal riding clothes and top hat, she entered the bedroom and curtsied.

"I'll take those." Lavanya took the clothes and laid them out on a black, crushed-velvet ottoman. "Be a dear and run me a bath." Lavanya knew she needed to be on point tonight, and a nice soak would warm her up and clear her head. On her way to the bath she grabbed the daily reports from her vanity where Chloe had put them.

Her bath was a haven. Chloe adjusted the taps, laid out her

robe and warmed towels, and left her. Soft lighting set off the sparkle of the veining in the rainforest marble that covered the walls and floor of the chamber. The brown and green veins seemed to flow through the natural stone just as the Arges River flowed through the valley below the castle. Lavanya climbed the steps to the raised tub and lowered herself into the warm water. Tiny bubbles tickled her skin as they floated to the surface, and she sighed as her tension slipped away. Then she retrieved the household reports from the counter and leaned back to read them.

The first report was about Ms. Belle Reed. She was unhappy with the size of her rooms and had moved up to the main level into one of the suites normally reserved for humans. Her servant had stayed with her during the day and protected her from accidental sun exposure instead of finding his own room. Well, if Belle's servant was up to the task, she wouldn't change their arrangements.

Belle wouldn't be easy, and Lavanya had known that going into this. Belle had been making her own flamboyant way in this world for more than two centuries, and finding a mate for her was a serious challenge. She'd been linked to Jesse James, Billy the Kid, and most recently, a former governor of Louisiana. There had even been a movie made about the time she spent in Louisiana as a burlesque queen. Belle was used to getting her own way and enjoyed being independent.

Arthur Rand would suit her perfectly. He was tall and lanky with an unkempt appearance but a brilliant mind. His appearance and simple approach to life would be the exact opposite of compact, red-headed Belle's vivacious energy, and he wouldn't compete with her for attention or dominance. However misleading Arthur's demeanor, he was no pushover. Belle would test him this weekend, but in the end Lavanya knew Arthur would step up and tame the fiery Belle. Lavanya couldn't wait to watch the fireworks. *Priceless.*

Another volatile couple had already made a connection. Tru and Naasir had spent the night in each other's company. It was lovely to see that her tattooed, tough-talking friend had found something to like in Naasir. Really, what wasn't to like? Naasir was six feet, four inches of muscled ebony, bald by choice, with a stylish gray goatee. Plus, the man had the deep, penetrating voice of a god and enough charisma to fill this castle. She was so happy for them. Yea! One down and three to go.

Licking her finger again, she flipped through the housekeeping reports. How she wished the castle would modernize, but the staff would make no changes without her father's approval. Since he's been sleeping for the last 60 years instead of an email she was stuck with paper reports. *Irritating.*

"Chloe," Lavanya called out, tossing the reports aside. "Have the other villagers arrived to stand in as the prey?" She glanced down at her fingers, they were beginning to prune. Time to finish her bath.

"Yes, Mistress, my cousins are being placed around the mountainside as we speak." Chloe put Lavanya's lotions on the vanity. As she placed the Chanel No. 5 on the counter, Lavanya remembered she wouldn't need it.

"I won't be wearing any perfume this evening. It interferes with my sense of smell, and I don't wish to hinder any competitors in the hunt."

"Yes, Mistress." Chloe put the perfume away and wrapped Lavanya in a fluffy, chocolate brown bath sheet as she stepped down from the tub.

"Chloe, see if Dylan's here." Chloe curtsied and left the bathroom, and Lavanya dried off enough to begin moisturizing. Dylan, her personal stylist and servant, went everywhere with her. Traveling with an entourage was a bit eccentric, but she did it anyway. And Dylan was the heart of that group.

After a moment she heard him in the next room ranting about the weather. He was in a tizzy.

"This mist will wreak havoc on her hair," he said. "Chloe, be a dear and get me some of the Moroccan oil from the case."

Lavanya loved to listen to him tearing through a room. Plus, it was amusing to watch poor Chloe try to keep up with him and his mess. He was a wonderful hairdresser and artist, but neat he would never be. His appearance and the appearance of his one and only client, Lavanya, were always perfect. But he could leave a wake of tissues, hair bushes, and color stains a mile long.

He burst into her bath chamber, clapping his hands.

"Okay, darling, we have ninety minutes to bring you into your spectacular self. Chop, chop!" he said. He was in his early 40s now, but he still had a youthful appearance. Dressed in designer boot-cut jeans and an Armani T-shirt, he lit up the room. His sense of humor was showing in the huge ornate cross stitched into the top of his worn cowboy boots. Even after 20 years together, he still enjoyed poking fun at the old vampire myths.

"Yes, darling, make me beautiful," Lavanya said as she moved to her dressing room and sat at the mirrored vanity.

"The schedule says riding tonight. Is that still the plan?" He took Lavanya's long black locks in his hands and turned them over, running his fingers through the mass. Dylan's own hair was short with just the perfect amount of curl to make women want to touch it. It was hilarious how many old ladies walked up to them and wanted to touch his hair. To his credit, he was very gracious and pretended not to love the attention, although Lavanya knew he adored it.

"Yes. We're planning a scavenger hunt on horseback." Lavanya answered.

"I'll make sure I'm nice and tucked in then. I wouldn't want to be anyone's prize. Except yours, of course," he said with a wink.

"Don't be ridiculous. You know I wouldn't hunt humans. Well, we are hunting humans, but they're not the prize." Lavanya couldn't hold in the laugh.

"Dear, you know I love you. As long as I'm not on the menu, I can handle it. All right. Let's get down to business." Dylan looked around the room. "Where's your top hat? I have to decide how I want to do your hair. The wind up here is a bitch, and I need to attach the hat so you won't lose it along the way. Plus, make sure you hair doesn't impede your ability to see."

"Chloe brought everything out earlier and set it on the ottoman." Lavanya pointed to her ensemble. "There's my riding outfit, and the hat is on the bust of Joan of Arc next to my gilded mirror." The hat was one of Lavanya's favorites. Made of coal black velvet with a satin band, she always felt like the Mad Hatter when she wore it. It sat to the side and had a curved brim to give it just the right touch of whimsy.

"Can your gilded mirror take us home? This is a dreadfully dull, cold place, and I miss the color of Miami. Don't you?" He tried the hat this way and that to decide on a hair style. "It's so gray and cold I had fruity pebbles for breakfast just to see a rainbow of colors."

"Oh, you big baby, we'll be here only a few weeks. You know that. So what's really going on?" Lavanya had an idea about what was bothering him. "Ah, none of the clients' servants meet your needs?"

Because he was a trained stylist, people were always surprised to find out that Dylan wasn't gay or bisexual. However, women flocked to him. Something about his fun and exuberant personality guaranteed a steady stream of willing partners. And true to his good nature, he usually stayed friends with his conquests.

"No. Can you believe it? Am I becoming too picky in my old age?" He laughed a little and glanced in the mirror.

"Maybe you're developing some scruples," Lavanya said with a grin.

"Oh, god. I hope not. I'll give the stable one last look this evening while ya'll are out having vampire fun. There's bound to be something I missed on the first go-round." He placed the hat on the vanity and reached for the Moroccan oil. Pouring a big dollop in his hand, he looked at her reflection. "Are you ready to be made over?"

"Do your worst," she answered with a mischievous smile.

And he did. An hour later she was released from his grasp, fully coiffed and looking striking. The striking part wasn't too hard since she was a world of contradictions. Pale skin, coal almost blue black hair, black cherry lips and violet eyes surrounded by charcoal liner. The outfit didn't hurt either. Her riding clothes were immaculate, and she carried her favorite accessory: a whip. She loved to slap it against her palm to get people's attention—so much fun to be naughty. Little pleasures made living worthwhile, especially after 75 years. With one good smack that stung her palm, she left her dressing room. Now she just needed someone to be naughty *with*.

Okay—enough of that. She'd start wishing for her own mate if she wasn't careful, and that wasn't going to happen. She'd found lots of fun Mr. Wrongs, but no Mr. Right. No one could truly understand her life. She'd had human lovers and vampire lovers, and both could be wonderful. But trying for any lasting relationship was just too complicated. She couldn't tell a human about her real life or her need to feed on blood. Sex was just no fun at all when you had to be so gentle. It was like having sex with a sugar sculpture: squeeze too hard and it cracks, and with all that sugary goodness just under the surface, all you really wanted was to take a bite out of it. She could feed off humans, but then she had to clean their memories, and that just seemed wrong, plus a lot of trouble.

Vampires, on the other hand, were wonderful in bed because they weren't so fragile, and depending on their age, they'd had a lot of practice. But they couldn't go out in the day with her. They couldn't brunch at Morgans, stroll through the zoo, or just bask in the sun. She felt trapped when she was in a relationship with a vampire.

"You look melancholy, darling." Dylan placed his hand on her shoulder. "Why so blue, when you look ravishing?"

"No reason, just work." She placed her cold hand atop his for some warmth.

"Have some fun tonight. You love to ride, and everyone will be off searching for a long while. If I know you, you've hidden those people well, haven't you?" Dylan gave her a light squeeze. "So go and just run. The horses probably need a good workout, anyway."

"You're right. I do need a good ride." *In more ways than one*, Lavanya thought, but didn't say. She watched him pick up his many makeup brushes and hair tools. "Happy hunting to you, too. I'll be keeping the vampires busy until well past midnight. You can take your pick of the servants, but as always…be nice."

"Honey, I am nothing if not *nice* to the ladies." And he gave her a wink.

With her own preparations for the evening complete, Lavanya hurried to the parlor to check that everything was set for her guests' arrival. There she found Andrei, her father's butler, stoking the fire.-

"Mistress Draculesti." Startled, he almost dropped the poker. "Good evening."

"Andrei," she said, nodding. "Is everything ready for this evening?"

"Everything is set for the hunt, and the servants have all been hidden throughout the hills." Andrei replaced the poker and dropped his gaze to the floor. Many of the servants were in awe of her father and, by extension, Lavanya. She wished they would treat her as just a friend or employer, but she couldn't do anything to change how they felt.

"Did Renfield help you with the placement of the volunteers?" She wanted to find out if Renfield had known about the hunt, as he'd teased earlier.

"Yes, Mistress, Master Renfield had some good ideas and mapped out a few yesterday morning."

"Very well. Thank you, Andrei. If all the hu—" Lavanya caught herself. She hated to call them "humans" to their face, because doing so just emphasized that they were food. She started again.

"If all the volunteers aren't found by midnight, we might have to call you back in to help. I don't want anyone out there freezing to death just for a game."

"Yes, Mistress, I'll be happy to help you, as always."

"Thank you, Andrei."

"Mistress." He bowed his head and left the room.

Lavanya surveyed the parlor, examining the prizes, bar inventory and cigar humidor. Everything had been set out perfectly.

She crossed to the large window that overlooked the mountains and a small piece of the Arges River valley. The wind howled around the castle and the cold chilled her skin, but it wasn't the only reason for her discomfort. She had a bizarre urge to stop the hunt.

As she stared at the darkened sky, a sudden pain gripped her, and a powerful pull from her father rocked her back. An urgent, stabbing need to go to him overwhelmed her. She doubled over and clung to the window sill. Her breath caught as though the wind had been knocked out of her. Lavanya struggled to stand up and breathe as the sharp pain tore through her diaphragm.

The sound of shuffling feet alerted her that the first guest was coming down the hall. She swallowed the pain and pushed the premonition aside to appear normal as her guests entered. As she straightened, she noticed the moon was full for the second time this month. A blue moon.

The moon, her pain and Helgaleena's dream were related somehow, Lavanya knew it. But tonight, she couldn't act on her knowledge. Tonight was for entertaining her guests.

CHAPTER SIX

The Couples

Phillip Murray and Lauren McDowell were the first to arrive for the festivities, and both seemed in good spirits. Lauren strode confidently to the high wingback chairs in front of the fire. She was a contradiction of sorts, but Lavanya respected her flare and style. Lauren was dressed in an English riding jacket, including a linen hanky sticking out of the breast pocket, denim pencil-thin jeans, and red-and-black cowboy boots with aces in every suit spread across the sides. Somehow she made it all work together beautifully.

Combine her style with her long, curly, chestnut hair, strong square jaw, and deep, caramel brown eyes, and you had a striking beauty. But the best thing about Lauren was her attitude. As she sat enjoying the fire, she pulled out an exquisitely made pipe, filled it with tobacco, and packed it. Then she struck a long match on her boot and lit it with the ease of someone who smoked a pipe every day.

Phil, on the other hand, was one hundred percent personality. His attitude and sex appeal had nothing to do with looks and everything to do with his individuality. He stood five feet eleven, was balding, and had an acne-pocked complexion and a physique that proved he'd been turned later than most. Yet you were drawn to this funny man with a wicked sense of humor and a devious smile. Lavanya noticed that Lauren turned toward him, and he responded with a randy smile. *Lovely.*

Lavanya joined them at the fire.

"Phil. Lauren. How are your rooms? Is everything to your liking?"

"The rooms are very accommodating. You thought of everything. Thank you, Lavanya." Phil never turned away from Lauren.

"Yes, I'm happy with the rooms. It's wonderful to get away for a holiday and see the castle again. Thank you." Lauren's lips

43

curved up on one side as she looked at Phil through the sexy smoke billowing out of her pipe.

She turned to Lavanya. "How's Vlad?"

Lavanya was caught off guard.

"Oh, that's right. I forgot you've been to the castle before. My father is doing well. I'm sorry he couldn't be here this weekend."

Lavanya remembered very well that Lauren had been a friend of her mother's and had visited the castle frequently before she was turned. However, when Lauren became a vampire, Vlad purposefully distanced the two women. After her mother died, he just avoided Lauren out of habit. And Lavanya pretended to be ignorant about the whole mess. Not a perfect system, but it worked.

"I haven't seen him in years," Lauren said, smiling as the smoke from her pipe billowed around her face. "It's been too long. I wish he could have made it to this weekend get-together."

"I'm sure he'll be sorry to have missed your visit." Lavanya smiled and turned to Phil, trying to change the subject.

"How are you finding the castle? Is it how you thought it would be?"

"It's wonderful, my dear, although not quite as cobwebby as I had pictured." He laughed.

"You look so much like your mother, with her violet eyes," Lauren said, seemingly stuck in the past. "I wish she could have known you. She would have been a wonderful mother. I'm sorry I haven't kept in touch with you or your father."

"As I said, he'll be sorry he missed your visit. I'll be sure to tell him you inquired about his well-being." Lavanya never advertised that her father was in a deep slumber and had been for over 50 years due to his grief over the loss of her mother.

Luckily, as more guests arrived, she had an excuse to discontinue the charade with Lauren. She left the happy couple and moved forward to greet the next pair.-

"Anya, this place is awesome!" Tru burst into the room, her raspy voice leading the way.

Tru could squeeze every ounce of fun out of a day, and Lavanya could tell that her friend was on her way to making a memory tonight. They'd been close for years, and Lavanya loved Tru's tough, chic, street style. Tru's white, spikey hair and ruby red lip color stood out against her pale skin and the black leather biker outfit she wore, allowing her to create a shock wave when she entered the room.

She patted Naasir on the arm and almost skipped over to the fire, dragging him with her. Her energy was infectious, and Lavanya found herself energized just by her friend's presence.

"Why don't you spend more time here?" Tru demanded. "It's so cool! The place is like a fuck'n museum, so quiet and creepy. I love it! I slept like a baby this afternoon." Lavanya noticed the smile Tru gave Naasir and didn't believe for a minute that the castle had anything to do with Tru's restful afternoon.

"I'm so glad I got you here, and I'm happy you're enjoying yourself. You deserve it." Lavanya gave Naasir a nod of approval. Tru was a friend, and she'd explained that to Naasir before she'd made the introductions. Lavanya knew he would be the calm in the storm that was Tru.

Where Tru exuded untamed energy, Naasir was calm, chained power. He arrived tonight dressed casually in a navy and black handspun silk polo sweater. The V-neck giving away a peek of his handsomely muscled chest. Heavy black slacks and black ankle boots finished his ensemble. His cigar was Cuban and hand rolled.

"Naasir, I assume that everything is to your liking, as well?" Lavanya asked.

"You assume correctly, Lavanya. Everything is good."

His deep voice had a mesmerizing effect on every woman in the room. As it rippled over her, Lavanya felt as if she were the water and he the stone. But his voice really did a number on Tru. Her breath caught, and her body sank just a fraction. She looked and dressed like an ass-kicking street warrior, but she actually swayed. *Ain't love grand?*

Raz and Uki arrived together and seemed equally happy with the arrangements. Raz wore heavy, military-style clothing, and yet she was the picture of feminine sexuality with her tight, army-green sweater hugging her taut muscles. Uki, on the other hand, had on an old-fashioned fedora and traditional English riding attire. Both seemed smitten with each other and joined the group around the fire.

"I can't wait to get outside tonight." A strange gleam entered Raz's eye. "The moon is bright and full. It lights up the night with its magic. Mwhahahaha," Raz laughed like the Wicked Witch of the East. Uki gave her a gentle tap on the arm for her shenanigans.

"You are so ludicrous, Raz," Uki commented. "It's a lovely night for a ride. Thank you for inviting us, Lavanya."

"You are most welcome, Uki. Raz. I trust that you both had a nice daytime rest."

"Yes." They both answered at the same time, giggling a little.

"Wonderful. Please enjoy the fire. I'm sure that Belle and Arthur will be with us momentarily, and then we can go over the rules for the hunt."

Lavanya turned to the rest of the group by the fire.

"Would anyone like a bite before the hunt?" She knew they wouldn't; it would impede their sense of smell. But decorum necessitated that she ask.

They all smiled and declined. Her guests chatted about the terrain and the Kabardin horses as they waited for Belle and Arthur. Lavanya had assumed that the couple would make a fashionably late arrival and had set the time table accordingly. True enough, 30 minutes later the two entered the parlor looking irritated with each other.

"Honey, I'm sorry to be so late," Belle said. "Traveling is not my thing, and I just could not wake up tonight. Plus, the water pressure in the shower reminds me of the little New Mexico hacienda that Billy always used to love. And now I just can't do a thing with my hair at this altitude." Belle managed to drop a tidbit of her infamous past with Billy the Kid while she called attention to the ravishing, flame-red locks of her hair. The beautiful, curly waves cascaded over her shoulders, looking perfect.

"I do apologize for your discomfort, Belle," Lavanya said sincerely. "I hope that your new room is better suited to your tastes and your servant is protecting you from the ravages of the sun."

"Yes, he's got me all tucked in. And thank you for the room switch. I was miserable in that little room below." Belle smiled and turned toward the bar. Her spurs tinkled as she walked. Befitting her western past, she was dressed as a cowgirl, complete with vest and spurs.

"I notice that you're wearing spurs." Lavanya wanted to warn her against them. "I have to tell you, our mountain horses aren't accustomed to spurs, and they're strong and temperamental. Be careful how you ride, because I wouldn't want your mount to get away from you."

"Don't you worry, sweet pea, I can handle anything that goes between my legs or has a trigger." Her laugh was infectious. Everyone chuckled, and her late arrival and petty complaints were forgotten.

"Good evening, Arthur. I trust you slept well?" Lavanya turned her attention to Arthur and smiled warmly at his disheveled appearance.

"Yes, Miss Lavanya, your hospitality is overflowing." He said it with a wink and a bow, while deftly raising his whiskey glass. Even though the liquor had little or no effect on him, he must still enjoy the taste. The household reports noted Arthur had a bottle-a-day habit, and she'd already instructed her buyers to have supplies delivered tomorrow.

"I'm so glad you're finding our hospitality to your liking," Lavanya said, nodding to his empty glass. "I'd love it if you'd join me this evening for an absinthe nightcap. I have it imported from France, and it's a wonderful experience. I have so few friends who indulge."

"Humm, the Green Fairy, I would be delighted, my dear." He ran his fingers through his long, unkempt, sandy hair. Because of her strange gift, Lavanya knew that Arthur and Belle would be a match, but it still baffled her. Arthur looked like a scraggly English bum. His black suit, with its pencil-thin pants, was in desperate need of pressing, and a blood stain showed prominently on his loosened tie. Belle was a complete opposite. She looked every bit like the country burlesque queen she was. Lavanya had a hard time not gawking at the extreme couple.

Lavanya explained the rules and showed everyone the prizes, and then they proceeded to the stables. Each couple found their bag containing a shirt that had been worn by a human courier who now sat hidden in the countryside holding a huge gift-wrapped box containing other goodies. The couple who returned first with their human would win the grand prize.

The hunt began.

LYNNE STEVIE

CHAPTER SEVEN

Chasing the Blue Moon

Zev's breath turned to steam in the cold night air as he raced toward Vlad's ancestral home. He had to get to the castle before midnight, or the deal was off. The bloodsucker wouldn't budge on the deadline.

He was lucky that the ground wasn't frozen this time of year, so he made good time cutting through the dense forest. Still, the timing would be close. He knew now why the vamp had offered up the two women. The added strength he'd gotten from feeding was the only thing keeping his legs moving. As much as he despised the bastard for manipulating him, he reveled in his power now.

All that mattered was saving his family from the curse that enslaved them. It didn't matter what he had to do to free himself and Inez. He would do it.

****

The wind was fierce, and Lavanya was glad that Dylan had taken extra care to pin her top hat so well. The air smelled of the wood and coal fires burning in the castle. The moon was full and low in the sky. It created waves of light and dark as it played peek-a-boo with the heavy clouds that surrounded the castle.

The Kabardin horses, huge and glorious, were bred especially for her father so they weren't squeamish about vampire riders. Lavanya's mount, Samson, the biggest stallion, carried her down the cliffside trails into the valley. As he ran, his heavy breath puffed from his nostrils as thick as smoke. To set the mood of a traditional hunt, Lavanya had let out the Borzoi Russian wolfhounds. Their howls rang in the darkness. Astor, her favorite and the one Buttercup enjoyed terrorizing the most, was at her side.

Lavanya let the others hunt while she enjoyed the ride. The countryside was beautiful in its ruggedness. All the mountain trees

49

were full, and their branches drooped with the weight of dew and moss. She cornered a few foxes and let Astor have fun scaring them with his bark before calling him off and urging Samson to the river.

The clouds hung thick and opaque, obscuring the moon and casting long and oddly shaped shadows across the landscape. Lavanya had the strangest sensation of being watched; her night vision allowed her to pierce the gloom as she scanned the forest for danger. Nothing unusual moved in the darkness, so she relaxed as Samson slowed his gait, crunching gravel under his hooves as they reached the river's edge.

Satisfied that nothing was out of place, she dismounted and let Samson and Astor drink their fill as she wandered over the rocky terrain to a boulder. She relished the quiet of the night. Water lapped hungrily at the shore, and a cold mist touched her face. The flap of bat wings drew her attention to the sky for a moment. Samson's big tail swished and Aster shook his head, creating a little shower of water as his ears flapped back and forth. The sounds soothed her nerves, and she closed her eyes and leaned back to enjoy the solitude. She so seldom got a chance to be alone.

Astor dashed over to plant a big wet doggie kiss on her face. Laughing, she ducked her head as he shook off the rest of the water, spraying cold water all over her white shirt.

"Astor, enough." She rubbed his big head and long snout and watched Samson step in front of her.

"All right boys, are we ready to get back to the others?" Both males shook their heads no, and snot and water flew all around her again. "I—"

Samson's head shot up and his ears swiveled as Astor growled and pressed his ears back against his head. She grabbed Samson's reins and stood to listen again to the night air to see what might have alarmed them.

Samson pulled and whinnied as he tried to free himself from her grasp. Astor clung to her side.

"Boys! What's gotten into you?" She held tight to Samson's reins and breathed in the night air, hopeful for a taste of what had spooked the animals. The night was silent except for the white noise created by the thrumming within her own body. She smelled the usual smells of earth and water and mold from the forest floor, but a new scent overlaid the others: the smell of a lightning strike in the desert.

Someone—or something—screamed, breaking her intense concentration and startling the animals again. Her adrenaline kicked in, along with the instinct to hunt. The thirst was all-consuming, and if she was this hungry, the other vampires would be even more so.

Her mind clouded with thoughts of blood. Her mouth watered and her fangs descended in anticipation of the warm liquid. Lavanya tugged on Samson's reins to get him to cooperate. As she swung up into the English saddle, another scream broke the silence. Samson reared. She kept her seat, but he nearly landed on Astor.

The scream had come from the east, toward the castle and the stables. Her control was close to slipping. She fought the urge to get to that scream and claim the prey for herself. In the back of her mind she knew she needed to separate herself from the bloodlust, but she still hurried toward the sound.

"Samson, go!" Lavanya shouted and kicked him into a gallop. They took off through the woods with Astor on their tail. The heavy, moss-covered trees blocked the moonlight and created a blanket over their heads so thick that it was difficult to see, but Samson's hooves dug into the rocky mountain side as he raced up the trail. The massive stallion covered the distance in less than half the time it took them to get down to the river.

As she topped the last rise into the stable area, she pulled hard on Samson's reins and skidded to a halt in front of Clyde, the stable manager. Humans and vampire guests alike looked shell-shocked, and the panic of both amped her hunger. Damn, it took everything she had to pull her fangs back and address Clyde. She gritted her teeth and willed herself to stay in the saddle and upwind from him. She didn't even want to chance getting a whiff of his fear.

"What happened?" Lavanya felt like spitting as the saliva infused with venom filled her mouth. She swallowed instead.

"I don't know, Mistress," Clyde said.

"I heard a scream. It sounded like a woman. Who's still out on the cliff side?" She began counting the people gathered around. She picked out Tru and Naasir holding their human by the arm.

Her vision slipped past them and then returned to Tru's strained face.

"Naasir, get Tru back to the castle. Now." He looked offended at her blunt order and then seemed to think better of it as Lavanya pointed to Tru's extended fangs. Tru hadn't been a vampire long, only 30 years or so, and her control wasn't what it should be on normal occasions. At her best, she was impetuous; at her worst, she was wild. Now was not a good time to let her lose her cool—both because the humans were under Lavanya's protection, and because Tru would hate herself tomorrow if she attacked someone.

"Of course, Lavanya," Naasir wrapped his arm around Tru's waist to turn her away from the human man that she now had a death grip on. The human was smart. Rupert had been with Lavanya's family for years, and he didn't try to object or pull away. He would know that any struggle would send Tru into feeding mode. However, anyone would have to be truly dead not to see and smell his fear. His eyes were glassy and a fine bead of sweat had broken out on his forehead. He was a man on death row waiting for a reprieve.

"Tru, we have won. Let's leave this to the others and return to the castle." Naasir held his other hand out to Tru, willing her to release Rupert and take his in hers. "Come, darling, I assure you, I will take care of your hunger."

Naasir had a slight English accent, and even Lavanya thought his deep voice could penetrate a woman's body like a fine whiskey, burning her throat and warming her from within. Combined with his fierce stare, he obviously promised complete satisfaction. Tru staggered, and the hold of the blood lust broke, replaced by pure lust. Luckily for Rupert, Naasir was damn near impossible to ignore. Tru released Rupert and turned to Naasir, burying herself in his embrace.

With Tru in good hands, Lavanya turned her focus to the others. Lauren and Phil were without a human prize, and they both looked shaken. Their horses were panting.

"Phil, Lauren, do you know who screamed?" Lavanya asked as she steadied Samson, now prancing with pent-up energy and fear.

"It was our human female who screamed." Lauren spoke without emotion, but her fangs gave her away. She was stimulated by this event more than she wanted to show.

"What? You found the human?" Phil turned to her in surprise.

"You haven't fed," Lavanya said. "Why did the human scream?"

Lauren's tone was furious. "I was tracking her using the clothing you'd given us. Then the smell of blood overpowered everything, and I followed the trail to the human. Just as I got close, a big black wolf attacked me." She turned in the saddle and looked down at her side. A large rip in her jeans and another in her leather boots exposed a nasty gash in her leg.

The horse was fine. The attack had been focused on her.

"Lauren, why didn't you call to me?" Phil was shocked.

"At first I thought the attack might just be part of the hunt—an obstacle. I attempted to fight the wolf, but as you can see, he was good—too good. One of the Borzoi hounds arrived and caught the wolf's attention, or I might not be here now. I thought to find you," she scowled at Lavanya, "to see if this was somehow part of the game."

Uki and Raz arrived with their human, dismounted, and came over to get a look at Lauren's injuries. The wounds should have been healing by now. Instead, they looked fresh and deep. All eyes turned to Lavanya for an explanation.

"I can assure all of you, this is not part of the planned hunt." Then something registered. "A hound?"

"Yes," Lauren said. "Just a few moments ago, one of your wolfhounds came to my aid."

Phil dismounted and reached up to help her out of the saddle as Lavanya searched the crowd looking for Astor's floppy ears. She barely heard Belle and Arthur ride up with their human in tow.

"Clyde, get everyone inside. See that Lauren gets all the help she needs. Then get two men, arm yourselves, and come to the Cave of Swallows where Giselle was hidden."

She kicked Samson into motion. He reared and then they thundered in the direction from which Phil and Lauren had come only moments before.

Astor could get himself killed trying to save the human. She wanted that black wolf's pelt for this attack. It would look lovely by her kitchen entrance and serve well as a doormat for servants' muddy feet.

LYNNE STEVIE

CHAPTER EIGHT

Magic Smells Like Cardamom

As Lavanya galloped toward the Cave of Swallows, she could smell blood and the musky, wet dog smell of Astor. But his scent was overlaid by a thick cardamom and clove smell that clung to the electrically charged air. What was it?

She took another deep breath and tried to gather more information from the wind, which swirled around her and whisked her hair into her face. The hat and her hairdo—as well as her vanity—were long gone in her haste to get to Astor and the young girl.

Magic: that's what she smelled.

Samson skidded to a halt about forty feet from the cave at the sound of large jaws snapping. Lavanya nearly shot over his head as he stopped. She regained her balance just to hang on again as he reared and jerked his head around to retreat.

"Samson! Whoa, boy." *So much for a sneak attack.* Lavanya slid off the plunging horse and ran across the rocky terrain toward the cave. As she rounded the corner of the cave opening, the warm air from the cave whooshed past her, bringing the scent of human blood. Giselle had been paired with Lauren and Phil. The wolf must have injured her as well.

Suddenly hungry, her fangs descended and her mouth watered. She licked her lips. Then she forced herself back to the rock wall. *She knew this girl and her family.* Lavanya needed to save her, not eat her. She fisted her hands and tried not to taste the breeze.

Astor's bark brought back some control. Lavanya again edged around the corner of the cave opening. She gasped when she saw a huge black wolf barreling down on Astor, who was standing protectively between the wolf and the girl.

Astor was a big dog, standing well over three feet at his shoulders, but this black wolf was twice that size and easily three hundred pounds. His coarse hair was the color of dull onyx; only his paws were splashed with white. The wolves native to the area were brown with black-tipped fur and a stripe of black down their backs, and the largest grew to only about one hundred seventy pounds. Where had this animal come from?

Astor retreated a little and the wolf pushed forward again. As he leaped, Lavanya got a better look at the beast, which looked like a wolf in every way except for its head. Instead of the long face of a wolf, it had almost a feline-shaped snout, whiskers, and slanted black eyes.

"*No!*" Lavanya commanded. Hoping to stop the beast's attack, she drew on her father's power like a junkie drew on a coke straw. She wouldn't be surprised if he woke up just to see what happened.

The wolf staggered, but didn't stop. He was upon Astor now, his snout and lips pulled back to display the largest set of canine teeth Lavanya had ever seen.

She threw herself into the tight confines of the cave and using every ounce of her vampire enhanced strength and speed, she backhanded the wolf. He flew across the small area and hit the opposite wall. He snarled and spit, struggling to get upright even as he hit the moist stone. He lunged, snapping and biting, and she crouched to repel him and protect Astor. She threw him off again, but his ferocious fangs ripped her palm.

As he catapulted through the air, his eyes caught hers and she saw something more than animal intelligence in his gaze. His eyes turned a greenish hazel, almost luminescent, unlike those of any wolf she'd ever seen. Even in the dark confines of the cave she knew that this was no natural wolf.

He hit the wall with a bone-crunching crash and a deep growl. Lavanya staggered to her feet. Her father could call all beasts. So far, she'd been able to manipulate only humans, but she'd never faced a need this desperate. She put all her will into the words.

"*You will stop!*" She stared into the creature's iridescent green eyes as it stood and shook out its fur. His tongue grazed his nose and she saw him taste her blood on his snout.

His head snapped up. A strangled growl echoed through the cave as he stretched his jaw and sang to the moon.

Lavanya took the opportunity and charged at him. She caught him off guard and slammed him to the ground, his neck in her hands. She could kill him now. She was ready to break his neck.

The beast snorted and let his tongue hang out of his mouth in the canine version of a happy face.

Several things happened at once. Astor stood, letting her know he was okay. Giselle took a breath, which rattled in her lungs. Lavanya was momentarily overwhelmed with relief and hunger. Astor was alive, and now she knew that the girl might live, too. But then, like a stray cat, with the smell of the blood gurgling out of the girl's mouth, the hunger came back.

The wolf pulled free. Too late, she tried to regain control, but the beast was already on his feet. Lavanya rolled to the left, putting herself between the wolf, and Astor and Giselle.

The beast stared at her as she crouched, ready to attack. Then he bowed his head to her as a formally trained horse would do in a competition. One leg stretched forward, and his head and eyes turned down.

She thought about rushing him again, but his growl stopped her. It was not the fierceness of the growl, but the humanity in it that caused her to pause.

Confused, she took a moment to study the large animal. Her eyes saw him—black as night and big as hell—but her nose didn't smell animal. She smelled magic.

She stepped back toward Astor, and he rubbed against her hand and growled at the wolf. The wolf showed his teeth, but didn't attack. Lavanya stood straighter and dared the wolf with her gaze. No one moved.

The noise of the others approaching broke the spell. The wolf turned his head toward the entrance of the cave and then back to her. As she watched, he rose up on his hind legs and melted into the air. Nothing but the crackling of magic and the smell of cardamom remained when Clyde and the two other villagers entered with their weapons drawn.

"Men, put down your weapons." Lavanya ordered. "The wolf's gone." They blinked a few times, and then looked around the cave.

The scent of blood tackled her now that the wolf was gone, and she turned her attention to the back of the cave. The young girl lay on the cold, hard earth. Beaten and bloodied. Lavanya's mouth watered, and her hands started to shake at the sight.

"Gentlemen, I must leave the area. I have taken care of the wolf for the moment, but you must move Giselle." She gritted her teeth against the hunger, but her fangs got in the way. All she managed to do was bite through her own lip.

"Mistress, I know her family and I will take her there."

"I trust that you will take care of this child." Lavanya said, pushing herself to the opening of the cave. "See that she gets the best medical care."

"Yes, Mistress, please do not trouble yourself." He took a step forward and held his hand out in invitation for her to leave.

She ran to the mouth of the cave. Astor followed. The fresh, cold air filled her nose and burned some of the bloodlust away. She took another deep breath and, along with the wet forest smells, she also caught a touch of cardamom. Lavanya whipped around to survey the area, but saw nothing except trees and wilderness. Still, these mountains held many places where a wolf could hide.

"Move her quickly, gentlemen. The beast may yet return. This may be his den. And Clyde—I need a full report of her injuries and anything that she can tell me about the attack."

"Yes, Mistress." Clyde bowed, and Lavanya ran before the scent of Giselle's blood made her do something she'd regret.

"Samson!" The fresh air helped clear her head, but it didn't help her find her horse. *Coward.* Samson was probably back at the stables by now so she and Astor began the journey down the mountain side. He ran with her for a few moments, and then she heard him fall behind. Lavanya retraced her steps and found him limping and panting.

"Astor, buddy, come to Mommy." She knelt, held out her arms, and he hobbled over. Lavanya could only smell her own blood from the wound on her hand, so he hadn't been bitten or cut. She gently went over his legs and didn't detect any breaks, but he could still have a fracture or a sprain. Lavanya rubbed the soft wavy fur of his neck, and he leaned his thin head into her hand. She winced, but ignored the pain. With her vampire blood wounds healed quickly so she tried not to dwell on the pain.

"Aww, baby, why did you try to take on that big, bad wolf?" She gave him another little snuggle and then stood with him in her arms. "You little hero."

As she walked back to the castle with Astor, she worried about her meeting with Helgaleena tomorrow. *Dream, my ass.* She looked up at the second full moon of the month. Helgaleena's beast had arrived right on schedule.

Damn clairvoyants. Why did every message have to be like a riddle?

LYNNE STEVIE

CHAPTER NINE

Marked

Lavanya pushed through the heavy, iron front doors of the castle, spouting orders to the servants who came running. Within minutes, guests and servants packed the large receiving hall. Lavanya caught the eye of her maid in the crowd.

"Chloe, get Dylan," she said. "I need him to look after Astor until I can get a doctor to look at his leg."

"Yes, Mistress." She curtsied and then ran toward the stairs and the servants quarters.

"Renfield, Giselle is badly injured, and Clyde and the other men are taking her to her family's home. Please have a doctor there when they arrive."

"Of course. Are you injured, Mistress?"

"I'm fine, Renfield. Have you taken care of Lauren? Her leg has a deep wound, and I'd like you to look at it personally." Lavanya wanted Renfield to view all the evidence from the evening, because she wanted his opinion on the events. He might have some insight about the wolf and the magic she smelled. Or he might have some history to draw upon that might explain the attack.

"Of course, Mistress."

"And please meet me back in the parlor when you're finished."

"Of course." He headed up the stairs to make arrangements for Giselle and to see Lauren.

Now that immediate needs were taken care of, Lavanya had difficulty holding onto her calm facade. Who would dare to attack one of her guests at her father's castle? The idea made her furious.

"Are you all right, Anya?" Tru rushed up. "Did you see the wolf?" She rubbed Astor's fuzzy gray head. "Or did you scare him off, big guy?" Naasir trailed a step or two behind Tru.

"I'm fine, thank you, Tru. Please don't let this worry you."

She looked out at the crowd. Belle and Arthur were also there, waiting for a report.

How should she handle this disaster? Then it came to her: with a lie, of course. Lying and secrecy came with the territory when you were Vlad's daughter.

"Tonight was an unfortunate accident, and the wolf will be dealt with," she said, raising her voice so everyone could hear. "I frightened and injured him this evening, and finding him will be easy now. Everyone will recover, and I will have the beast made into a new entry rug for all to step upon."

"Darlin', that's the spirit." Belle chuckled and bumped Arthur with her hip.

As if on cue, Dylan barreled down the stairs. All the focus turned to him.

"*Ohmygod.*" He brushed Tru and Naasir aside, his eyes wide and shocked, as he dashed to Lavanya. "What the hell happened to you, and what have you done to your hair?"

"Dylan, I'm fine, but my hair and hat are casualties from a rough ride through the forest." Lavanya gave him time to meet her gaze. "Right now I need you to look after Astor. He was playing hero and may have hurt his leg."

"Of course, honey, anything you need."

Dylan put his arms around the dog to take him from Lavanya, but she remembered that Dylan, although her servant, wasn't as strong as a vampire and Astor weighted more than one hundred twenty-five pounds. Arthur caught her hesitation and stepped forward.

"Allow me. Where would you like me to take him?"

"Please put him in my rooms. Thank you, Arthur." Lavanya eased Astor into Arthur's arms and patted the wolfhound before turning back to the men.

"Dylan, will you get Astor's bed and show Arthur the way to my suite? I'll be up to relieve you as soon as I can."

"You go up, Arthur," Dylan said. "I'll get his bed and meet you on the third floor." Arthur headed up the stairs as Dylan went in the opposite direction.

"Let us all retire. In light of everything that's happened and the hour, I shall give out the awards for the hunt tomorrow evening.

"As long as you're sure you're okay, Anya?" Tru placed a hand on Lavanya's arm.

"I'm fine. Please go ahead. The excitement is over."

"All right. If you need me, just yell, K?" Tru gave Naasir's hand a little squeeze, and they left for their rooms.

Lavanya entered the parlor, where the warmth of the fire engulfed her as soon as she crossed the threshold. She allowed herself to take a deep, centering breath and watched the orange-and-yellow light from the huge granite fireplace flicker over the walls. Wrapping a blanket from one of the chairs tightly around her, she stumbled to the bar. With shaky hands she poured herself a full glass of whiskey from the Waterford crystal decanter and took a long sip before she dropped an ice cube in the glass.

Setting the glass on the chesterfield table, she curled up in the wingback chair and ran her fingers through her tangled hair. Lavanya noticed the tremor in her hand; she needed to feed. She'd used too much energy today, and she'd used all her strength to cloud the minds of all present in the foyer. She hadn't allowed anyone to see her wound, but now she opened her right hand to examine the deep tear.

Lavanya hissed, as pain tore through her. The cut was deep, but at least it had stopped bleeding. The edges looked puckered and brownish red, like the skin had been cauterized.

The strange color of the wound and extreme pain had to be some sort of reaction to that wolf's bite and the magic that surrounded him. If it had been a normal wolf, she would have healed by now. Hell, if it had been a normal wolf, it never would have gotten the opportunity to wound her. That thing's speed and strength were obviously part of its magic.

What could create such an animal? Damn it! She hoped Renfield had some answers.

A light tap at the door drew her attention. She straightened up, dusted off her shirt, pushed her hair out of her face, and unwound her legs where she'd curled into a ball from the pain.

"Enter." Her voice was slightly deeper than normal, but that was the best she could do with the pain engulfing her. She was careful to fold her hands together and hide the wound.

"Renfield," Lavanya sank back into her misery and reached for her drink. "How is Giselle?"

"I'm sorry to inform you that she hasn't regained consciousness. It's doubtful that she will if no 'intervention' is taken." He raised his brow and came to stand in front of Lavanya's chair. She leaned back in the chair and let out a sigh. *He wanted her to intervene.*

"Renfield, I've never changed a human. Can nothing be done? What are her injuries?" She downed the rest of the whiskey. Renfield took the empty glass and looked at her with disapproval.

"Anya, you know that alcohol impedes your abilities, and you need to be clear-headed tonight." He carried the empty glass back to the bar.

"I know that you've never changed a human," he continued. "I'm merely pointing out the facts. She won't make it if you do not intercede and give her immortality. Let me see your hand." He reached for her.

"How did you know?"

"You know that mind tricks don't affect me. Plus, I've seen to Lauren's leg. I had to use quite a bit of power to persuade her to let me heal the wound, by the way."

"All right." Lavanya felt defeated. She held out her hand. When he probed the wound, she came out of her seat.

"Stop." Lavanya hissed as loud as she dared. She tried to pull her hand back and failed. She sometimes forgot that Renfield was her father's servant, not just his confidant. He could draw on her father's strength when the need arose, just as she could. Between the two of them, they had really tested the old guy tonight. And the night wasn't over yet.

"Hold still and let me look at it," Renfield scolded her.

"It wasn't a normal wolf." Her fangs had descended from the pain and the stress, and she almost bit through her lip again for the—hell, she didn't know how many times she'd lost control tonight. "Have you seen anything like this before?" she asked, wincing as he poked.

"Yes, I'm afraid I've seen this type of wound before." He released her hand. "I need to know exactly what happened, Anya."

Lavanya walked to the fire, suddenly freezing as her body used all her extra energy to heal the wound. With her back to Renfield, she explained finding the girl lying beaten, and Astor trying to fight off the wolf.

"Renfield, why didn't the beast just kill Astor?" She turned away from the fire to see his expression. "He could have easily done it."

"I'm not sure. Continue with your recantation of the events, please." He was so still that she wondered if he was breathing.

Turning back to the fire, she told him all she could remember—the cardamom scent that filled the air and the crackle of magic when the wolf rose up and melted into the night.

"Well?" She turned around and was surprised to find him standing behind her holding her glass full of whiskey.

"Thank you," she said and reached for the glass. Before she could take it, Renfield grabbed her injured hand and poured the whiskey over the wound.

"Do not scream. I must clean out the beast's poison." And then he pushed her hand down into the flames.

Two things happened at once. The pain blinded her, and Renfield grabbed her mouth to hold back her howl. The pain was over quickly, but it was white hot and brought stars to Lavanya's vision.

When she could focus again, all she could see was Renfield's bristly beard. She drew back and licked her lips. *Blood.* She'd been feeding on him. She'd never drunk from Renfield before, and the taste was pure ecstasy. His blood was like hundred-year-old scotch. It burned all the way down and warmed her soul.

"Renfield," she said, trying not to breathe in his scent. It took all her strength to stop, to resist tearing his flesh from his body and bathing in his blood.

"I was prepared for you to feed. Anya, you will need this extra strength to save the girl and fight the poison. Feed, child, I'll heal." He raised his head, offering her the soft, thin skin of his neck. She couldn't stop. With a growl she tore at his neck and drank deep. Somewhere inside, Lavanya hoped that she'd be able to stop. And somewhere deeper, in a dark corner, her vampire hunger hoped that she wouldn't.

"*Lavanya! My child. You must stop feeding. Renfield is my servant, and you have taken all that I can afford to give.*" Her father's voice rang in her mind.

"*Daddy, I can't stop.*"

"*You must find the strength. NOW, I command you to stop.*"

His will wrapped around her like a fur coat

She drew back and growled, "*Yes, Father!*" She was ravenous and mad as hell at having to stop feeding, but Vlad's voice was impossible to resist. The body she'd held fell to the floor. She pushed away to obey her father's command and moved as far away as she could. Across the room and writhing in the power of the blood, she realized what she'd done.

"Renfield?" Her sanity came back in a rush as she watched his still body. "Renfield! I'm so sorry." Lavanya wanted to go to him, but she was too afraid that his scent would make her attack again, and he couldn't afford to lose any more blood. She was paralyzed by the fear that she'd killed him and the incredible buzz she felt from his powerful blood.

Then she smelled cardamom and felt a crackle in the air like static electricity. The balcony doors burst open and a man—wild in dress and by nature—strode through. His hair hung past his tanned shoulders in tangled, dark waves, and his eyes were hazel green and deep-set. His beard was scraggly, like he'd forgotten to shave for a few days. He wore only a black tank top hanging out of his dirty, worn Levi's.

Lavanya snarled and leaped to angle herself between the intruder and Renfield. Feeling the effects of the blood and extra strength from her father, Lavanya's adrenaline spiked. She wanted to kill.

"What have you done?" he asked as he tried to get to Renfield.

"You are the beast who attacked what was mine. I know your scent. I will kill you and bury your bones along the shore. How dare you come into my home?" She crouched to attack.

"You stink of him." He moved to circle around her.

"Of course I stink of him, I just fed. But not to worry. I'm still hungry, and you look like a tasty morsel." Lavanya lifted her head and smiled, letting her bloody fangs show. Then she beckoned him to come to her as she used her voice to make him answer. "Who are you?"

"Zev." He resisted her pull, but he spoke the truth.

"Why have you come here, Zev?"

"I was summoned." He spat the words and continued to struggle against her command to come to her side. "I see you bear my mark." A ferocious grin formed on his whiskered face as he looked up from her wounded hand to gaze in her eyes. "Did it burn?"

She looked down now and noticed for the first time that the wound was healing, but a scar was forming.

"How dare you mark me!" she screamed as she attacked him. They tumbled over the wingback chair and into the bar. Crystal fell from shelves and banged off the wall and the hardwood floor. Lavanya landed on top of him and went for his throat. Zev grabbed her tangled hair and pulled her head back to keep her teeth from sinking into his flesh.

The smell of cardamom wafted through the air, and Lavanya tingled with electric pulses as he held her at bay with his strength and his magic. But Zev couldn't get the upper hand. He tried to roll her over to get a better advantage, but she held tight with the strength of her father surging through her veins.

At a stalemate, she changed tactics and used her manicured nails to rip into his arms. He howled in pain, but didn't release her head. As she concentrated on digging her nails into the arm that held her, he worked the other arm free and slapped her hard in the face. The jarring from the slap forced them both to release each other. Lavanya scrambled to her feet, rubbing her jaw where he'd hit her and snarling with rage, while Zev held onto his bleeding arm and snarled back.

"Zev, Lavanya, stop this absurd behavior," Renfield croaked.

Lavanya's growl died in her throat as she angled her head toward Renfield, never taking her eyes off the intruder.

"Renfield," she sighed with relief, happy that he was still alive. Then she realized that he knew this man, or witch, or whatever he was.

Chloe's frantic voice and knock drew everyone's attention. "Mistress, Mistress, are you all right? I heard you scream. Please, Mistress, answer me. Let me in." Lavanya looked to Renfield before she answered.

"Well, are we okay?" Lavanya asked.

"Yes, tell the child we're fine and to leave us. Then help me up." He looked tired and pale.

"Chloe, we're fine. The wind just knocked over the bar. Please get Renfield a dinner tray and place it in his quarters, then go on to bed." Lavanya gave Chloe a little mental push.

"Yes, Mistress." She sounded dazed. And then they all heard Chloe's shoes on the stone floor of the hall as she retreated to the kitchens. Lavanya returned her attention back to Renfield and the stranger.

"Both of you, help me up," Renfield said. Lavanya moved to help him, but as the intruder started forward, she hissed at him.

"Stop it, Anya. Zev has been summoned here by your father."

That stopped her. She looked the stranger over, noticing his eyes again.

"Make yourself useful and pick up that chair for him," Lavanya said, her voice full of malice. She felt Zev's muffled growl ripple through her, but he obeyed. She helped Renfield sit in the wingback chair and pulled the table back up beside him.

"He needs orange juice," she told Zev, pointing toward the back wall behind the cabinet they'd knocked over. "There's some in the bar fridge." While Zev went to get the juice, she took the opportunity to talk to Renfield.

"Why did you let me feed like that?" she asked. "I could've killed you."

"You will need your strength, and I knew your father would not let you harm me. Although it's been a long time since anyone's bitten me, and I'd forgotten how badly it hurts." He touched his neck.

"Let me fix it, please," she said, leaning in to lick the wound. Without the healing saliva, her bite could leave a scar and might not heal for weeks.

"Yes, dear, you better do that. I don't want anyone to know that you drank from me tonight."

For a moment Lavanya was lost in the blood lust again. She could smell his blood, and it was a powerful force. Her fangs descended as she fought the urge. She delicately traced the wound with her tongue. *Ah, just one taste…*

"Here's the juice." Zev startled her. "Maybe you shouldn't be the one to heal him. You're still shaking with hunger." His tone was condescending and he pissed her off, but that meant she could focus on her anger instead of hunger. She could thank him for that. But she wouldn't.

"Shut up and clean up this mess." Then she turned her back on him, knowing that Renfield could see him and wouldn't let him harm her. Lavanya could hear Zev taking in rough, angry breaths.

"Zev." Renfield pushed weakly to sit up straighter in the chair. "Please clean up as much as possible. We don't want anyone to be suspicious." He leaned back and closed his eyes.

"Yes, sir." Lavanya listened to Zev's heavy boots retreat to the bar across the room, but she focused on Renfield—getting him comfortable and nourished. She opened the bottle of orange juice.

"Renfield, you can't fall asleep yet."

"I know, dear." He opened his eyes, and his exhaustion was plain to see in the way his lids drooped. Lavanya held out the open bottle of juice.

"Take a big drink and I'll finish healing you."

Renfield did as she asked, even though he looked too tired to lift his head. When he'd had enough, she leaned into him again, healing Renfield's wound like a dog cleaning its paw. Her mouth watered, and she thought of anything and everything besides the yummy smell coming off his skin. To a human, it was sort of like licking a juicy steak, but not being able to take a bite. All the while she pretended she didn't hear Zev in the background cleaning up.

How did this perfectly planned weekend getaway go to shit in a matter of hours? Lavanya didn't have a clue.

After a minute the wound was sealed, so she blew on Renfield's neck. The gash was looking better, but sometimes blowing on the wound sped the process and calmed the victims. Goose bumps broke out on Renfield's flesh.

"Thank you, dear." He cleared his throat and seemed to be feeling a little better.

"Here." Lavanya handed him the orange juice, and Renfield gulped the cold drink. When he finished, he set it aside and gave her a tired smile.

"I'm guessing that you have a few questions?"

"Always stating the obvious." Lavanya smiled at him and then remembered they had an audience. She turned to take in the damage to the man and the room. The room looked okay, considering what they'd done to it only moments before.

Most of the crystal hadn't shattered, probably because the wood floors had a lot more give than the stone floors in other parts of the castle. Zev had swept up the broken glassware and mopped up the spills. Renfield had stopped them before they could cause serious damage, so they might get away without anyone knowing that they'd been at each other's throats.

Lavanya pushed the other wingback chair next to Renfield's and repositioned the tables. As she dragged the bearskin rug back where it belonged, she caught Zev staring. She bared her fangs, challenging him.

"I had plans for a brand new wolf pelt at the foot of my bed," she said. "It would give me pleasure to wipe my boots on it every night. Know where I could find one, Zev?"

He acted like it didn't bother him, but she could feel and hear his pulse quicken. Lavanya smiled, satisfied that she'd ruffled his fur.

"I would expect nothing less of a *frigid* vampire." He ran his hand down his lean body, the fire's light showcasing his muscular outline. "You have a powerful wolf in your bedroom, and your only thought is of your boots. *Tsk, tsk.* A little cold, are you?"

His mocking smile infuriated her. She pulled her arm back lightning fast to smack his smug face.

"Anya!" Renfield stopped her.

Lavanya halted mid swing with the force of his voice. She lowered her hand, but whispered her warning.

"This business with my father can't last forever, and then we'll see how you look stuffed. No one comes into my territory and hurts my people or my guests. You will pay for it."

He looked amused, which only infuriated her more.

"Me." He laughed, grabbing a handful of nuts from the bowl that somehow had managed to survive their fight. "I didn't hurt anyone except the brown-haired vamp who attacked me. Hell, I didn't even scratch that stupid dog, who deserved to be killed. Renfield, you saw the wounds on the girl and the dark-haired vamp. Are they consistent with my style of attack?"

Renfield coughed and pulled forward in his chair.

"Lauren's is your work, yes. But the girl was beaten, very badly. I hate to have to tell you this, Anya, but she was raped, too. A wolf did not do the damage done to her."

She was dumbfounded. "*What?*" She focused on Zev, her face contorted with anger. "Rape is the most evil thing. I will kill yo…"

"Anya, I do not believe it was Zev. Your father has been increasingly restless because he knew that some danger was coming. He sent for Zev to assist me in protecting you."

"Protecting me—are you kidding? This shithead attacked me!"

"Whoa, whoa, whoa!" Zev slammed his fist on the bar. "You attacked me, remember? I found the girl there, beaten. When the female vampire stuck her nose where it didn't belong, I gave her a small scratch for her trouble. Lucky for her, my claws don't carry as much poison as my teeth when I'm in animal form. So I scared her away. Then your pet yipped at me and you attacked me. When I realized that your scent linked you to Vlad, I stopped. But oh no, not you. You insisted on attacking me again. You got what you deserved."

He smiled, his eyes cold. "It burns doesn't it?"

Lavanya snarled. She wanted him dead.

"Renfield, I don't care what my father thinks. Get rid of him tonight, or I will. It must have been him that injured Giselle. He was the only person there."

"Anya...Anya," Renfield stood on shaky legs. "I don't have the strength to explain everything tonight, but you'll have to get used to him being around. At least for a little while. Now you must go to the girl and change her. She's innocent, and it's a waste for her to die when she can live. Plus, she may have information about who attacked her. We owe her our assistance."

That took the wind out of Lavanya. She'd put the girl in harm's way, and now she'd give her immortality. Would the girl thank her or curse her for it? Some people were glad at first, but then over the years, when everyone they knew died, they hated you for the *gift*. Others thought you damned them to hell and hated you right from the beginning. Either way, it ended badly.

"Does her family know? Do they approve of what I have to do?" Lavanya placed her hands on her hips and stared at Renfield's tired face.

"They asked for it."

"Okay." Lavanya closed her eyes for a moment and took a deep breath to calm herself, but the smell of cardamom surrounded her. "I'll freshen up. Renfield, can you arrange to bring her to me?"

She needed to focus on helping Giselle now. She'd never turned anyone before, but she'd seen it done and she knew she'd need to stay with the girl during her first day of sleep. Watching

Giselle's body die would be difficult, but she'd awaken tomorrow at sunset and be immortal.

Later she'd have time to reason with Renfield and kill Zev.

"Yes, dear, I've already made the arrangements."

He always was two steps ahead of her.

"Of course," Lavanya murmured. She waved a hand dismissively in Zev's direction. "Renfield, what are we to do with the wolf? I fear for your safety. I won't leave you alone with him." Lavanya let the hatred she felt cloud her features in a silent warning.

"I'll be fine, dear, you needn't worry. Especially since Zev will be with you."

Lavanya and Zev both protested at the same time, but Lavanya won the floor.

"Renfield, you can't be serious! I'm going to be holed up with the girl all day tomorrow here in the castle. Why on earth would I need him with me?"

Renfield touched his neck where she'd bitten him.

"Lavanya, I'll be down most of the day myself recuperating from this, and you need to have someone with you for your own safety until we find out who attacked Giselle. I hope your father will communicate through dreams tonight and explain more, but there's no guarantee. Right now Zev will be your shadow. Danger's coming. This attack wasn't random."

"How am I supposed to explain his presence in my chambers, or even in this castle?"

She turned back to ask Zev. "How the hell did you get up on the balcony, anyway?" Even in a wolf's form, he couldn't have jumped or climbed onto the balcony without coming into the castle first.

Zev smiled. "I'm proficient at many things."

"Renfield!"

"Zev," Renfield chided him. "He acquired a lot of magic from his mother's side of the family, and he can take other forms besides a wolf. He'll be an asset to us, Lavanya. Please try to get along, will you?"

Renfield took a step and wobbled a little, but he looked better. His color had returned to his cheeks, so she knew he'd be fully recovered in a few days.

"I'm going to my chamber to rest," he said. "I don't want the two of you fighting any more this evening. Lavanya, you have a job to do. You know what needs to be done."

Then he focused on Zev. "You, Zev—do not antagonize her any further, or she will make a rug of you before I can wake and stop her." He hobbled to the door as Lavanya watched him. He seemed older than she had ever seen him look before.

"Be sure to eat the food that Chloe brought to your room before you go to sleep," she called to him. He didn't respond. "Renfield?"

"Yes, I will eat. You two behave yourselves. I'll see you tomorrow evening. If you need me, just call my rooms."

"Get some rest. I know what to do." Lavanya was saddened by what she must do, but it didn't change the fact that she had to do it. Zev stood at ease with his hands behind his back, like a military soldier.

"Come." Lavanya patted her leg and gave a little whistle, like calling a dog. "I have things to do to get ready for Giselle's arrival."

"Do not order me around like a pet or a servant. I'm not your servant." He sounded furious.

"Are you sure? It seems as if, through my father, you *are* my servant. He did summon you didn't he?" Lavanya gave him her biggest smile.

"I'm here to protect you and Renfield as part of the deal I made with Vlad, but I'm *not* anyone's servant. Got it, Princess?"

"Yeah, yeah. Let's go." Lavanya pushed past him. *Princess*, she fumed. It sounded condescending, and she hated the title. She turned to confront him before heading to her rooms.

"My name is Lavanya, you idiot…"

He was gone. Just gone. Nothing there, not even a mist or film like when someone disappears in the movies. He was just there one moment and gone the next.

"Great," she whispered to herself. She could only hope that he'd decided to stay in the kennel with the other dogs. Lavanya trudged to her suite, suddenly tired and apprehensive about the events to come. She'd sworn that she'd never change anyone into this life. Tonight she'd break that promise, and tomorrow evening she'd plan her attack on Zev. Then she'd take care of her guests and teach a child how to feed off a human. Busy, busy, busy.

CHAPTER TEN

A Roach By Any Other Name...

Lavanya entered her suite as quietly as possible, but Astor and Buttercup heard her. They both raised their heads off the bed, and she saw both of their tails twitch.

"Hi, babies, how are you?" Their tails moved from a twitch to a full wag as she went to give them some affection.

"'Bout time you made it to bed." Dylan was lying on her lounge by the fire. The light lit his face, and he looked tired.

"Darling, what the hell happened tonight?" he asked. "A simple weekend in the country has turned into something completely different. The rumor mill has you training a wolf to attack your own guests. They're speculating that you wanted Phil for yourself, so you trained a wolf to attack Lauren. Or that you have some sort of curse on you, or my personal favorite, that you were having an affair with the girl and wanted to get rid of her. So, what's the truth?"

"Dylan, how's Astor?" Lavanya entered the dressing room, eager to get out of her ruined clothes, leaving him sitting by the fire.

"Astor's fine. I think it's just a little sprain or something. I'll take him into town tomorrow and have it looked at to be sure."

Dylan stood at the entrance to her dressing room now. "So answer my question. Are any of the rumors true? Are you having an affair with Phil or the girl?" He grinned as he came into her dressing room and helped her get out of her ruined things.

"Don't be absurd, Dylan. It was just an unfortunate accident. I'm not having an affair with anyone. You know that."

"Yes, and what a pity. You need to get laid," he said with a wink.

"Dylan, really."

"Enough joking. Let me run a bath for you. It'll help you relax. You seem all keyed up." Dylan tossed her robe over the screen she used to change behind.

"A shower will have to do. I need to hurry. They're bringing the injured girl, Giselle, to the castle tonight. I'll be asleep for the entire day tomorrow, and I hope you get some rest too, because I'll need you to help me get ready tomorrow night for the dinner and concert. Oh, we'll also have another guest with us tomorrow."

"Who?" Dylan called from the bath.

"Giselle will be joining us. I'd like you to help her get ready, too. She'll be on her worst behavior, so be sure to watch for signs of hunger. I'll be here, too, so it'll be fine, but I wanted you to know." Lavanya came out from behind the screen, fastening the tie on her dressing gown. Then he registered what she'd said.

"Wait. The girl who was attacked tonight. You're going to revamp her?" Surprise was written all over his face. Lavanya sat down at her vanity and pulled her hair out from the back of her gown. Dylan grabbed the brush and began to work it through the tangles. Lavanya closed her eyes after she saw him pull a leaf from under her heavy curtain of hair.

"Her family has requested it, and I can't let her die. She was hurt doing a favor for me." Lavanya kept her eyes closed, not wanting to see the hurt and anger on his face. Dylan had requested the change several times. But Lavanya knew he'd be happy only for a little while. Then as he watched everyone die, he'd hate her. She couldn't bear it if she saw hate in his eyes.

She'd tried to explain it to him. She was a monster. She didn't want to change her loved ones into monsters, too. Tonight she could have killed the girl with her thirst. What if she changed Dylan and then he killed someone he loved? He'd never forgive her. She was born into this life. Would she have chosen it if she'd had a choice? Of course, she'd never know the answer to that question.

"Dylan." She used the voice that influenced people. "You do not wish to become a vampire."

"Of course, Lavanya, you are very sweet to take care of her. I would be happy to help her tomorrow." He didn't skip a beat—he just went on with their original conversation, although there was none of the jealousy in his voice that had been present a moment before.

"Thank you, Dylan. Will you come and get Astor and Buttercup in the morning?"

"I'd be happy to take little Buttercup for a walk, too. Plus, it'll give me a chance to evaluate Astor after he's slept on his leg overnight."

Lavanya took the brush and held his hand for a moment. "That'll be all, Dylan. You can retire for the night."

"All right." Dylan kissed her cheek and gave her a little hug. "Don't worry, it'll all work out. She'll make a lovely immortal, and if her family requested it, you shouldn't feel guilty."

"Thanks." Lavanya didn't look at him, and he left without another word.

Guilty was but one of the emotions swirling through her. Rage was more at the forefront, along with frustration. Who would dare to attack Giselle in Vlad's territory, and why would Vlad fear for her safety? Her money was still on Zev. How could her father trust a magic-wielding shapeshifter? She slammed down her brush and stood. She needed to shower and wash away all the dirt from the tumbling matches she'd had with Zev.

She looked at her hand. The surface of her palm was still pink from the fire. The skin was healing quickly, as normal, but a fine, jagged scar was visible.

"Damn it!" She used her other hand to rub the skin, and it felt different, too. The scar was warmer than her normal body temperature. She fisted her hands and looked at her reflection again.

"He is going to pay for marking me," she promised herself. What kind of magic did he have? She was immortal; nothing had ever hurt her before. As she looked at the scar again, a tingle of fear, an unknown feeling, trickled up her spine. *Just another reason to get rid of him quickly.*

A fly buzzed her face. Lavanya waved her hands to drive it away, but it just kept dive bombing her. She backed away from her vanity and headed into the bath to get away. She needed to hurry, so she quickly undressed and stepped into the stone shower.

Lavanya's shower was cut short when she heard the house phone ringing in her suite. She grabbed a towel and hurried out to catch it.

"Yes," she said into the old-fashioned telephone.

"Mistress, the men are bringing Giselle up to your room per Renfield's instructions. Do you need anything...any help?" Chloe swallowed.

"No, Chloe, I don't need any help. Just bring me the evening reports and see to everyone's needs during the day tomorrow."

"Yes, Mistress." Just then a cockroach ran across Lavanya's bare foot, and she yelped into the phone. Buttercup and Astor growled.

"Mistress, are you all right? Mistress?"

"Chloe, I'm fine." She bent to look under the bed to see if the roach was still visible so she could kill it, but it was gone. "I just saw a cockroach."

"A what?"

"A big bug! I want you to see to it that we have an exterminator come to the castle next week."

"I'll call one right away and schedule it."

Lavanya caught sight of the roach as it headed into her dressing room. Buttercup stood next to Astor as if she were protecting him with all her three-pound might.

"That'll be fine, Chloe. Bring the reports right up." Lavanya hung up the phone, grabbed one of her satin slippers, and headed into the dressing room after the roach. In the corner she found a nest of roaches and began to crush them. She'd never seen a roach here in her father's Romanian fortress. At her home in Miami, she saw them all the time, but never here.

The towel came undone and fell to the floor in a puddle around her legs as Lavanya tried to smash the bugs. The damn things moved like a swarm, she'd never seen anything like it. Her blows did nothing and then... she smelled the cardamom.

"Damn it, Zev!" She pulled a big sweater off the shelf as she yelled at him. "Show yourself!"

All of the black cockroaches flowed and moved together to combine into one mass. Lavanya stepped back pulling the sweater down as the air crackled and the mass of roaches grew and melted into Zev. She rushed him and held him by the neck against the wall.

"What the hell are you doing in my room?"

"I was told to stay with you, and that's what I'm going to do." He smiled and pulled her hand away from his neck, so she slapped him with the other one. It zinged with the pain of the slap and the healing scar. He caught her hand before she could swing at him again and brought it to his mouth, licking the scar his teeth had created. It burned, and she pulled away.

"What the hell is wrong with you? I don't care if my father is your best friend. If you ever touch me again, I'll kill you. Or better yet, I'll do a little research and see how I can trap you in one of your many shapes. Maybe a little friend for Buttercup—a cat she can chase. Declawed, of course. That'd be fun to watch."

Astor limped to her side and growled, showing his teeth to Zev. He seemed to be feeling better at least. Buttercup, on the other hand, was jumping at Zev's legs. The little dog wanted him to pick her up. Traitor! Lavanya couldn't believe it. Buttercup never liked anyone new.

"Oh, Buttercup. You little sweetie." Zev bent to pick her up and nuzzled her face. If she'd been a cat, she'd have purred. It was plan to see from her body language that she adored him.

"Why does she like you? She never likes anyone new. Have you been in here before?" Lavanya placed her hand on Astor's head to silence his growl.

"Yes, Buttercup and I are acquainted, but no, I have not been in your personal suite before today," Zev said, petting Buttercup like they were old friends. "I assumed you would like to keep my arrival a secret, so I disguised myself as something inconspicuous. I decided a roach might be up your alley. Who knew you were the kind of woman to take matters into your own hands and try to kill a whole colony?"

"If you knew anything about me, you'd know that's exactly the kind of woman I am. Buttercup, come here." The tiny dog looked up at her from her perch in Zev's arms. Then she snuggled back against his hard chest, tucking her head under his prickly beard.

Lavanya was furious and stormed into the main room of the suite. Strangely, though, as she stomped away, a question popped into her head. *How would Zev's beard feel scratching down her back and over her ass?*

Was she crazy? *Stop thinking like that*, she warned herself. Then she realized that her ass was probably sticking out and that he'd been here watching her all along.

"Get out of my sight and out of my rooms." Lavanya pointed toward the door. "Go protect Renfield."

Without saying a word, Zev sat Buttercup down. Lavanya stooped to pick up the mutinous rat, tucked her under her arm, and rubbed her soft neck.

Zev stretched out on the bed. "Sorry, no can do, Princess. I stay with you. But I know you have guests, so you can choose. What would be the easiest animal for you to explain? Dog, cat— you name it and I can do it."

"What kind of witch are you?" Lavanya couldn't help the question. She'd never seen anyone who could change forms with such ease.

A knock sounded at the outer door.

"No time for an explanation tonight. Time is ticking by. What would you like to spend the night with, Princess?"

"I don't need a bodyguard and don't call me princess." Lavanya hissed.

"Whatever, Princess. What shall it be? Not a fly. I tried that, and you didn't seem to like it."

Another knock sounded at the door. *Damn her overprotective father.*

"A trained rat, it suits you." She crossed her arms under her chest.

"Ha, ha," he said as he rolled his eyes. Then she watched as his eyes wandered over the deep V in her sweater and down to her barely covered assets and naked legs. Lavanya stood up straighter and pushed her breasts out farther.

"On second thought, how about a snake?" she said, smiling as he stared. "I'd love a new pair of boots."

A third knock at the door made them both turn. When Lavanya turned back, Zev had shrunk down into a scraggly black rat terrier. Astor growled, but didn't move. Buttercup, on the other hand, wiggled in Lavanya's grasp until she let her down. The little minx jumped around Zev until he yipped to play with her. Lavanya left them to it and went in search of some clothes.

"Just a moment," she yelled, running to her dresser. She pulled on a soft pair of leggings and ran her fingers through her hair. After a quick glance in the mirror, she was ready to answer the door. Or as ready as she'd ever be.

"Gentlemen." Renfield, looking pale and tired, stood with the assembled men of Giselle's family. One man in the middle held

Giselle in his arms like a baby. He seemed comfortable with holding her. Her father, Lavanya guessed.

"Please come in," she said, moving back so they could enter. Giselle's father—she'd guessed right—spoke first.

"Mistress Lavanya Draculesti, I bring you my child. She has been brutally attacked in your territory. I request your assistance. We have been your family's servants for generations. Please grant my daughter your immortality." He stood, holding his child, surrounded by the men of his tribe, to announce his formal request.

"Gentlemen, Renfield—please leave us. I would like to speak with Giselle's father alone."

Giselle's breath was very shallow, and her head hung off her father's arm. Lavanya could smell death spreading over her like a pungent perfume, which killed her hunger. Without life to warm it, blood tasted just like rancid milk.

The men looked to their leader, holding his daughter. He nodded. Renfield handed Lavanya the household reports and then addressed the men.

"Gentlemen, we can wait downstairs in the parlor," he told them. Lavanya was grateful for his help as he herded them out and shut the door.

"Please, lay her down." Lavanya watched as he spread her out on the bed. Giselle's father lovingly sat beside her and brushed her golden blonde hair off her pale face.

"Giselle was under my protection when this attack took place, and I want you to know that I do *not* take it lightly. I have already found the wolf, and he will be dealt with. However, it seems he was not responsible for all the injuries your daughter sustained. I have to ask. Has she said anything that would give you any idea who could have done this to her?"

The man's eyes were red when he looked at Lavanya, but what was worse was his broken expression.

"No, Mistress, she never regained consciousness." Then his gaze went back to his child.

"Sir, I know that you're grieving, and I'm sorry for your loss. But making her into a vampire will not bring *her* back to you."

He started to rise in protest and Lavanya held out her hand.

"I'm not refusing your request," she said. "But I want you to understand what she will be." Lavanya let her fangs descend and her face relax into her true nature. She removed any hint of mind control so he could see the monster. He would see her as she was when she fed. Her eyes turned to a deep red, and her mouth got bigger to accommodate her teeth. She knew what she looked like when the monster came out. She'd seen it once in the mirror and never wished to see it again.

"We're a little part devil and a little part animal, all wrapped up in a package that we can make look beautiful to humans." He pulled back from her gaze and closed his eyes.

"I'm aware of what you are, and I understand that she'll have to learn to control the hunger. I also know that she'll not have children." He took a deep breath and his voice waivered on the next words.

"But she's my only child, and I cannot watch her go into the grave knowing that she could live. I watched her mother die, and I will not survive Giselle's death." He bowed his head and pleaded. "Please."

"What of her desires? Would she want to live forever and watch everyone around her get old and die? Will she curse you for giving her this half-life when she watches her friends get married and have children?"

"She's a practical girl. She would want to live." He looked up into her red eyes and his sincerity was evident.

"Very well. Leave us." Lavanya turned away as he said his last good-bye to his child.

When she heard the door shut, she turned back to the bed and swallowed the bile that had risen in her throat. Even though she was a vampire, she'd never taken a life or changed a human. And she didn't want to do it now.

The girl took a ragged breath, and Lavanya, her mind made up, didn't hesitate. She attacked her.

When she couldn't drink anymore of Giselle's rank, almost dead, blood, she took her to the shower and let her bleed out. Then she opened her own vein and forced the blood down Giselle's throat. Lavanya was glad for the privacy the shower provided. She didn't want Zev to see the tears that slipped down her cheek.

After a long night of fighting and watching a young girl die, Lavanya was exhausted. She would need to feed tomorrow. She wrapped Giselle in animal skin blankets and laid her in her own bed to sleep. With a chill settling deep in her bones, she pulled the heavy shutters over the stained glass windows and balcony doors. The fire's flames flickered against the stone floor and gave the room a warm glow. Lavanya kicked Zev off her chaise and lay down on the lounge by the fire. Sleep took her as she wondered how the girl would awaken—glad or sad.

Zev lay down on the floor beside Buttercup and waited until he was sure Lavanya was asleep before changing back into his human form. As he stood from the change, Buttercup danced around his feet.

"Shh, little lady," Zev whispered. Then he picked up the little troublemaker and placed her at the bottom of the chaise with her master. She did a couple of circles and settled when Zev draped a blanket over her head. As he backed away, Lavanya's voice startled him.

"Sorry…now…I had to…" Lavanya tossed, obviously agitated even in her sleep.

Zev pulled the blanket up and tucked it around Lavanya, too, and she settled back into peaceful sleep. He'd been curious when Lavanya took the girl into the bath, so he'd changed into a fly and watched Lavanya complete the blood exchange. The last thing he'd expected to find was Lavanya crying in obvious grief over revamping the young girl. The only other vamps he'd met were all for adding to the ranks of the undead. Zev had never expected this bitchy vampire princess to have a heart.

And her smell, what the hell was up with that? Zev had been momentarily blinded by it when she'd struck him earlier. Then he'd licked her hand and she'd tasted just as delicious as she'd smelled. He felt himself move behind the tight jeans he'd manifested himself in and quickly moved away from her.

Shit, absolutely not. Zev wouldn't let his dick get in the way. He had a job to do. Keep Lavanya safe and find out who hurt the girl. Soon he'd be free of all these bloodsuckers.

Zev checked out the rest of the suite and made sure everything was safe before returning to the bedroom to watch over Lavanya and the girl. As he sat down beside the door, he hoped he wouldn't have to be the last of his line. If Vlad kept his side of the bargain and lifted the curse of servitude, maybe he'd have a chance at a normal life.

CHAPTER ELEVEN

An Unexpected Guest

Lavanya awoke to a girl's high-pitched scream so sharp and piercing that she was glad she didn't keep any crystal glassware in the room. She sat up immediately and regretted the move, holding onto the edge of the chaise, waiting for the spinning to stop. Then she remembered why she felt so bad and who would be screaming.

"Giselle, stop screaming," she commanded. The poor girl was shaking, of course, holding the blankets to her chest, frantic and scared of everything she saw. Her skin was the color of milk, and her blue eyes would be beautiful again once she fed and learned how to use her magic.

"Mistress? I...I'm sorry. I should be hiding?" She looked down at her hands clutching the blankets.

"Giselle, you'll be fine. Do you remember anything about last night?" Lavanya asked, still trying to wake up.

"I took the clue and went to the cave, as instructed. I waited to be found and brought back to the castle." Her face shut down. "Pain." She screamed again. "No. No! *No!* Please, Mistress, why?"

Zev, still in his mutt disguise, howled softly and jumped up and sat beside Giselle. She took him in her arms, sobbing into his fur. Then her head shot up, she scented the air.

A knock sounded. *Chloe.* Giselle threw Zev to the floor and vaulted to the door. Lavanya got there just in time to stop her from opening it.

"Chloe, step back from the door," Lavanya instructed, blocking Giselle's advance. "Giselle, I know you're hungry, and we're getting you someone."

Giselle's eyes were blood red. Fresh venom ran down her chin as she struggled to get to Chloe. Lavanya slapped her.

"Giselle! Stop this. You've been revamped and you're hungry. But you must show me that you can control yourself, or I'll have to destroy you."

Giselle huffed in fury, but stepped back. Then some of her

sanity seemed to come back. She looked at her pale hands and then brought them up to her mouth to wipe away the drool.

"What have you done to me?" she asked around her swollen fangs. Fear wrapped the young girl up and brought her to her knees.

There it was, the question that Lavanya had been dreading all her undead life. The reason she'd never revamped a human.

"Giselle, you were injured last night." Lavanya tried to calm her with her voice. She approached her with her hands out in a universal sign of peace.

"No!" Giselle shouted. She leaped to her feet, hurtling over the footboard to gaze in the mirror by Lavanya's bed. The scream of torment that tore from her throat when she took in the reflection of the monster in the mirror could be heard all the way to the valley below the castle. All the dogs howled along with her as she stared at her new fangs and pale porcelain skin.

Lavanya wrapped a blanket around her and folded her up in an embrace. After Giselle quieted, Lavanya told her what she knew of her attack and that her father thought she would want to live, no matter what. They sat together on the floor for more than an hour, Lavanya telling her what had happened and Giselle nodding her head.

In the end, Giselle's father had been right. Giselle was practical and didn't blame Lavanya for revamping her, although she was shaken and refused to look in a mirror. She had no recollection of the attack. She remembered the pain of being beaten and raped, but it was like a dream—only broken pieces of the whole came to the surface. The memory of dying and the hunger she felt now drowned out everything else.

Her first feeding went as well as could be expected. Lavanya was there to pull Giselle free and heal the wounds she inflected on the village men who volunteered to be her firsts. With Giselle fed, Lavanya passed her care off to Renfield, who was looking much better.

Lavanya grabbed a bite from one of the servants and then returned to her suite. A wonderful quiet greeted her. Her rooms were empty of dogs, new vamps, and servants. She showered, and when she returned to her bedroom, she noticed that the ever faithful Chloe had brought up some sweets—just what she needed to put her in a happy mood. After the feeding and a few nibbles, her strength returned. That was important, because she still had guests to attend to this evening. As she finished her third croissant, Dylan crashed in with the latest news and gossip.

"Darling!" He entered, clapping his hands. The man certainly could scoop up all the oxygen in the room. "We need to get you ready and caught up." He raised his brows. He had something juicy to tell her.

"Okay, what's the news?" Lavanya winked at him and licked her fingers clean of the final bits of buttery goodness. He almost skipped to her sitting area in front of the fireplace. He took a seat next to her on the chaise, scooching her over a bit and sucking the last bit of jam off her thumb.

"First off, Astor is fine, just a little sprain. Doc said to keep him calm for a few days and he should be good as new."

"Thank you for taking him. Was Buttercup civil to you?" A little sigh of gratitude escaped her, and she squeezed his arm.

"Don't think anything of it; Buttercup is such a little lady. She's running around the castle somewhere now, and I put Astor in his kennel." He rubbed his hands together.

"So, annnyway, back to the good stuff. Everyone is talking about your fighting off the massive black wolf and saving the damsel and the dog. You are such a bad ass, bitch." He winked.

"Yes, yes, we all know what a bitch I am. So what else happened while I was busy watching a young girl be reborn into evil?" She dabbed at her lips with a linen napkin and pushed a croissant toward Dylan.

"I can't, darling." He pushed it back and shook his finger in her face. "We don't all have the terminator's metabolism." He got up and went around the chaise and ran his fingers through her wet hair.

"Anyway—"

Lavanya had to smile. Dylan could always be counted on to find out everything that wasn't in her housekeeping reports.

"Tru and Naasir are inseparable," he said. "You called that one. Over the top, and Tru is so giddy. I would've never imagined it. Actually, all the couples are doing well except maybe Lauren and Phil. I'm not sure about them. Maybe it's because she was injured last night, but something just doesn't sit well. Anyway, no one's been too distracted by the events last night."

"Good. I was worried they might be upset."

"Not at all. If anything, they loved the drama of it. *Wolf attack!*" Dylan used his hands as if he were lighting up a billboard. "*Girl barely survives! Lavanya Draculesti comes to the rescue!*" He shook his head.

"Please. Come on, up and into the chair before I give you the biggest surprise." He took Lavanya's arm and dragged her into her dressing room and the vanity chair.

"What?"

"We have another guest in the castle." He grabbed both the blow dryers and, with one in each hand, began blowing her hair around her face. Then he turned the chair and angled her head down as he whipped her hair into a fury. Finally satisfied, he pulled her back up to a sitting position and stashed the dryers back in the drawers.

Talk about enjoying drama! Lavanya grabbed his arm. "*Who arrived today?*"

"Harry Connick, Jr. and his lovely wife arrived. He's wonderful—even dreamier in person, I might add. That southern accent is to die for, and his wife is beautiful."

Lavanya nodded. "I was expecting him. He's putting on the concert tonight for our guests. They have such divergent tastes; I needed someone who could appeal to a wide audience. He fits the bill perfectly—he's a wonderful musician and showman, and he's from New Orleans, so all our little eccentricities won't shock him too much. Practically every other home in Louisiana is owned by a vampire, so he's used to the undead. But surely, that's not the mystery guest, is it?"

"Nooo. Of course not." Dylan answered. "I knew he was coming and even picked out the Stella McCartney dress for you to wear for the concert." He began to mold her black hair into her trademark 1940s wave. "I've changed my mind though. Do you still have that red fox wrap?"

"I'm sure it's in the dressing room. Why?"

"Honey, you just wrestled a wolf. You deserve to wear fur. It'll be symbolic. Plus, I want you to stand out. The red fox worn with the black tuxedo dress that's open to your belly button is a showstopper."

"Why on earth would I want to stand out? I'm here to get these couples mated, not draw attention to myself."

"That's why I want you to look your best."

"Dylan," Lavanya said sternly, a little tired of his games.

"Okay, okay. A friend of your father's arrived this afternoon."

"What? Has Renfield met with him yet?"

"I don't know, but he has the suite next door, so *shush*." He put his finger to his lips.

Renfield and the staff knew that she always kept this floor empty. *Hmm.*

"He wouldn't happen to be tall, dark, and handsome in a wild beast sort of way, would he?" She raised a brow as he plucked her eyebrows and laughed.

"Tall and dark maybe, but wild beast, no." He shook his head. "More of a computer geek or book worm vibe. Glasses, cleanly shaved. No pocket protector, but that's just because no one uses those anymore."

Who could that be?

"Something just tells me that you need to make a strong impression that's all." He laughed again and blew her a kiss. "Call it hairdresser intuition."

"Far be it for me to go against hairdresser intuition. Does this geek have a name?" She knew it had to be Zev in another disguise, but she also knew she needed to make sure everyone saw her as a strong, independent woman, especially him.

"I overheard him speaking to Uki, and she called him Bob, or something. I couldn't catch the rest."

"Thanks for the tip. I'll be sure to get to know him."

By the time Chloe gave her the daily reports, she was caught up on everything. Lavanya didn't learn anything new from the reports, but Chloe did remind her that she'd missed her appointment with Helgaleena.

"Chloe, please get word to your grandmother. I'm sorry I had to miss our appointment today. See if I can come by tomorrow. I still want to talk to her about that dream," Lavanya said, putting on the red fox shawl.

"Yes, Mistress and… you look stunning tonight."

"Thank you, Chloe." Dylan had done exactly what he said he would. The fox shawl was the same color red as her lips, and the tiny chain that held the top of her black tuxedo dress together barley contained the creamy white flesh of her breasts. She finished the outfit with a pair of Christian Louboutin red snakeskin stilettos.

She'd show Zev, the geek, that she didn't need a chaperone or a bodyguard.

CHAPTER TWELVE

An Uninvited Guest

Lavanya entered the grand hall where Harry Connick, Jr. and his wife, Jill, were enjoying a cocktail.

"Harry, Jill, it was so good of you to come. My guests are so excited to hear you tonight."

"Lavanya." Harry kissed her cheeks and stood back for his wife to do the same. "It was my pleasure to come. It got us out of the city for a few days and away from the kids."

Jill playfully slapped at his arm. "Harry! But it is nice to be alone." She winked playfully at her handsome husband. "Lavanya, I'm so glad to finally meet you. I wanted to thank you personally for your contribution to our music program for kids in the city. Your generosity is overwhelming."

Jill took Lavanya's hand. As a testament to her comfort around vampires, she didn't flinch from the cold, marble-like texture of her skin.

Class act, Lavanya thought.

"I was happy to do it," she said. "Louisiana is dear to all our hearts. You open your doors to us at every turn, so I wanted to return the favor. Who knows? Maybe I can help spawn another musical genius like this one." Lavanya poked Harry.

"Ah, shucks," Harry laughed. "Don't embarrass me. I have to perform tonight."

"Enjoy the party, and if you need anything, please don't hesitate to ask." Lavanya started to step away, but Harry caught her arm.

"Are you kidding? You made jambalaya tonight that was as good as my momma's. Don't tell her I said so, but I might never leave."

"With your permission, though, I'll tell my chef you said so," Lavanya smiled. "He'll be pleased to know that he got it right." After all, he'd been working on the recipe for a week.

Like a good hostess, Lavanya moved around the room and

checked on the refreshments and preparations for the concert. Everything was going well, so she decided to find her clients and remind them of the concert, which was scheduled to start soon.

"Hi, doll. How're ya holding up?" Belle asked as Lavanya entered the main parlor. Belle and Arthur were playing cards by the large entry doors.

"I'm wonderful. How are you two this evening?" Lavanya stopped to look at their game. "Who's winning?"

"Belle, of course. She's a card shark." Arthur smiled up at Lavanya with his ever-present glass of whiskey in his hand.

"Old habits die hard," Belle replied with a devious smile.

"Yes, they do." Arthur finished his drink and then shook his empty glass, letting the ice rattle. Lavanya smiled and motioned for one of the servants to refill his glass.

"Live and let live," Lavanya said. "We all need our vices, as long as they hurt no one." She smiled as servant refilled Arthur's glass with his favorite whiskey: Wiser. "Enjoy."

"I'm sorry I missed having a nightcap with you last night. How's the dog?" Arthur asked.

"And the young one?" Belle added.

"Thank you for asking. Astor is doing fine, and Giselle's first feeding went well. Renfield is an excellent and patient teacher." Lavanya smiled even though she felt as though her guilt were pouring out.

"That's great. She's more prepared than most, being brought up in your household. She'll do fine—good stock around here." Belle winked and carefully slid an ace of spades from her vest while Arthur swallowed some of his drink.

"Thank you Belle...and don't beat up on him too badly." Lavanya winked back at Bell and excused herself. Tru and Naasir were standing next to the fire speaking to a tall stranger. Lavanya guessed it must be Zev in his new disguise. She joined their little grouping.

"Tru, Naasir, how are you this evening?" Lavanya hoped to startle Zev, but he didn't even jump.

"I don't think we've met." The man held out his thin hand. "I'm an old friend of your father."

Lavanya looked down at his hand, not wanting to touch him.

"I'm very upset he isn't here," the stranger said. "I had hoped

92

to see him on my way through this country." He said all this as if it was a formal announcement rather than a greeting.

Lavanya was stumped, but she shook his hand. Maybe Zev could change his personality when he changed looks, because Zev definitely had more personality than this man.

"I'm...sorry. He's away on business in the States." Lavanya absently wiped her hand off on her skirt. "If you'd called, we could have saved you the trip."

Tru reached out and squeezed Lavanya's arm. "I can't wait to see Harry Connick, Jr. His voice is dreamy." Tru was always so enthusiastic, she could infect a whole room. Even Lavanya was excited now.

"I know! He is amazing, and such a wonderful person, too," Lavanya said.

"Plus, who doesn't love him in *Hope Floats*?" Tru and Lavanya giggled a little and the men stood and stared around the room.

"He'll be starting soon," Lavanya said. "I'm going to see if I can find the others so everyone is here on time. Have fun, you two." Lavanya turned to go, purposely ignoring Zev dressed as the geek.

"Lavanya Draculesti, I was hoping to get a moment to discuss some things with you. Do you have someplace private where we can talk?" The geek caught her by the arm, and Tru and Naasir took that as a sign to move on through the party.

Lavanya looked at where he held her arm and then back up into his face with a hard stare. His eyes were a dark, muddy brown today.

"You don't want to push me any farther." Lavanya pulled her arm away and whispered so only he could hear, but her eyes said *back off*. "You've caused enough trouble."

In the hall she brushed off the exchange with Zev the geek and continued her search for the other two couples. Uki and Raz and Lauren and Phil weren't in the main rooms, so she checked the private parlor to see if they were having dinner. Lavanya had her staff set up a safe environment for her guests and donors to share the experience. Dinner was an intimate experience for both the vampire and the donor. Vampires could manipulate the mind of humans by giving them soothing thoughts, feelings and memories so they didn't feel the pain. But if the vampire wasn't careful, the human could become too enthralled—and even addicted—by the vampire's bite.

Lavanya had seen a few sad cases and heard stories of hunters putting down rogue vampires who enjoyed turning humans into slaves. A chill went through her at the thought of those creatures trained to kill her brethren. Her dad kept a list of the top hunters, and if he felt it necessary, he contacted them. That's where a lot of the fear and legends came from. So many of her kind got off on the pain and fear, it created a bad image for them all.

Nowadays most vampires policed themselves, and any revamped children they made were their responsibility, too. Thinking of that, Lavanya remembered Giselle. She should check on her to see how she was coping. With Renfield as her teacher she should be fine, but the girl was still Lavanya's responsibility. She gave herself a moment to worry about Giselle before she opened the door slowly and slipped inside.

Uki and Raz were huddled on one of her Hermes loveseats with a lovely young man nestled between them. Raz was dressed in a light sea green leather halter and pants. The shirt showed off her washboard abs and her beautiful, dark brown skin. Uki looked stunning in a simple black satin halter jumpsuit and heels. The color matched her silky black hair perfectly and looked amazing next to the bright white of the loveseat. The pale light that reached them reflected off their shiny skin.

Lavanya watched from the shadows as they fed on the young man, Uki from his throat and Raz from his thigh. He wore only white briefs, and he was enjoying himself immensely. If the smile wasn't proof enough, then his erection made her confident that he was feeling no pain.

Lavanya's mouth watered at the soft suckling sounds, and she absently licked her lips when a small trail of blood dripped down his muscled, hairless chest. As much as she wanted to join the fun, she didn't move toward them. First, it was their first meal together, and this weekend was for them to bond. Besides, it could be dangerous. Vampires are territorial about their food and will strike out without thinking if interrupted mid feed. It was an excellent sign that Uki and Raz were eating together. It meant they were getting along exceptionally well. Lavanya forced herself to turn away.

She caught sight of Lauren and Phil exiting the room through the servants' entrance. Their behavior seemed odd, so she followed them. The door opened into a long hall with the servants' quarters on either side. By the time she opened the door, they were gone. No door creaked to let her know they'd just closed it, and no noise alerted her to which room they might have entered. For that matter, they might very well have continued down the hall and out into the kitchen.

That's the route she decided on, thinking they must have been checking on their servants or in need of something for Lauren's injury. Wasn't Lauren healing as she should? The last thing Lavanya needed was more curiosity about the wolf attack.

She pushed into the kitchen, hoping to find them speaking to the housekeeping staff or their own servants, but it was empty except for Victor, her personal chef. From the delicious smell of cinnamon and yeast, he was baking. As always, he had his ear buds in, probably listening to some sporting event.

Lavanya tiptoed across the room to surprise him and get a closer look. He was getting things ready for tomorrow's breakfast. Fresh cinnamon rolls were still hot in the pan, his secret recipe icing dripping off the sides. The smell was heavenly, and for the second time tonight, her mouth watered. At least this time her fangs didn't descend.

From her vantage point, she couldn't make out exactly what he was stirring until he grabbed a handful of chocolate chips and tossed them into the batter. Ooh, *brownies*. Victor tasted his concoction and then added more chips.

"Yummy." She smacked her lips and startled him.

"What are you doing?" He shook his curly, red hair and took the ear buds out of his ears.

Lavanya slipped her hand under his arm and tried to dip her finger into the bowl. He always put extra chocolate chips and syrup in for her.

"Get out of that." He batted her hand away before she could get any. "You have the biggest sweet tooth of any vampire I've ever served. Are you sure you suck blood from your victims, not sugar?"

"If only I could survive on sugar and chocolate. That would be heaven, Victor." She winked at him. "You know anyone sweet enough to satisfy me?"

"Don't tempt me, you naughty girl." His husky voice filled the room, and his belly shook with his laughter. "What are you doing back here? Shouldn't you be out there with your guests?"

Then she remembered why she was in here.

"I was looking for Lauren and Phil, two of my guests. I thought they came through here. Did you see them?" Lavanya moved around him and grabbed a couple chocolate chips.

"Nope," he leaned his huge body against the counter, blocking her from the chocolate. "No one but me and the little scamp over there waiting for crumbs." He jerked his thumb to the little bed he kept under the kitchen island for Buttercup. Lavanya scooped up the little dog and gave her a snuggle.

"Where's your new friend?" Lavanya asked her, then turned back to Victor.

"Hey, Victor, have you seen the little black stray that was running around with Buttercup today?"

But Victor's hazel eyes looked glassy, and he seemed uneasy on his feet. His grip tightened on the counter's edge as if he needed extra support.

"Victor, are you all right?" She put Buttercup down and helped Victor onto a seat at the island butcher-block counter. "Here. Sit down."

"Yeah, I just feel light-headed...tired." His eyes closed as he sat on the stool.

Victor was the picture of health—this wasn't right. Lavanya looked around, but no one else was in the kitchen, and nothing looked out of the ordinary.

"Victor?" She shook him, and he flopped over against the counter. "Victor, wake up!"

"La...." He mumbled something and turned to pudding in her arms.

"Victor?" She caught him and balanced him against the butcher-block island. What should she do? She didn't want to alert the guests, not after last night's catastrophe.

She laid his top half amid the cinnamon rolls and trays, wedged the stool under his butt, and dashed for the phone by the main entrance. Helping humans live wasn't her specialty, but

Renfield would know what to do.

But before she could grab the handset from the wall-mounted phone, the large, no-personality Zev entered the kitchen from the formal part of the castle. Dylan was right: tall, dark, and geeky.

"Oh, you." She moved to go around him. "I don't have time for you right now. Get out of my way. I need to call for help. Victor's collapsed." Geek Zev didn't move.

"Excuse me, *hello*, trying to get to the phone." He just stared at her. Then Buttercup came out of her bed like a shot, growling and snarling like some kind of crazed hamster.

What the hell? Buttercup loved that stupid Zev.

A chill when up Lavanya's spine. She stepped back. Animals and hairdressers, she trusted them both.

She sniffed the air.

"Lavanya Draculesti?" The stranger stepped toward her, and she backed up another step. The kitchen was suddenly too quiet and too small. She bumped into the island and had to catch Victor so he didn't slip to the floor. In her haste, a tray of cinnamon rolls crashed to the floor.

With her next breath she smelled the cinnamon rolls, the chocolate from Victor's batter, and the orange juice on the breakfast trays. She even smelled the jambalaya that was cooling in the walk-in freezer. What she didn't smell was cardamom.

She looked down at Buttercup, who still barked and snarled at the geek. But the sound of Buttercup's bark seemed miles away. Lavanya shook her head a little, pulled at her ears, and opened her jaw in an attempt to hear better. When she moved her head, it was too large and too heavy for her neck to hold up. She tried to focus on the stranger. His smile was fuzzy.

"Who are you?" She was sure it wasn't Zev. The stranger's face seemed to waver, like ripples in a pool of water. He was using some sort of magic to change his appearance, and now that she was aware of it, the magic was breaking down.

"Iluziewyaski!" Her father had taught her a little from the old country, and now she was happy she'd paid attention to his lesson. The word was supposed to disable illusionary magic.

And it did. Her vision and hearing rushed back as she surfaced from the illusion. The man was small—almost a dwarf in his true form. His face was pale and petrified, like meat hanging on a skeleton. The few strands of hair he had left were white, and his teeth were black.

As all her senses came back full force, she could barely stand the putrid smell of the mummified zombie standing in front of her. Her hand went reflexively to her nose to block the smell. Lavanya hadn't seen a zombie in fifty years, and she'd hoped never to see one again. They were disgusting creatures with no moral or emotional ties, only mindless machines.

"What's your name?" she asked. "Bob, is it?" Maybe he'd slip and give it to her. Names were crucial to controlling zombies. Necromancers held great power over the dead, largely by using the person's true name in conjunction with a difficult spell. If she could learn his true name, she might be able to find out who sent him.

Now she remembered that he'd never really introduced himself. It hadn't bothered her at the time, because she'd thought it was Zev. *Shit, where was Zev.*

"I am many people. Today I was your father's friend, visiting at Renfield's request. This evening I am a minion who will be rewarded after a job well done." The dwarf bag of bones lunged for her, but she was ready.

"I don't think so, you little piece of shit." She jumped aside and raked her long, ruby red nails across his face, aiming for his eyes. He was quicker than she thought he would be. She missed her mark and slammed into the island. Victor fell to the floor from the impact.

Something dripped from her fingertips and she looked at her hand. She had raked off rotting flesh from the zombie's face, and it was now plopping onto the stone floor.

Lavanya shuddered and hissed. A startled Buttercup yelped and ran for cover. Now that the zombie assassin wasn't tampering with the sound, Lavanya could hear the party going on in the parlor. Harry had started to sing. Lavanya held her scream in. She didn't want to alert anyone. No need to broadcast that a zombie assassin was in her kitchen.

What the hell had happened to her little weekend vacation in the country?

"Damn it," she hissed as the zombie struggled with his balance and stepped on her cinnamon rolls.

Shaking free of the sticky icing, he quickly regained his footing and went at her again. This time she needed to find a weapon sharper than her fingernails—something that would cut through his bones, not just the rotting skin. She couldn't kill him, because he was already dead. She needed to dismember him and hope that when she got to a few choice parts, he'd tell her who sent him to save those said parts.

Lavanya grabbed a butcher knife from the magnetic rack on the wall. The zombie couldn't get away. Her position blocked the exit to the courtyard, and now she had a knife.

"I ask you again. Who are you?" She lunged hummingbird fast and sliced his neck almost to the bone. He reached up to his decaying face, and when his hand came down, it was covered in the black ooze that dripped from the wound. He looked up at her with those hollow, muddy gray eyes that all zombies have no matter what their eye color was when living, and roared at her.

"I got in trouble for having fun with the girl last night and then missed getting you because of that wolf. Then this human got in my way next." The vile thing kicked Victor. "I will not fail my master again."

"I will cut you into tiny pieces and throw you out for the rats to eat for what you did to Giselle." Lavanya's anger rushed through her, causing her to vibrate with expectation. Her fox shawl flowed around her arm as she yanked a larger serrated knife from the wall. She was sure that her eyes were now the same color red as her fox. Her fangs were out in rage and hunger—hunger for his death, not his black blood.

As Lavanya stared at the grotesque figure, the wounds she'd inflicted healed. She sniffed the air again. He wasn't a vampire, but he certainly healed like one. A vampire's servant, then.

"Who are you pulling your healing power from? Who's your master?" She gripped the thick, black handle of the knife.

"None of that is important to this conversation." He opened his hand and threw something at her—a small, white ball. Lavanya jumped away and it missed hitting her, but as it hit the floor a small tremor went up her spine. *Shit.*

Lavanya lunged at him over the island, tucking the blades close to her forearms she went for his head. She cut his arms, but he managed to protect his face. She slashed again, but her attack wasn't as fierce. Her muscles were slowing. She was losing her strength.

Thinking quickly, she pretended she was more affected by the spell he'd thrown at her than she actually was. She'd have one chance before whatever he did had its full effect on her, and she'd be prepared to take it. She needed him off guard and soon. Come hell or high water, he was not getting her.

She made a show of moving her arms in wide circles and missing the zombie. The putrid face smiled, and she could see all the way through to his black tongue. She pretended to stumble.

"What have you done?" Lavanya held on to the counter to show how weak she was. The zombie moved to attack. She let her head fall forward, waiting for her chance to strike. She watched his feet as he inched closer. Almost there. One more step. Almost…

The kitchen erupted with a loud bang, and a burst of electricity like lightning blew her hair into her face and rippled the red fur on her wrap. The zombie jerked to stop and Lavanya smelled something new: cardamom.

No!

Snarling and growling, Zev half man and half beast burst into the kitchen. Now the smell of cardamom was overpowering, and the stranger sniffed the air and stepped back toward the courtyard exit. Lavanya stood, shaking like a newborn colt, wanting to get the zombie with the knife. If she could just pin his arm to the butcher-block counter, he wouldn't be able to run. But before she could stab him, the zombie bolted for the courtyard.

"Shit!" Lavanya slurred like she had a handful of rocks in her mouth.

Now that he was gone, she allowed herself to stagger and sit heavily on the stool where Victor had been. "Why…did you scare him away?" she asked Zev. Even in his partial wolf form she could see his confused expression.

"I had him, and now," she yawned, very tired, "he got away." She'd propped her head up on the island, but she was just too sleepy. She made a pillow out of her fox shawl and slumped over on the counter as gracefully as possible.

"I want some chocolate…and I want to make sure…call Renfield and put Victor to bed. Nite… ni…"

Zev went to the swinging door leading to the courtyard. In his wolf form he had a tremendous sense of smell and could track the zombie if he took off now. As he started out the door, his foot crunched down on something, and he stepped back to get a better look. It had been a round capsule. He smelled it. A witch's spell. *Shit.*

He whipped around to look at the scene. The cook was done. His chest wasn't rising and falling with breath. Lavanya was still breathing, but it was very shallow. He changed immediately back into his human self.

"Lavanya?" He ran to her side, catching her just before she fell on top of the cook.

He should have never left her alone. Zev had been tailing her as a fly, but when she went into the kitchen, he figured she'd be safe for a moment while he checked out her guest's rooms for anything out of the ordinary. He never anticipated an open attack like this. *Shit.* A zombie with a witches spell. What were the odds?

"Lavanya, you have to wake up." Zev tried to shake Lavanya awake.

"Damn, you can change fast..." she slurred. "Learn magic like that or you born..." Her head slipped back down on the counter. "Ouch. My head rattles and..." she said and swallowed like she was holding back vomit.

"Lavanya, stay with me."

"You let it get away... let me sleep." She tucked the red fox under her head better. "Don't tell Dylan I'm sleeping on my fox shawl, he'll kill me. Shh...Okay."

"Lavanya, wake up." Zev tried to sit her up.

"Stop poking me!" she said, swatting at his hand. Then she slipped off the counter and into Zev's arms, unconscious.

"Shit." He looked down at her draped over his arm. She was small, but very powerful. He could feel Vlad's power surrounding her even as she lay helpless.

And with that power came breathtaking beauty. The tuxedo jacket she wore, which had barely covered her when she was standing, had malfunctioned, and one perfectly formed nipple stared him in the face.

Nice. He shook his head and tried to ignore the puckered, dark pink skin. He wasn't sure how much of the spell had hit her, but he knew what had to be done. He also knew she'd be pissed about it. Frankly, he was pissed too. But his bargain with Vlad was ironclad. He had to protect her if he wanted his freedom. He looked down at Lavanya's beautiful breast.

"Zev. May I ask why you are staring at Mistress Lavanya's breasts?"

"I...shit." Renfield scared the crap out of him. But there was no time to explain.

CHAPTER THIRTEEN

"I Used To Be Snow White, But I Drifted." Mae West

Lavanya reached out and held fast to the thick wood counter. She would have slipped to the floor if not for that strong butcher-block island. She struggled to rub her forehead on her forearm and shielded her eyes as she opened them. They were so dry it felt like her false eyelashes were glued together.

"Lavanya?"

"Renfield? Is that you?" She couldn't focus, but she sooo needed it to be him.

"Yes, dear, I'm here, as well as Zev." Lavanya felt Renfield's hand on her shoulder. "Can you stand? We need to get you out of the kitchen."

"Okay." Her mouth was wet and she wiped it with her hand. She hoped she wasn't drooling on the counter. What had that little zombie done to her? How long had she been out?

She stood, but the kitchen spun around her in a whirl of scents: cinnamon, chocolate, and cardamom. As she steadied herself, she noticed blood on her hand. It wasn't the zombie's, because it was red, not black. She raised it to get a better look and then she wiped her lips again. She'd fed, and not very neatly. The last remnants of the blood tasted like nothing she'd had before. Strong and powerful, like the soil here in her father's homeland.

Renfield's mouth was turned down in worry. However, what worried her the most was Zev standing there, holding his neck. Blood seeped through his fingers. She immediately spat on the floor.

"Oh no! Renfield, you let me feed from him! A witch shifter. *Why?*"

"I'd just walked in to find you—very unladylike, I might add—slumped in his arms. Before I could do anything, you were feeding. And I know better than to get in the way when you're eating." He looked to Zev for an explanation, as did Lavanya.

"Look, it was either this," he pointed to his neck, "or let you

103

eat your pastry chef." He shrugged his shoulders. "I've heard of the way you covet his cinnamon rolls. Besides, I needed you to have a little of my blood to counteract the zombie's spell."

"*Zombie?*" Renfield looked back at Lavanya.

"Yes, and if he hadn't interrupted," Lavanya jerked her thumb at Zev, "I would have had him nailed to this island."

"Yeah, right. How were you planning to nail him in your sleep?" He looked exasperated.

"I was acting, you idiot. The magic hadn't affected me much yet, but I was playing it up." Lavanya grabbed a towel, wiped her face, and brushed the food crumbs off her red fox. "I was hoping to stab him, maybe cut off enough stuff or pin him down so he couldn't move. After you scared it off, I stopped fighting the effects of the magic." Lavanya let go of the counter as the dizziness wore off.

Renfield just stood and looked at both of them as if they were children and had made a mess in the kitchen.

"I would've had him if I hadn't stopped to take care of you!" Zev said, checking his wound to see if the bleeding had stopped. "Once you slipped off the counter and almost landed on the chef, I was afraid to leave you." He held up a small white pellet. "And it's lucky for you I didn't."

"Why?" Renfield asked. "What's that?"

"This held a Snow White curse," Zev explained.

"A what?" Lavanya said, almost laughing.

"Snow White. Don't you read? Hell, you've at least seen the movie."

"Of course I've seen it—the original release, not that remastered stuff. What does the movie have to do with that capsule?" Her head was clearing. Not much longer now, and she'd be as good as new. Zev's blood was potent. She felt awesome. Not that she'd tell him that.

"This would have put you into a sleep as deep as death, and only true love's kiss could have woken you, Princess."

His tone was so condescending, she could have ripped his head off.

Zev chuckled. "I'm guessing you haven't found your true love, so my donation of blood and a bit of my magic was the only other option. If I'd gone after the zombie, it would have given the

CHAPTER FOUR

Who Ya' Been Eatin'?

Zev was cold, his head throbbed, and his mouth was dry. He felt like he'd put away a whole bottle of tequila, but he couldn't remember drinking anything after he spilled his beer. Maybe this is what it felt like to be sick.

A moan escaped as he searched for his old patchwork quilt. His grandmother had made the thing of cast-off clothing, extra thick for the winter nights in the wilderness of the Romanian mountains. As he swept his arm around the bed, he heard a strange sucking sound, like the noise his feet made when he walked around the muddy river bank in the village.

Zev opened his eyes, but his lids scraped like sandpaper and his vision was blurred. All he could make out was the color brown, so he scrubbed his hands across his face to wipe away the last of the grogginess and clear his sight.

His hands felt crusty against his skin. He stretched his face and opened his eyes again. When he did, his fingers curled into fists. Vampire blood was everywhere. Like day-old maple syrup, it crusted on his hands, pooled under his body, and soaked his grandmother's quilt. His cabin was a bloody mess.

"Fucking vamps!" Anger racked Zev again as he remembered the message and the way it had been delivered last night.

"Watch yer mouth, Wilkie." The old woman's voice was strong and deep, showing none of the frailty a woman her age should have. It broke through Zev's anger like nothing else could.

Only one person called him "Wilkie"—his grandmother.

"Babcia, Inez." He pulled himself back through the mess until he could rest against the wall. "What are you doing here?" He flung out his hand to remove some of the blood, but all he managed to do was fling the thick, brown syrup across the room.

"Wait, let me guess." He hung his head in surrender. "You had a dream." Inez was a czarownica, a witch, and her power was legendary, as was his family's. Supposedly they were decedents of

31

the original Gana, or mother earth herself, but Inez would never talk about his mother, her past, or the fact that they were almost immortal.

"Of course I had a dream. Do ya think I'd be sittin' here sewing', looking at you in a pool a blood, calm as day, if I hadn't had a dream? I knew you'd be needin' me this mornin'." Inez tied off her stitch and cut the thread with her teeth.

"You're a mess," she said, setting her sewing aside, away from the blood. "Go on now and get cleaned up. Then ya can tell me, who ya been eatin'?"

****

Zev watched as the brown water dripped off his fingers. He'd been in the shower for so long, working to get the blood off, that the water was ice cold. But it was the memories of the night before that made him shake with rage.

"Yer not a teenager, Wilkie." Inez beat on the thin, wooden door. "Come out of the bath now. You need to hurry."

Fucking vampires. Zev leaned his head against the tile wall. Vampires were the scum of the earth, scheming, manipulating pieces of shit. He could believe nothing else—especially not after last night. The memory was hazy, but he recalled the two women who'd entered his room and sliced their own wrists. They'd covered him with their blood as he lay, unable to move, held captive by the dark mist that weighed him down.

Their blood had gushed out of the open wounds and, at first, they seemed to enjoy the warm flow as if it were a lover's touch. They writhed about, massaging their blood like a thick lotion into their own skin and his. He sensed the evil in them calling out to his demon, but he also saw the fear in their eyes.

Zev had finally found his voice and screamed at the bloodsucker he knew was controlling them—Vlad Dracula. Too good to do his own dirty work he'd used the women as puppets. They dutifully laid out Zev's assignment. Then they offered him their lives in the form of a drink.

The women were evil so Zev didn't think twice before he took what they offered. Their twisted and demented souls infused him with strength. As he savored the power he'd taken from Vlad's spell longer to set in and I wouldn't have been able to reverse it. Lucky for you, I'm a 'rare' talent."

"What?" Lavanya stared at him.

"'Rare.' Get it? Bloody…rare? Come on, babe, that's funny."

Lavanya hissed and lunged for him. Renfield swiftly blocked her.

"Don't ever call me anything other than Mistress Lavanya. If you ever call me *babe* again, you'll regret it."

"Whatever." Zev laughed, and Renfield blocked her angry advance.

Not willing to hurt Renfield to get to Zev, Lavanya calmed and straightened her jacket. "Renfield won't always be here to protect you." She peered around the servant and licked her fingers. "You're an idiot, but you taste divine. I can't wait to get another taste."

Zev growled then, defiance shinning in his iridescent wolf eyes.

"*Enough.*" Renfield slapped his hand down on the butcher-block counter, and even Buttercup ran for her bed. Both Zev and Lavanya gazed at the floor in submission. Her father's voice could cause that in the meanest bastards.

"I need a full report of what happened today," Renfield said. "Who is this person and how did he enter the castle? Then I need to know what exactly this magic is and how they came about it." He looked at Zev.

"Yes, sir." Zev stood straighter, but kept his eyes to the floor.

"Anya, do you feel well enough to go to your guests?"

"Yes." She straightened her dress and repositioned her boobs. The little chain had come unfastened, and if not for the fox wrap, she would've been flashing Renfield. She noticed Zev looking at her breasts. She hated to admit it, but after tasting him, she felt a little lust mixed with the anger.

Damn. She had to focus on the moment. Anyway, she was just feeling the adrenaline rush. That was all.

She was sure of it.

Zev couldn't help looking at her breasts. Damn, she knew how to display her assets. He checked the wound at his neck again. It had stopped bleeding. He'd never been bitten before. It was strange and…sexy as hell. He felt desire rip through his whole body every time she drew on the wound. He licked his lips as the thought of tasting Lavanya moved across his mind.

"How are my hair and makeup?" Lavanya asked Renfield. "Do I need to freshen up?"

"You look fine," Renfield told her as he helped her fix her hair. "Only about half an hour has passed since anyone saw you. You can tell them you were checking on Giselle, who's doing well. She'll make a wonderful asset to our family. You did exceptionally well in turning her."

Lavanya bent down to check on Victor. "What about Victor? Will he be okay?"

Renfield looked to Zev.

"I'm sorry, no. He won't wake again." Zev felt bad about that, but there was nothing he could do.

Lavanya grabbed a knife from the counter and threw it, picking a target to the right of his head. He ducked as the knife sailed past his head, thunked into the wall behind him, and stuck perfectly. Was this woman crazy?

"Shit!" he yelled. "Watch what you're doing!"

"That—that—zombie cretin killed my friend! And my favorite pastry chef!

Renfield picked up Victor and hoisted him over his shoulder.

"Zev, what about a true love's kiss?" the servant asked. "Victor was married once, we could see where she is."

"That might work, Renfield, or the witch who made the spell might be able to reverse it." Zev shrugged. "I just don't know."

"Okay." Renfield addressed both of them. "I'll try to contact Cherie, his ex-wife. But for now, clean up this mess and pretend nothing happened."

"*What*?" Lavanya said, her voice furious.

"Lavanya, think logically," Renfield said, carrying Victor to the cellar door. "This is someone close to us. Most likely it's someone here this weekend. He found an opportunity to kidnap you and maybe force your father to wake or show his resting place. We must make him believe we're oblivious and hope he makes a mistake."

Lavanya watched Renfield descend into the darkness of the cellar with Victor. She didn't look at Zev or even seem to realize that she was talking out loud.

"Why would any of the vampires I brought want me or my father under some spell?" she asked.

"How well do you know your guests?" Zev asked the obvious question. He leaned against the back counter and waited.

Lavanya seemed to jolt back to the present. "I have to get back."

And that's all the thanks he'd get for saving her life.

"You're welcome, Princess." He tossed the little white capsule at her. She caught it midstride with ease and continued out the door.

He had to hand it to her. She was a pain. But she was hotter than Lara Croft and Morrigan Aensland put together.

CHAPTER FOURTEEN

A Different Kind of Hunger

Zev set to work cleaning up the mess from the zombie attack. He found a broom in the back closet and piled the spilled food and dishes for the trash, but he couldn't stop thinking about Lavanya. *What a bitch.* Not even a thank you. He saved her life, and she was pissed that he scared away a zombie.

A zombie, *shit*, he'd never even seen one before. Heard plenty of scary stories from his grandmother and her people, but he'd never actually seen one in action. And a Snow White potion, *damn*.

Why did he have to owe the big guy so much? It was true that Vlad had saved his life, but how long was he expected to pay? Going against a necromancer so powerful that he could resurrect a zombie that looked alive to all of them, that was suicide. Whoever orchestrated this had to be extremely clever and very close.

Lavanya had a lot of people here this weekend, which meant lots of potential suspects. He should just start a fire and kill all the bloodsuckers. Would that set him free from Vlad? Zev smiled at the thought as he swept up some more of Lavanya's precious cinnamon rolls.

Why would anyone want to hurt her? Sure, she was a pain in the ass. But...the only thing that popped into his mind was that she had nice tits. A picture of her perfect pink nipple hovered in his mind. He shook the vision from his head and pushed the broom bristles harder into the kitchen floor. That train of thought would get him into trouble, and he had about all the trouble he could handle at the moment.

Zev wanted to get out of here and leave her on her own. But if he did, Vlad would just summon him back.

"Huh, she was *acting*, my ass." He chuckled as he remembered her laying her head on the counter as he came through the door. It was a good thing he hadn't gone after the zombie—she wouldn't have made it.

He'd let her feed from him. No one had ever tasted his blood.

He wasn't a vending machine. But seeing her fall into that deep sleep had been too much. What the hell was he getting himself into? He'd made sure to block his emotions from her—and she'd seemed out of it—so no harm had been done. But she did bust him eyeing her boobs later. In the future he'd have to be more careful to hold that hunger at bay. *Focus.* He just needed to finish this job and get the hell away from her and this castle.

He'd heard through the door before he changed that the zombie was working for someone. Renfield was right—it had to be someone here at the party. No one would trust a zombie to finish the job unless they could witness it. But what could anyone hope to gain from harming her? The Snow White was a tough curse to make, and why would you want her to sleep? She'd be of no use to anyone. If someone wanted her gone, why not just kill her?

Renfield clomped upstairs from the cellar, bringing him out of his thoughts.

"Zev, what do you know about zombies?" Renfield asked as he helped Zev sweep up the last of the food and stuff it into the big trash container.

"I know enough to stay away from them." He put the trash can away and turned back to Renfield. "But what has me worried is that he fooled all of you with his appearance. The necromancer who's controlling him has to be extremely powerful and close by. And that Snow White potion is ancient. Most of us who remember the old magic are gone. I doubt five people in the world remember how to make it, and none of them besides me are here this weekend."

"So we have a very powerful necromancer who knows ancient magic and wants to take or kill Lavanya. But why?" Renfield went to the main door and peeked out. Then he turned back. "Master was smart to alert us. I only wish he could elaborate more. I rather hate puzzles."

"Me, too." Zev leaned against the counter. "Just tell me who to kill, and I'll finish the job and be on my way."

Renfield shook his head. Of course, Renfield didn't know whom he should kill. If he did, he'd speak right up.

"Why would Vlad tap me, anyway?" Zev had been dying to ask that question ever since he got here. "I'm surprised he'd want me anywhere near his progeny." Little Buttercup came out of her bed just then and jumped up on his legs, begging to be picked up. Zev obliged her and tucked her under his arm.

"I don't know, Zev. But I'm glad he did. Obviously, we are in need of your special genetic makeup for this dilemma. If what you say is correct, no one else would have known how to undo the sleeping spell." Renfield tiptoed to the servant's door and looked out into the hall. Zev guessed he was checking to be sure no one was listening in to their conversation. Then he returned to the center of the kitchen.

"You are officially invited to this weekend gathering," he said. "No more hiding in the background protecting her from afar. You'll be Lavanya's date for the remainder of the festivities."

"Whoa!" Zev shook his head with vigor. "Don't even go there, Renfield. She'll never agree, and I won't trail around after her like a puppy. So just forget about it. There has to be another way to explain my presence."

"How else do you expect to protect her? You cannot stay in animal form for extended periods. Besides, no one will believe she has a pet wolf.

"I can be a fly." Zev protested. Getting closer to her would just fuel the desire he already felt. Not an option.

"You cannot hold that form all weekend and you know it. As her lover, you'll be expected to be by her side at all times and sleep in her chamber. Therefore, you can protect her when the zombie or its master tries for her again."

He hated that he saw Renfield's logic. *Shit.*

"Fine, I can pretend. But *you* have to tell her. I don't want any part of that."

"I'll inform Lavanya. You need to ready yourself for a grand entrance into the festivities." Renfield looked Zev over and then said, "I would change into something more suitable if I were you."

This was the worst job he'd ever had. Why should he change? Who gave a crap about what Lavanya's guests thought? He had on black leather pants, a T-shirt, and his custom heavy boots with the soft leather soles—the same clothes he'd been wearing earlier. When he changed form, his clothes changed, too—and then changed back with him, thanks to his mother's magic. Very convenient.

Renfield wanted him to dress up? Fine. He used his magic to

add his black-and-red leather motorcycle jacket to his ensemble. As a benefit, this outfit would probably also irritate Lavanya.

"Ah, much better. Don't you think?" Zev smiled at Renfield while he straightened his jacket. Renfield shook his head, but didn't object. "So—do I need to come through the front door, or can I just take up residence and go meet everyone?"

"Give me a few minutes to break the news to Lavanya, and then you can just join the party. Try not to push her too hard. She's under enough stress without your adding to it."

"Please. The princess hasn't seen stress yet." Zev's smile turned devious.

"I hope the Master knows what he's doing," Renfield whispered to himself as he pushed through the door. But Zev had one more question.

"Renfield, the girl who was attacked last night—what would she have to do with this? Why attack a human on Vlad's territory? What purpose does that serve?"

"It's a good question, Zev, and I'm afraid I don't have an answer for it. However, I'm certain we shall find out."

Renfield left, and Zev decided to see what he could overhear from the servants while Renfield broke the news to Lavanya. He changed into the little black dog form, and Buttercup immediately came up to tag along. Zev nuzzled his little partner in crime, and they pushed through the swinging door into the servants' entrance.

CHAPTER FIFTEEN

How To Introduce Your Lover

"Lovers! But I can't stand him." Lavanya's eyes widened in shock. "Renfield, that is not acceptable. I will not agree to anything that involves me pretending to be with that dog."

Lavanya put her foot down. Literally, she stomped her red heel on the stone floor. When Chloe had brought her to speak to Renfield, she'd hoped that he had news. Maybe he'd caught the zombie or even the necromancer who was controlling it. She hadn't expected that he'd try to coerce her into pretending that Zev was her lover.

"Lavanya, do you have a better idea?" Renfield asked. "Remember, he did save you from the zombie. And he knew enough about the magic to save your life."

"But..."

"The Master, your father, trusted him enough to summon him to protect you. Do you want to second-guess his decisions?" Renfield raised one eyebrow.

"Renfield, that's not fair, and you know it. I'd never second-guess him, but I won't be forced to call Zev my lover in front of my friends and clients."

"One of whom is trying to kill or kidnap you. Please don't forget that."

"We have no proof that it's one of my guests," Lavanya whispered as they spoke outside the main entrance to the castle. "Do you know the background checks they had to go through to get an invitation? I've personally known or reviewed their backgrounds for at least three years." She wouldn't give in without a fight. None of her guests wanted to kill her. She'd bet on it.

"Three years is nothing to a vampire, and you of all people should know that. Your father has been asleep for more than fifty. This could be an enemy from hundreds of years ago."

"I understand that someone could have hatched an elaborate plan to gain entrance into the castle. And I understand that they would see me as a link to possibly hurt my father." Lavanya ran her red nails through the silky fur of the red fox. The feel of the fur was…comforting. And…erotic. Her body was still humming from taking in Zev's blood. She'd never felt such a craving. If she was honest with herself, she'd admit his blood wasn't the only thing she wanted from him, but denial was easier. The hunger to touch him was powerful and it frightened her.

"However, I don't understand the connection with all this and Giselle," she said. Maybe she could get Renfield off course. "Why would anyone after me or my father attack a young girl? She didn't have anything to do with us, except that her family is in our charge. Has she remembered anything of the attack?"

"No, and that's a puzzle too. Maybe the trauma was too much for her to process. The human mind is fragile. Maybe in time she'll remember. We have to be patient."

Renfield smiled. "Nicely done, but changing the subject doesn't change the fact that you need extra protection, and your father sent Zev for the job. He needs to be around you at all times. Do you have a better idea as to how to accomplish that task? Would you prefer that we just call him a bodyguard?"

"I don't wish to explain a bodyguard to my guests, and furthermore, I don't *need* a bodyguard."

"You can't tell me that when you were in the kitchen—"

"Yes, yes, I understand how Zev saved me in the kitchen. But I also remember how he let the zombie go. Haven't you thought for a moment that he might be a part of this plot?" Lavanya crossed her arms, her red fox throw soft against her face.

"I have your father's vision to confirm Zev's intentions, plus Vlad has held control over Zev since he was born." Renfield said. "I've never known your father to be wrong about a tie like that before." He reached out and caught Lavanya's hand where she was worrying a callus on her thumb.

She'd about run out of excuses. If she didn't want to admit that she was afraid of her own desires, she was stuck. He could see it, too, the bastard. He had that smug smile on his face instead of his normal stoic appearance.

"Renfield, please don't make me do this. I…" She could think of no other way to follow her father's advice and keep Zev close. He could stay in dog form for a while, but then he wouldn't be able to communicate with her. If there was a threat, she needed to be able to understand his plan of attack or retreat. She wasn't in the mood to play the "What is it, Lassie?" game. So she gave in.

"Okay," she sighed. "Fine. You win."

"It's done. Zev should be arriving at the party in a few moments, and you can introduce him as your lover, friend, or whatever suits you. But he stays with you at all times. I'll have his things moved into your suite, and I'm having the chamber next to yours searched for any traces of the zombie as we speak. Maybe they attacked the girl knowing that you'd put me in charge of her upbringing, so I'd be out of the picture today, making you an easier target." He shrugged his shoulders.

"Maybe." Lavanya thought for a moment. Something had been bothering her all day. "I've never revamped a human before. It was...not what I expected. I thought she'd be more emotional about the change. She had to give up a normal life, having children. I was surprised how easily she adjusted to the feeding and...I just didn't expect it to be that way."

"Every human is different. It's true, she has adjusted remarkably to her situation. Perhaps that's because she was brought up here at the castle. Giselle understands better than most what vampires are, not some faux Hollywood image." He placed his hand on her crossed arms. "You did the best job possible. You told her father the truth and asked for his approval. It was all that you could have done under the circumstances."

"Thanks, Renfield. I'll be more help with her once these guests have gone. I'll postpone my flight back to the States and stay a while to help with her education."

Lavanya looked up as the sound of laughter floated out of the large entrance door.

"Speaking of guests, I better get back. As Ricky Ricardo would say, I have a lot of 'essplaining to do' about my new lover." She rolled her eyes.

"Do you remember *Father Knows Best*? That's another show you used to enjoy."

She hated it when Renfield treated her like a child. And now he reminded her of how much she missed having a father.

"Yesss, Renfield, I remember. I'm doing my best to follow his instructions. But I wish he'd just wake up. Send in lover boy when he gets back from doing whatever it is he's doing."

Lavanya's chest ached with heaviness, and one nagging question wouldn't leave her alone.

"Do you really think one of them," she pointed toward the laughter coming down the hall, "could be behind all this?"

"I'm afraid it's highly likely that one or more of them are behind these events." Renfield left as quietly as a spider walking up a wall.

Lavanya re-entered the parlor where everyone was having a great time playing charades. She was sure her smile looked genuine, but she felt a softball-sized knot in her stomach. When she looked around the room, all she could think was, *which one of them betrayed me?*

Tru excused herself from the festivities, a serious look on her face, and took Lavanya's arm, turning her away from the group and leading her toward the bar. Tru was very shrewd when she wanted to be, and Lavanya didn't think anyone noticed her friend's worried look.

"What happened?" Tru asked. "That fake smile can't fool me."

"Nothing. Why?" Lavanya tried to put real emotion behind her smile.

"That's better. But if you don't want the rest to get suspicious, you better give that smile more oomph." Tru laughed as if they were having a funny conversation. To all the others, Lavanya realized, they looked just like two women engrossed in girl talk.

"I won't press you, but I know something's been going on this weekend," Tru said now. "You're too distracted, you're not yourself. Don't tell me it's just because you had to turn that young girl. She was ready, and you did what you had to do with her family's blessing. When you're ready to talk, I'm available. Okay now, laugh."

Lavanya laughed heartily, and it felt good to release some of the pent-up energy.

"Oh thanks, I needed that." She squeezed Tru's arm. "Nothing's wrong, it's just been a crazy weekend. I hope I haven't put a damper on your fun." Lavanya looked back over to the group. They had quieted as they watched Arthur act out some silly charade.

"Not at all, doll face. I just know you better than the rest." Tru waved to Naasir.

"I see this weekend is working out well?" Lavanya nudged Tru.

"You were right, he is hot." Tru fanned her face and a sweet blush warmed her pale cheeks, which was something special since vampires aren't easy blushers.

"I knew you two would be perfect for each other." Tru liked to look so rough with her spikey, white hair, but Lavanya knew that under that tough street exterior was a sweet person... hiding. As small as she was at barely 5 feet she'd developed a tough shell around herself to protect herself physically and emotionally even when she was human. Tru surprised Lavanya by looking back at her with a serious expression.

"You find love for others," Tru said. "When will you find it for yourself? You deserve to be happy, too." Tru smiled. As Tru brought home the reality that Lavanya always avoided, she almost had time to feel sorry for herself.

"Babe, there you are. I've been looking for you for an hour." Zev strode through the room in black leather, looking like an ad for a European motorcycle company. With his messy, black, wavy hair loose and his muscled body barely contained by the leather, he looked every bit the part of a playgirl centerfold.

Damn, Lavanya hadn't gotten the chance to tell Tru or anyone else about her *lover's* arrival. And he called her *babe.* He was insufferable! Worse, she was sure her fury showed on her face.

And then he took her in his arms and planted a soft, intimate kiss on her lips. Despite herself, her lips responded all on their own and softened at his touch. Anger or lust: Lavanya didn't know which heated her system, but she was on fire. While her mind was awash with the soft sensation of his lips covering hers, he let his kiss trail down her neck just below her ear where he whispered into her skin. "Remember, we're supposed to be lovers."

"Hi, and you are?" Tru didn't miss a beat.

Zev pulled Lavanya up and tucked her under his arm while Tru stared at them with her mouth open wide enough to catch flies.

"I..." Befuddled, Lavanya was too dazed to answer her. It really had been too long since she'd taken a lover. That was her only excuse for the way his kiss affected her. It had just been too long. That's all. Surely it wasn't his talent as a kisser.

"Hi. Zev." He reached out and took Tru's hand, but he looked down at Lavanya. "Haven't you mentioned me to your friends?"

Lavanya noticed that his eyes lingered on the little chain that held her dress together. She immediately stood straighter and found her voice. *Damn*, this man could mess her mind.

"No, I didn't see the need." Lavanya tried to pull away some, but Zev held her locked to his side. "You surprised me with your visit."

Tru was giving Lavanya the big eye, so explanations were in order.

"Tru, this is Zev. He's a friend of mine, but he doesn't live in Miami. That's why you haven't met before. Zev, this is a good friend of mine, Tru. We're neighbors in Miami." As they greeted each other, Lavanya noticed that Naasir was making his way to Tru's side, and the others had stopped playing the game and were waiting to be introduced to the madman who'd just groped their hostess. *Great.*

Lavanya introduced Zev to the couples. Everyone, including the Connicks, greeted him and gave Lavanya raised brows of appreciation behind his back. They'd be gossiping for months about this. Soon after, the Connicks took their leave, and her vampire guests settled into private conversations. Lavanya tried to pull away from Zev, but he held tight to her waist.

"Let go of me." She commanded through gritted teeth as she smiled up at him.

"Ah, ah, ah. We mustn't let anyone be suspicious." He smiled down at her and pulled her in closer. Which smashed her breasts against his leather-covered chest and pushed them up even farther. The fox wrap made a perfect frame for them. Lavanya felt his appreciation growing against her stomach. She glared up at him.

"If you don't release me, I'll make you pay for it later." She dug her nails into his arms.

"Ooh, promises, promises." He laughed, but released her. "Renfield had all my stuff put in your suite, and while I was waiting I did a little sniffing around the servants' quarters. I'll fill you in later." He took a glass from the bar shelf and dropped some ice in it. "So, how about you? Did you hear anything in the mindless chitchat?" He poured a shot of Wiser over the ice and handed the glass to her.

"I...how did you know I like whiskey?"

"You're not that hard to figure out. You got any beer in this little fridge, or just juice for all your victims?" He chuckled as he searched the shelves, finally taking out a bottle of Kirin, a Japanese Lager, and popping off the top. "This'll do."

The staff was trained to think of every eventuality, but it still pissed her off that they had beer.

The evening went without any further drama and Zev behaved himself, but Lavanya was exhausted. She couldn't wait for the night to be over. Uki and Raz were the first to excuse themselves. Then Tru beckoned her over. Out of the corner of her eye, she saw Naasir join Zev.

"I want full details tomorrow evening, do you understand?" Tru grabbed Lavanya's hand and pulled her back into a corner where she could ogle Zev more.

"Tru, really..."

"Oh, no, you don't. There is a story to tell and I want it all."

"Did you tell Naasir to keep Zev busy while you grilled me about our relationship?"

"Damn right, I did."

"There really isn't anything to tell. We're just...friends, nothing serious."

"Are you kidding me? He's hot. I'm young and not as practiced as I should be, but he doesn't smell like a vampire and he's not exactly all human. What is he?" She nearly salivated in anticipation.

"You're correct. He's not a vampire." Tru really didn't need to know more.

"Come on, tell me. I'll just get Naasir to tell me later."

"And I will tell Naasir to make you figure it out on your own. It'll be good practice, since you never take your senses seriously."

"Pleaasse." Tru drew out every letter in the word.

"Night, Tru." Lavanya hugged her.

"I want full disclosure tomorrow," Tru whispered. "Oh, and I'll let you know what Naasir thinks of him tomorrow, too. You know how men can be with handshakes."

They both peeked over at the men to see them grip each other's hands.

"I swear we haven't evolved as a species at all," Tru said, still watching. "It's like watching two animals sniff each other."

Lavanya burst out laughing. Tru had no idea how close she was to the truth. Naasir and Zev looked at them with raised brows, but Lavanya had managed to rein it in by the time Naasir and Zev joined them.

"Good day, Lavanya...Zev." Naasir took Tru's hand and started away.

Lavanya caught Tru's eye and winked. "I'll talk to you tomorrow, Tru. Thanks."

Zev pulled her into him and wrapped his strong muscled arms around her waist, crowding Lavanya with his big body and whispering into her hair.

"You shouldn't be so friendly with her. She's a suspect and so is her date."

"Don't presume to know my friends, and don't tell me who to confide in," Lavanya said with a smile. She pulled herself as far away from his chest as she could—but that really wasn't far, since he had incredible strength and she didn't want to cause a scene.

"Whatever." Zev released her to attend to her guests and nodded as the couples mingled and said their good days to each other.

Belle and Arthur were still playing cards. And as much as Lavanya wanted to join the fun couple for a nightcap, the dog boy would have none of it.

The only people Lavanya didn't see to say good day too were Lauren and Phil. *Again.* Not that she wanted his help, but she thought he should know.

"You asked earlier, and I feel the need to let you know that Lauren and Phil have been unusually absent for part of this weekend. She was injured, by you." Lavanya looked to see his expression...nope, no remorse in his eyes at all.

"Anyway, they haven't been participating in the weekend's activities like the rest of the guests. That's all I'm saying."

"That's a lot for you, Princess." He watched Belle and Arthur. "So, you know Tru personally, but the rest are clients through Love Bites. Right?" He snickered.

"Count. On. Love." Lavanya corrected him. "Yes, Tru is a friend. However, they all went through extensive background checks before I took them as clients." Lavanya motioned to the maid to refill Arthur's glass. "Really, you've met most of them now, does anyone strike you as crazy enough to mastermind a kidnapping or murder by necromancy? This is all insane. It just doesn't fit."

"I agree, but it doesn't change the fact that someone executed a complicated plan to either take you or kill you. I don't know what their motive is, and I don't give a shit. I'm here to stop them, and that's what I'm going to do. I owe your father, and that's that." Zev finished his beer and set the empty on the bar.

"Interesting. I wonder what my father holds over your head, and why of all the people he could have called, he called you. Both questions plague my mind." She turned to go, but he pulled her back.

"Where do you think you're going?" He looked down and smiled.

"I'm going to say good day to Arthur and Belle and then I'm going to bed. What's it to you?" She didn't realize it, but she had stepped back and pulled her arm free.

"Easy, babe, we're supposed to be in this together."

Lavanya closed her eyes to try to calm herself. "Don't call me babe. Besides, do you have a better idea?

"Actually, bed sounds good to me." He smiled and pulled her into an embrace.

"Ugh, go take a cold shower." She smiled back.

"I'm sure we could find a better way to spend our day than a cold shower."

"Yeah," Lavanya looked him up and down as if checking out a prime cut of meat, "if I didn't despise you, maybe. Na, probably not." She pulled free, put her fake smile back on, and walked to the table where Belle and Arthur were still playing cards and laughing.

Belle's eyes sparkled with mischief and Arthur was eating her up with his. They were at ease and yet excited by each other. Suddenly a tiny tinge of jealousy reared its ugly head as she watched the couple. *Equals.* What would that be like?

"Good day to the both of you, I hope that you're enjoying the weekend."

"Yes, yes, it's always good to get out and meet new people. By the way, whatever happened to that tall chap? The friend of your father. You know, I never got his name." Arthur looked at Belle to see if she knew it.

"Sorry, hon, he never said. Funny, because I asked twice and both times he avoided the question." Belle looked to Lavanya for a name.

"Oh, he's just one of father's accounting people, boring as the walking dead," Lavanya said, trying for dramatic flair. "After meeting with Zev and me, he decided to take his leave. He shouldn't have barged in on our weekend, anyway. I'm sure my father will have his head for that." Lavanya smiled brightly, hoping that if they were involved, they'd get the veiled threat.

"No harm done, dear. Just curious, that's all." Arthur tipped his drink up.

"Come on, big boy, let's get upstairs before you turn into a bat," Belle said. Lavanya caught her wink at him and he smiled.

"Have a good day. Please let us know if you need anything."

Lavanya moved along to Lauren and Phil, who'd just slipped back into the parlor.

"Darling." Phil held out his arms, took Lavanya's hands in his, and gently kissed each cheek. "This weekend is turning out to be so much fun. Thank you for inviting me. And thank you for introducing me to Lauren." He released her hands and put his arm around Lauren.

"I'm so glad you're enjoying yourselves." Lavanya looked to Lauren for confirmation that she, too, was having a good evening. Lauren smiled.

"Thank you for inviting me after all this time." Lauren seemed to be picking at the fact that I hadn't invited her before now.

"Well, I don't spend much time here, but I'm glad that you're enjoying it," Lavanya said. "I was a little worried about you earlier this evening. I could have sworn I saw you entering the servants' quarters. Is your leg healing?"

"I didn't notice you." Lauren laughed, but she looked embarrassed. "Were you following us?"

Lavanya just smiled and waited for her to continue.

"Oh, it's not a big secret. Phil and I are discussing an extended vacation after this weekend. It's been wonderful to get away from our territories and just relax with others. We were checking in with our servants to see if the others at home were having any problems with our absence. And my leg will be fine in a few days, thank you."

"That's wonderful news about the trip," Lavanya said with real enthusiasm. "I hope you both can get away." Lauren and Phil took their leave, and Lavanya watched Zev saunter over. His body moved more like a large cat than a dog—all contained power ready to pounce at any moment.

"Ready for bed, babe."

Damn, if he wasn't tempting. Lavanya buried the impulse to say yes and smelled the air again. Along with the cardamom was his human skin, the smell of the outdoors, and something darker, like the musk of the forest. Her mouth watered and it wasn't because of blood lust. She swallowed and stopped scenting the air. Anymore and she might do something she'd regret in the morning.

"You so annoy me. Let's go." Lavanya stepped out of his way and around him. The last thing she needed to do was accidentally touch him.

LYNNE STEVIE

CHAPTER SIXTEEN

What a Tease

Zev noticed the way Lavanya had sidestepped to avoid brushing against him. However, he could smell a sweetness coming off her skin that made him hard. She was aroused, but she wouldn't make it easy on him. Not that it mattered. He had no intention of becoming mixed up with a prima donna princess.

Still, he couldn't help but watch the way her ass moved as she walked, and the long line of her leg in the red stiletto heels. He allowed her to lead the way up to the third floor, but when they got to the entrance of her suite, he walked in first. After all, she was *not* on the menu and this was his job.

Lavanya pushed past him. Oh yeah, she was like a thorn stuck in his paw: maddening.

"And just who are you tall, dark, and menacing?" A man sitting on the chaise reading a tabloid magazine looked up as they entered. His presence surprised Zev and a growl slipped out. Gotta be more on guard. Like he hadn't learned that lesson once already today.

Lavanya elbowed him and kicked off her shoes, obviously not surprised by the man's presence.

"Good evening, Dylan. Don't let this overgrown hound bother you." She walked right into the man's—evidently Dylan's—arms.

Zev's inner demon woke up at the site of Lavanya in the arms of another. The Rakshasa demon didn't like it.

"Darling," she said as she kissed the guy's cheek. "I'm exhausted and in need of a shower. Plus, I broke a nail fighting off a zombie tonight." She held up her fingers to show the broken nail to Dylan, who seemed shocked.

"Heavens, how long have you been wondering around with that broken nail and chipped polish?" He *tsk-tsk*ed and invited her to sit beside him on the chaise, taking her hand in his. "I thought I brought you up better. You must fill me in on all the details. But first, what's with the chaperone?"

At least the guy eyed him with more respect now that he'd had a good look. Then he blew it.

"Or is he here for fun?"

Oh hell no!

"Oh, Dylan, stop teasing him." Lavanya playfully slapped at his arm. Go on and run me a bath please." Dylan got up and dropped his magazine on the chaise.

"So will Mr. Personality be staying?" He went into the bath and then stuck his head back out. "Maybe he's dinner?" His laughter could be heard in the suite over the crackling of the fire.

Dick head.

"Enough, Dylan." Lavanya went over to the fire. She looked tired.

"Why can't you just eat *him*?" Zev commented as he plopped down on the gray silk expanse of her bed. Then he tossed pillows to the floor until he came up with Buttercup in his hands. "I thought I heard you under there." He pulled her into his lap and lay back on the remaining pillows.

Lavanya was watching him—maybe she was admiring his chest again. He cleared his throat and she quickly turned back to the fire. Yup, that's what she'd been admiring.

"Don't get too comfortable," she said. "You'll be sleeping on the chaise." Lavanya took off the fox wrap and undid the chain that held her gown together, releasing her breasts. The jacket still covered her nipples, but just barely.

"There's a bathroom and shower in the suite next door if you need to use them," she said. "I'm going to change. Be out of my bed when I return." She headed off to the bath, the gown moving and sliding down her shoulders as she went.

Buttercup stretched and then curled up on Zev's lap. He sat for a moment, not wanting to move, his leather pants suddenly tighter than they had been only moments ago. Any movement would be painful to his swollen cock. As the blood flow slowed, he patted Buttercup on the head.

"Thanks for shielding me." The last thing he wanted Lavanya to know was how much he wanted to throw her down and bed her. Then he got up, settled Buttercup back on the pillows, and went next door to take a cold shower.

Lavanya had a big smile on her face as she entered her changing room where Dylan waited to help her get ready for sleep.

"You naughty girl, did you strip right in front of him?" Dylan said with a mischievous smile.

"Not all the way." She gave her own wicked grin in return.

"And you call me a tease." He held out her robe and she wrapped up in it and sat at her vanity. He began brushing out her hair. "Now that we're alone, tell me what happened. Were you serious about fighting off a zombie?"

"Yes. Take a look." Lavanya held up her hand, and he inspected the nails again. She had the fingernails of a vampire, as strong and sharp as the blade of a knife. They rarely broke, and keeping them trimmed required endless maintenance.

"We'll have to trim them all to match." He pulled out the straight file and clippers from the vanity. "Did you, I mean, how do you kill a zombie?"

"It's gone for now. The problem is that we don't know who sent it or why. Father sent that animal to protect me." She motioned to the outer rooms.

Dylan set his supplies on her vanity, pulled a footstool over, and took her hand in his.

"Well, stop teasing him. He doesn't look like the type to appreciate teasing. On the other hand," he reached for the clippers, "it's been years since you've taken a lover. What better way to keep your protector close?" He wiggled his brow.

"Not my type." Lavanya said, a little too quickly.

Dylan bent back over his work. "He's not a vampire." He looked up to see her shake her head in confirmation.

"So what is he? No one with that much sex appeal or animal magnetism is simply human." He sat back and admired his work for a moment and then reached for her other hand.

"That's a good question, and one that I plan to ask Renfield. You're right—Zev's not *just* human, but I haven't ever seen his sort of magic. He's powerful, and he must be very strong if father believes he can protect me, but I'm not sure what he is."

Lavanya looked around conspiratorially. "I have to tell you, I fed from him tonight." Dylan made a little o with his mouth.

"And..." He stopped doing her nails and waited for a response. Anya licked her lips.

"I don't remember much, but he tasted sooo good." She waved her hand so Dylan would get back to work.

"What? Back up. What happened?"

"Well…"

Zev materialized in the door and cleared his throat. "Are you almost ready for bed?"

Dylan and Lavanya both jumped.

"Get out of my dressing room! I'll be with you in a moment." Lavanya watched through the mirror as he shook his head at her. *Keep the specifics of the attack to ourselves*, he seemed to say.

"He startled you," Dylan said, shaken. "How come you didn't hear him? You always hear everything."

"Dylan, will you do me a favor?" No one had ever been able to sneak up on her before, and she didn't like the feeling. "Keep your ears open around the servants. I have an uneasy feeling that all this—Giselle, the zombie, Zev—it's all connected to the clients here this weekend." She took her hands back and reached for her hand cream.

"Of course, love. Anyone in particular you'd like me to concentrate on?" He looked determined.

"Don't get into trouble poking around, just keep your ears open." She didn't want him to get hurt trying to find something out.

"Darling, I am the epitome of discretion, you know that." He got up and blew her a kiss from the doorway. "Are you sure you don't need me to stay tonight?"

"Thanks, Dylan. I can handle him. Will you tell Chloe to leave the reports in the outer suite, and I'll need her here a little earlier tomorrow evening to finish my nails."

"Sure, hon. Can I get you anything else?"

"No, that'll be all. You're a peach." At the last minute Lavanya remembered the cover story for Zev. "Oh, and if anyone asks, Zev is my friend. End of story." Dylan winked at her as he left.

Zev was glad he'd arrived just in time to stop her from spilling everything to her hairdresser. How clichéd. Sneaking up on her had been fun, though. She'd looked like that had never happened before. It made him laugh and also worry for her safety. She was too used to being a pampered princess and a vampire. They all thought they were indestructible.

He knew better. She needed to understand the real danger. That zombie tonight could have killed her—yet he'd chosen to use the Snow White curse. What use could Lavanya be if she were asleep? Speaking of sleep—

He looked at his watch. Damn, she'd been in there for two hours! What was she doing? He'd showered and changed into sweats, and he'd taken his time because the cold shower was exactly what he needed to chill his arousal. Still, he was back in here within thirty minutes. Dylan had left an hour ago, and she still hadn't emerged from her inner sanctuary.

Zev got up from the chaise where he'd been reading her evening reports and paced. The reports held nothing he didn't already know. Everyone seemed happy in their accommodations, everyone had fed, and all volunteers were accounted for. Blah, blah, blah. The new vampire Giselle was acclimating to her new life extremely well. Zev guessed she'd grown up around people eating other people, so it wasn't a big shock when she had to start sucking the blood from her friends and neighbors.

Zev paced some more. The longer she kept him waiting, the madder he got.

Lavanya took her time in the bath and dressing, finally choosing a long, black silk gown and robe that looked great next to the gray silk of her bedding. She'd be damned if she'd hide behind clothing or change her routine in the least just because he was out there. She wondered what he wore to bed. Was he a boxer, brief, or commando guy? *Yummy.*

She had to stop it. That kind of thinking would get her into trouble—and she still didn't trust him. There was just something about him that set off all her senses.

Lavanya checked her reflection in the mirror before sliding on her robe. Renfield had never been wrong before, and if he said her father trusted Zev, than Zev wasn't the enemy. But she didn't have to like him.

With her robe tied, she opened the door to her bedroom and felt the heat of the fire on the silk material almost immediately.

Zev stood in front of the huge fireplace in loose sweats and nothing else. *Oh my!* The tight cotton T-shirt hadn't lied. He was rock solid, with broad shoulders and tight washboard abs. His chest was covered in a light coating of dark hair that tapered down to a thin line. Her mouth was suddenly dry.

Lavanya tightened the belt on her robe and crossed to the tray with her absinthe and the evening reports, which someone had already rifled through. When did he decide to make himself so at home?

"Do I even need to read these, since you've already gone through them?" She carried them to one of the chairs by the fire.

Zev watched as the thin robe she wore fell to the side when she sat, exposing the long line of her leg. He turned away from her before his body could betray his desire.

"Those reports held nothing of interest. Although you should know that Renfield told everyone the cook went on an errand for you. So he won't be missed for a while." Zev bent and stoked the fire for something to do.

"Okay." She leaned back and closed her eyes. "I'm sure his daughter will be suspicious, but I'll think of something. Is there nothing you can do to bring him out of the deep sleep?"

"Time will tell. If he got what you got, then no—unless you know who his true love is or we find the witch who made it."

"Victor's wife left him years ago. I have no idea if he's been seeing anyone since. His daughter might. I'm going into the village tomorrow to see an old friend. I'll send Chloe to visit with her and see if she knows anything about a lover."

"It isn't wise to be away from the castle. Your father's magic protects you some here. Plus, it's easier to control who gets in and out.

"Mr. Zombie made it in easy enough. Plus, you." Lavanya turned her attention back to her reports.

"Yeah." He found it hard to talk—or even think—as he looked at her. She sat back in the chair, her long, black hair flowing past her shoulders, and the black gown still open to reveal her legs. He dragged his mind back to the problem at hand.

"But I'm here now, and I'll decide where you go and who gets time with you." He turned back to the fire to keep his lust out of her sight. "Why do you want to go into town tomorrow?"

"Chloe's grandmother is a childhood friend. Chloe gave me a message from her and now I need to see her. I've put it off for too long." She sat up and put the reports back on the tray. "I'm going tomorrow."

She stood to make her absinthe. "Would you care to join me? I can call down for another glass."

He watched as she trickled the liquid over the sugar cube and the frothy mass foamed up in the glass. Her tongue came out of her rosy lips and raked across her full mouth.

"No. Thanks, I don't drink absinthe," he said. He needed something to distract himself from the urge to grab her and kiss her like she needed to be kissed. He put another log on the fire even though the room already felt too hot.

"Buttercup and I did a little snooping after our scare in the kitchen." He eased over to the chaise, where he'd laid out a pillow and some blankets. He needed to sit down if he wanted to conceal the bulge in his pants.

"What type of magic allows you to switch between animals with such ease?" Lavanya asked out of nowhere.

"If I told you, I'd have to kill you," he said, grinning. "Sorry."

"I'll just find out tomorrow," she said, looking madder than a Cockroach at a tap-dancing recital. "So what did you find out on your little walk with Buttercup?"

"Not much, I'm sorry to say. However, I thought it was odd that Lauren and Phil's servants should seem so friendly. They let Buttercup and me in while they chatted, and it sounded like they were old friends. Any ideas about that?"

Zev leaned back, closed his eyes, and crossed his arms behind his head. He didn't want to see her in that damn silk robe that brushed against her nipples every time she moved.

Do the job and gain his freedom. The contract his grandmother signed in blood with Vlad more than a hundred years ago had sealed their fate. Their family and any descendants were destined to be a servant forever. He was the last of his line, and one way or another, this agreement ended with him. Either Vlad would let him go, or his family line would end. He would not bring a child into this world unless he was free. Besides, he was the big guy's assassin and screwing Lavanya was definitely not in the fine print. He had a feeling that if Vlad found out he'd even considered it, his freedom would be the least of his worries. But he'd overheard her hairdresser say it had been years since she'd taken a lover. What a waste of a beautiful woman. Certainly she could have her pick of men. Hell, she ran an internet dating service for the most eligible vampires in the world. Why hadn't she found one for herself?

Lavanya had no idea why Phil and Lauren's servants would know each other, and furthermore, she couldn't be bothered to think about it when Zev was stretched out on her chaise looking like sex on a platter. And if this damn gown didn't stop rubbing against her hard nipples, she'd have to go back into a cold shower. As it was, she'd never be able to sleep knowing that he was just a few steps away, all warm and toasty. She could feel his body heat from where she sat, and his arousal was easy to see. Curse him.

"Sorry, I have no idea why the servants know each other," she said. "I check out the clients, but not the servants. I don't even know who they're bringing until I ask them the names for the plane tickets."

"Do you still have the list of names for the trip?" He asked without opening his eyes. *Maybe he's tired*, she thought.

"Yes, it's in my tablet."

"Good. I'll need the list tomorrow morning. I can do some homework while you sleep the day away," he said with a brief smile.

"I guess you don't know me very well," she said as she sipped her drink.

"What's to know? You're Vlad's progeny. End of story."

"That's just the beginning of the story. So what time will you be getting up tomorrow?" she asked.

"Let's see," he looked at his watch. "It's four in the morning now, so probably around noon. Why?"

"Eight hours sleep. You need that much." She sat her empty glass on the tray. "Tell you what. I'll be getting up at ten. Why don't I copy the itinerary and guest list and leave them here for you? Because by noon I'll already be in town visiting my friend."

He sat up and glared at her. "How?"

Lavanya rose from the chair. *He knew nothing of her half-breed status.* "Either get up earlier and do your homework, or I'll leave without you."

She walked over to the fancy paper lanterns that lit the sitting area and turned them off. The dim light that remained displayed his rough features perfectly, and she enjoyed his confusion way more than she should. *Damn*, she wanted to touch him—just close her eyes and let her fingers wander over the sculpted muscles of his chest and back. What would it be like to spend the night with an equal?

Lavanya turned off the rest of the lights. "Goodnight, and try not to snore."

He huffed, but didn't respond to her jab. She turned out the last light on the nightstand by her large, silver, canopied bed. But before settling in, she reached for her phone and texted Renfield. She needed her questions answered about Zev, or he wasn't staying with her any longer. Then she set her alarm for eight-thirty. She'd live without her regular eight hours of sleep.

Zev was stunned by Lavanya's admission. She could go out into the light. He'd never known a vampire who could stand in the sun. Not even Vlad himself could go into the sun. How could she?

Between the arousal she generated in him and the mystery behind what she was, he'd never get to sleep. He reached for his phone and set the alarm for nine in the morning. Then he texted Renfield. He had questions, and he needed a few answers before he got in any deeper. A vampire out in the day. How did that work?

If the plan was to protect her, he needed to know everything about her.

LYNNE STEVIE

CHAPTER SEVENTEEN

Hairdresser's Intuition

Lavanya awoke before her alarm went off and tiptoed into her dressing room to get ready for her meeting with Renfield. She hurried to wash her face and run a brush through her tangled, black hair. It hadn't been an easy night. She'd tossed and turned, knowing that Zev was just a few steps away. The musky scent of their combined arousal filled the room until she almost got up and opened the doors.

She grabbed the first clothes she saw—a simple, white, button-up blouse and skinny jeans. It was chilly, so she also grabbed her UGGs for warmth and comfort. She didn't need to dress up or wear makeup, because none of her clients would be awake at this unnatural hour for vampires.

She peeked out of her dressing room to make sure the path to the door was clear, and when she looked over at the chaise, Zev was gone. Damn, he was already up. She hurried to the door, still tugging on her boots, hoping he'd gone for a shower and she'd find Renfield before running into him.

She could have spit when she came into the solarium and saw Zev sitting and eating in her normal spot.

"So you can be an early riser if needed," she said as she walked to the table that was always set out for her and Renfield. Of course, this was way earlier than their normal meal, but she'd alerted the staff last night after Renfield had texted her that he'd meet her early.

"Yep." Zev said as he shoved the last cinnamon roll in his mouth. *Damn it.* The last cinnamon roll, and there wouldn't ever be any more of those, either. She wanted to throw a fit, but decided against it. Zev already thought of her as a spoiled princess, no need to give him more fuel for his thoughts.

"Where's Renfield?"

Zev raised his finger for her to wait as he chewed the gooey dough.

"I just got here and…" he swallowed, "he hasn't arrived yet."

Lavanya almost growled, and not just because she was hungry for the stupid cinnamon rolls. Zev looked even yummier this morning than he had last night. His hair was damp, and it hung in waves. He'd obviously dressed while still wet from his shower, because his cotton T-shirt stuck to him deliciously. The stubble on his chin was trimmed neatly, and before she could stop herself, she remembered the touch of his lips on hers when he kissed her in the parlor. A shiver ran through her body.

"You cold?"

"No, I'm irritated." *And frustrated.* "You're in my seat, you ate the last cinnamon roll, I'm up early, and Renfield isn't here yet." She fisted her hands on her hips and she actually stomp her foot a little. *So much for not throwing a fit.*

"That's quite a list." He licked his fingers and took a big drink of coffee.

"Is that chicory I smell?" As he gulped his coffee, the scent wafted over to her. She imagined Bourbon Street.

"It is. You like chicory in your coffee?" He seemed surprised.

"I live in the States, and that's definitely New Orleans coffee. Is it the original New Orleans coffee?" She tried to get a better smell of the delicious aroma.

"I'm impressed that you know your coffee. It's Café Du Monde, of course. All the others are just imitations. Don't you think? The kitchen staff went all out for Harry and his wife, so I couldn't resist." Then he held up a cup and she relaxed a little.

"Thanks." She sat and let him pour her a cup. Just then Amelia came through the swinging door with a plate full of beignets. *Oh, there is a god.* She barely waited for the maid to set the tray down before she grabbed a hot confection, thickly dusted with powdered sugar, from the top of the stack. The first bite was heavenly. Almost as good as blood and infinitely sweeter. She followed that with some of the thick, black coffee. Maybe later she could make some café au lait. All the pleasures of home.

Zev watched as Lavanya practically made love to the beignets, and the look on her face when she sipped the coffee almost made him take her right there on the dining table. He'd never seen someone eat with so much sensuality. It didn't help that she looked so warm and casual in the cotton button-down and jeans. He imagined her in one of his shirts. It would be big on her and fall below the curve of her ass. She'd have nothing on underneath. She'd lie in the middle of her huge bed with the covers messed up all around her. She'd have a content and sleepy smile on her beautiful face. A smile that can only come from a good and thorough fucking....

"Sir?"

"Zev." Lavanya snapped her pale fingers in front of his face, bringing him from the vision. "Amelia wants to know if you'd like more coffee."

"Yeah, thanks." He coughed a little and shifted in his seat to readjust his hard-on. *Damn, he might need another cold shower.* Then held out his cup for the maid to fill.

Lavanya wondered what he'd been thinking about so hard that he didn't hear Amelia. And where the hell was Renfield? He was never late for a meeting—it was a running joke between them. She noticed Zev staring at her and suddenly felt self-conscious about the way she was devouring the beignets.

"What?" She set the pastry down and sipped the rich coffee.

"How are you different from other vampires? I know you're Vlad's offspring, so that should make you more powerful, but even he can't be out in the sun. What makes you different?"

Ah, there it was. She wondered if he'd be upset that she wasn't fully vampire, or if he'd be upset that she wasn't fully human.

"I could ask you the same questions. You can change shape at will, although I think the wolf-beast is your preferred or more dominate shape? Plus, you have your own magic, which is powerful enough to combat the Snow White curse. So?" She raised her brow and waited for an answer. The silence stretched between them.

Then something hit her—something with tremendous force. The momentum ripped her out of her chair, knocking it over and upsetting the dishes on the table, and threw her against the wall. Her head slammed against the plaster, and her chest felt crushed. She heard Renfield's voice in her mind: *I won't leave you, Master.* Then her father's rage burst forth.

"*Run, my child, run. RUN!*" He shouted in her mind and then cut the connection. She was adrift. For the first time, without his powerful love or Renfield's guidance. Alone.

"No." Lavanya whimpered and held her ears against his entreaties. "No, no, no, Father...Renfield, please." But they were gone.

Zev watched in horror as some force picked Lavanya up from the table and threw her into the wall. The impact cracked the plaster and cut her head open. He reached her side just as she went into seizure. He held her through the violent jolts and spasms and heard her grief as she begged for her father and Renfield.

He grabbed a couple of the linen napkins littering the floor and pressed them to her head to stop the bleeding. When the flow stopped, he carried her to a soft chair in the sun room where he could see her better. *Damn it.* He'd been sitting right in front of her, yet he'd been powerless to help her. He hadn't felt any magic or otherness in the room. What the hell had happened? Feeling her limp in his arms was agony. She couldn't be hurt. He wouldn't allow it.

"Lavanya, come back. Can you hear me?"

She didn't respond. He laid her on the sofa and wiped the blood off her head with the napkins. Then, using only his fingertips, he examined her scalp. Thank god there didn't seem to be any fractures, just the head wound from the force of the impact.

"Amelia!" he yelled. "Get Renfield! He's supposed to be down here!"

"I'm sorry, sir." Amelia wrung her hands. "But none of us have seen him this morning."

"Then go check his rooms. Find him now!" He spotted a young boy picking up the fallen dishes.

"You!" he shouted.

"Yes, sir." The boy sprang to attention.

"Go to the kitchen and put some ice in a bag for her head. Then find a first aid kit if you have it."

The boy ran off without a word. With nothing else he could think to do, Zev ran his fingers over her face and through her bloody hair.

"Lavanya, wake up. I need to know what happened." He said

it as much to himself as to her.

When she didn't respond, he opened up his own magic to see what else was around him and if he could help her that way. His magic was like a seventh sense, as much a part of him as his eyesight or taste or smell. No one had ever explained why or how he could manipulate the world around him, but he used that part of him to examine her on a cellular level. He checked for internal injuries or a brain hemorrhage. He found nothing wrong with her. Vlad's smell on and around her was strong—more powerful than he had ever noticed before—but maybe that was because he was so close to her now.

Zev ran his hand through her hair again and looked at her face. She was beautiful, even more so than she had been last night. The sunlight played with the blue-black streaks of her hair, and because she wore no makeup, he could see the natural color of her skin and lips. He wanted her to open her eyes so he could stare into the deep violet color and see the passionate spirit within her.

"Sir, the ice." Zev took it from the boy and lifted Anya's head just enough to place the ice on the back of her head where the skin was broken. The bleeding had already stopped, but the ice would help any swelling. He had no idea if she'd be okay—she wasn't like any other vampire he'd known. He knew that most vampires could recover easily from a fall, but she didn't fit any of his preconceived ideas of a vampire.

"Where's Renfield? Has anyone found him yet?" He asked the servants who hovered around their mistress.

"No, sir," Amelia said. "And it's not like him to be gone without word. We're sending out people to search the grounds now."

"Find Chloe and Dylan and bring them here. They're her personal servants, yes?" He needed to find someone who knew her. Maybe she fainted a lot, or maybe she was injured. Maybe she'd been injured before, just like this. He had no way to know.

He'd never felt more helpless, and he didn't like it. He wanted action. Change. He shook from rage, excitement—even fear—and his body wanted to change to his beast. The beast didn't feel fear.

Dylan stumbled into the solarium, shielding his eyes from the sun. He looked as though he hadn't woken yet. He still had marks on his face from the pillow, and his eyes didn't seem to want to stay open. At first he didn't notice the overturned chairs and food on the floor.

"Lavanya, darling, why on earth are you up at this hour, and in God's name, why do you need me to be up, too?"

"Dylan, we're in trouble," Zev said. He turned to the servants. "Let him in."

When a path was made, Dylan awoke in a panic.

"Oh, my god. Lavanya!" He looked around at the mess and the frightened servants. Then he caught sight of Zev and took a step back.

Zev tried to force down his anger, but he was sure that his eyes were black flames. Stress always brought on the change. His control was normally rock-solid, but Lavanya's hurtle across the room and her subsequent injury—and his inability to help—were pushing him. His Rakshasa demon wanted to take control.

"Lavanya was injured and Renfield can't be found," Zev said. "I need your help."

"Of course. How badly is she hurt?"

"Take a look for yourself." Zev turned to the servants. "Somebody—send in Chloe. Everyone else leave. *Now!*"

Dylan touched Lavanya's face and hair, then checked her pulse. "What happened?"

"I don't know. We were having breakfast and generally pissing each other off like normal. Then she flew against the wall screaming, as if someone or something was crushing her. She hit her head." He showed Dylan the wound, now almost healed.

Dylan felt her head. "That's it?"

"That's it!"

"And?"

"And now she won't wake up. There's no other magic around her—I would know. She only smells of her father, and her body's in perfect shape except for the head wound, and hell— that's almost healed. Why isn't she conscious?" Zev jumped up and paced the room, running his hand through his hair.

"What can you tell me, Dylan? What happened here? What is she? If she's a vampire, how can she survive in the sun?"

"What did she say exactly when she was hit?" Dylan asked.

"How the hell should I know? It was something about her father and no, no, no, and then Renfield, please."

He paused, towering over Dylan, to gaze down at Lavanya. "Will she wake up?"

"I don't know. Where's Renfield?"

"No one can find him." Zev fought to control his emotions when her eyes twitched. He bent down to speak to her again.

"Lavanya, can you hear me?"

"Father…" she said on a sigh.

She was alive. Zev bowed his head in overwhelming relief. Never in his life had anyone affected him so much. What would he do if she didn't come back?

Dylan patted her hand.

"Lavanya, darlin', its Dylan, I need you to sit up." Zev watched, impatients and worry tightening his body as Dylan took her arm and helped her to sit up, then held her as she started to cry.

Lavanya had never felt as alone as when Dylan held her. The pain of the attack had been Renfield's and it was brutal and searing, but the pain when her father pushed her out was almost more then she could bear.

"Dylan, Father's gone. He's cut our connection. I can't feel him. I don't know if he's okay. Renfield's hurt too. I felt it. I felt it all." She was overwhelmed by the silence. Her father had always been there, to provide strength when she needed it, and Renfield, through him, was always with her, as well. He'd told her to run. He'd known he was in danger, and he cut her out to save her. She was sure of it.

She opened her eyes to see Dylan and Zev. The obsidian glow of emotion in Zev's eyes caught her by surprise.

"What happened?" he demanded. "One minute you were fine, and the next you were flying across the room."

She decided right then and there to trust him. If her father sent him—and Renfield believed in his abilities and trusted him—then she had no choice but to trust their last actions. Plus, she wanted to trust him with her secrets.

"I'm connected to my father as he sleeps," she said. "I'm sort of a lifeline, or he's my lifeline. I…it doesn't matter. Through that tie, I'm also somewhat connected to Renfield." She sagged, unable to go on.

"He sent me, you know, Zev said, which somehow reassured

her. "Your father contacted me in a vision and told me he needed me to protect you. Renfield knew that, too."

"I know."

"I trust him," Dylan said, smiling and taking her hand. "Hairdressers intuition, remember? Go on. Tell us what happened."

She looked into Dylan's eyes for support.

"Renfield was ripped away, and the connection was severed. The last thing he said was that he would never give up Father, and then he was gone." She clutched her chest.

"It was awful, so much pain. Renfield is in so much pain." She couldn't blink back her tears and felt them trail down her cheeks.

"You shouted 'Father, no, no.'" Zev was pacing again, running his long fingers through his thick tangle of hair. "What did you mean?"

"He told me to run, just before he cut me off, and I lost my connection to him and Renfield." She squeezed Dylan's hand and wiped the last of the tears off her cheeks. Chloe rushed in and ran right to her mistress's side, pressing a cool, damp cloth to Lavanya's forehead. Lavanya looked up to Zev.

"I told him no. I won't run."

CHAPTER EIGHTEEN

Start At The Beginning

Zev had tried every logical thing he could think of to make Lavanya leave—to run—as her father had instructed her to do. But she refused to leave when Vlad and Renfield were in trouble. Even knowing that Vlad had shut her out to save her, she wouldn't be swayed.

Even Dylan tried to talk her into going into hiding to get a better picture of who or what might be behind the attacks. But she would have none of it.

"No daughter of Vlad would cower in hiding," she'd replied when Zev mentioned returning to the States for a few days while he tried to discover who was responsible.

Who was responsible? Who could be powerful enough to take Renfield? Plus, the new vamp Giselle was missing, too. Had the same force taken her? He could find out, if he had time and he wasn't worried constantly about protecting Lavanya.

Lavanya had finally confided to him that Vlad was asleep—really asleep. No wonder he hadn't heard from him in years. His resting place was close, but she wouldn't tell him exactly where. Which irritated him, but he understood. What would he have done 100 years ago if he'd had that information? Would he have tried to destroy him? Maybe. Probably. Yes.

But that was then and this is now. Now he was here to protect Lavanya, which was why he was following her black horse into the little village of Arefu in the valley below the castle. Lavanya was determined to visit with her childhood friend Helgaleena. She believed Helgaleena might know something about the situation. Helgaleena was some sort of a seer, and she'd warned Chloe about a dream she'd had.

Zev didn't like it. They were too exposed. But he couldn't change Lavanya's mind, so here he was in dog form, trailing after her.

Samson and he hadn't exactly made friends, so he was forced

to stay back instead of running alongside Lavanya. Most animals have a nose for magic, and if they smell it, they avoid it. It wasn't unusual, but what was unusual was the way Buttercup adored him. *Women.*

Zev watched as Lavanya dismounted to walk Samson into town. Everyone stopped what they were doing and nodded or bowed to her as she walked beside her horse. It was like an old western movie. If he looked around, would the women be grabbing up their young 'uns? He shook his head as only a dog can when they're confused by humans.

The ride into town was long—and felt longer on horseback. Lavanya's head hurt, which she'd never admit, and she'd never felt more alone than she did at this minute, now that the ties to Renfield and her father had been cut. The mountain air and the smell of the earth—her father's earth—helped clear her head, and the land gave her strength. She had a feeling that before the weekend was over, she'd need all the strength she could get.

The residents of Arefu knew something about strength. The village had survived thousands of years in a hard country. Harsh mountainous conditions and constant struggles with invading enemies, fought off with her father's help, had toughened its people.

As she entered the town, most of the villagers bowed their heads slightly as she passed. Lavanya sometimes forgot that Vlad was revered in this small town, and she was a princess. She remembered her position and stood straight, nodding solemnly to the awestruck townspeople. Lavanya was proud to be Vlad's daughter and proud of these tough people who called this cold mountainside home. She greeted a few of the merchants, accepting with thanks the hand-woven scarves and jewelry they offered her. She hadn't been back to town to see its people in a long time— more than 25 years. She'd been hiding in Miami, she understood that now. Well, no more hiding.

Zev looked cute as an Irish wolfhound trailing behind Samson. Lavanya worried about how Helgaleena would react to him. Would she know that this was the wolf she'd warned Chloe about? Lavanya had tried to come alone, but this was a good compromise. Zev had been right about assuming a disguise. Everyone knew she bred the large dogs, so no one in town would question why she had one with her today. Zev trotted beside her, and she rubbed his head every now and then.

As for herself, she knew that she looked stronger than she felt. She needed to put forth a confident and strong appearance, because that was what her father would expect and what his people deserved. Thank god Dylan had helped her get ready, because she'd been in no shape to do anything after the pain she'd been in this morning. He'd pulled her hair back in a low ponytail gathered at her neck just above the white turtleneck of her cashmere sweater. The hounds tooth jacket, leather pants, and black riding boots completed the outfit. Of course, Dylan wouldn't let her leave the castle without false eyelashes and red lipstick, and now she was glad. Because of him she looked presentable. Hopefully, all the trouble of getting here wouldn't be in vain and Helgaleena could help her.

Lavanya had nowhere else to turn, so she'd decided to start at the beginning. Helgaleena had predicted a wolf, and that had come to pass. Maybe she could help Lavanya figure out what was happening now.

Helgaleena's gift was hard to describe. She didn't actually see the future as much as she just knew certain things. Normally, she reported only good news. She'd be the first to know who was expecting a baby, sometimes even before the woman knew she was expecting. And she always knew what the sex the baby would be, and she could sometimes tell about other medical ailments, as well.

A few young women stood by Helgaleena's front porch—waiting to speak with her, Lavanya guessed. Many were pregnant and held their stomachs protectively as she passed by. Their fear washed over her like the humid air of Miami in August. If she'd worn glasses, they would have fogged.

Lavanya glanced to the sky, where the gray clouds seemed to follow her. She'd heard stories of her father manipulating the weather of these mountains, but this was the first time she felt the pulse of the earth in her own fingertips. She willed a small patch of sun to peep through the clouds, and the sky obeyed her. The sun rained down on her, Zev, and Samson, painting them in brilliant light. Lavanya closed her eyes and enjoyed the warmth on her skin. The women gasped, dropped their heads, and backed down the steps away from her and the door to Helgaleena's home.

"Stop that." The woman who'd been her sister in many ways chastised her from behind the screen door. "You'll scare them silly. Plus, you needn't be advertising your powers." Startled, Lavanya focused on the clouds, which now drifted together again.

At eighty years, Helgaleena looked frail and old, and Lavanya didn't recognize her voice, which was no longer that of the girl she had known, but that of an old woman. But Lavanya could see that Helgaleena's mind was still sharp, and her eyes reflected deep intelligence behind the little glasses she wore at the end of her nose.

"Helgaleena, it's been too long." Aware of the audience on the street, Lavanya didn't move to enter the home, but addressed her from where she stood.

"Yes, it has." Helgaleena stepped out onto the small porch and held onto the railing.

"Joseph!" she yelled. In a moment, a boy, all awkward, gangly legs and arms who couldn't have been more than fourteen, appeared from the back of the yard and ran up the side steps.

"Yes, G.G.," he said before he saw Lavanya.

"We have company." Helgaleena nodded toward Lavanya.

"Yes, ma'am." When the boy turned to see who was there, recognition flooded his innocent face.

"Mistress," he said, a little breathless, and bowed his head.

"G.G.?" Lavanya asked Helgaleena. She wasn't familiar with this name.

"This is my great-grandson Joseph." Helgaleena grabbed his arm and nudged him down the steps until he stood in front of them. The pride in Helgaleena's voice made Lavanya long for something that she would never have: family, children.

"Joseph, this is Princess Lavanya Draculesti, daughter of The Prince, Vlad Tepes."

Oh hell, she'd used her full name. Lavanya heard Zev sneeze as he bumped into her leg. Obviously, he enjoyed hearing Helgaleena call her a princess. She knew she'd hear about that later. She extended her hand to the young man.

"Hello, Joseph, it's good to meet you." She met Helgaleena's eyes as Joseph bowed and kissed her hand. When he stood again, his eyes looked unfocused and his breathing was more of a pant.

Lavanya stepped back, not sure what was wrong with the boy, but Joseph held on tight.

Zev growled low in his chest.

No, this couldn't be happening! Lavanya had manipulated the clouds and now she had be-spelled this poor boy without even trying. Her father had been notorious for his magnetic draw for all things female, but she had never experienced anything like this. The boy looked at her as if he were seeing a goddess.

"Joseph." She yanked her hand back as Zev, still growling, leaped in front of her.

"*Zev.*" She pushed her knee into his shoulder, trying to shove him out of the way, but even in dog form he was stronger than she.

"Joseph," Helgaleena said. "Take Lavanya's horse out to the pasture and give him a drink." Helgaleena waited a moment, but the boy didn't take his eyes from Lavanya. Zev growled again.

"*Joseph.*" Helgaleena moved quickly for an old woman and stood before Joseph in an instant. She snapped her fingers in his face and he blinked, coming out of his reverie. "The horse to the pasture. Then go on with your chores."

"Ah." He looked longingly at Lavanya and Zev growled again, breaking the boy's concentration. "Yes, ma'am." His hands shook, but he took the reins and led Samson away to the back of the property. Helgaleena looked at Zev.

"So, you seem to have found your beast." She laughed, but the girlish giggle coming from her stooped body sounded wrong. "I may have been wrong about the control part. I think a better word might have been *power*—you have power over the beast. Yes, that is better."

She laughed again and patted Zev's head. He gave her a warning bark and shook off her hand. Helgaleena stared at Zev, a look so foreign and lacking any warmth that Lavanya almost backed up to get away from it.

"This one doesn't like the reins you've fit on him, and you're not even aware of the influence you have on him." Helgaleena shook her head and went into the house, holding the door open for Lavanya in welcome.

It had been a long time since Lavanya had been inside. The house hadn't changed much in the past fifty years, but it looked different to her eyes now. Lavanya had grown up in this place with

Helgaleena, and yet she'd never belonged here as Helgaleena had. Lavanya knew every creak on the steps and every moan of the wind against the stone tile roof, but this house was Helgaleena's family home and had been for hundreds of years. The front door was solid oak, heavy but short. If Zev had been in his human form, he'd have had to stoop to enter. Even now, Helgaleena kept to the old traditions and tied cinnamon above the door to ward off unwanted spirits.

Lavanya felt the difference—that she was an outsider—now more than ever. She'd been an orphan that Helgaleena's family had taken in for a time. With a heavy sigh Lavanya crossed the threshold, but Helgaleena blocked Zev from entering.

"Ah, ah, ah—I don't allow animals in the house. You can wait out here on the porch."

"Grrrraaawr." Zev looked at Lavanya.

"She's right," Lavanya answered. "I want to speak with her alone."

"Grrrraaawr." Zev didn't budge from the doorway.

"Zev, wait on the porch. If I need you, I'll call." No one ever contested or disobeyed her orders, and she didn't like the feeling now. Zev still didn't move from the doorway.

"Enough!" Helgaleena said. "Dog, I know you're here to protect her. I promise she'll come to no harm in my home." Her words were law, and even Zev backed down. He stepped back out the door and sat facing them. Helgaleena shut the door in his face, just missing his muzzle.

"Now," Helgaleena turned to Lavanya, "would you like a drink?"

"Helgaleena, it's only one in the afternoon." Lavanya smiled at her beautiful, wrinkled face. Helgaleena's face was marked with age, but the only deep lines were smile lines. And they were extremely deep.

"So?" Helgaleena put two coffee mugs on her kitchen table and, from the cabinet under the cast iron sink, pulled out a bottle filled with a clear liquid. No label marked the bottle's contents. For all Anya knew, it was rubbing alcohol.

Helgaleena poured the liquid into the two mugs and motioned Lavanya to come to the table. She sat in one of the old wooden chairs, handmade so long ago they were almost black with age.

One sniff of the cup and she knew she was in trouble. This homemade brew—called white lightning in the States but Pervach here—was more potent than rubbing alcohol. Lavanya could almost feel it burn her throat just from smelling it. Helgaleena held up her own glass and took a healthy swallow.

"Ahhh. That'll keep your heart tickin.'" She smiled at Lavanya in encouragement, raising her eyebrows and waving her hand to prompt her to drink. Lavanya took a deep breath and gulped down a shot.

"Whew!" Lavanya swallowed again to keep it down and nodded her thanks to Helgaleena. "That'll put hair on your chest, as Renfield would say." She bowed her head at the thought of Renfield.

"Helgaleena, I need to know about your dream."

"I told Chloe not to bother you with such nonsense as my dream," Helgaleena said, narrowing her wrinkled eyes at Lavanya. "I'm guessin' you were feeding and pried it outta her?"

"Yes, I was feeding. Do you need to remind me that I must feed on your grandchild?" Lavanya huffed. "I've never forced her to feed me."

"What's happened?"

"Your dream first." Lavanya needed to hear the full dream before giving Helgaleena any of the specifics. She didn't want to sway Helgaleena's memories or lead her into any conclusions before she'd heard the entire dream herself.

"Lavanya, you know I don't always understand what they're trying to tell me." Helgaleena reached out and took Lavanya's hand. "Sometimes I just get pictures and sometimes random words. Why do you want to know? You never believed in my gifts."

Lavanya's own magic sparked to life, and she caught a glimpse of Helgaleena as a young girl dancing in the fields. Helgaleena wanted to be young again. Just as quickly as the image formed, Helgaleena pulled her hand back and rubbed it on her apron. She looked angry. Lavanya didn't blame her. She wouldn't want anyone messing around in her mind, either.

"Helgaleena, I know how it works. But something that didn't seem important at the time might be important now, and I don't want to influence your memories. A lot has been happening."

"I can see that." Helgaleena tilted her head toward the door.

"It may not be evident to either of you yet, but you will have power over each other." She sat up straighter.

"All right then. The premonition came to me in a dream. He—" she tilted her head toward the door again, "was a black wolf. The control you have over him he will not admit until it's almost too late. You'll both have to choose a course of action that'll affect the other. I won't say any more about that."

She dusted off her skirt with her rough hands. "I also felt deception and a feminine aspect."

"What woman—" Anya began to ask, but Helgaleena held up her hand.

"Don't ask me, Sister. I can't tell you anymore than I can tell you what the wolf would look like as a man." She looked up at Lavanya with mischievous eyes.

"So, how does he look?" Her cracked lips pulled apart in a devious smile.

"Oh, Helgaleena, you never change."

"I hope I don't, but that doesn't answer my question." She sat forward conspiratorially, and so did Lavanya.

"Good, really good." Lavanya smiled and sat back in the chair.

"Excellent." Helgaleena turned back to the business at hand.

"In the dream, a tidal wave was about to crush you. The wave, I think, represents emotions, and you are spinning around and around, so you cannot see the tidal wave approaching. Someone is deceiving you, Anya, and that person could cost you your life or the lives of your loved ones."

Lavanya slumped in the chair, contemplating Helgaleena's words. Which of her friends would betray her like that?

"Now, I have a question for you." Helgaleena looked out at the afternoon sky. "Did you manipulate the clouds? Have you discovered a new gift from your father?" She seemed excited by the prospect.

"I'm not sure, but yes, I think I did. I don't know how. I just asked for a little sun, and the clouds parted."

Lavanya gazed at the old woman who'd once shared this cottage with her. "Helgaleena, what am I going to do? Something terrible has happened to Renfield. And someone is trying to find Father. He cut me off, Helgaleena. I can't feel him anymore. He told me to run."

Helgaleena smiled, which baffled Lavanya.

"You're not running, are you?" Helgaleena poured each of them another shot.

"Of course, I'm not running." Lavanya tossed back the drink, which stayed down better than the first one had. She wasn't sure if that was a good sign or a bad sign. "I need to ask for a favor." *A huge favor.*

"If I can."

"I want you to cast the runes for me."

"I don't do that." Helgaleena put the bottle back under the sink and gathered the glasses.

"You have your mother's set of staves, and she was an Erulian—a rune master." Lavanya kept her seat, although it was difficult not to go to Helgaleena and try to force her to help. She knew that would never work. Helgaleena had to want to help her.

"Renfield and Father are depending on me, Helgaleena," she said. "I need to know who's behind this."

Helgaleena gripped the counter. Silence flowed over Lavanya like a quilt, heavy and warm, almost suffocating.

"Why are you asking me for this? You never took the divinations seriously. For that matter, you never took my dreams seriously."

"You predicted him." Lavanya motioned toward the door, to Zev. "I'm desperate to find out who's betraying us. Please, Helgaleena, do this for me."

"One question," Helgaleena said. "That's all I'll give you." She looked to the door. "Ah, why not? You won't believe what they say, anyway. But that's all I'll do. Those staves are cursed."

Helgaleena turned away, and Lavanya hated herself for what she was making Helgaleena do. Helgaleena believed that to ask for a divination—to see your fate—was too presumptuous. And that the answers could be so construed in your mind that you would never really know what the truth was. But Lavanya needed all the answers she could get. She'd worry about the consequences later.

Zev howled, one long, soulful cry, and then scratched on the door.

LYNNE STEVIE

CHAPTER NINETEEN

The Runes

"Curse these old legs," Helgaleena swore as she lowered herself to the floor to prepare the casting space.

"Here…let me help you." Lavanya reached for her arm, but Helgaleena batted her away.

"Just because I've aged, don't mean I need yer help." The bitterness in her voice made Lavanya step back. Helgaleena's face lost the grimace of pain as she settled on the floor. Only her sharp inhale let Lavanya know she was still hurting.

"Fine." Lavanya sighed, throwing her arms up in defeat. Helgaleena's frail body shook as she laid a clean, white cloth on the old wooden floor and pulled each corner until the crisp fabric lay flat. It reminded Lavanya of Velka, Helgaleena's mother. As children, the two of them used to hide in the large cabinet by the door and watch Velka read for the women of the town. They'd question the sex of the child they carried or whether their husbands would return from their travels. When Velka died, it was like losing her mother all over again.

Lavanya looked around the room. The old pedestal table used to be a honey color, but now it was blackened with age and seemed smaller than she remembered. She caught a glimpse of herself in the age-scarred mirror that hung on the wall behind the table. Her reflection looked the same as always—no wrinkles; no gray hair; vibrant, violet eyes; and plump, red lips. She was frozen in time.

She hadn't been in this house in more than twenty years. She understood why she'd stayed away—she never again wanted to grieve the loss of a loved one. She'd taken the coward's way out and left after Velka passed away. She'd pushed the pain away by leaving, but absence hadn't changed the facts. Helgaleena was aging and would die soon. Then her only tie to her human self would be eradicated.

Helgaleena struggled to her feet. Then she worked her way around the cloth, tracing Thor's hammer in the air and creating a protected environment ideal for divination.

"You must think of your question now," Helgaleena said, looking at Lavanya with cloudy, gray eyes. "It must be precise."

Lavanya put the past behind her and focused on the events at the castle. She watched Helgaleena pull herself onto a stool at the southern tip of the cloth.

"I need to know who is trying to harm us." Lavanya stood behind Helgaleena so she could see the staves as Helgaleena cast them.

"Pull your chair up, Anya. I cannot have you leering over my shoulder."

Lavanya pulled her chair to the side of Helgaleena's.

"I'm ready," she said.

"Clear your mind of everything except your question," Helgaleena ordered. She picked up the black bag that held the staves and shook and stirred them. "We must ask the goddesses of fate for help. Recite with me this passage from the Voluspà."

> *From there come the maidens*
> *with knowledge of many things*
> *three from that sea,*
> *which stands beneath the tree;*
> *one is called Urdhr,*
> *the other Verdhandi,*
> *they carved on sticks,*
> *Skuld the third.*
> *They laid down the law,*
> *they choose the lives*
> *of the children of men,*
> *the fates of men."*

Lavanya repeated word for word what Helgaleena said, even though she thought it was nonsense.

"Lavanya, clear your mind." Helgaleena placed a hand on Lavanya's leg, stopping her nervous foot-tapping. "I can feel your anxiety, and you need a calm mind to cast."

Lavanya stopped fidgeting, took a deep breath, and shook her arms out.

"Better. Now, picture the words of the question in your mind."

After a few moments Helgaleena handed her the black satchel. "Shuffle the runes, and ask your question out loud."

Lavanya took the bag and shook the small wooden staves carved with runes. "Who is trying to harm my father?"

"Repeat after me, 'Runes rown right rede'!" Helgaleena shouted to the sky.

"Runes rown right rede."

"Pick out three runes from the bag one at a time, and repeat what I say as you lay them on the cloth. Do not turn them or change their direction. Lay them down in a vertical line exactly as you take them out."

"Okay." Lavanya pulled the worn leather straps apart and took out the first rune.

"Urdhr, that which has become," she said after Helgaleena with the first rune. "Verdhandi, that which is becoming," she said with the second. The second rune landed face down, so Lavanya reached to flip it.

"Do not touch them again." The old woman slapped her hand away. Lavanya was surprised at how fast Helgaleena had moved. She picked out a third rune.

"Skuld, that which shall be," she said as she lay it on the cloth.

Helgaleena closed her eyes as if praying. Lavanya, edgy again, tapped her boot on the floor. Helgaleena cleared her throat and sneered at her through lids opened only to slits. Lavanya stilled.

"Odin, may I read the runes aright!" Helgaleena said and took the first rune in her hand.

"That which has become is Sowilo—the sun. ⟩ It stands for energy, health, and life." Helgaleena grinned.

"There's a Norse legend about the sun," she said. "A young girl, chased by a great wolf that wants to devour her, drives around the sun in a chariot."

Lavanya whipped up her head to stare at the door. "It's just an old legend, Sister."

Helgaleena smiled at Lavanya's discomfort and reached for the second stave. As she turned it over, she hissed.

"*What?*" Lavanya asked, almost coming off her chair.

"Shush!" Helgaleena evaluated the second rune. "That which is becoming is Isa—ice. | It stands for confusion, frustration, or stagnation in its natural form. However, in the merkstave position—face down—it represents blindness, treachery, and betrayal."

"Who would dare try to deceive us?" Lavanya jumped up in rage.

"*Sit down,* or I won't continue. You knew there was a plot against you before you ever set foot in the door. Stop being shocked by what you already know. It's a waste of energy."

Lavanya knew that she was right. She took her seat again and Helgaleena reached for the third and final rune.

"That which shall be is Eihwaz—the yew tree. ↑ The yew is a long-living evergreen and a symbol of immortality. However, it is also the thirteenth rune, so it represents a turning point or transformation."

The thirteenth rune—why was that important? Lavanya racked her brain. Then she remembered. Thirteenth—the death card in the tarot deck.

"Death," she said softly.

"Yes," Helgaleena confirmed. "But the death of one thing can also be the rebirth of another. Odin believed that with any transformation or rite of passage, we must enter the Hell Realm to gain the knowledge and acceptance of our own mortality. As well as learn the mysteries that can be learned only from the Dark Lady of the Dead."

Helgaleena dusted off her worn skirt and sat straighter in her chair. "To close, repeat after me."

"Wait!" Lavanya protested, but Helgaleena continued her closing.

> *Now are H'ar's sayings said in Har's Hall*
> *Helpful to the sons of men*
> *But of no help to sons of Etins.*
> *Hail the one who speaks them*
> *Hail the one who knows them,*
> *Gain, the one who grasps them*
> *Hail those who hear them!*

Lavanya repeated everything Helgaleena said without really

hearing herself finish.

"It is done." Helgaleena clapped her hands and then held them up to the gods, just like a blackjack dealer in a Louisiana casino.

"That's it? How am I supposed to know who's trying to kill us if the reading doesn't give us any names or descriptions? What does it all mean?"

Helgaleena shook her head. "This is why I don't do readings anymore. They're always accurate, but no one ever sees that until after my counsel comes to pass. Maybe seeing our own fate is impossible."

"That which has become your energy and health, that which is becoming a betrayal, that which shall be a transformation. Her condescending smile irritated Lavanya.

"Death," Lavanya spat. "Just say it."

"Death comes to all of us. Death of our childhood, our innocence, and, yes, finally our bodies or our souls. You're not listening to me. We're done!"

"But who? Helgaleena, in your dream you saw a woman betray me, but the runes say nothing of a woman. The runes talk of betrayal and transformation. What does it mean?"

Helgaleena went to the kitchen and retrieved a slip of paper and pencil, which she handed to Lavanya.

"Write your question and then write all the answers that were given in the correct order. Ask yourself how each rune relates to the question at hand." She sat on the stool and pulled the white cloth up by the edges with all the runes placed in the middle.

"Or not," she continued. "You've never believed in divination. As a child you laughed at my mother and her silly wood chips. She told me you wouldn't believe until it was too late and your future was set."

"That can't be!" Lavanya grabbed her arm. "Wait! I have another question."

"No. You were given a negative answer in the Verdhandi—betrayal. We must not ask any more runic questions today." Helgaleena looked down at where Lavanya held her arm. It turned red under Lavanya's pale fingers.

Lavanya released her, then scribbled the rune answers on the slip of paper. But after she finished, she still felt no closer to a solution. And the piece of paper seemed to burn her hand. To ease the sting, she switched the pencil from hand to hand and rubbed her palms on the smooth leather of her riding pants. Finally, frustrated and frightened for Renfield and her father, she walked to the door.

"I have to go." She opened the door and felt the weight of an approaching storm bearing down on her skin. "Thanks for the warning about Zev, and the reading, I guess."

"Wait."

"I can't, I have to get back." Lavanya stepped out onto the porch. The wind had picked up while she'd been inside, and it tossed her hair around her face, as if the sky was irritated with her for her earlier interference.

"Wait!" Helgaleena startled Lavanya by grabbing her arm.

"What? I thanked you for the help, now I must leave." She was impatient now. Visiting Helgaleena had been a waste of time she just didn't have. Plus, she felt a strange resentment and anger radiating in the small cabin.

"I have something. It was with the runes. I'd forgotten about it."

"Helgaleena, I must go." Lavanya yanked her arm free and fought the urge to run.

"You must take it. It was mothers."

Lavanya stopped. Velka was the only mother who'd truly known her for what she was, and she'd always treated her as a daughter.

"Here." Helgaleena held out a necklace and Lavanya leaned over so she could place it over her head. When she stood, an oval pendant fell between her breasts. The metal was as heavy as iron. Helgaleena's family crest was on one side, and on the other, a symbol that resembled tiny pitchforks with connected lines through their handles, making a giant snowflake.

Lavanya rubbed the symbol between her fingers. "What's this for?"

"It's a bind rune. The snowflake symbol is the rune for Helm of Awe. It's for protection, among other things."

Lavanya slipped the pendant under her sweater.

"Thank you, Helgaleena. Your mother meant the world to me. Now, I must leave." She was already backing away as she spoke, her body and her instincts pushing her away from the small cabin that was once her home. She'd come here for answers, and she was leaving with a piece of paper and an ugly new necklace. It hadn't been the visit she'd hoped for.

LYNNE STEVIE

CHAPTER TWENTY

Double, Double, Toil and Trouble

"Guard," Renfield cried out, but he couldn't make himself heard. The screams of the other patients pierced his heart and his sanity. Their shrieking voices surrounded him. His master would come for him, he always came, but why couldn't he hear him?

"Master, please answer me. Master, I need you."

Renfield awoke to silence and pain. He'd been dreaming of the old asylum and the patients. His hands went to his head and then his chest. He was alone.

"Master..." The pain of the severed connection to Vlad was still fresh in his body and mind. Renfield rocked himself on the bed until the pain dulled some. When he'd first started hearing the Master speak to him in his mind, he'd been terrified and misunderstood it. He'd assumed he was insane. But now the hollowness ate at him. Without Vlad's power supporting his body, he wouldn't live long.

Lavanya! He'd cut his tie to her as soon as he felt the attack on his connection to Vlad, but she had to have felt it. He hoped she was all right. He sat up on the second try, but he had to wait until the ringing in his ears stopped before he could open his eyes and look around. The pain in his chest was still strong, but not debilitating like it had been. He hadn't been alone in his own mind for centuries. It would take some getting used to.

He looked around at his prison. At least this time it was fresh and clean.

On legs weaker than a baby's, he staggered over to the window, which took more time than he'd thought possible. Through the decayed slates of the shutters, he could see the sky and mountains. The landscape was familiar—he was still in the castle—but...

Renfield looked around the room. It was round and made of stone, and it looked out *over the Arges River*. He was in the "first wives tower." How could that be? Vlad had made sure no one would ever see this tower room again; he'd walled it up after she jumped to her death.

This was the one place that Vlad would never think to look for him.

He reached out to open the window and then realized it wouldn't help. He was so far up no one would hear him, and jumping meant certain death. If he got the window open, all he could do was let in more cold air. His hand fell from the latch.

He hobbled to the door and tried the handle. Of course, it was locked.

This room was a prison, but it wasn't the cell he'd once known. All his mind could see was the small room at the asylum all those years ago where he'd wished for death. To his eyes the floor wasn't stone—it was dirt, and the shutters covering the windows were rusted iron bars.

He paced the room to clear the last of the fatigue from his mind. The last thing he remembered was Chloe bringing him his evening reports. With the Master's help, he'd felt good, even though he'd donated a lot of blood to Lavanya the day before. But when Chloe set the tray down, he noticed that it also held orange juice and a dinner plate. Assuming that Lavanya was still worried, he finished off the lot of it and helped Chloe take away the empty tray. He remembered the door closing as she left, but he never made it back to his chair to read the reports. Poison, of course, but who and why? He supposed that anyone would have access to the kitchen, now that the chef was gone.

After a short time the door lock clicked open and Giselle entered the room with a tray.

"Giselle?" He started toward her, but her smile stopped him in mid-stride. Her lips curved upward, but her red eyes were filled with horror. Lavanya had had a book when she was a small child where you could move the flaps to interchange the eyes and features of a face. That's how Giselle looked—she had the eyes of a terrified person and the smile of a psychopath.

"Hello." Giselle's voice was loud and clear, yet flat. She brought in a tray of food and a pitcher of water and sat them on the bedside table.

"Giselle, are you all right, dear?" Renfield took two steps toward the door.

Giselle stepped in front of him, blocking his exit. Her movements were jerky, as if she were fighting for control of her own legs and arms.

"We brought food. You cannot leave, until you tell us where your master sleeps."

"Giselle, who took us?" Renfield yelled as Giselle began to close the door. Tears of blood shimmered in her eyes.

"Double, double, toil and trouble." Then something jerked her back, and the door slammed shut.

Renfield heard Giselle's agonizing scream and knew her pain was real, unlike that of the imagined patients and their phantom screams he'd heard earlier. He rattled the locked door and then pounded on it.

"Don't hurt her, you bastard!" he shouted.

When her cries finally ceased, he slid down the door to sit on the cold, stone floor. *Double, double, toil and trouble.* What could she be trying to tell him? The quote was from Shakespeare's *Macbeth*. Renfield had been distracting Giselle from her hunger when he'd given her his old copy to read. Why would she risk so much to quote Shakespeare?

"Master, I wish I could hear you," Renfield said to the walls. He looked at the tray of food. He couldn't see under the silver dome, but the room was filled with the scent of chicken and Renfield's stomach growled. He wouldn't give in to the hunger, though; he couldn't afford to be drugged again. And he wasn't a novice at either physical or psychological torture. Vlad would come. He just needed to be patient.

CHAPTER TWENTY ONE

"Each Of Us Makes His Own Weather..." by Fulton J. Sheen

Zev waited in front of Helgaleena's door listening to the women, but after hearing of Helgaleena's dream about a wolf, he stopped listening. The bullshit fortunetelling made him sneeze. He shook his big head to clear it and afterwards noticed a scent he had to follow.

He searched the old porch and then wandered down the steps and around the house. What he found surprised him. The earth smelled of witchcraft and death.

No one had told him that Helgaleena was a powerful, yet primitive, dark witch. Zev wondered if Helgaleena even knew her own strength—or if the strength came from the land itself or the home that nestled on it. So much of the magical power in this region was tied to the land and the families that settled here thousands of years ago.

Zev finished his search just as Lavanya headed down the path from the house. Helgaleena put something on Lavanya, and she tucked it into her shirt. But the look of fear and anger on Lavanya's face made him forget everything else. He ran to her side, but she seemed lost in her thoughts and acted like she didn't see him. She didn't say a word to Zev, even when he bumped his large head against her or pushed Helgaleena's grandson away when he brought Samson around for her. She seemed too preoccupied—too anxious—even to notice the weather as the sky darkened with heavy, black clouds. She just climbed on Samson's back and spurred him into a gallop toward the castle and its safety.

Zev ran through the darkening forest following Samson's big swishing tail, rethinking what he'd overheard. The old woman said that in her vision, she'd seen a wolf, and Anya would have power or control over it. But he hadn't heard her say what power. Vlad had power over some animals; maybe the witch saw that power awakening in Lavanya. It had to be that.

The thought settled him, because he knew he wasn't like any

other shifter. He didn't become the animal; the animal became him, giving him all their talents and traits. He didn't lose himself, so Lavanya wouldn't be able to control him with her new abilities. Besides, who could say if he was the wolf in the old woman's dream? *Crazy old witch.*

The quiet forest and the coming storm set Zev's every nerve on alert. The only sounds were the crunch of leaves and gravel under his paws and Samson's snorts. Every now and again Lavanya cleared her throat as if she were trying to clear away some bad thoughts. When a gust of wind whipped through his fur, causing the hair along his spine to stand up, he looked skyward and noticed that the puffy, white clouds of earlier had thickened into a dark, black layer that blocked out the sun.

Zev had seen the clouds move outside of Helgaleena's, but he hoped Lavanya hadn't instigated the change. After she cleared her throat harshly several times, he trotted closer to get a better look at her. Her face was pale and confirmed his assumption: The weather was mirroring Lavanya's mood. The clouds were heavy with her tears and fear. She wiped a tear from her face as the first fat drops of rain hit his nose. Thunder broke the silence of the forest, and Samson reared, his hooves narrowly missed striking Zev.

If the clouds were any indication, Lavanya would have to release her boiling emotions soon, so he needed to get them out of the weather as quickly as possible. Samson wasn't handling Lavanya's outbursts well. Any more thunder and he'd buck her off, and then they'd be stuck walking back to the castle through her emotional storm—*literally.* Having run these hills for centuries, he knew of a cave around the next hill. If memory served, it was big enough to tie off Samson on one side so he'd feel safe from the weather.

Zev barked to get her attention, but she was lost in her sadness and didn't hear him. He had to howl to get her to hear him.

"*What?*" She tried to shield her eyes from the wind and rain that now came down in sheets.

Zev barked again and darted off the forest trail. He heard her curse and pull on Samson to make him follow. He'd forgotten how tightly the forest could close around you when you left the trails. Samson was a big horse; Zev hoped the path he took would be big enough for him.

"Zev, wait up!" Lavanya dismounted and led Samson through the think underbrush.

Zev almost wished he couldn't understand what she was saying. He was pissed listening to her curse him for dragging her through the heavy overgrowth. When another crack of thunder and lightning shook the sky, Samson reared again, almost tearing the reins out of Lavanya's hands.

"Don't worry about the thunder, Samson," Lavanya said, trying to soothe the big horse, but he was scared and plunged against the reins, and she couldn't manage him. So much for the thought that she had control over animals.

"Zev," Lavanya said, struggling with her horse, "where are you taking us?"

It was time to change back so he could talk, or she'd leave his ass and go back to the trail. He pulled in the magic he needed from the forest around him, and with the spirits' help, he altered his shape.

Lavanya watched as Zev raised his head to the sky and howled.

"You stupid animal, I…" she yelled at the wolfhound and then there was nothing but a shimmery bubble. She could see through the thin barrier, but it distorted the dense forest. She reached out to touch it, to find out if she could put her hand through the bubble and see it on the other side. But when she got close, the bubble burst, liquid sparks popped, and Zev stood in front of her, wearing his trademark leather pants and nothing else. His eyes were closed. Her hand almost touched his chest. She pulled her hand back before he opened his eyes.

Lavanya's anger flared.

"Great!" she yelled to be heard over the wind or because she was pissed—or both. "Now you can tell me why the hell we got off the trail in the middle of a storm!"

"Samson's a pain in the ass, and he won't calm down until the storms over. There's a cave up ahead we can use for shelter to wait it out."

"Fine, but the way in better not be any tighter than this, or Samson won't make it."

"He'll make it. It's not far." Zev set off on the narrow path

167

through the heavy forest.

Lavanya held tight to Samson's reins and pulled him along. The horse fought her at every step. The path really wasn't wide enough for him, and now, as she cried, the rain came down in driving bursts. She could barely see Zev through the rain and tears, so she reached out and grabbed the loop in the back of his leather pants.

"What!" Zev jumped at her touch.

"I can hardly see you with this rain, you idiot! Plus, you're leading us into heavy brush. Just turn around and get us out of this." Lavanya's voice was strong, but it cracked just a little. She'd never felt so alone, and she hoped that her voice hadn't given away too much of her emotions. Lavanya had left Helgaleena's even more worried for Renfield and her father than when she'd arrived. They could be dead and she wouldn't know.

No! She could not allow herself to think that way. If she were honest with herself, she'd admit that she needed to touch Zev—and not just because it was hard to see through the storm. *But denial is a wonderful thing.*

"Hang on; we're almost there." Zev took a deep breath, like an animal scenting the area, and pushed on through the forest.

She was just about to curse Zev again for getting them lost when the forest opened up, and he lead them into a perfect cave. The opening was big enough for Samson, yet it faced east, so the rain didn't come inside, and the floor was dry.

Lavanya shook off the water and surveyed the interior of the natural cave. It was big and open, and the dry earth crunched under her feet. Even with her excellent immortal vision, she couldn't see where the cave ended.

"Here you go, you're safe now," Zev said, reaching for Samson's reins. The horse reared up and Zev took a step back.

"All right, Samson, whatever you want. Lavanya, there's room over there to tie him, and he'll feel safe and secure away from the storm and *me*." Zev showed her a small alcove that was almost like a stall.

"You can tie him off here to these roots, and he should be fine." Zev stepped out of the way so Lavanya could tie up the large horse. "Get him settled and I'll look for some firewood."

Lavanya tugged the thick vine roots, and when they didn't

give, she figured Samson was as secure as he could be under the circumstances. With her hands finally free, she wrung out her hair. The dripping water made her think of something else she needed to take care of.

"Hey, Zev, I'll be right back." She headed farther into the darkness in search of a little privacy.

"Where do you think you're going?" Zev was in front of her before she had time to blink, and he reached out and grabbed Lavanya's arm. She jumped back a step. Her sight had adjusted to the darkness, and she could see water droplets clinging to the dusting of hair on his bare chest. Lavanya watched as a drop ran down his abs to disappear behind the loose waist of his leathers. Before she could stop herself, she licked her lips, wishing she could lick the water off his skin.

"To the bathroom, if it's okay with you," she said with her hand on her hip. "Now get out of my way."

"But…you're a vampire. You don't need to *pee*."

"Yeah, well, I wouldn't if I didn't like to eat and drink. But I really like the stuff." She looked down to his hand on her arm. "If you hadn't noticed, a few things are different about me. Remember, we had brunch together today in the *sun*. Now let go."

"What are you?" Zev pulled her closer and smelled the fresh rain and wild emotions that swirled around her. Lavanya pulled away and stomped into the shadows.

"I could ask you the same thing, dog! Do you mind, or do I have to pee in front of you?

"I'll get the fire going." Zev returned to the mouth of the cave.

Lavanya rubbed her arm where his hand had been. It was warm. His hand was rough and strong, and yet he hadn't hurt her. Shaking her head, she edged deeper into the cave to make sure she was out of his sight.

Zev found plenty of branches and dead leaves that would be good to build the fire, but he felt that he could start the fire with his thoughts alone. He'd never experienced such an overwhelming desire to touch another person—especially a vampire. Usually vampires were enemies, and their very nature repulsed him.

But with Lavanya, his feeling was the exact opposite. Just touching her arm had him craving more. If they had to stay in this cave for any length of time, he'd go insane. Not to mention, his pants were painfully tight. Her skin was cooler than his, yet it wasn't cold like a normal leech, and that one touch had sent a shot straight to his cock. Without realizing it, he started walking toward the back of the cave and her.

What was he was doing? *The fire.* He needed to start the fire. He tried to concentrate on that task, but when that didn't stop the throbbing in his dick, he gave in and stooped to adjust the hard-on he'd developed when he'd touched her.

Lavanya returned to find Zev rousing the fire. When he heard her approach, he stood and faced her. He was still wet and his hard body glistened in the fire's light. The dark brown leather clung to him like a thin skin, outlining his muscular legs. As her eyes devoured him, she couldn't help but notice the bulge in the front of his leathers. Suddenly, thirsty her fangs descended. She was hungry. She pulsed with thoughts of his arousal and she felt her body weeping for him. She licked her lips and wiped her palms on her wet pants. Her breath came faster and her heart hammered in her chest. She'd never felt such a physical need for another person before.

Lavanya looked up from his pants as Zev raised his head and sniffed the air. His nostrils flared, and a low growl rumbled in his throat as his eyes darkened and locked onto hers. This was one man she didn't have to be careful or gentle with. She launched herself at him.

He caught her as she wrapped her legs around his hips. The force would have knocked them flat, but he was fast and gloriously strong. As he caught her, he turned and pushed her to the rock wall, almost as if the motion were choreographed. She greedily savored the thrust of his arousal trapped behind the rough leather laces as it brushed up against her core. She was lost to a primitive need for him. She was all instinct with no thoughts or doubts.

"Ah…" Lavanya licked the water from his neck, shaking with anticipation when her fangs brushed his skin. She wound her hands through his hair and pulled his head to the side, all the while rubbing her heated center against his hard length. He felt thick and long through the tough material that separated their bodies.

"No." Zev caught her hands and held his head back while he

still had her lower body pinned to the rock wall. Lavanya hissed at him and tried to pull her arms free, but he held her firmly. "Not yet, princess. I want to taste you first."

"Now. I want you now." Lavanya looked down at where their bodies touched and felt Zev shudder. He released her hands, and she went to work on his string-tied leathers.

Lavanya lowered her legs to stand and pushed him back so she could unlace his leathers to release him. Zev's hands went for her sweater, and everything came off together in one swift movement, leaving her naked from the waist up. At the same time, she pulled his pants open. She sighed as she gripped his long, thick shaft. He was all natural, which meant there was extra velvety skin at the tip and more for her hands to explore.

Zev cupped her breast as Lavanya gripped him. He was desperate to get her undressed, and his fingers couldn't work the buttons and zippers of her pants fast enough. He used his magic to remove the rest of their clothes and throw them in a pile by the fire to dry. He knew he shouldn't waste magic on such a frivolous act, but at the moment he just didn't care. He had to have her naked.

He was rewarded for his efforts by a delicious sigh as Lavanya realized she was naked and stroked his cock. Zev bent his head to taste the sweet, red nipple that had been torturing him ever since he saw it peek out of that dress she had on yesterday. It was puckered, beautifully rosy, and felt like silken ripples in his mouth. The scent of her skin set him on fire. It was sweet like honey. No woman had every smelt or tasted as good to him.

Lavanya tilted her head back and a sound came out of her mouth that told Zev he was doing something right. Even as she enjoyed his touch, she continued to stroke his hard shaft and he grew harder and thicker under her hand.

As he suckled her, he let his hand trail past her belly button and down her hip to the luscious honey at her core that he wanted to consume. As his fingers brushed her soft, thick folds, he felt her shudder. He couldn't wait. He plunged one finger into the center of her, and she bucked against his hand.

"I want you now!" Lavanya was frantic to have him inside her. Every nerve ending sent shock waves to her core, and she needed release like never before. "Please."

Lavanya panted, surprised that she was willing to beg. Still holding him, she tried to maneuver his thick staff where she needed it most, but he refused to allow it. Instead, he drew his finger out and then use his hand to dance over the delicate inner folds of her opening. She was so wet he slipped up to the beginning of her and back to her ready opening again and again, causing ripples of pleasure to crash over her and through her. The pressure built until she couldn't hold in the climax any longer. It burst through her like the lightening that lit the sky. Lavanya's legs buckled forcing her to release her hold on his shaft and grab his shoulders. Zev held her in place working her with his hand and supporting her while her body shook with pleasure. She pushed herself against his hand and threw her head back in total ecstasy. She felt like a wild thing, the pleasure stripping her of all her careful restraint.

Zev was amazed that he'd managed to hold himself back long enough to give her climax. His desire was a monstrous need, like he'd never felt before. With her body still wet and open to him, he supported her hips and pulled her down on top of his hard cock, burying himself in her while she still felt the aftershocks of her first climax. She growled huskily as he filled her and he met the sound with his own deep purr. As the ripples of her body squeezed him he forced himself to hold still, wanting to savor the feel of her body wrapped around him tight and warm. Her legs squeezed his waist and her panting breath filled his ears.

As she adjusted to his body invading hers, she whispered his name. Zev pulled back shocked at the feeling of possessiveness that invaded his being at hearing his name slip from her lips. Zev watched her as she rode him. Her eyes were partly closed and her luscious lower lip was between her teeth. She was beautiful, as she took her pleasure from his body.

Her eyes flew open then catching him watching her. The depths of emotion he saw in them undid him. He buried his face in her neck so she wouldn't see his own need. Now he knew what the old witch was talking about. Lavanya had him under her control. He'd do anything to be inside her. Before he could think that thought through, Lavanya pulled him deeper into her body. Slowly she guided her core over his hard shaft. The feeling of her body's tight grip stripped away any rational thought.

Lavanya relished the feel of Zev's hard body joined intimately with her own. She threw her head back and growled at the sensations assaulting her. He filled her completely, but she needed more. More of his panting breath on her neck, more of his deep kisses, more of his strong arms wrapped around her. More. She was crazed with need. She moved her body over his and dug her nails into his back. He was torturing her with is stillness. Yearning to feel him move deep insider her she pushed away from the wall and forced them both down to the ground. Straddling him and finally in control Lavanya grabbed Zev's hands from her hips and pushed them up above his head. By the light of the fire she could see his eyes. They were darker than she remembered, almost black and his hunger was evident in his piercing gaze. But there was something else, some emotion, a longing.

As she moved on top of him, she tried to get a vision of his desires. Normally she knew immediately what another person's greatest desire was or what they wanted in life. However, she got nothing from Zev. She could feel and see his desire for her at the moment, but he was a blank slate as far as her talent was concerned. Lavanya freed his hands so she could run her fingers over his rough bearded chin. Cupping his face she leaned down to take his mouth with hers as she slowly moved herself above their joined bodies.

Zev gave her no reprieve. His hands free again, he grabbed her hips, and pulled her down hard onto his thick cock, sending all thoughts out of her mind. She screamed her pleasure to the cave ceiling. Then he sat up with her and suckled one of her nipples again, as if he couldn't get enough of the taste of her skin. With a speed that took her breath, he flipped them over and pinned her under him, entering her more deeply controlling her more thoroughly.

Lavanya wrapped herself around Zev as he released his control and pounded her core. Flickers of pleasure and pain danced in her mind, like fireworks. Lavanya dug her nails into his shoulders and nipped his neck as a shudder rocked his body.

"Zev...I want to taste you..." Lavanya raked her fangs over

his nerves and muscles of his neck as the heat built in her core.

"Do it!" Zev yelled as he drove himself deeper into her body one last time.

His climax tipped her over the edge, too, and the sensation was tripled when she reared back and bit his neck. His sweet, hot blood filled her throat as she rode the waves of the orgasm. The taste was better than anything she could imagine.

Lavanya opened herself to him and tried to hide in his climax the pain that he must be feeling from the bite, but she couldn't sense any pain in him. As the waves slowed and thought returned, she tried to feel his mind. She couldn't. Still impaled, she licked his skin to heal it, but it was already healing. She pulled back and looked at him. He was smiling. Then he swiftly rolled them over and pulled her hips tighter onto his body. She could feel him growing harder insider her. She was sure that he'd climaxed, too.

"I thought…" she said, looking down.

"Not to worry, sweetheart, I enjoyed it." Zev winked at her. "I just stay hard longer than regular men. Wanna go again?" He wiggled his eye brows at her.

Lavanya felt naked in a way she never had before. She pulled away. This…connection—whatever it was—scared her. Her insight into other people had never failed her. Until now.

"What are you? I can't feel your desires and thoughts like I normally can." She stood and grabbed her clothes, which had dried while she'd been mindless with pleasure. Confused, she turned away from Zev and pulled on her sweater. What had she gotten herself into?

"Funny, I just asked you the same question." Zev stood and grabbed his leather pants. He pulled them on, focusing on the fire rather than her. Trying to give her some privacy and dampen his desire. So far, that wasn't working. He could smell her delicious scent on his skin and his body wanted more. No amount of looking away was going to change that.

"I'm the daughter of Vlad the Impaler—Dracula—and Eva Maria, the actress," Lavanya said as she slipped on her lace underwear. "I'm the only known vampire who was born into this life. That's what makes me different. My father trusts you enough to send you to protect me, so there's no reason why you shouldn't know. And you are?" Thunder filled the quiet moment as she challenged him, willing him to tell her what made him different.

Zev couldn't take his eyes off her black lace underwear, although it didn't seem to cover enough to be called underwear. It was more like a black lace ribbon. All he could think about was tearing it off her with his teeth. His shaft throbbed, reminding him that he was ready to have her again.

Lavanya snapped her fingers to draw his eyes up to her face, even though she enjoyed his looking at her with obvious hunger.

"I'm up here," she said.

"Wait—you're really his *daughter?*" He pulled the leather lacing of his pants closed and crossed his arms over his chest. "I didn't know that was possible."

"As far as I know, it's never happened before, but my father's unique. I think I was a surprise to him, too." As Lavanya picked up her pants, Helgaleena's old medallion necklace fell from the folds and landed on the cave floor. "That was a good trick with the clothes, by the way. You're handy." Lavanya forced her feet through the tight legs of her riding pants.

"Thanks, but you haven't seen anything yet," Zev purred as he glided over to her. He moved like a large snake, all muscle and pent-up energy.

Lavanya backed away from him, hopping as she pushed her legs in her pants. She needed a clear head, and she wouldn't be able to think if he touched her.

"You never answered my question," she said. "What are you?"

"It's a long story." Zev kept moving toward her, his eyes dark again.

Lavanya held her hand up to stop his advance. "Yeah, well, I told you my story. Now you tell me yours."

Zev stopped just before his chest touched her outstretched hand.

"Or you'll...what?" His smile looked even more devious in the fires glow.

"Just because we had sex, don't think you can manhandle me whenever you want." Lavanya was frightened at her need for him. And she knew better than to touch him. "We need to get back to the castle. Maybe someone has heard from Renfield."

Zev looked to the opening of the cave.

"Yeah, you're right. Just don't get mad or sad again, and we should have clear skies back to the castle." Zev stepped back and then jumped as if something stung his foot. "What is that?" he asked as he rubbed his foot on the ground.

Lavanya looked at it. "Oh, my necklace. Thanks, I would have forgotten it." Lavanya bent to retrieve the medallion.

"Seriously?" Zev said with a chuckle. "It has a leather strap and it's made of wood, I can smell it from here. Nothing personal, princ...Lavanya, but you don't look like the hippy leather jewelry kind of gal."

Irritated at his assessment of her, Lavanya rolled the oval medallion in her fingers to feel the cold rough surface. "I know it's not my normal style, but Helgaleena gave it to me today. It's not wood. It's metal or...iron, anyway."

"Oh, it's wood, trust me." He pointed to his nose.

Lavanya rolled her eyes.

"Helgaleena said it would protect me and bind me somehow to her family. Velka, her mother wanted me to have it. She raised me and... It's not important. It's just a necklace." Lavanya shoved it in her pocket. Irritated at his assessment of her, plus she remembered he hadn't answered her first question.

"Don't change the subject. Tell me how you wield this magic." She pointed to her clothes. "And the shape-changing thing."

"What does it matter, what I am? I'm here to protect you, and that's it." Zev walked to the cave opening.

"It matters to me." Lavanya grabbed her boots and followed him. "I want to understand what makes you different. I've never met anyone like you before. You defy my abilities. I want to understand."

Zev stopped at the opening and looked out at the still, dark sky. Lavanya grabbed his arm.

"Hey, what did you mean by 'just don't get mad or sad, and we should be able to get to the castle'?" she asked. As she looked at him, his eyes started to darken and she took a step back and released his arm.

Zev looked back at the sky.

"Come on," he said, as a small smile turned devious again.

"You have to have realized that the weather mirrors your mood. You need to learn some control soon, or you'll really mess with the meteorologists in the States."

Lavanya thought about the clouds moving before visiting Helgaleena, how she'd been in a foul mood before the rain started, and how it started only after she swiped away a stray tear that had escaped her control.

"Why? And why now?" She looked at the sky, thinking that she'd try out her new talent.

"Ow!" She jumped. The necklace in her pocket sent a chill up her side, taking away any thought of the weather. She took the necklace out of her pocket and inspected the markings.

"What happened?"

"I don't know! It just seemed to get cold and sent a chill through me or something."

"Let me see that thing." Zev picked up the necklace by the leather strap instead of touching the oval disc. He instinctively didn't want to touch the medallion. Its magic wasn't conducive to his—he'd found that out early when he'd stepped on it. He looked at it carefully.

"What did Helgaleena say it was for?"

"She said it was her family crest on one side and then on the other was a Helm of something for protection. It was supposed to bind me to her family and protect me."

"I'm not familiar with Odin or the northern magicks, but the symbol looks familiar." Zev strained to see the odd carving, but before he could get a good look, Samson reared and stomped his large hooves. Zev looked around to see what had gotten into the horse. Samson was straining at his reins, trying to pull free from his tether. Lavanya took the necklace from Zev and tucked it into her pocket before going to the horse.

"Samson! What's gotten into you? Enough!" The horse snorted and put his head down to be patted, but he pranced and stomped the dirt floor of the cave, edgy and anxious with fear.

"What could—" Lavanya started, but stopped when she saw Zev crouched low, ready to attack whatever came through the cave opening. His normal tan skin tone was transforming into black granite, with white veining like soap stone running throughout.

"Zev?"

Zev felt the presence of magic, black and evil, eat at him, and he reacted without thinking by hardening his skin, ready for whatever was thrown his way. Samson had felt it first, but he wasn't far behind the large animal. They both knew it was bad.

Giselle stepped into the cave. She walked with an obvious limp, and her head was tilted unnaturally to the side as she approached Lavanya. Zev thought that after being revamped, she should move with strength and grace, not like a rag doll on puppet strings.

"Mistress, help me," Giselle slurred. "I didn't want…" She fell to her knees and screamed loud enough to echo in the cave. The bats awoke, flapping their large wings and hissing in aggravation at the disturbance.

"Giselle," Lavanya said, stepping forward, but Samson wouldn't budge. *Smart horse.* That gave him enough time to put himself between her and the girl.

"Mistress, please." Giselle had eyes only for Lavanya and crawled toward her. *What did the vamp want?*

"What's happened to you?" Lavanya dropped Samson's reins and looked beyond her to the front of the cave and then back. "Is Renfield with you?"

"No. He…is…away." Giselle's voice was soft, and it seemed as if each word was an effort to get out. He glanced at the cave opening for a second—all the time in the world for Giselle to lunge at Lavanya and stab her in the shoulder. Lightening crashed. He moved with his inhuman speed and yanked Lavanya away before Giselle could stab at her again.

Giselle was all arms and legs, flailing and wind-milling as she tried to get to Lavanya. Zev thought it looked as if she were fighting herself and the strings that controlled her movements.

"Giselle! Control yourself, or I'll be forced to kill you!" Zev shouted as he hauled Lavanya back to where she'd left Samson.

"No!" Lavanya yelled.

Zev ignored her. Her opinion didn't matter. He had a job to do.

He looked down at Lavanya and saw her dark mahogany blood staining her sweater. Rage took what little control he had.

He flew back to Giselle and backhanded her. The black blade she'd used to cut Lavanya flew from her hands and landed beside the fire. She was convulsing and screamed for help. Zev wasn't a vampire, but he knew enough to understand that part of the process of revamping included the bonding between sire and offspring that should have made it impossible for her to hurt Lavanya. Even if Giselle were possessed by something evil, as she most certainly was, her bonding should have trumped it.

"It's my fault!" Lavanya cried and moved toward the girl. "Don't hurt her!" Lavanya looked at Giselle's shaking, huddled form.

Zev pulled Lavanya back.

"Get out of the way, Lavanya," he said. "Somehow she's been possessed, even with your blood binding her. Whoever you and your father pissed off is powerful. She's a threat, but I'll make sure she won't hurt you again."

"No, Zev. It's my fault. I didn't bind her to me. I didn't want to take away her free will." Giselle looked like she was in a lot of pain—she must be fighting the possession.

"What! Are you kidding me? You must be the only vampire in the world with a conscience." Zev paced across the cave. The activity must have relaxed him some, because his skin lightened, yet it still looked as hard as stone.

"I know, I know. I'd never revamped anyone before, and I've never forced anyone to feed me or bound them to me sexually. Excuse me for having human compassion!" Lavanya pulled the woman into her arms and held her while she shook. "Yelling at me isn't helping Giselle. How can we help her?"

Zev noticed that Lavanya had stopped bleeding and acted like she wasn't hurt. That helped his control. She was as strong as a vampire, even though she felt soft in his arms. He needed to remember that.

"I don't know how to help her. She has your blood in her. Can you bind her now?"

"I don't know, but I think it's her only chance." Lavanya cradled the girl and rocked her as if she were a child.

"If we could kill the person who was controlling her, maybe

179

she'd be released. But unless you have some new insight into whose doing all this, binding her is all we've got." Zev still paced, his body desperate to change into the beast and kill the threat that Lavanya seemed determined to protect.

"Try it," he said. "We don't have a choice, and we need to get out of here and back to the castle as soon as possible." Zev felt danger in the air, and his beast felt exposed now that their enemies had found their hideaway. The skies were still dark with unshed tears, but they had to leave soon, whether Lavanya got her emotions under control or not.

"Giselle, I'll try to pull you out of this." Lavanya pulled the struggling girl into her lap and positioned her so she could exchange blood with her again. It was the only way to bind her. Zev watched the cave opening for any sign of the threat his beast could sense.

"Giselle, can you hear me? Do you understand? I'm going to bind you to me."

"Mistress, help me," Giselle whispered.

"Lavanya, just do it!" Zev yelled. He wished she'd stop pussyfooting around. She should have bound Giselle when she was vamped in the first place.

"I'm so sorry, Giselle," Lavanya whispered and then bent to take her neck.

"I am, too," Giselle said as she jammed her fingers into Lavanya's not-yet-closed knife wound. As Lavanya screamed in pain, the girl went for Lavanya's exposed neck.

Zev jumped to help her. He tried to pull Giselle off, but he was too late. The girl had already sunk her sharp teeth into Lavanya's neck.

"Don't pull her. She'll rip out my throat." Lavanya could heal almost any wound, but this would be a bad one if he couldn't get Giselle to release her. Lavanya was trying to choke the girl enough to make her let go, but Giselle didn't let up. It was as if she didn't care if the blood went down her throat as long as she killed Lavanya.

"I can't get her to release," Lavanya slurred, losing blood way too fast. "Try to open her jaw."

Zev tried to force the girl's mouth open, but the vampire was strong with Lavanya's blood, and whoever had possessed her had to be strengthening her, too.

"Lavanya, I can't get her to release without hurting you, too." As he struggled with Giselle, he watched Lavanya's blood spurt between the girl's teeth, down the front of Lavanya's body, and pool on the ground.

"Zev...I need." Lavanya struggled to keep her hands on the girl's neck although Zev could tell she didn't want to kill her, probably out of some crazy sense of guilt.

Zev had had enough. His rage consumed him and he couldn't watch Lavanya suffer any longer.

"Hold on!" He released Giselle's jaw and winced as he saw her teeth sink more deeply into the soft skin that he'd just been kissing. Circling behind the girl, Zev called forth the strength of the beast he carried and the earth magic he held from his mother. He howled as he felt the change come on and saw claws extend from his fingers. He looked down at Lavanya's scared face as he drove his claws into the back of the girl and pulled out her heart. The girl expelled one last breath and fell lifeless in Lavanya's arms.

Vampires were immortal and could live forever without aging a day. However, nothing could live without its heart or head. Zev had learned that a long time ago.

Lavanya reached for the torn skin of her neck as the girl lay dead in her arms. The tearing was extensive, but she'd survive.

"Zev?" Lavanya looked up into the black eyes of a beast. He panted staring at the heart as if he wanted to eat it. When she called to him, she saw a little of Zev slip back into place. His eyes turned from black to golden, and he looked in confusion at the heart he held. When he looked back to Lavanya, he smiled at her—not a happy smile, but a smile of satisfaction.

He was part beast and part man. His powerful claws and black skin sent a shiver through her. She should have been terrified. But she knew that he wouldn't hurt her. That smile said that both man and beast were happy that she was alive, that they had saved her. His smile was possessive and protective.

"Lavanya," Zev said through sharp teeth as he walked toward her. Then he seemed to remember the heart in his hand. He threw it into the fire. The quiet flames flared up to consume the blood and flesh. He pulled the girl off Lavanya and threw her on top of the fire, too. The fire exploded, thankful for the new fuel. Zev watched the flames dance, consuming the body of the vampire who'd hurt Lavanya. The beast in him roared in triumph. The sound echoed through the cave and agitated Samson, who pulled against his reins.

"Samson, stop!" Zev ordered, and the horse understood and obeyed the beast's command. With Samson settled and the dead vampire taken care of, he turned to Lavanya.

He didn't care that the beast was still in control. Both of them needed to feel her safe in his arms.

"Zev." Lavanya's voice was weak from the mauling she'd endured from Giselle, and it was obvious that she was struggling to speak. She pointed at him, holding her neck and shuffling back to the cave wall.

"Zev!" She looked weak, but determined to keep him away. Zev stopped and panted, waiting for her calm down.

She's scared of me. How stupid could he be? Of course she was frightened. He was hideous when the beast took control, and the beast was almost fully in control of him. He looked down at his black, marbled skin and the bloody claws of his right hand. He stepped back to give her space and tried to control his demon. He'd never let anyone see him this way, but he'd been in a rage when Lavanya had been hurt.

Lavanya was frantic to get Zev to turn around and see the zombie that stalked him, but he was too focused on her to notice. It was the same zombie that they'd fought the night before in the castle. Her torn throat made speaking impossible, but she struggled to the cave wall. She needed the wall to help her stand and be ready to fight.

"Zev! Look *out!*" She got the words out just in time. Zev leaped sideways, and the zombie's deadly blow went left of center and scraped down his arm. Sparks flew as the zombie's blade struck Zev's odd, black flesh. Blood oozed from the opening as Zev bellowed in fury.

The cave's stone walls shook, and Lavanya covered her head as silt fell from the ceiling. As the dust settled, she watched Zev's black skin close around the wound and heal. Zev lunged for the smaller male, but the zombie was surprisingly fast on his feet and got away. Lavanya was reminded of her own fight with the creature, and yet she was still surprised at its speed and agility.

The zombie tried to circle around and get to Lavanya. She felt her neck. The skin was tight, and the scab was huge, but she was healing. Zev's blood had to be helping.

She crouched, ready to defend herself, but Zev got to the nasty creature first and threw him across the cave. As the zombie tried to recover, Zev grabbed Samson's reins and pulled the large horse over to Lavanya.

"Go back to the castle!" Zev thrust the reins into her hand.

"I won't leave you here!" She couldn't let him fight the zombie alone. This was a powerful enemy, it would take both of them to finish it.

"The hell you won't." Zev grabbed Lavanya and threw her across the saddle. He slapped Samson on the rump to get him moving.

She barely had time to find her seat as the animal tore out of the cave in a panic.

"You fool!" Lavanya looked back to see the zombie rush Zev and tackle him to the ground. The creature had the brute strength of a vampire. How could anyone get this close to her without her knowing they had such powerful black magic? But Zev also had an incredible amount of magic, and she'd had no idea. She still didn't know what he was or could do.

Lavanya pulled back on the reins with all her strength.

"Samson! Whoa, whoa, boy," she said, and Samson stopped. She was in no condition to fight. She knew she should make her way back to the castle and safety. But nothing about Zev or her feelings for him were logical, they just were.

She turned Samson around and headed back to the cave. *Like hell* she'd leave Zev to fight her fight. *Over her dead freaking body.*

A crack of thunder lit up the sky. *Crap.* She needed to get control of her emotions, or she'd drive the poor farmers crazy with this weather thing. Samson pranced, shaking his head in agitation, but he followed her command and headed back to the cave.

Lavanya stopped Samson at the top of the rise just before the cave opening and tied him off. Hoping for a surprise attack, she crept to the opening to appraise the situation. The two men, and she used that term loosely, wrestled in the back of the cave. It looked like one of the cage matches she'd seen in Miami, except instead of humans fighting, this was a horror film come to life.

Zev was an evil God, with a man's body the color of onyx with white veining. He had the head of a wolf, but the mouth and teeth of a large cat. The zombie looked like something conjured in Frankenstein's lab. Its skin—the parts not missing chunks—was as gray as old meat that's been left out on the counter too long, and its eyes bulged from small, dried sockets. Lavanya was certain that Zev's sharp teeth and claws were responsible for those missing chunks.

Watching the two creatures fight was eerie. As she gazed on the scene, she glimpsed something black and shiny lying by the fire—the black blade that Giselle had attacked her with. Zev was fighting brilliantly, and he'd win if the contest involved only brute strength. But that wouldn't be enough if the zombie pulled out a Sleeping Beauty or some other magic. Lavanya knew from experience how powerful this creature's magic could be.

Lavanya made her move. She crept to the fire and grabbed the blade. It was old and looked like black glass, obsidian and powerful. She rolled the blade in her hands and tested the weight. It was well made, and she always had a place in her heart for a well-made blade. As a child growing up here in the mountains, she'd learned how to hunt and use knives. However, other than showing off for Zev yesterday in the kitchen, it had been years since she'd had to throw one with precision or in tight quarters.

The zombie had focused on something over Zev's shoulder, and then he darted to the left. *Lavanya.* Shit! That damn stubborn woman would be the death of him.

He'd smelled Lavanya as she entered the cave, but he'd tried to block the zombie from seeing her. Now it was too late. The little maggot was on a mission to get her.

Zev dove for him, and they barreled to the other side of the cave. He needed to keep the creature as far away from Lavanya as possible. For the second time today, he and the beast were in agreement. They wanted to rip the zombie to pieces. Neither of them cared to find out who had raised him or who controlled him.

Zev just wanted him in pieces and in the fire.

He roared as he ripped out another piece of the zombie's side. He'd caught the thing and dug in his claws right at the thick, meaty side of the torso. The zombie snarled, and Zev's stomach lurched at the smell of rotting flesh. As the zombie squirmed and thrashed on the cave floor, Zev flung the rotting meat from his claws.

"Lavanya, what the hell are you doing?" He saw her standing behind the fire watching them. She looked ready to jump into the middle of the fight. How was he supposed to protect her if she wasn't willing to protect herself?

A sharp pain in his thigh caught him off guard. The bastard zombie bit him. But the whoosh of air on his calf as the obsidian blade flew past confused him until he looked up and saw the satisfied look on Lavanya's face. He'd rolled away from the zombie before he realized it wasn't necessary— Lavanya had nailed the zombie's shoulder to the cave wall with the black blade. As he fell to one knee in pain, he saw the zombie struggle against the blade. Then Lavanya was at his side.

"Hold still and let me see how bad it is." She pressed Zev's hard-as-stone chest back to the ground.

"The zombie," Zev said, struggling to sit up. "I have to burn it."

Lavanya pushed him back and looked at the bite on Zev's thigh.

"He's not moving for a minute. Lucky you were wearing leather, plus your skin." She ran her fingers along his forearm. "It feels as smooth as slate or granite." She tore his leathers to get a better look at the wound. "It's only a small bite mark. Why are you in so much pain?"

"His teeth carry mold and decay. I am of the earth, and that fungus is trying to take over my healthy cells, just like mold on bread." Zev cracked a pain-filled smile. "It's painful for the bread."

"Rotting from the inside out—a fitting end for you, demon!" the zombie panted, sounding strained. "A painful death for trying to protect his unnatural offspring!"

With a terrible scream, the creature tore his arm off to free himself from the knife stuck in the limestone wall. He lumbered toward them with something in his hand.

"I'll be rewarded as you wither and die!" The zombie spoke in the voice of a woman. Lavanya had heard that voice before, but where?

"No!" Lavanya screamed. Zev grabbed her and rolled them away, covering her with his body.

"Close your eyes!" Zev instructed. "Close your eyes and hold on!"

Zev began chanting in a language Lavanya had never heard before. Small pieces of sand hit her skin like shards of glass in a whirlwind. So she tucked her face to his stone chest and held on tight. The wind pulled at them with such ferocity that even her hair hurt as it whirled about her head.

"Zev!"

"Don't open your eyes!"

Lavanya buried her face in his shoulder and hung on as the sand stung her skin and the ground shook beneath them. The storm seemed to last forever, but finally the wind died down and the sand settled.

"Okay, you can open your eyes. It's gone." Zev coughed and rolled them over so she was on top.

Lavanya coughed to clear her lungs and wiped her face. The cloud of dust and sand was so thick she couldn't see the fire through it. "What did you do?"

"Just a little prachova burka, as my grandmother would say."

"A what?"

"A dust storm. Like a hurricane or a tornado, I blew him away. Literally."

"But were still here." Lavanya opened her eyes to stare down at Zev. "Hey, you're back to you. Your hazel eyes are nice to see."

"Thanks." Zev smiled. We're still here, because I was the center of the storm. He was really being hammered by the wind and rocks." Zev ran his hands over her shoulders and cupped her face in his hands. "Hey, are you all right?

"Yeah, I'm fine." Lavanya pulled back from his touch and—conscious of her location on top of him—slid off and stood up.

"Good. You stupid woman."

"Shh…" Lavanya scanned the dust-filled cave.

"You can stop looking for it." Zev gasped and winced at the pain in his leg as he sat up. "It's gone."

"Oh, you're still hurt." Lavanya bent to look at his wound and then registered what he'd said. "What do you mean, *stupid?*"

"I mean, I told you to get the hell outta here and back to the castle! I had everything under control until you came sneaking back." Zev pulled his torn leathers away from the wound and swore at the greenish cast to his skin, now pale again after his transformation. Not too bad, but it was going to hurt for a while.

"Whatever you say, twit." Lavanya pushed his hands away from the wound.

"Did you just call me a twit?" Zev asked as she looked at his leg.

"Yes. It means idiot."

"I know what it means." Zev sucked in a pain-filled breath as she poked at a tender spot. "I just haven't heard that in a while."

"I'm not an expert on wounds of any kind. But whatever you are, I think that needs attention. Let's get out of here before the zombie comes back." Lavanya put her arm under Zev and helped him up, then dusted them both off.

The entire cave had been sandblasted. Every surface was covered in dust, and the fire was out.

"How did you make a dust storm?"

"I'm a man of many talents. Let's get out of here."

"Zev. The zombie called you a demon. Are you?"

"I'm no more evil than you are, Lavanya. Come on. We need to get back to the castle."

Lavanya didn't know what to believe, but others had judged her evil often enough for her to know that she wouldn't assume someone else was evil. Zev had saved her again, and that was enough for her to trust him. For now.

"I left Samson tied just down the path. He can carry you."

Zev was grateful that she'd dropped the subject. He didn't want to see her face when he told her he was part Rakshasa demon. What a freak he was—black-marbled skin like stone, claws and teeth like an animal. How sexy a picture was that? He was surprised she wanted to be this close to him after seeing his beast in full form.

But she felt perfect tucked up under his arm supporting him. They both were worn out. She lost a lot of blood when Giselle attacked her, and now he needed to feed, as well. Maybe he could just change to wolf and hunt. Animal blood and meat might be enough.

He knew that was a lie even as he thought it. He needed human blood to fix this infection. He wondered if Lavanya's blood would taste sweet. She was strong. Maybe he wouldn't have to kill to feed. Maybe he could give up searching for evil souls to take.

No. He shouldn't think that way. He didn't want to get any more involved with her than he was now. *Was he involved?*

"Hang on." Lavanya helped Zev lean against the wall of the cave opening and ran back into the cave. She grabbed some of the fresh dirt and dust from the fire and sprinkled it over the pit.

"Dust to dust," she intoned. "I ask of the God that Giselle prayed to: please take her into your arms. Giselle, I'm sorry I failed to protect you, but I promise to avenge you."

She stepped back from the glowing embers and saw the zombie's arm still attached to the cave wall by the black blade. Furious that he'd gotten away, she pulled the knife out and stuck it in her back pocket.

"Next time, I'll nail your heart to the wall," she vowed. Finished, she returned to Zev.

Zev looked at Lavanya curiously, but he didn't ask what she'd been doing. Lavanya helped Zev outside, and it felt wonderful to be out in the fresh air. They staggered to Samson's hiding place. She wasn't prepared for what she saw. Samson lay on his side. The ground was torn up from his struggles, and a small tree was broken in two under him where he fell. A warm steam came off his ravaged body. His neck had been torn open. He didn't move.

"Samson?" Lavanya let go of Zev and ran to her horse. Foam had built up on his mouth and nostrils. He'd put up a fight, but he was gone.

Zev watched Lavanya fall beside her horse, and he felt her pain. The zombie had found another way to hurt her. The clouds above them crashed with thunder as her anger built. He needed to get her to the castle to feed and to safety.

"Lavanya." He limped to her side and pulled her up from Samson's large body. "We need to go. I know it's hard, but try to control your emotions until we get back to the castle." Zev looked up to the darkening sky.

"Why are they doing this?" she cried. "Who would do this?"

"We'll find out. But your father has made a lot of enemies." She'd lived a sheltered life for too long, in his opinion.

"I know who my father is, but why would his enemies come after me, and why now? I've never been a part of Vlad's life. Hell, for most of my life he's been sleeping. Ever since my mother died, it's like he died, too. I haven't seen him. I know he did evil things, but that was a long time ago."

"Come on," Zev said, putting his arm around Lavanya. "Let's get out of here before it starts to storm." They started down the mountain, both of them tired and in need of blood and food.

Lavanya pulled in her emotions and tried to think of something positive to get them through the forest without any further weather upsets. What a pain in the ass it was to be tied to the weather in this way! She really didn't need this right now. Adding up all the things she had to do brought to mind her favorite movie. She began to laugh, hysterically.

"I hate to ask, but what could possibly be funny?" Zev asked as if he were scared to hear the answer.

"'Tyron, you know how much I love watching you work.'" Lavanya twisted her favorite quote to suit her own crazy list of things to do. "'But I've got a formal dinner to plan, my clients' love lives to arrange, a zombie to murder, and a betraying bitch to track down. I'm swamped.'" She burst out laughing again.

"Get some rest." Zev's hazel eyes caught the late afternoon light and sparkled with mischief. "If you haven't got your health, then you haven't got anything."

Lavanya froze. "You just quoted *The Princess Bride?*" She couldn't have been more surprised.

"I have a good memory." Zev smiled at her. "It felt good to hear you laugh. You feeling better?"

"No. But that released some tension." Lavanya put more steel in her spine. "I'll feel better when the zombie and its master are dead."

"I like the way you think," Zev said. "Let's get back to the castle and get ready for tonight. This'll be over soon."

LYNNE STEVIE

CHAPTER TWENTY TWO

An Old Wives Tale

Lavanya left the trail they were on and led Zev through the heavy brush surrounding the castle wall.

"Where are you taking us?" Zev complained as a heavy branch hit him in the shoulder.

"Well…" Lavanya pushed thorny bushes away from the moss- and mold-covered stone wall and ran her hands over it. "I didn't want to get pinched strolling through the entrance hall looking like—*there it is*—the survivor of a bloody war."

Zev leaned forward to see what she'd found.

Lavanya grabbed the small projection in the wall, turned it, and pushed. The section of wall moved with her, swinging in like a giant stone door. Branches and vines clung to the stone, allowing only a slight opening for them to squeeze through.

"Nice," Zev said, smiling. "I'll have to remember that."

"Yeah well, desperate times call for desperate measures." Once inside, she repositioned the wall and swept some dirt and leaves back to cover the slight scraping on the ground made by the stone door. "I don't want to answer any questions about Giselle or our appearance. So I figured a less public entrance might be more prudent."

"Smart," Zev said with a slight lift of his brow.

"I might take that as a compliment, if you didn't look so surprised," Lavanya said with her hands on her hips.

"I'm impressed, not surprised. And you're right, there's no need to announce the fact that we've been fighting a zombie." Zev looked around the walls of Poenari Castle. "Now, which way?"

"Come on." Lavanya took Zev's hand and pulled it over her shoulder to help him the rest of the way. He hesitated at first, as if he wanted to refuse her help, but then he pulled her close and tucked her under his arm. She wasn't sure if she was helping him or if he was holding her—and she didn't really care. Either way it felt good.

She led him through the remains of the old servant's quarters. Not that anyone would know that's what it had been. Now it was just a few crumbled walls and hearths.

"This section of the castle was destroyed in the 1800s when a landslide took most of the servants and the building and deposited them in the river," she said as she scooted out from under his arm and kicked at the rocks surrounding a large iron door.

"When Vlad rebuilt, he added rooms to a new northern wing for the servants and their families. So this part of the castle has been forgotten." Lavanya kicked at the loose stones until she found her hidden key. The lock resisted at first but finally turned, and she opened the door to a crumbling stone stairway.

"This used to be the main entrance for the servants coming and going from the castle to their private quarters," she said. Now the stairs were a broken patchwork of stones that were missing a few chunks here and there.

"Is that safe?" Zev asked.

"We just fought off a zombie; I think we can handle a few old castle stairs. Come on."

She led Zev up the old servant's stairway, careful to remember which stones were loose and which were sturdy. The covert journey through the ruins and up to her rooms brought back a deluge of memories from her childhood and had her heart pounding. She smiled even in the midst of her worries, and a small chuckle escaped her lips as they reached her door.

"What are you laughing about now?" Zev's voice was low and rough.

"Sorry, sorry. I was just remembering all the times I used this route to break free of the castle as an adolescent." Lavanya's laugh caught in her throat as she gazed from his muscled chest to his hazel eyes. "Until today, I've never sneaked a man into the castle."

Zev crowded her against the closed door. Her hand fell from the doorknob and her mouth watered as his body heat teased all her senses. She longed to touch his warm skin with an urgency that surprised her. She placed her palm against the taut muscles of his abdomen and drew in a ragged breath. He smelled of soil and dust. She drew in another breath and smelled his sweat, the musk of his skin, and blood. Intoxicating.

Long ago she'd given up any hope of having a relationship

with anything warm-blooded. She'd learned the hard way that human men might be warm, but they were weaker than she and couldn't hold up to her lovemaking. Her body knew them as prey only. For decades she'd been content to lay only with other vampires, telling herself that she didn't need to feel the warmth of a lover's body to warm her cool skin.

Lavanya moved her hand up Zev's torso to rest against his beating heart. She swallowed hard and licked her lips at the thought of all that delicious warm blood pumping through his large form. She was hungry. But when she looked up into his dark eyes, she knew that he'd never be her prey.

Her body tightened and her breath caught. Not in anticipation of feeding, but of his warm touch.

Zev's eyes darkened and his nostrils flared as lust swamped his normal restraint. Lavanya's cool hand resting on his chest put out the fire of his pain while it stoked his desire to have her again. He pressed her to the door and attacked her mouth. Her hand caught in his hair and pulled him forward. His hands went to her ass and hoisted her up while she wrapped her long legs around his torso and devoured his mouth.

Lost in the sound of Lavanya's hungry growls and the feel of her core shamelessly rubbing against his shaft, he didn't hear the doorknob turn until it was too late and they fell through the door. He took the brunt of the fall on his side rather than crushing Lavanya, but they still ended up a tangled mess on the stone floor.

Tap, tap, tap. They both looked up to see Dylan's black, cross-engraved Italian leather boot tapping against the stone floor.

Zev couldn't help it; he burst out laughing. Lavanya pushed against him to free her legs.

"What's so funny?" she asked, sitting up and straightening her sweater.

"Oh, come on," Zev said, still laughing. "Sneaking in late at night, copping a feel, and then your brother busting us. This reminds me of *my* adolescence!"

"Did you get caught often?" Lavanya purred.

"Only once." Zev stilled. "But it was worth it." He winked and slapped her ass.

"Hey!" Lavanya swatted his hand, but missed. Rolling her

eyes at Zev, she let Dylan help her up.

He tried not to wince when he stood and his injured leg took his weight.

"Oh, God, your leg!" Lavanya said. She reached out to help him, but he didn't want her babying him. He waived her off.

"It's fine," he said, straightening. "I just forgot about it for a minute. Something else on my mind, I guess." He looked at Lavanya. Yeah, babying him was the *last* thing he wanted from her. He felt a small surge of satisfaction when a small moan escaped her throat.

"Okay, you two. Don't make me get the ice bucket." Dylan, that damn cheerleading chaperone, clapped his hands to draw their attention back to himself. "Focus, people," he scolded as he shut the door. "Now, what the hell happened to you? It'll take you days to wash off all that dirt, and we're already running late for the party. The clients have been up for over an hour, and they've been asking about you and Renfield."

Lavanya looked like she'd been kicked in the gut.

"No one's heard from Renfield? I was hoping…"

"Nothing. Not a trace." Dylan headed for the bath.

"Sorry, Dylan. We got stuck in a storm, and I don't really have time to tell you all the gory details. But the zombie is missing his arm." Lavanya pulled the knife from her back pocket and laid it on the mirrored table by the door. "And Giselle is gone."

"I'm starting your shower, and I already know Giselle is missing. Wait!" He turned back. "That's what you meant, right?"

"No, she's *gone*. Samson's dead too." Lavanya's voice sounded hollow, and she looked empty and defeated. Zev wanted to support her, but his leg wasn't really up to it. She lowered herself to the vanity.

"Don't sit on that!" Dylan shrieked. "You'll get dirt everywhere. Get into the bathroom. You, too, Zev. You're filthy. Go next door and get cleaned up."

Lavanya looked so tired Zev wasn't surprised when she sagged onto the decking around the tub. The best thing he could do for her was let Dylan take care of her.

He kissed her and left for his own suite. They could make up for lost time later.

"Giselle and the zombie attacked Zev and me," Lavanya told Dylan, tugging at her boots. He came over to help her take them off.

"She was possessed," she said. "Zev had to kill her or she would have torn my throat out." Lavanya pulled down her collar to show him the scar.

"Uggh!" Dylan gasped at the sight of the wound. "Oh, honey, I'm sorry. But I'm so glad you're okay. *Are* you okay?" He checked her over for more injuries.

"I've been better." Lavanya watched as Dylan held her boots out as if he wanted to throw them in the trash.

"That's it." Dylan threw her boots into the tub. "No more leaving the castle until we catch this monster, and we're going home as soon as this client weekend is over. We need to get back to the States. Now, get in the shower; we don't have time to pussy foot around. Your dinner party starts in one hour, and we have to wash and dry your hair, so don't dawdle in there."

"Dylan, I need to feed if I'm going to make it through this evening. And I have to check on Zev."

"He went into the other suite to shower. You check on him, and I'll call a donor for you. But hurry!"

"Thanks." Lavanya, barefooted and dirty, wobbled to the door connecting Zev's suite to hers. She heard his deep voice, so rather than knock, she eased the door open. Whom could he be talking to?

"No," Zev said. "Lavanya doesn't know about the agreement."

Hearing her name, Lavanya halted halfway through the door. And instead of alerting Zev to her presence, she kept quiet and watched him pace while he talked on the old castle phone, a black, rotary dial model. His back was to her as he continued his conversation.

"She saw more than I would have preferred.... Yeah, I know. I usually have more control.... No, I'm not distracted. I have my eyes on the prize, don't worry. We won't be servants to the bloodsucker any longer."

Bloodsucker! Lavanya had heard enough. She entered the suite and slammed the door shut behind her.

Zev turned and saw Lavanya's large, angry eyes. He wondered

195

how much she'd heard. Enough to make her mad, he guessed by the look of her.

"Inez. *No*. Feeding from Lavanya is not an option. But I need blood to heal. Will animal blood work?" Zev watched as Lavanya started to pace.

"Yeah, I know," he said into the phone. "But that has to wait until I catch the necromancer. No way!"

Lavanya stopped and stared as Zev burst into a loud, coughing laugh.

"I'd forgotten that," Zev said, shaking his head. "I remember. Yes, yes, I got it. Okay, I'll call if I need anything. Love you, too, old woman."

Zev hung up the phone, still smiling. But he quickly lost the smile when he saw Lavanya's scowling face.

"Bloodsucker, huh?" Lavanya sounded furious. "And my blood's not good enough for you. I guess that tells me all I need to know." She stomped toward the door.

Typical woman, Zev thought as he watched her huff and puff. After overhearing half the conversation, she was ready to storm out. Very Scarlett O'Hara and *Gone With the Wind*. He waited for her to slam the door again as she departed.

Lavanya was furious over Zev's bloodsucker comment about her father and her. She reached the door, intending to walk out on the bastard, but her curiosity trumped her anger. *Damn it*. Zev hadn't had any trouble kissing her earlier, so why the bloodsucker comment now? He bewildered her, fascinated her—and stirred her body to life.

As Zev's scowl turned up into a curious smile, her anger left her on the exhale of one deep breath. She wanted to learn more about a man who could turn into an animal and yet quote *The Princess Bride*.

"Who were you talking to?" She watched Zev relax his stance and hobble over to the chair by the window.

"My grandmother." He winced as he lowered himself into the chair. "I figured she'd know how to fight the infection from the zombie bite." He pulled back the torn leather to examine the wound.

"And did she?" Lavanya asked.

"Yes, that's what was so funny." Zev smiled, and Lavanya couldn't help but feel warmed by it.

"What did she say?" Lavanya pushed away from the door.

"I need to eat garlic." Zev burst out laughing and so did Lavanya. "Don't suppose you have any in your room?"

"I don't have any in my room, but we have plenty of garlic in the kitchen." Lavanya joined him and looked out the window. "It's an antifungal herb, right? Almost as good as penicillin."

"Yes, it is."

"I don't know anything about you." She looked into his hazel eyes. "Do you need blood to heal? You've fed me twice, you must be hungry."

She turned away from his piercing gaze and focused at the night beyond the window.

"I've never given my blood to anyone, except Giselle. That didn't turn out too well." Lavanya exhaled. "But I could get someone for you if vampire blood isn't suitable."

"Lavanya." Zev took her hand in his. "I said I wouldn't take your blood because you can't afford to lose any right now—not because I didn't think you were good enough."

He stood next to her. "And I'm sorry you heard my comment about your father. We're not exactly on the best of terms." He sat on the stone windowsill and pulled her in to rest against his chest. As he brushed his hands through her black hair, she snuggled into his embrace.

"What's going on between Vlad and you?" Lavanya's breath tickled over Zev's skin; his scent was delicious. "What does he hold over you?"

"It's a long story. It has to do with my birth." Just then a knock sounded on the connecting door.

"Lavanya, dear, Stephen's here to feed you," Dylan said through the closed door.

Lavanya felt a low growl rattle in Zev's chest.

"We need to hurry if we're going get to dinner before midnight," Dylan pleaded.

"Lavanya." Zev's voice was rough from the unreleased growl. "Isn't there a woman you could feed from?"

Lavanya snuggled closer, wishing she could feed from him instead of the human donor, and loving the fact that he cared who she was with.

"You prefer to share me with another woman?" Lavanya purred while rubbing against his chest and nipping at the tender skin of his neck. "That's something to think about later. However," she pulled away abruptly and Zev groaned, "right now we don't have much time. Will you be able to come down tonight?"

"I'll be fine, it's just a scratch."

"Dylan," Lavanya called out. "Did you have a chance to get something for Zev to wear to dinner tonight?"

"Yes, and it'll coordinate with your gown perfectly. Now get in here."

"I better go. Press line two on the phone and that'll get you the kitchen; they can bring you anything you need. Even *garlic*." She stepped through the door, but turned back with a mischievous smile.

"Zev."

The silky tone of Lavanya's voice worked like a charm and brought Zev to his feet. "Yeah."

"I don't like to share... at all. See you at the party." Then she shut the door.

Zev wanted to pull her back into the room and bolt the doors. They could spend hours in the big bathtub and then a few more in bed. He wanted a taste of her so bad his mouth watered. He took a few steps toward her door before he remembered his wound and his obligations.

"Damn," he whispered to himself. He'd told her it was no big deal, but he really could use a feeding. He leaned against the door. He couldn't allow himself even a little taste of her, because the demon would want it all. The Rakshasa wanted everything from their victims, blood and soul. But maybe with her it would be different. He'd felt the demon's rage mix with his when Giselle attacked her. Lavanya was part human and part vampire—strong with Vlad's blood. Zev pushed the thought away. He couldn't risk her life.

He turned back to the phone and pressed two. While he waited for the kitchen to pick up, he cradled the heavy old telephone to his ear and stretched the thick cord to the large closet. The only thing besides a robe was a tuxedo. *Oh, hell no.* He closed the door.

"Yes, this is Zev. I need five cloves of garlic, two large steaks, rare.... Yeah, a roast will do. Thanks, and be sure to have garlic on hand for the next few days, too." He started to put the phone down and thought of something. "Oh, do you have fresh mint?"

With his food ordered, he decided to grab a cold shower, because he still needed to clean up, and if he didn't cool off, he'd storm through the connecting door and rip the human male to pieces. He'd lied to Inez about being distracted; he just hadn't known how much Lavanya clouded his mind until now.

Lavanya took the blood she needed from the donor, clouded his mind, and made a note to see if Uki and Raz wanted to take him home with them. He'd been hooked on them since they'd fed from him the other night, and he wanted out of Arefu. Now as she sat in Dylan's chair of torture and listened to Chloe complain about the mess in the bathroom, she empathized with the young man's need to get away.

"Chloe!" At Dylan's loud voice, Lavanya jerked in her seat. Which in turn caused more hair pulling from Dylan.

"Sit still," he scolded. "Chloe, I need more bobby pins. Be a dear and get some from the drawer in there." Dylan had blown her hair dry, trimmed the ends, and curled it. Now he was teasing and pinning it into an up style with one long tail that hung down on the side.

"Thank heaven for the gown and your long hair," he said as he worked. "We should be able to camouflage where you were attacked."

"Here they are, Dylan." Chloe held out the pins.

"I need the black ones, not the silver ones, *please*." Dylan rolled his eyes in the mirror as soon as Chloe had her back turned.

"Be nice, Dylan, you didn't say which ones you wanted." Under normal circumstances, Lavanya loved being in the middle of their bickering, but she was anxious tonight and didn't have the patience to be diplomatic.

Chloe returned with the correct bobby pins.

"Mistress, I found these in the pocket of your riding pants." Chloe held out the necklace from Helgaleena and the notes she'd taken on the divination.

"Thanks, Chloe, I'd forgotten. Just..." Lavanya looked for

some place to set them between all of Dylan's shears and combs. "Just give them to me." Lavanya held the bundle of papers and the necklace in her lap. While Dylan worked, she played with the leather strap of the necklace and eyed the papers. She had a nagging feeling that she'd missed something important today.

Zev felt a little stronger after consuming the meat that the kitchen delivered. The garlic wasn't as easy to stomach, but he managed to swallow all of it and keep it down. He would need several more daily doses to kill the infection if he didn't feed soon. The thought of eating more of the pungent bulbs made Zev want to find the zombie-controlling necromancer and devour him sooner rather than later. The urge to feed on the evil creature clouded his vision.

It was night, and the Rakshasa was ready to hunt. Zev had extraordinary night vision from two sources. His natural earth magic helped him see in the dark because he could access sources of electromagnetic radiation. His demon side gave him an extra layer of tissue in the back of his eye, which reflected light back through the retina and increased the amount of light it could capture. This extra tissue layer was also the reason his eyes shone in the dark.

Zev felt his skin prickle, and pain spread through the bones of his face as he yearned to change into the demon and feast. He took a deep breath and tried to clear his vision, but the demon wanted out. He looked up at the night sky, deep purple through the old glass window, then at the clock on the table. There wasn't time.

No, he had to make time.

Renfield beat his bloody fists against the heavy wooden door.

"Giselle—whoever's out there—let me out. The Master will kill you for this!" Renfield was rewarded for his efforts by the sound of silence. Exhausted and worn, he slid to the floor. He'd gone through the room for more than an hour, trying to find a way to pry open the door or remove the hinges, and he had nothing to show for it except a room full of broken furniture. As the cool air chilled his sweat-soaked skin, he put his head in his hands and called to Vlad again.

"Master, please wake up. Send me a sign. I must know if

you're all right." Renfield felt a hint of their connection. It gave him hope that their enemies hadn't found Vlad's resting place yet.

Renfield's stomach growled. The forgotten tray that Giselle had brought earlier was under the window. He eyed the cold food. As another growl rolled through his stomach, he shifted to his hands and knees and crawled over to it. He picked up the chicken and settled beneath the window. As the cold stone chilled his back, he turned the chicken breast over in his hands, then he threw it over his shoulder and out the window, followed by everything else on the tray. He screamed his rage at the cool night beyond the window.

The temperature was dropping rapidly, and his breath was a mist in the darkening room. His captors had left firewood in the old hearth, so he stumbled over and started the kindling with the long matchsticks they'd left him.

He was cold, exhausted, and hungry, but he couldn't give up hope that Vlad or Lavanya would find him. He pulled the old mattress off the bed and dragged it in front of the fire. Then he curled up on it and, with the musty blanket pulled up to his face, released himself to sleep.

The forest called to Zev. If he hoped to keep the demon in check, he needed to ground himself. He could transport his body outside on a wave of the earth's energy, but that would require power he might need later. So he used the same hidden route that Lavanya had taken earlier to enter the castle.

As he quietly worked his way over the rubble of the ruined servants quarters, he heard two animals snarling and growling. He tilted his head and crouched low to the ground, the predator in him taking control of his actions. He scented a couple of silver foxes, and he growled once low and deep to let them know they needed to move along. He glided around one of the ruined walls to see double sets of eyes trained on him, glowing in the moonlight. In their mouths they each carried—he lifted his nose to the wind and sniffed—a small morsel of frayed meat.

Zev growled again, one more deep, low growl, and the fox on the left dropped his meal and ran for the cover of the thick forest. The fox on the right went in the opposite direction, presumably to enjoy the spoils of the conflict.

Satisfied that they weren't a threat, Zev surveyed the forest surrounding the castle. The sounds of the night quieted as the animals hunkered down to hide from the predator now in their midst. Zev raised his gaze to the cloudy night sky and lifted his arms to the energy he felt under his bare feet. He opened himself to the electrical rhythms and free electrons flowing from the earth and allowed its healing energy to fill him as his grandmother taught him. The energy raised the hair on his body, and the smell of ozone filled his nostrils as it swirled around and within him. The electrical charge, like a slow river of light, invigorated him, and he drank in the power the earth gave willingly. The torn and infected skin of his thigh sizzled as it healed, and his mind cleared as the earth reset his hormones and oxygenation to optimal levels.

The demon inside howled at the invasion of the positive energy. For it alone kept the demon from totally controlling him, body and soul. Although, Zev loved the strength and the ability to change forms that came from his father, the Rakshasa demon, he detested the evil within him. It was forever hungry for human souls and blood. Without his close tie to the mother earth and her elemental light magic his soul would have been lost to darkness long ago.

After he had his fill of the earth's electrical recharging energies, he used some of his illusionary magic to create more suitable clothing for the evening. He could wear only natural fibers, the less processed the better, so he created a leather suit. He chose a dark, dirty brown for the front and back, with large buttons and pockets, like a traditional suit. Then he added a mandarin collar and sleeves to match made of fine, black wool. He paired that with a brown, cotton t-shirt and black leather pants. After adding his customary leather-soled boots, he was done.

He hated to go back into the castle and lose his connection to the earth, but he needed to get back to Lavanya. He was uneasy about leaving her alone inside. She wasn't really alone, he knew that, but he just felt the need to keep her close. And he always trusted his intuition.

Walking back to the ruins, he felt the tingle of metal beneath his foot and stopped to retrieve the item—a bent and twisted piece of silverware. As he studied the piece, he heard a faraway cry on the wind. He searched the forest night to determine its direction, but just as he heard it, it was gone. He threw the fork aside and moved fast and sure through the old ruins, his heart beating fast with his need to get to Lavanya.

CHAPTER TWENTY THREE

Dinner and Dragon Shears

"You're officially done. Now for the dress." Dylan retrieved her dress from the closet, and Lavanya stood with Helgaleena's gifts still clutched in her hands. Helgaleena had told her to wear the necklace for protection. Lavanya placed the papers on the vanity and dropped the necklace over her head when Dylan caught her.

"What are you doing with…that?"

"Helgaleena said I needed to keep this on. It has some sort of family magic or something."

"Absolutely not. This dress is a custom Eriani. I won't let you ruin the lines of the gown by wearing that junk." Dylan held his hand out for necklace. "Give it to me."

Lavanya lifted the necklace carefully over her hair and handed it to Dylan. He held it with just two fingers and studied it for a moment.

"Ugh," he said with a shiver. "I don't know, dear, it gives me the heebie-jeebies." He tossed it on top of Lavanya's discarded notes. Rubbing his hands on the fabric of his pants as if to clean them, he turned her to face the antique three-panel dressing shade and the beautiful gown that they'd chosen for tonight's festivities.

Lavanya sighed. The gown seemed frivolous and outrageous now, with Renfield gone and Giselle dead.

"Lavanya?" Dylan asked.

"I'm just not in the mood to put on a show, Dylan." Lavanya's violet eyes glowed red with anger and sorrow.

"I know, but you need to go out and show this bastard that you aren't to be messed with. You are the only daughter of Vlad the Impaler. You will not be troubled or frightened by anyone or anything. The best way to catch them is to confront them, and by showing up sparkling and confident tonight, you'll piss them off. Hopefully, that'll make 'em stupid enough to come at you face to face. You and Zev, together, can beat them. Then we'll find

Renfield and make sure your father's safe." Dylan pushed Lavanya toward the screen. "Now get dressed."

"I love you, Dylan." Lavanya gave Dylan a hug.

"Yes, yes, I know." Dylan gave her a gentle squeeze before releasing her to her task. "Now get going."

Zev got back to the suite just as Lavanya stepped out of her rooms. His breath caught in his throat when he saw her. *Holy shit!* Her hair cascaded over her shoulder in a shiny, black wave that rippled like a waterfall as she moved. Her shoulders were bare and so smooth that her skin looked like a bowl of cream. Her dress was a strapless, black, sequined number that hugged her body and sparkled in the light. Plus, the front was an amazing piece of art. A line of emeralds and crystals formed a tail that started at her calf and twisted up around her hips to her breasts, where it formed a dragon's head. Its jaws were open, and black feathers jutted out to simulate smoke streaming from its mouth.

"There you are." Lavanya's voice barely broke through to him. She smiled, gathered her skirt, and walked toward him like a small slice of heaven.

"Anya, you look amazing." She might have said "thank you," but he wasn't sure. He could lose himself in her. *Damn it*, he thought. It might be too late already.

As she reached him, he changed the color of his jacket panels from dirty brown to silver gray and his t-shirt to black to better match her gown. She noticed the color change.

"You're handy with clothing. Is this what Dylan picked out for you?" She pulled back to get a better look, as if she knew that Dylan had nothing to do with his wardrobe choice.

"Not exactly." Zev winked at her and tucked her hand in his arm.

"How do you do that?" Lavanya asked as they walked.

"Just one of my many talents." Lavanya rolled her violet eyes at him, and for the first time ever, he wanted someone to understand him. He stopped her in the hall.

"Truth," he said. "I don't know how it works, but I can create any natural fabric or material—just no plastic or synthetic stuff." He leaned his head down, rested it against her forehead, closed his eyes, and bathed in the smell of her skin and soft perfume.

206

Lavanya shivered in his hold, but her arms moved to circle his waist in a comfortable embrace.

"Thanks." Lavanya's voice washed over him.

"For what?"

"Letting me...telling me the truth." Lavanya's small hands caressed his lower back and he knew he had to tell her everything.

"Lavanya, I'll get you through this, and we'll find out what happened to Renfield. But you need to know when this is all over, I may not be able to leave you." He rubbed his face against her neck and cheek, loving the feel of her cool breath and soft skin against his rough whiskers. Physically and emotionally his body hungered for her more than he'd ever thought possible.

"I hold a Rakshasa demon inside of me, Lavanya." Zev tilted Lavanya's head so he could see into her eyes. "You asked me what your father held over me. He killed the demon that raped my mother and protected me and my grandmother when my mother died in childbirth. We have been sworn to serve him ever since."

"Zev, I'm sorr..."

"I don't want your pity, but you have to know that I'm part demon. What you saw in the cave is barely held in check by my elemental magic and strength of will. Rakshasa are man-eaters. The demon always wants to feed on human flesh and blood, he wants their human souls." Zev stepped back to allow Lavanya space if his announcement frightened her.

Lavanya couldn't believe what Zev told her. Her pulse spiked at the knowledge that he truly was a demon. A sane woman would be heading for the hills. She'd never seen a demon herself, but the horrific stories of their destruction of humans and anything else in their presence were legendary. Even as he admitted that he wanted to kill and feast on humans, her heart sang at the thought of having someone not leave her, of having *him* not leave her. Then she remembered the beast he'd become in the cave and the way he'd torn out Giselle's heart. Still, she'd looked into the monster's eyes without fear. Why? She reached up and cupped her hand against his strong jaw.

"Zev, the demon didn't want to hurt me when we were in the cave, did it?"

"Lavanya, I'm sorry. I normally have better control. But when

Giselle attacked you, I went crazy and—"

"Shh, not I, *both*." Lavanya felt a calm come over her as she remembered looking up into the face of the beast.

"What?"

"I mean both of you. I don't understand how you share one consciousness or body, but I looked into the demon's eyes, Zev, and it didn't want to hurt me or eat me. Well—" she chuckled, "not in the literal sense of the word, anyway. Zev, I don't fear the demon."

"It's dangerous, Lavanya!" Zev stepped back farther, but his arms still reached out to her, his head turned slightly to the side like an animal waiting for her command. Lavanya reached for his hand to pull him into an embrace. That was all the invitation he needed.

He moved fast and surrounded her with his huge body, pulling her against him and lifting her off the floor. His hold was crushing, but his kiss was a soft brush of his lips. He pulled her in as the dry, cracked dirt of the desert absorbs the first drop of water from a storm. She kissed him back, clinging to his promise of warmth and intimacy.

"Shit, girl! You're surrounded by bedrooms. Pick one." Tru's husky voice broke the moment. But when Naasir cleared his throat, Zev released her so fast Lavanya almost stumbled off her Louboutins. Zev kept her tucked under his arm and angled his body in front of her. She couldn't see his face, but Tru stepped back and Naasir stepped forward.

She shrugged off Zev's arm to embrace Tru.

"Hey, girl," she said. "You look wonderful." Tru was wearing a black leather bustier with a full, draping skirt in leather to match. The skirt was open in the front to reveal Tru's trademark black leather pants with crimson detailing in the front of the thigh. "Your dress suits you perfectly," Lavanya said, admiring the gorgeous outfit.

"I hate wearing dresses, so this was the best of both worlds!" Tru laughed. "But damn, girl, that outfit is bitchin!" Tru ran her hand over the delicate feathers at Lavanya's neck.

"Thanks." Lavanya cupped her hand over her mouth for effect. "Are the men standing down, or do we need to get Dylan out here with some ice water?" Tru's giggle came out a husky gurgle as she peeked over Lavanya's shoulder.

"I think we're okay. I felt a draft as they deflated their puffed-out chests." Tru slid back to Naasir.

"Stand down, babe," she said as she slapped his ass.

"Can you blame us for being territorial over the two of you?" Naasir pulled Tru close and looked at her with a healthy dose of obsession in his eyes. Then his gaze moved over Lavanya with none of the heat she'd seen for Tru and rested above her left shoulder.

"Zev, Lavanya." He nodded hello. "Tru was anxious and wanted to check on you, Lavanya. Please accept our apologies for interrupting."

"No apologies necessary." Zev put his arm around Lavanya, his body relaxed as his hand circled Lavanya's waist. "I don't handle surprises well, and I'm not normally surprised. But my powers of concentration are being tested this week." Zev looked at Lavanya as if she were an ice cream sundae on a hot summer day. Then he licked his lips.

"Lavanya! Are you blushing? Oh, my God, I am loving this!" Tru shouted.

"It's just the feathers." Lavanya brushed the black plumes away from her face. "They irritate me."

"So, ladies," Naasir held out his arm to Tru. "Can we escort you to the party?"

"Of course, thank you for reminding us, Naasir." Lavanya took Zev's arm.

"Dracul—dragon? Oh, hell, Lavanya, how long have you had that dress?" Tru asked.

"What?" Naasir asked as they walked down the hall.

"Lavanya's father—his surname—Draculesti, Dracul, Dracula," Tru said. "It stands for Order of the Dragon or the Devil. And now she's wearing a dragon dress." Tru waved her hand in front of Lavanya's dress as they walked.

"Ah." A light came on in Naasir's eyes. "Very clever, Lavanya."

"Thanks. I had it commissioned for a special event years ago, but it came out so beautifully that I thought if I had the chance, I'd wear it here. It reminds me of my family's history." Lavanya squeezed Zev's arm for support as thoughts of her father reminded her of the danger they were all in.

The soulful sound of a violin reached the foursome as they came to the large landing at the top of the grand staircase. Servants finalized details or served cocktails. It was the exciting first few moments of a party when everyone arrived looking wonderful, no one's feet hurt yet, and the men still had their ties tied. The promise of a good time still sparkled in everyone's eyes. However, all Lavanya could think of was that someone was trying to kill her and her loved ones.

"Gentlemen, would you be so kind as to give Tru and me a moment alone?" Lavanya saw disapproval in Zev's hazel eyes, but she didn't care. She needed to warn her friend about the danger. Lavanya pulled Tru toward the closed library doors.

"Lavanya, can't this wait?" Zev trailed after the women. "The party is starting, and you'll be missed if you're late."

"We won't be but a minute." Lavanya opened the large double doors and stepped aside so Tru could enter. Zev stepped around the ladies and entered the room before Lavanya or Tru could move.

"I'll turn up the oil lamps for you." Zev glared at Lavanya as he passed, obviously not happy with her idea of talking to Tru alone.

"Thank you." Lavanya kept her voice as sweet as honey. Tru looked baffled, which was understandable, since neither of them was into drama or girly talk.

"Hon, go on down, and I'll catch up in a minute." Tru kissed Naasir on the cheek, and he tenderly took her hand in his and kissed her palm.

"Take your time. I'll be waiting," he said with a wink. "Zev, care to join me?"

Lavanya noticed Tru and Naasir watching Zev as stalked through the dark room turning up the lamps as if he were hunting a tiger instead of just walking over their hides. The room was really lost in time with the tiger skin rugs and the stone walls, dark wood and large hearth. Her father had not even allowed them to install modern lighting in the library. He preferred the oil and candle light to the modern glow of electric lights for reading.

"Zev, we'll just be a minute," Lavanya said. Zev turned back and Lavanya saw his eyes glow with a cold florescence. Tru took a step back, and Lavanya had to force herself not to do the same.

"Zev," she said.

Lavanya watched as Zev reined in his beast. He closed his eyes and when he reopened them, he was just Zev again. Lavanya felt Tru take in a deep breath and relax at her side.

Zev strode back to where they stood in the doorway. "Ten minutes. Any longer, and I'll be in here."

"Don't be so possessive; it's just a little girl talk. I want Tru's opinion on the weekend and some of the other couples." Lavanya used the only excuse she could think of at the moment.

Zev stalked out of the room, and Tru took a seat near the hearth. Lavanya closed the doors behind the men and sighed.

"All right, what's going on?" Tru asked.

"Am I that obvious?"

"Not really. If I hadn't seen the way you kissed him, I'd say that you just wanted to get rid of his possessive ass. But there's more. He wasn't being a possessive lover—he was looking this room over for danger. And he seemed angry that you wanted to talk to me. Now, what the fuck's goin' on?"

"He's angry. He doesn't know you, and to him, everyone's a threat right now."

Tru patted the seat next to her, and Lavanya joined her friend on the large leather sofa.

"We really do have only ten minutes, so here's the Reader's Digest version," she said in a rush. "Someone is threatening me and my father. They've already tried to kill me twice, and Renfield's missing. My father somehow got word to Zev, and he's here to protect me. I wanted you to be aware of the danger for your own safety. Zev's not really my lover. That was just a story to get him access to the party."

"Um hmm." Tru's brow lifted.

"Well, I mean I didn't know him before this weekend. I guess we're lovers now."

Tru covered Lavanya's hand with her own. "I get it, and I am glad he's here. I haven't decided yet what he is, though."

Lavanya gazed into Tru's intelligent eyes. "What do you mean?"

"I saw his eyes glow a little while he was checking the room a few minutes ago. He's scary as shit! But I'm feeling only good vibes toward you. The rest of us—" Tru paused. "He could probably kill any of us without remorse. But as long as he's good for you, I can overlook that."

"Thanks."

Tru smiled, her fangs visible in the dim light, as her husky laugh cracked through the somber, silent room. "Damn, it's fun being a monster. You never know what you're gonna see next."

"Tru, I can't tell you about—" Lavanya started.

"No worries," Tru interrupted, patting Lavanya's hand. "I figured you'd need to keep quiet about him, and Naasir must not have seen his eyes or he wouldn't have left me here with you. No one will be the wiser about him. Now, what do you need from me?"

Lavanya gave her friend a hug and smiled. "Thanks. Just keep yourself safe and let me know if you get any weird vibes from any of the other guests. I trust your input."

"Well…there's no love lost between Lauren and your father. But you already know that."

Lavanya shook her head. "Yeah, he has a history with her. She might still be angry because he didn't revamp my mother, but I just don't think she'd be capable of—well, everything else that's been happening."

"Gotcha. I'll defer to you on that one. Plus, I'll keep my eyes and ears open." Tru looked at her big, black Tissot men's watch and chuckled. "We better get going before Zev busts down the door."

"Ha ha, he's not that bad. And I can't believe you're wearing that huge men's watch with a formal gown." Lavanya loved to tease Tru about her quirky sense of style. It felt normal, and she was glad she'd told her friend about the possible danger.

"You know me better than that. I love this watch. Its waterproof, and I never take it off. Besides, this isn't exactly a girly formal gown." Tru stood and let Lavanya admire the black leather leggings and high heeled biker boots under the split skirt. Lavanya rolled her eyes and laughed.

"Thanks, Tru, I needed that." Lavanya hugged her friend. "Come on. We better find those men." Lavanya took her friend's hand to lead her from the library. As the two walked to the door, Tru tried to tug her hand away.

"Lavanya, you're crushing my hand," she said, but Lavanya

couldn't release her. "Lavanya! Let go!"

Lavanya heard bones crunch as she looked down at her own hand and Tru's white knuckles. *She'd hurt Tru.* Anger rushed through her like a flame, but she released Tru's hand. She turned her rage toward the heavy wooden door, jerking so hard that she pulled it free of the top hinge. Tru, holding her injured hand, scooted past her and ran to the top of the stairs. Leaning over the railing she spotted Zev pacing at the bottom.

"Zev! Help! Lavanya—"

Zev appeared in front of her. "What?" He grabbed her shoulders.

"Something's wrong with—" Tru looked back into the library, and Zev released her and rushed in.

Lavanya's eyes glowed red in the dim light of the library. Zev leaped to her side, but as he reached for her, she hissed and crouched to strike him. He held his hands out and took a step back. Anger and pain radiated from her.

"Lavanya, it's Zev," he said. "I'm here to protect you. Remember?" Lavanya didn't move but stayed crouched and ready to attack.

"Tru," Zev called. "What the hell happened in here?"

"I don't know," she said from the doorway. "Everything was fine. We were laughing. She took my hand to lead me out, and then she just started crushing it. She let go, ripped the door off the hinges, and I ran for you. I've never seen her like this. I have no idea what set her off, but we have to help her." Tru stepped into the room, and a low growl echoed through the coffered ceilings as Lavanya warned Tru not to come any closer.

"Lavanya, its Tru, honey, please tell us what's wrong."

Zev watched as Lavanya looked to the right, as if she could see through the wall of the library into another room.

"Dylan!" she said. She pushed past Zev and Tru, moving faster than Zev had ever seen a vampire move. She was no more than a blur, even to his sensitive eyes.

"Tru, get to Naasir and tell no one what's happened." Zev didn't wait for her to answer. He zeroed in on Dylan and willed his body to his location.

He appeared in Lavanya's suite of rooms just as Lavanya crossed the threshold and barreled into him. They both smacked down on the gleaming, black stone floor. He smelled fresh blood. Lavanya must have, too. He tried to hold her, but she moved too fast. She was out of his grasp and gone.

She had to get to Dylan. She could feel his rage as if it were her own. But what really cost her was feeling his fear.

She scrambled out of Zev's grasp and half-crawled, half-ran to her changing room, splitting the side seams of her dress in her desperate need to find him. It had taken her too long to realize that what she'd been feeling was Dylan's fear and anger. She'd always tried to block the emotional connection that came with the master/servant relationship. Now her stupid attempt to give him privacy might be what killed him.

As she entered the changing room, the smell of blood hit her hard. Her fangs pushed down and venom filled her mouth. A thick spray of blood splashed the wall and dripped from the paper lanterns on the far side of the room. *Oh, God, please don't let me be too late.*

"Dylan!" She frantically scanned the ruined room for her friend and servant. Blood-covered clothes and her beauty products, a testament to her vanity, littered the floor. A shot rang through the room and echoed off the stone walls. She raced into the bath suite, following the blood splatter and sound of the shot. Dylan stood over the zombie with his SIG 9mm in one hand and his Kenchii Dragon shears dripping black blood in the other.

"Dylan?" Lavanya reached out to him, but Dylan put up his hand, gun pointed to the ceiling, to stop her advance.

"Anya," Dylan panted. "Stay back!" His eyes held pure rage. Like looking into a Kansas City tornado, Dylan held a fury that was barely contained. Lavanya took a small step back and landed against Zev.

The zombie moved, and Dylan shot it point-blank in the face. Black fluid from the rotting body sprayed the room and rained down on the dark green and brown granite. The color looked like a river of blood as it blended in with the rain forest granite. A few drops landed on Lavanya's face, burning her cheek. She gasped and wiped away the vile, poisonous liquid.

"Zev, get her out of here," Dylan yelled as he bent over the body of the zombie and dug into its chest with the sharp, dragon-etched scissors. He grunted as the point of the scissors broke through ribs and muscle. The strong shears scraped along the stone floor as Dylan worked to cut out the zombie's heart and kill it for good. Lavanya was mesmerized by the sight.

"Lavanya! Chloe's been hurt. She's out there." Dylan motioned with his head without looking up. "Go help her."

Chloe was hurt? Lavanya straightened up.

"Zev, stay here and help Dylan." Lavanya turned to go without doubting that her direct order would be carried out.

"Dylan, don't pull out the heart—" He was too late. *So much for asking it about its master* "—yet." Zev watched as Dylan stood up over the zombie, holding it's dripping heart in his hand.

"Stay with her," Dylan said through grinding teeth. "I'll burn its heart in the tub. You, protect her."

Zev tried to reconcile the two conflicting images of Dylan. How could this ditsy hairdresser, who fussed for hours over Lavanya's outfits, be the same person who'd taken down a zombie? Was now cutting its heart out and ordering Zev around? Zev shook his head to clear it.

"Don't hurt yourself thinking too hard." Dylan stepped over the lifeless zombie and tossed the creature's heart into the huge stone bathtub.

Zev smiled a wicked smile. "Just wouldn't have guessed you had it in you, *hairdresser.*"

"Anyone can just go in there and kill someone, but you can't get information from a corpse." Dylan walked across the bathroom and reached for a towel before he turned back to Zev to see his reaction.

"Fuck," Zev said, leaning against the door frame. "That's a Navy SEAL's quote."

"Now I'm the one who's surprised." Dylan wiped off his expensive shears. "A dog that can read. You know the saying?"

"Yeah, but *you* were a Navy SEAL?" Zev shook his head in surprise.

"Yes." Dylan put the towel down and looked at Zev. "Don't ever underestimate me or Lavanya again."

"Did you get anything from the zombie before you finished him off?"

"Not much." Just then they heard Lavanya cry out Chloe's name.

"Go help Lavanya and I'll fill you both in after I'm done."

"That's what I was thinking." Zev jogged out to help Lavanya and found her cradling her personal maid.

"She's alive, Zev." A light pink tear stained Lavanya's porcelain skin as she gazed at the young woman.

"Call a doctor. I'll get her into bed." Zev bent to pick up the young girl.

"I'll get her," Lavanya said, holding onto the maid with fierce possessiveness and strength. "Call the kitchen ask for Hilde. Tell her to fetch Helgaleena."

Zev hesitated. Helgaleena, a black witch, was the last person he would have thought to call.

"Now!"

Fine. He stumbled through the shattered room to the house phone. He remembered to dial two for the kitchen.

"Hello, Hilde, Mistress Lavanya needs you to call Helgaleena and have her come to the castle immediately. Well—" Zev looked up to see Lavanya nodding her approval. Okay, so he could tell Hilde why they needed Helgaleena. "Chloe's been injured, and she needs medical help."

As he put the phone down, Dylan flew out of the dressing room smelling like sulfur and rotting vegetables. He dashed to the balcony doors and opened them wide.

"Sorry, honey, this isn't a pretty job." Dylan took a deep breath of the cold, fresh air and then began picking up debris as he made his way to the bed where Lavanya held Chloe. "How is she?"

So the silly, flirty Dylan persona was back in place over the tough-as-iron man he'd just seen in the bathroom standing over a zombie corpse.

"She's alive." Lavanya held out her hand for Dylan, and he took it.

"How are you?" she asked. "Are you hurt? I was so worried; I didn't know. Dylan, I would have been here sooner if I'd known. I felt your fear and anger; I just didn't recognize them as yours. I tried so hard to give you privacy, but I was blocking you when you needed me most. Forgive me."

"Shh, honey, I'm fine." Dylan looked down at Chloe's

216

ravaged body and blood-stained face. "I just wish I'd heard him before he hurt Chloe."

"What happened?" Zev asked. Dylan looked to Lavanya first, and she shrugged her okay. *She trusted him.*

"She was cleaning up your dressing room as I put everything away in the bathroom. She was whining about me, she always had to clean up my messes. Blah, blah, blah." Dylan gently pushed Chloe's blood-soaked hair off her face. "I tuned her out."

Dylan got up off the bed and went to the bathroom.

"She's always complaining," he yelled from the smoke-darkened room. "She's such a pain in the ass sometimes." Then he came back with a wet towel, bringing the icky, burnt smell with him. "But you know I love her."

He kneeled down and gently wiped the blood from Chloe's face with the wet cloth. Chloe took a deep breath as the cool towel touched her face.

"Chloe?" Lavanya gasped. But Chloe didn't respond. Lavanya grabbed her shoulders to try to wake her, but Dylan stopped her.

"It's okay, honey," he said. "It's a good thing that she's out of it. Her mind isn't ready to feel the pain yet. Let her be."

"Lavanya," Zev interrupted her. "You can feel her health and life force if you settle yourself down. You know she's not dying, just as I do. She's injured and unconscious, but she's strong." Zev watched as Lavanya closed her eyes and took a few deep breaths.

Lavanya opened her eyes and smiled up at Zev. Then returned her attention back to Dylan. "Thank you for saving yourself and Chloe," she said.

"Dylan, continue. What happened after you stopped the zombie from attacking Chloe?" Zev demanded.

"It was strange. The thing was so focused on her. Even after I shot it, it ignored me and went for her. Finally, I dragged it into the bathroom where I keep my Kenchii shears. They're real silver. I hoped they'd be strong enough to cut out its heart."

Dylan raised his eyes with a devilish grin. "They were. Do you think I should put that in my review?"

"*What did you learn from it?*" Zev thundered. He'd lost patience with Dylan's recount of the events.

"Did you have time to question it before you killed it?" Lavanya looked surprised. "I felt such fear in our connection."

"Fear for you, Anya, and Chloe. Yes, I questioned it."

Zev wondered if Lavanya noticed that the hairdresser Dylan changed back into the soldier when he spoke of killing.

"It knew only that its master was a woman and that it was after the lady of the Castle Vlad, Lavanya Draculesti. Zombies aren't exactly intelligent creatures, and I doubt if this one was very smart even when he was alive." Dylan sighed. "It was more like a homing pigeon in the way it ignored everything except trying to get at Chloe."

"Great," Zev grumbled. "That narrows it down." He paced around the ravaged room. "You've got—what?—five or six women guests, plus who knows how many women working around the castle. It could be anyone."

"She'll be fine, honey." Dylan handed the washcloth to Lavanya and fussed with the bed cover, straightening it as much as he could with a bleeding woman and a furious, scared vampire princess spread out over the top.

When he moved on to the rest of the room, Zev finally noticed that it was a train wreck. Furniture was trashed; books, clothes, and china were strewn and torn or broken on the floor; and worst of all, blood was splashed everywhere. Chloe had put up a good fight before Dylan hauled the thing off her.

"Hilde, hurry up, girl. I may need yer help." Helgaleena's loud voice filled the hall, and they all turned to see her enter Lavanya's suite. She was flanked by a huffing and puffing Hilde, still in her apron from her work in the kitchen, and her nephew, Joseph. Helgaleena raised her head, her long, gray braid falling behind her as she sniffed the air.

"What happened? I smell something rotten." Then her eyes drifted to where Lavanya lay with Chloe. "So this is my patient."

Buttercup shot out from under the bed and barked at the threesome as they stood in the doorway.

"'Chaos is a friend of mine,'" Dylan said, leaning over and whispering to Lavanya.

"Get this rat out of my way!" Helgaleena shouted over Buttercup.

"I hate it when you quote Bob Dylan." Lavanya whispered back. Dylan had never been a fan of Helgaleena's. "Will you get Buttercup?"

"I got it." Dylan retrieved Buttercup, looking happy that she'd made it through the fight. "Come here, you little scamp. Zev, I'm putting her in your suite."

"Fine." Zev moved a chair out of the way and opened the door to his room. As Dylan passed, Buttercup snarled and barked at the old witch, which made Zev smile. He reached out and scratched the tiny dog on her ear. It calmed her some, and Dylan set her in one of the big chairs in the room. Zev shut the door on her as she started circling for a comfortable spot.

As Zev shut the door, he noticed that Lavanya was now pacing in a tight pattern. She smiled at him. It warmed him from the inside out. But why would she smile at him? He looked around to see what about all this destruction might make her smile. There was nothing.

"Hilde, bring me my bag!" Helgaleena shouted, and the young girl jumped to action and came to the old woman's side. "Lavanya, what happened to my granddaughter?"

Lavanya backed into Zev's arms, and he felt her settle as he wrapped his arms around her.

"A zombie attacked her," Hilde and Joseph hissed.

Helgaleena organized her supplies, laying out little packets of dried herbs and the mortar and pestle. "Did you destroy it?"

"Yes," Lavanya said.

"We've burned the heart," Dylan added. "But we still need to burn the body."

Lavanya pulled free of Zev and knelt by the edge of the bed. "I can feel her, Helgaleena. She's strong, and she'll be okay. Won't she?"

"You better hope so." She ripped a thin, white cloth down the middle and set it aside. "Hilde, get me some clean water." Then she turned back to Lavanya. "It's only luck that I was here tonight to tend her. You need to take better care of those around you, Lavanya."

"I—" Lavanya pulled away from the bed.

"First, Giselle is attacked. Now my granddaughter is attacked in your room. In your castle!"

"Yes, Helgaleena, and we were attacked after leaving your house today. I told you it was serious then, but you couldn't help me. Could you? You wouldn't ask another question or help me

219

interpret the vague answers from the rune reading. Now we're both paying."

"Ladies!" Zev stepped between them. "Focus. Helgaleena, you take care of Chloe. Dylan see to it that a room is ready for her when she can be moved. I'm sure she won't want to wake up to this messy memory."

Helgaleena nodded and ripped another piece of the cloth with white-knuckled hands.

Zev looked around the room. "You—" he said, pointing to Helgaleena's nephew, "—will help Dylan dispose of the body." He held up his hand to stop Dylan from commenting. Take it out Lavanya's escape route and burn it." He caught Hilde as she returned with the bowl of water. "You stay here and clean up this mess as best you can and help your grandmother."

"Yes, sir." Hilde put the bowl down and began picking up broken glass.

"Lavanya, Zev, you too have a castle full of guests waiting for you." Dylan reminded them. "The vampires will have heard the gunshots, so you can be sure they're all down there gossiping. Did you shoot Zev, did he shoot you? And so on. You need to decide what you want to tell them."

CHAPTER TWENTY FOUR

And Her Little Dog, Too

"All right. You're right, Dylan." Lavanya rolled her shoulders and tried to focus. She needed to return to her guests, but as she stepped away from Zev's embrace, she felt a cold breeze on her legs. Her dress was ripped at the seams on both sides all the way to her hips, and splotches of black zombie rot and flesh had mixed with Chloe's burgundy-hued blood to cover the scales of the beautiful, sleek dragon. Now it truly stood for the Dracul, as Tru had pointed out.

"Dylan, can you…?" She held out the sides of the dress, now flapping unflatteringly like a snake sheading its dried skin. Dylan got the hint.

"I'm on it." He picked his way through the debris to her dressing room. "I could use a change of clothes, too. I'll see what's still wearable in here." As he disappeared into the dressing room, Lavanya turned her attention to Zev.

"I'll go down there and confront everyone. Helgaleena's right about one thing. I'm responsible for the people under this roof, and I want them warned and on guard. I don't want anyone else hurt."

"I'm right behind you, honey!" Dylan, wearing a clean, vintage Rolling Stones t-shirt and jeans, came out of the dressing area with her travel bag of toiletries, creamy white coat dress, and Buttercup's matching jacket draped over his arm. He stopped to look over Zev.

"What?" Zev glanced down at his own clothes, which were still clean and presentable.

"I assume you can take care of coordinating your own wardrobe, since you didn't need my help earlier." Zev ran his hand over the gray leather of his jacket sleeves, changing them to a buttery tan color. Dylan looked at the clothes he'd picked. "That'll do."

Lavanya led the way into Zev's suite. By the time they got into the room and closed the door, Zev's clothes were all changed to complement Lavanya's. All the gray was now light tan, and the black t-shirt had turned into a caramel color to coordinate with her winter white jacket dress.

"Can you teach me to do that?" Dylan asked.

"Sorry, you kinda have to be born with it. But trust me, you don't want it. Everything comes with a price." Zev shrugged.

"That's always the way, isn't it?" Dylan sighed.

Zev moved to the big chair, picked up Buttercup, and then sat down with her in his lap. Lavanya noticed the look of relief as he sat down. His injured leg must be hurting more than he let on.

Dylan threw the doggie jacket with matching collar and hat to Zev. "Since she loves you, she'll let you dress her. Put this on her." Then he pushed Lavanya toward the bathroom.

"Why on earth do we need to dress the dog?" Zev asked.

"And why did you pick out white for me to wear?" Lavanya asked. "I never wear white. It's such a..." she searched for the right word. "Virginal color?" Lavanya sputtered.

Zev laughed, which was so irritating. Just like a guy.

"You said it. Not me." He held up the tiny doggie jacket as if it were Barbie doll clothes and he'd been caught playing house.

"You're going to go down there and tell them that you just killed a zombie," Dylan said. "You've only been gone for about an hour and a half. Whoever sent that zombie thinks you're dead right now. They're ready to celebrate. When you show up, fresh as a daisy, crisp and clean, holding your little dog, it'll throw them off. They'll be furious, and my hope is that their anger forces them to make a mistake. I want you two—" he motioned to Zev to get started with Buttercup's dress, "—*three* to piss them off with your calm, in-your-face attitude."

"Nice." Zev bowed his head to Dylan.

"Warfare is not always about who has the biggest weapons, although when it's needed, I have a big weapon." Dylan smiled and for just a moment Lavanya saw the killer behind the stylish mask.

"Dylan!" Lavanya rolled her eyes and grabbed the clothes he'd hung on the bathroom door. "Help me get ready."

"Good luck with Buttercup—she doesn't really like to wear clothes." Dylan laughed and followed Lavanya into the bath room.

"Great." Zev sighed and shifted Buttercup on his lap. She raised her head briefly, then sniffed his injured leg and moved slightly to place her head on his other leg. "Yeah, I know it's not pretty, but at least it's getting better. Now let's get this thing on you."

He unbuttoned the small straps and held it up to look at it, then set it on Buttercup's back to try to figure out how to place it.

"Arf!" The little dog voiced her opposition to the clothing. Then she sneezed and quickly turned around in his lap, finding another spot farther under his arm to curl up. He reached under the little dog and pulled her out from her hiding spot.

"Arr roof," she warned.

"Grrrraaawr," Zev replied, making sure she saw his sharp teeth.

"Yelp." Buttercup dropped her head. She tucked her tail between her legs and shook.

"I'm sorry." He scratched behind the little dog's ears. "Listen, I'm not happy about it either, but you're part of the show, too, so you have to get dressed."

Zev pulled the hood over her tiny head and hooked the strap under her chest. Her ears flattened and she shivered and wobbled on his legs like she couldn't walk correctly with the jacket on. The beret that strapped under her snout was over the top, and Zev felt bad about putting it on her. Finally, the heavy collar.

"Oh, hell no, are these real diamonds?" He asked Buttercup as if she could answer. She just sneezed again and dislodged her hat.

Lavanya was ready to face her guests, but as she opened the door, she heard Zev talking. Who could he be visiting with?

"I feel your pain, little one," he said. "I know what it's like to want to be free of these clothes and..." he picked up Buttercup's diamond-studded tag, "chains."

Lavanya stepped back into the bathroom, closed the door, and leaned her head against it. For a little while she'd forgotten that Zev was here, helping her, because of a debt he owed her father. Not, she reminded herself, because he cared for her.

"Uh-oh," Dylan saw her reaction. "Did Buttercup bite him? I never should have asked him to dress her; you know what a little bitch she can be." Dylan set the makeup case down and moved toward the door. But Lavanya blocked him.

"No, it looks like Buttercup is dressed. I just…"

"What?"

"I just remembered that he's here only because he owes my father some debt. He's here to gain his freedom."

"Well, he seems to be doing a good job. When your father gets back, tell him to release him from this debt. Problem solved." Dylan returned to packing up his tools. "Wait." His hands slowed as he put the last of the makeup brushes away. "You think he'll leave as soon as this is over. That's what has you worried?"

"I didn't say I was *worried*."

He backed into the vanity and folded his arms across his chest. "Well, I wondered. You both seem casual about everything, but I know you're not a love 'em and leave 'em kinda gal. So, I'm guessing that what I interrupted at the door to your suite wasn't your only tango?"

"Nope." Lavanya studied her reflection in the mirror for any flaws and then rubbed her lips together and pouted toward the mirror to check if the lipstick was on properly.

"You naughty girl!" Dylan slapped her ass, shocking her into standing straighter. "When did you find time?"

"Dylan?" This…thing she had with Zev, it wasn't a laughing matter. At least not to her.

"Sweetie, you sound sad. Is your heart already gone?" Dylan asked, all humor fading from his voice.

"Oh, Dylan," Lavanya whispered. "I think it is." She rested her hands on the counter and sighed.

"It sounds to me like you've already been dealt your hand; now all you can do is play your cards and hope you have a pair of aces." Dylan looked at her for a moment. "Do you trust him, or does he make you crazy with doubt?"

"Yes. To both. He's dangerous. I know I shouldn't trust him, but I do."

Dylan started to pack again. "Well, you could tell your father never to release him. Then he'd stay as long as you want."

"I can't believe you'd even suggest something like that! I'd never do that to him."

The door to the bathroom swung open and banged against the marble tub. Zev stood there looking exactly like what he was—a beast; part animal and part man. His eyes had gone from hazel to dark brown, and the only thing to soften his look was poor little Buttercup tucked under his arm, shivering and miserable in her cream-colored coat and diamond-studded collar.

Dylan picked up her toiletries bag and started through the door. "Well, I knew you'd never do that, but I thought 'Mr. Eavesdropper' might want to hear it, too. Come here, little lady." He scooped up Buttercup. Lavanya and Zev remained frozen in place.

"Close your mouths, you'll catch flies," he said. "You have five minutes to get all the lovey-dovey stuff out of the way. Then you have to go downstairs, gather your guests, and get this talk out of the way before dawn." He made a show of checking his watch. "Ready. Set. Go!" He pushed Zev in Lavanya's direction, then left the bathroom with Buttercup.

"What's wrong with you?" Lavanya asked, turning back to the mirror and pretending to check her lipstick for the second time. Just as before, the deep red matte color was applied perfectly.

"Well, I heard you're not a casual lover." Zev sauntered over and leaned against the shower wall. "That surprised me. I figured from your reaction in the cave, you'd jump any man."

"You…" Lavanya turned and raised her hand to strike him, but Zev caught it just as she was inches from making contact with his face. His smile at catching her made her even more furious. He tugged on her arm pulling her closer and she allowed herself to be pulled into his body. When she was tucked up against him and his smile was triumphant, she kneed him in the balls.

"Oomph." He exhaled and released her so he could double over.

"How dare you talk to me like that!" Her eyes blazed red and her hands shook with rage.

"Lavanya, I was…*whew, whew*…kidding." He stood a little straighter. "Yes, I want my freedom from your father, but that has nothing to do with how I feel about you. He forced me here to protect you, but now it's personal. I…we—the Rakshasa and I—want to protect you for ourselves. We don't normally agree on much, and I just do my best to keep it fed and hidden away. But in this, we're in total agreement. Which terrifies me." Zev managed to pull himself straighter.

225

"Zev." Lavanya opened that part of her that could feel a person's true self and what they wanted in life. She waited for answers. Nothing. He was a closed book. Her gift was useless on him. So she looked into his eyes.

When their eyes met, her body took two steps toward him without her permission. His arms opened for her. She'd never felt this terrible need for anyone else. She'd had lovers, but nothing had prepared her for this. Dylan was right: it was too late, she just had to go all in and pray she had a winning hand.

"Whatever happens, I'll talk to my father about releasing you." She snuggled into his embrace and felt him wince when she made contact with his lower body. "Oh, and I'm sorry about the knee."

"Don't worry about your father right now; we have other vampires to burn. Hahaha." He looked down at her face. "Just kidding, and don't worry about the knee. My fault. A wise man once told me not to underestimate you. I won't let it happen again." A knock sounded on the open bathroom door. "Ahh, speak of the wise ass now."

"Funny," Dylan said. "Lavanya, the troops are getting restless. I've got this handled up here. Chloe is conscious, but sleeping. She's got a good bump on the head and a lot of bruises and scratches, but she'll be fine. We'll move her downstairs as soon as Helgaleena lets us. We may need the day to get your rooms livable, though."

He raised his brow. "I'll go out on a limb and say that you two are okay with sharing this suite for *resting* until yours is clean."

"Yuck. I gotta share with her?" Zev whined, and Lavanya elbowed him in the gut.

"Thanks, Dylan," Lavanya embraced Dylan. "I don't know what I'd do without you."

"Don't you worry about me, honey." Dylan wiggled his eye brows and pretended he had a cigar in his mouth. "'I intend to live forever, or die trying.'"

"That's our cue. If he's quoting Groucho Marx, it's time to leave." Lavanya grabbed Buttercup from Dylan and fled with Zev close on her heels as Dylan laughed.

"What's your plan?" Zev asked as they left the suite. He tried not to notice, but he couldn't help loving the little bit of black lace garter that peeked out of the full skirt as it separated on the long strides Lavanya took to keep up with him. He had to fight not to walk faster just so he could see more of her thigh.

"I think Dylan's right. If they see us and know they've lost their best weapon, the zombie, they'll be furious." Lavanya adjusted Buttercup against her and fixed her beret. "Maybe they'll make a mistake. Plus, I want to warn my clients of the danger. I don't want anyone else hurt."

"Yeah, it'll rile them up. That might be an advantage for us, or it might make them more dangerous. A cornered animal and all."

"I know, but what else can I do?" Lavanya stopped at the top of the large staircase.

"Probably nothing," Zev agreed. "But after we put on this show, I'm going to slip outside. I want to walk the grounds and see if I can whip up a little protection spell. I don't like that the zombie seemed to have free rein in here. I assumed your father had this place magically warded to keep out everyone who wasn't invited."

"You're right! I didn't even think about that. Chloe's family has hidden this castle magically for centuries. Anyone crazy enough to make it this far into the mountains can't see the castle—all they see are storm clouds and mist. Plus, they should feel an overpowering fear that makes them turn away. Her family's magic has always kept us safe from all the tourists who think it would be fun to find Dracula's castle." She rolled her eyes. "If you'd like, I can ask Helgaleena to help you. She should know what's in place."

"No," Zev didn't want to involve the old witch. "She's busy with Chloe right now. I'll just check it out. If I need her help, then I'll ask." His grandmother had taught him that a witch's magic always comes at a price, and usually a life was the cost. Mostly animals were used in their sacrifices, but Zev didn't want to take from mother earth when he could simply ask her for help. He'd smelled dark magic on the old woman, and he didn't want to disturb it if he didn't have too. He held out his arm for her to take.

"Okay, I'll defer to you on that. I don't know much about magic." She adjusted her dress and took his arm for the walk down to the gathered guests.

CHAPTER TWENTY FIVE

Game On

Everyone quieted as Zev and Lavanya entered the parlor, and even Belle and Arthur stopped shuffling cards and set their drinks down. The servants abandoned their duties and backed to the edges of the room.

"Lavanya!" Tru moved too fast and shouted too loud for her greeting to seem casual. In the middle of her rush to get to Lavanya, she seemed to realize her slip and slowed down to human speed. "Have you two been having a private party?" She hugged Lavanya and whispered, "Sorry, lame cover, but I was worried. Why did you change your dress?"

"We were starting to wonder if you two were going to make it tonight." Arthur picked up his drink and the ice clinked in the glass, showcasing the quietness in the room.

"No hard feelings here, sweetie, I can appreciate the attraction of other activities." Belle looked Zev over like she was sizing him up for a new pair of chaps.

Arthur coughed. "No worries, sugar," Belle said. "I can appreciate another's prize stallion without wanting to ride it."

Zev grinned and Arthur rolled his eyes. Lavanya looked around the room to locate everyone.

"I have a few announcements to make before the evenings over," she said. "Where are Lauren and Phil? And Raz, I don't see Uki?"

"Lauren and Phil just won a game of cards and took a break to check on their servants," Belle answered. "They're probably back at their rooms."

"Uki was handling some business on the phone, problems with her territory or something," Raz said. "Would you like me to get her?"

"No, stay and relax." Lavanya didn't want anyone out of her sight until this was done. "Zev, could you find them and ask them to join us? I'd like to have everyone together for this."

"Of course. Have a drink with Tru, and I'll be right back." He handed her and Buttercup off to Tru and left.

Zev hadn't made it ten steps before he found Uki talking to Helgaleena. He tried to hear a bit of their conversation before interrupting them, but Uki stopped talking and turned to him, looking expectant.

"Uki, Helgaleena." He nodded to the women.

"Hello, Zev," Helgaleena answered.

"Uki, I'm a friend of Lavanya. I don't think we met the other evening. My name is Zev." Zev suddenly felt like a third wheel in the conversation. "I wasn't aware that you two knew each other. Lavanya told me that this was your first time to the castle."

"Yes, that's true. We just met." Uki said.

"Dylan and my nephew brought Chloe down to rest in the suite on this floor, and Uki was kind enough to ask about her." Helgaleena said.

"I'm glad she's doing better, Helgaleena," Zev said.

"I couldn't believe that another of Lavanya's servants has been injured this weekend. Really, what are the odds?" Uki added.

Zev turned his attention to Uki. "Uki, Lavanya has some announcements to make tonight. The rest of the group is waiting for you in the parlor. I'm on my way to get Lauren and Phil now."

"Okay." Uki hesitated and then nodded to him and Helgaleena.

"Good evening, Helgaleena." Zev waited until they both moved away before he continued toward the servant's rooms in search of Phil and Lauren. *Women and gossip*. Damn, he'd seen fire in Uki's eyes. She couldn't wait to tell her friend that another of Lavanya's servants was injured. *Huh*, he chuckled a little. *Wait till she finds out how she was injured*. What a night this was going to be.

Zev headed through the vamp dining area and into the servants quarters and the long hall of doors. Now, which room? He walked down the corridor and stopped at every room to listen. He'd heard Tru mention Lauren as a possible suspect, and he wanted to see what the two vampires were up to before he announced his arrival.

"...Dracula will die."

It was Phil's voice. Zev itched to bust the door open, but he wanted to be sure no one else was involved, so he decided to listen a little longer.

"No, you're not even in the right level to find him," Lauren yelled.

"I'm way ahead of you, Lauren. You'll never catch up with me. Whahahaha." Phil answered.

Zev was confused. They sounded like an old B movie. But he didn't want to wait any longer. He twisted the knob as slowly as possible and opened the door just enough so he could see inside.

"Ingrid, stop lollygagging and get in here with our drinks," Phil ordered.

"Sorry, it's not Ingrid, and I have nothing for you to drink." Zev pushed the door all the way open and filled the doorway with his wide shoulders. "Whatcha doin'?"

Lauren and Phil stood and jumped in front of the table they were sitting at. Both seemed desperate to block his view.

"What are you doing, busting into our rooms?" Phil took a step forward. Zev matched his step with two of his own. His eyes had begun to glow with energy from the demon within him. He was hungry, and these two would do fine.

"Stop it," Lauren said, grabbing Phil's arm. "We're playing a game." She pushed Phil to a chair and then moved to her own.

"We found out online that we both love video games, so we made a little wager for this weekend," she said. "What better game to play than *Castlevania* while we're here—" she held out her hands "—at the real Dracula's castle? But they're kids' games. We didn't think Lavanya would get the irony, so we've been sneaking away to play. We're busted. I'm sure she'll be pissed, and I'm sure the others will think we're crazy for playing these games, but I won't let ya'll get into a fight over something this stupid." She pushed her bright, pink-covered game across the table.

"I'd love to see Vlad's face if he found out you were trying to track and kill Dracula in a kid's video game." Zev laughed and leaned against the door. Who'd have guessed these two formally dressed vampires liked video games? Life was always full of surprises. "But it's not any of my business unless you're actually trying to track and kill him?"

"What?" Lauren asked with real confusion written all over her impeccably made-up face. Phil looked to Lauren for some kind of signal that she understood Zev and came up empty, too.

Zev moved to the table and picked up the game case and began reading all about the game. "I'm a WoW fan myself, but I may have to get one of these little games for traveling." Satisfied they hadn't been planning anyone's death, he went back to the door. "I need you to come down to the parlor with me. Lavanya has a few announcements to make, and she wants everyone together before she does it."

"All right. Let me just turn everything off and we can go." Lauren began cleaning up the table.

"*No!*" Phil grabbed the game player from Lauren. "Just push pause. I'm winning, and I don't want to start over." Zev would have thought Phil was being paranoid, except the serious look in Lauren's eyes told him that that was exactly what she'd been doing. She'd been losing and wanted a re-do.

"Hey, have you guys ever played World of Warcraft?" He could use some new teammates for a raiding party, and these two obviously took their gaming seriously. They both looked up with a deer-in-the-headlights expression.

"Come on, let's get back to the others," he said. "I'll get your email addresses from Lavanya after this weekend is over and fill you in."

Lauren adjusted the straps on her red silk dress and shrugged on the matching silk jacket. Phil seemed somber as he, too, put his suit jacket on and buttoned it up.

"This isn't over, Lauren," he said. "I was winning."

"Hush, Phil. Something's wrong."

"I didn't say that," Zev clarified.

"You didn't have to." Lauren studied Zev for a moment. "Look, I don't know you from Adam. But Lavanya seems to trust you, so that tells me her father has vouched for you. But I don't trust Vlad. Lavanya is my best friend's daughter. Even though we aren't close, I still feel the need to protect her, and some really weird things have been going on this weekend." Her eyebrows shot up as she looked at Zev. "Especially the wolf that attacked me. Wolves don't get that big *naturally*."

Zev knew his eyes were his human hazel color, and she'd never seen him do magic, but she knew something was up. He felt a new level of respect for her and would have to tell Lavanya that

Lauren really cared for her.

"Come on," he said again. "Let's get back to the others. Lavanya will fill you in."

Lavanya felt disheartened. The evening was winding down, she'd made her announcements, and she was no closer to knowing who wanted to hurt her or where Renfield was. The longer she was separated from her father and Renfield, the more adrift she felt.

Startled, she jumped when Tru said her name. She turned from staring into the fire and her worries to find that Tru and Naasir were the only guests left in the room.

"You're exhausted," Tru said, touching Lavanya's arm gently. "When we turn into slugs and go to ground, you need to rest. I know you don't have to sleep during the day like we do, but you need your strength." Lavanya thought her friend must be reluctant to leave her alone since Zev had gone outside to do his magic ward thingy.

"Yes, mother slug," Lavanya joked, even though she was tired and sleep sounded like just what she needed.

"I'm not joking," Tru said with a furrow in her brow.

"I know, and trust me, I know my limits. I'm exhausted." After all the buildup before the announcements, she'd expected something to happen. Maybe not a big showdown, but something. Everyone had been surprised about the attacks, but no one stood out as an obvious suspect, at least from what Zev and she had seen. Most of them seemed excited. Not much surprised immortals, and they seemed to enjoy the sensation. No one had tried to kill her again, so maybe it wasn't one of her guests, but someone working their magic from outside the castle. She hoped Zev would have more information about who was behind all this when he returned from his scouting.

She led Tru to the door of the parlor. "It's almost light; you should get to your rooms. I'll just check on Chloe and then go to bed. Zev will be back soon, I'm sure. Now scoot." She gave Tru a little shove.

"All right, but Jackie, and Naasir's servant, Alfred—" Tru turned toward Naasir. "I still can't believe you have a servant named Alfred. Do you have a bat cave, too?" She smiled.

"Of course not, and I've heard all the jokes." Naasir held up his arms in defeat. "But his name is Alfred."

"Anyhoo—they're available if you need them," Tru said. "Tell Dylan to call."

"Thanks, I'll tell him. Although knowing Dylan, he's already got everything under control. Now get going, or you'll fry. And I'll have to clean you off the stone floor."

"You're probably right. Goodnight, hon." Tru gave Lavanya a little peck on the cheek and moved off.

Lavanya watched Tru and Naasir move down the hall arm in arm. She hoped they'd spend some time in Miami, where Tru had a nice little cottage. Lavanya would miss her if she moved to Africa with Naasir after this weekend. One thing was for sure—they were really cute together, and he seemed good for her. At least one positive thing had come out of this trip. She'd never seen her friend so happy.

Buttercup tip-toed through the tall-to-her, but short-to-everything-else-except-maybe-a-snail, grass as she sniffed and checked out her surroundings. She was much happier since Zev had removed the jacket and hat. Zev chuckled at the little dog as she walked.

"I swear it looks like you're walking with chopsticks for legs." Finally she picked a spot, circled it five times, and did her business. Once done, she ran back to him and shivered.

"Come on, Buttercup, let's see who's out tonight." Zev took five steps and then he heard a whimper. Buttercup walked slowly, as if she were walking through cotton candy and each foot stuck to the ground. She went about two of his steps and whimpered again and shivered.

"What?" Zev asked. He walked back and the tiny dog put her dime-sized foot up on his leg and scratched at him.

"Oh…come on," Zev moaned. "You can't even walk around the castle?" Buttercup scratched at his leg again. Resigned, Zev bent and scooped up the little dog. "Are you really an animal?"

"Woof!" she answered—or was just happy that he got the message and agreed to carry her.

Zev adjusted her under his arm and walked east. In a few seconds, his hand burned where he touched Buttercup on her belly. He moved her to his other side and wiped the palm of his hands on his leather pants. Then he continued to walk toward the stables. Now his other hand itched.

"What did you get into, you little scamp?" Zev looked at Buttercup's belly in the light from the moon and the overhead lights at the stables. Nothing showed except soft, white fur and pink skin. Her little ribs stuck out as if she were malnourished, but he knew perfectly well that between Dylan and Lavanya, the dog was spoiled rotten. Hence the reason he was carrying her around outside.

Nothing was visible on her skin. He ground his fingers into his palms, and although he couldn't see anything, he could feel fine grains like sand between his fingers and covering his palms. He raised his hand to his nose, and the smell of burnt earth filled his sinuses. Zev licked his open palm and salt burnt his tongue, but what really sealed the deal was the taste of blood.

Witch.

He opened his connection to the earth. He could feel her strength flowing through his body. His night vision was better than a human's, and he used it to look at the ground where they had walked.

He'd started his tour tonight at the kitchen entrance. Lavanya had given him the job of walking Buttercup, and she had a patch of grass that was hers, so he'd taken her there first. All around the entrance, a witch had burnt the earth. Zev kicked the grass and leaves just a little, and as he did, a path emerged.

Someone had cut the magic wards that protected the castle from uninvited guests. Now he was up against a black witch and a necromancer. His money was on two people. One person could have both talents—it would be difficult, not impossible, but not probable, either. Which made everything even more difficult. Now he'd have to track two people. Two very talented and dangerous people.

They'd already pissed off the necromancer by killing their zombie. Might as well start pissing off the witch by putting a little motherly love back into the ground around the back entrance. Zev smiled down at little Buttercup.

"Let's finish our tour, little one, and then we'll seal up these wards." When he was done, nothing would be able to get in without his knowledge. "This'll be fun."

Lavanya hung around the parlor for a bit longer than necessary, watching the staff clean and put everything back in order. Her father loved order and control, but Lavanya felt anything but controlled without Renfield to anchor her. As she stood at the large balcony doors and looked out at the shadowy mountains, she realized how much strength and confidence Renfield and her father gave her.

The sun's rays had begun to light the sky even before it peeked over the horizon. By now, all the vampires would be tucked away from its heat and light. A cool breeze lifted her hair, and her skin bristled at the feel.

"Good day, Father, Renfield. Come home to me," she whispered. The sky sputtered, and a light drizzle began to fall.

"Oh, crap." She took a deep breath, wiped her eyes, and tried to batten down the magic path that allowed her to affect the weather. Now she understood why her father was so controlled. He had to be.

"Please let this happen only here at the castle." The light drizzle turned to mist and then fizzled out as she focused on her breathing, then controlling her emotions. Now more settled, she turned away from the balcony. The parlor was all put back into place and clean.

Hilde seemed to be waiting for her.

"Mistress," she said. "Can I get you anything before you retire? Do you need to feed, ma'am?"

"Thank you, Hilde. I'm fine for now. Tell me, how's Chloe doing?"

"She's sleeping, Mistress. Gram Helgaleena says she'll be okay in a few days. Good-night."

She didn't want Hilde to go yet. What might make her feel more normal and not so adrift? *Routine.*

"Hilde, will you have someone bring me any household reports and my evening absinthe?" Lavanya felt better just thinking about the mundane activities. "I want to check on Chloe, so you can have them delivered to my adjoining suite. The one Zev is occupying." She'd dallied on the balcony to delay a confrontation with Helgaleena for as long as possible. She just wasn't feeling up to hearing of her failures again. But Helgaleena had been right; the people under this roof were her responsibility.

Hilde grinned hugely and nodded her approval. "Yes, Mistress. Right away."

Great. Now the entire household would know where she'd be sleeping today. Little gossips.

Zev and Buttercup had walked the full perimeter of the castle to see if the kitchen was the only entrance compromised by witchcraft or if the warding had other breaks. The front entrance was without a magical ward altogether, which surprised him until he realized that Vlad had other safeguards in effect there. When Buttercup yapped at the grand entrance, he'd thought only that she wanted to get inside, but he opened the door for her to enter, and she didn't go in. As he looked around, he noticed the small gargoyles positioned over the columns. They were subtle and appeared to be made of stone to match the large columns, but he could feel them reading his thoughts.

"You little bastards. Quit that!" Zev squinted up at them, and his mind relaxed when the little demons stopped probing his thoughts. They were perhaps twelve inches tall, but they crouched and their wings were tucked, so it was hard to tell. They looked slightly different. One had three larger horns spread across the head, the other had a row of bumps that formed a V above the eyes and small horns closer to where a human's ears would be. Neither of the small figures moved a muscle. But the Rakshasa demon inside him recognized the small terrors.

Very smart, Vlad. Let everyone enter and yet post sentries that can recognize evil in any form. Zev had never seen a real gargoyle, mainly because he never went into large cities. He wanted to see one move, so he found a long stick, climbed up on the pedestal of the column, and poked the ugly demon with the little horns on its head. The poor guy toppled over and fell to the ground. If it really had been made of stone, it would have broken. It didn't.

Buttercup barked furiously. Zev did his best to ignore her as he touched the rough scales of the gargoyle's arm. It looked like carved stone, but it felt tough and smooth, like crocodile skin. The image of a dragon popped into Zev's head. *This is what they would feel like*, he thought. He pushed a little and the thing rocked back and forth. It was small, but its claws looked deadly. It felt as cold as the stone Zev knelt on, and it seemed to be in some sort of deep sleep.

"Damn." If his blood had helped Lavanya fight off the Sleeping Beauty charm, maybe it'd work for these little guys, too.

Zev rubbed his finger across the rough slate stone of the entryway, then squeezed the scrape until a large drop of blood hung on his fingertip. He let the blood drop fall into the gargoyle's mouth. Zev was rewarded with a hiss from the one still on its perch above the entrance. It was the smaller of the two, but the response shocked him because he'd assumed the one he'd given his blood to would be the one to awaken.

"Hissss!" The ugly little demon jumped to its feet and spread its wings, which had to be twice the size of its body, reminding him of a bat. Puffs of steam escaped from its mouth like a tea kettle ready to shriek. Distraught, the gargoyle took flight and landed in a protective stance in front of its partner. Buttercup charged, and it snapped its wings, trying to hit the little dog. She snarled right back at the little guy and almost got a piece of its long, horned tail as he wrapped it around his body. Zev picked up Buttercup, but she struggled to get down and take on the gargoyle.

"At, at, at little brother," Zev scolded, shaking his finger at the gargoyle. "She's off limits. Understand?" Zev let his eyes go black and the Rakshasa looked out at the minor demon. The gargoyle opened its wings grabbed its partner and flew them both back to their perch above the entrance. Then the little demon hissed and roared back at Buttercup.

"Can you wake your brother so I can speak with both of you?"

"We are sisters, you cat-faced goblin." She stretched on her perch, fanning her wings out along her sides. "I am Usha, and that is Lilitu." She licked her lips with a blue, split tongue. "Thank you for waking us. Lilitu say you taste good, Rakshasa. May I have some?" Her claws scratched the stone of the column as she pranced in eagerness.

"I think not."

"Give me just a little taste to be fair." Her split tongue slithered out as she hissed.

"Usha, meaning the dawn, and sister of night." Zev pointed to the still sleeping gargoyle.

"Yes, that is our name and our meaning. Rakshasa, can I have taste?"

"Come down and take one drop to make it equal." Usha's eyes widened and her tongue shot from her mouth in excitement. Zev held his hand over his cut finger. "Just one drop."

"Yes, yes. Just a drop," said the creature. Zev squeezed his finger and as a drop formed on the tip, the little beast took flight. Zev just had time to put his hand up in the air before the gargoyle's mouth latched onto his finger.

"Just a drop!" Zev roared as the gargoyle dug in its teeth.

"What have you done to our Master, Rakshasa?" The little monster raged with her teeth still in his skin. "I have been asleep too long, and I can no longer feel him."

She'd probably read enough of his mind to know that he wanted Vlad dead, and from there she'd assumed he'd had something to do with their link being cut. Zev dropped Buttercup to the ground as gently as he could with an irate gargoyle biting his finger.

"It's true. I want him returned to the earth. But I'm tied to him in service, just as you two are. I've done nothing to harm him." He felt her in his mind again, and he let her see that truth. Then he shut her out. He couldn't blame the demon for trying, but he didn't want her rummaging around in his brain.

He also couldn't let her keep biting him, so he let his Rakshasa come out to play. He focused the change as best he could. He feared letting the demon have control, so he forced only his hands to change. His demon form had claws, very big claws.

"Hiss," she complained and let go of the hardened claw. Once on her perch again, she licked his blood from her lip.

"Look, you little shit—I applaud your tenacity, but don't try that again," Zev said, his eyes as dark as a black magic hollyhock and his hands now clawed to matched the gargoyles' hands in shape, but five times as large.

"We have the same Master, and you did not harm him. Why do you try to hide from me that which you covet?"

"What?" Zev shook his hand, which melted back into his human form. The Rakshasa was hungry, and forcing it back under his skin was increasingly difficult.

"We are sworn to protect this above all else—that which he will never give, his scion." The little bitch hissed at Buttercup, digging its nails into the column as she barked. "You want his offspring more than you want the death of our Master."

"Thanks for the news flash, but my dick has been telling me the same thing for days." Zev scooped up Buttercup "Enough!"

He was tired of dealing with the little gargoyle. "Will you be able to wake your sister?"

"Yes, we are both aware now, although she sleeps."

"Isn't one of you supposed to be awake at all times?"

"Yes, we guard this house for our master, but I cannot feel him anymore. Is he still here in this time?"

"We think so, but his connection to everyone has been broken and his servant Renfield is missing. Any ideas who slipped you a mickey?"

"A mickey?"

"Poison. A potion. Something to make you sleep."

"Ah, no. Chef did not feed us, and we were hungry. Lilitu is very lazy. She was to hunt for us a couple of nights ago, I think." The little thing scratched its bumpy head with its claw, which sounded like metal scraping over gravel. "She found a dead rabbit. It not taste good."

The creature spit over its winged shoulder. "Then I could not stay awake in the day, and she must never have woken for the night. You will find the one who did this and give Usha and Lilitu a piece."

The gargoyle hissed. "I will have its flesh."

Lavanya knocked lightly on the suite of rooms where Dylan had put Chloe and Helgaleena for the day. She saw the sun through the stained glass windows above the main entrance. It had just peeked through the mountains. She wondered if Renfield could see it, too. The thought made her sad, but she tried to rein in her emotions. It was getting harder to pull herself together. After she checked on Chloe, she'd get a few hours rest before she went out to search for Renfield. Lavanya started to knock on the door again when it opened.

"Lavanya." Helgaleena looked tired in a blue robe that was way too long to be hers. Her white hair flowed down around her bowed shoulders.

"I wanted to check on you both. Can I come in?"

"She's sleeping now." Helgaleena kept her hand on the door and didn't move back.

"I won't wake her, but I need to see that she's okay, Leena." Lavanya pushed through the door, exasperated by the old woman's small displays of power.

"I don't think it's a good time."

"And I didn't ask your opinion." Lavanya marched through the large outer sitting area to the bedroom where Chloe was sleeping. She stopped a few feet from the large, canopied bed. Chloe looked so fragile. She was pale, and a light sheen of sweat had broken out on her forehead.

"Is she feverish?"

"Yes, but just a slight rise. Nothing life-threatening."

"I'm so glad she's all right." Lavanya tip-toed to the side of the bed and sat on the edge so she could feel Chloe's brow and make sure her temperature wasn't too high.

"Yes, I'm sure you are. We wouldn't want you to lose your blood cow." Helgaleena spoke in a hushed tone, almost as if she thought that Lavanya wouldn't hear, but her fists were clenched so tight that her knuckles were white.

"Excuse me!" Lavanya's anger stirred as she confronted her sister.

"Where were you? Why weren't you there?" Helgaleena's fury filled the room and brought a cold draft that ruffled Lavanya's hair and turned her breath to vapor. "If you had been there, she never would have been hurt!"

"Don't you think I wish I'd been there to protect Chloe and Dylan?" The sky rumbled as Lavanya rose from the bed in a slow and deliberate move, her own anger mounting with every step she took toward Helgaleena. "They are my *family*. I would never want them harmed."

Helgaleena charged toward Lavanya like a train, but then fell to her knees and held her chest as if she'd been struck. "Aaugh," she groaned.

"Leena? What's happened?" Lavanya reached to pull Helgaleena up. "Are you all right?"

"Leave me!" Helgaleena pushed away Lavanya's hands. Then she stood and, one hand still pressing on her sternum, stumbled toward the bench at the end of the bed. She sat hard—fell—onto the seat.

"Helgaleena, what can I do to help you?" Lavanya said.

"I don't need yer help. I'm just an old woman. There's nothing you can do to change that." Helgaleena clutched the bedpost and leaned her head against it. "Leave us alone. Chloe needs to heal. We'll see you tomorrow night."

"Helga—"

"Just go!"

Lavanya hadn't thought it would be possible to feel worse, but she did.

Zev had agreed to bring the gargoyles a piece of the person who'd poisoned them if he could. The little demons made him nervous. He'd have to remember to call Inez and ask about them. She'd know more about what they were capable of doing. He wasn't sure, but he thought gargoyles could change size at will. Which meant that those tiny, ugly-in-a-cute-sort-of-way demons could grow as big as a bus whenever they wanted if somebody wasn't controlling them. Which he didn't really want to see.

For now he needed to concentrate on the job at hand—fixing the ward around the servants entrance. So with Buttercup sitting on the stone entrance to the kitchen, Zev focused his attention on that task. He'd just finished digging up and turning over the burnt and cursed soil around the door to the kitchen. The light drizzle that had started halfway through his work had rinsed away all the salt and prepared the ground for the next part—casting.

Zev sat on the cold, fresh earth and gathered his strength for the protection spell. He began by forming a circle in his mind— first, blue for healing and then an outer circle of gold light for protection. He spent time making sure that the circles were solid and three-dimensional, like a baseball or the earth itself.

He could feel the earth's power and energy coursing through his body, and all he needed now was to direct it and invoke the spirits' help. The ritual would take time, but after he was done the ground would be clean and this entrance would be protected again.

CHAPTER TWENTY SIX

The Master Is Awakening

Lavanya leaned against the wall outside Helgaleena's suite and closed her eyes. She didn't need much air to live, but sometimes the rhythm of deep breathing helped calm her. Two counts in through her mouth—she put her hand on her chest to feel it rise and fall—and two counts out through her mouth. Two counts in and...

"Mistress?"

The young man's voice woke Lavanya from her short, meditative exercise. She opened her eyes to see the boy she'd fed from earlier. "Stephen?"

"Mistress, are you okay?"

"Yes, I'm fine. Just tired." The boy seemed sick despite the smile on his face, as if he wanted to lean against the wall, too. "Stephen, how are you? You don't look well." Lavanya glanced around to see if anyone else was with him; she thought he shouldn't be off by himself. He was paler than he had been, and he had dark circles under his eyes.

"I'm good, Mistress, can I get you anything?"

"Where are you going?"

"I'm returning to Miss Uki and Miss Raz, Mistress." He swayed a little.

"I think you've spent enough time with them. Why don't you go to the kitchen and get something to eat."

"I've just come from the kitchen, Mistress, and I drank three glasses of orange juice and ate a healthy meal." He looked suddenly scared. "Please let me return to them for the day. They've both already fed and we shall just rest together."

Rest, my ass.

"Please, Mistress," the young man pleaded.

"Okay. For today. Please let them know that I will want to talk to them tomorrow evening. They need to take better care of the gifts I've allowed them to partake of if they plan on keeping in my

243

good graces." The boy looked relieved.

"Thank you, Mistress."

"I know you want to go with them when they leave, Stephen, but I won't allow it if they can't take better care of you."

"I'm very happy. They are very good to me. Thank you for permitting me to return." He shuddered, making Lavanya question her decision. But before she could change her mind, he hurried off.

She definitely would have a talk with the ladies about his care.

Lavanya dragged her body upstairs. The only things keeping her awake were the promise of her absinthe cocktail and the comfort of Zev's arms. "Yum," she whispered at the thought of Zev, picking up her pace.

She opened the door to Zev's suite and was happy to see that Dylan had moved a few of her things into the space for the night. Her silk rob was draped over the bed and a few of her cosmetics littered the vanity in the bath. Lavanya pulled open the joining door to her suite and surveyed the messy room.

"Doll, what are you doing in here?" Dylan came out of her dressing area, the end of a rolled-up rug hunched over his shoulder. Helgaleena's nephew held up the other end.

"I was just checking to see how you were doing."

"Once this is out of here," he patted the fat rug that looked like a zombie-stuffed burrito, "I'll be better. When you wake up, this should all be cleaned up."

Lavanya hurried to open the door of her suite for them. "Thanks Dylan, Joseph."

"Get some rest."

"Oh, I plan on it." Lavanya shut the door behind them and returned to Zev's room. Someone had started the fire, and she sank down on the big loveseat to get warm. The tray holding her absinthe cocktail was on the low table in front of the sofa, so she kicked off her satin heels and made her drink while the fire warmed and relaxed her. When the drink was thick and frothy green, she took a gulp that burned all the way down to her stomach and unwound her thoughts.

She closed her eyes for a moment, feeling herself sink into the cushiony feather pillows and letting the crackle of the fire settle her nerves. It seemed like a lifetime ago that this terrible night had started. Exhaling the negative energy, she opened her eyes, set the glass down, and picked up the reports. *Here's hoping for mundane problems, like not having enough Wiser's whiskey for Arthur.* Lavanya smiled at the thought of his funny, kind eyes. He and Belle had lingered in the parlor to offer their support. She was happy to see them already becoming the united force she had envisioned for the couple.

Really, all the couples seemed unified and happy with each other, which was great for business, but didn't help her with the problem at hand. Could one or more of her guests be trying to kill her? And if not them, then who? Anxious again and disgusted with herself for feeling that way, Lavanya went back to her reports, hoping that something would give her a clue as to who her enemy was.

Nothing. Lavanya slapped the reports down on the table after going over them twice. The big news was that everyone missed her head chef, and the staff was scrambling to make up for his loss and keep the kitchen going as expected. Of course, she knew where he was—on ice in the freezer. Lavanya still held out hope that if they found the necromancer, Zev could somehow wake up Victor.

Lavanya stood and started to pace, but she was just too exhausted. Between entertaining her guests and all the adrenaline bursts of the night, she'd used more energy than she had. Her arms and legs felt like lead, and she needed some rest or she wouldn't be good for anything.

On her way to the bathroom, Lavanya glanced at the large clock. Nine in the morning and Zev hadn't returned. *Hold it together, girl.* Zev had told her it might take a while to find the problem and then redo the wards or whatever to make the house safe again.

Instead of worrying, she washed her face and stripped off her white dress. Dylan had brought in a beautiful silk-and-beaded, white, see-through gown, but it seemed too fake for the occasion, made up, like doll clothes. She already felt naked around Zev since she had bared her feelings for him earlier, and he already knew what she was and who her father was. It was a strange feeling, and she liked it.

She decided to skip the gown and black robe, opting to wear nothing at all. The smooth silkiness of the sheets felt wonderful against her bare skin, and the pillow cradled her head. She closed her eyes, and sleep pulled her in like a wave burying the sand.

Zev was at one with mother earth. She gave him the power he needed to guard this patch and make sure that nothing that would harm Lavanya entered the castle. Zev pushed the bubble of energy carrying the golden circle. He pictured it as bright as the sun and just as powerful.

> *"A spell of safety here I cast,*
> *A wand of might to hold us fast.*
> *A shield before us and behind,*
> *To right and left protection bind."*

Zev grabbed the bowl of spices he'd pilfered from the kitchen pantry—cinnamon, nutmeg, cloves, and ginger—and sprinkled the mixture around the area in a large circle.

> *"To us may no ill wight come nigh,*
> *But only She who's Rede I cry.*
> *So mote it be."*

He also included a healing circle of blue for Chloe.

> *"I'll health I do tell,*
> *Run with this circle,*
> *Chloe is free and well."*

Lavanya awoke to the sting of a mosquito bite on her neck. Those little bastards and the no-see-ums were almost like the plague here in Miami. She swatted at the irritant.

"Mistress, I…"

It all came rushing back to her. She wasn't in Miami, and the mountains of Wallachia don't have mosquitos. She opened her eyes.

Stephen stood over her with a butcher's knife at her throat. He'd nicked her skin, and she could feel the small drop of blood trailing down her neck. Normally Lavanya wouldn't have worried about being cut or stabbed, because she was nearly immortal and her wounds healed easily. But at this angle, and with that knife, the young man could decapitate her. She wasn't sure if anything or anyone—except maybe her father—could survive that type of mortal blow.

"Stephen, what are you doing?"

"I...don't want...to ...hurt you." He strained to say every word. His muscles were as taut as violin strings in his neck and arms. He vibrated with energy, enough to shake the bed.

"Buttt...."

Lavanya felt the blade push into her skin.

The damp, cold stone of Renfield's prison chamber seeped into his bones. He ached everywhere. Without Vlad's assistance, his body seemed to be aging impossibly fast.

The night was dark, and the air was filled with the smell of the smoldering fire and mold from the moist, stone walls and floor. Renfield was tucked as close to the small fire as possible, drifting in and out of sleep as his body quaked from the cold. He wrapped his arms tightly around himself as if he still wore the straight jacket from the long-gone asylum.

"Reiny, Reiny, you must wake. Where have you gone" The little voice jolted Renfield from his nightmares. He shook his head to quiet his imagination.

"Reiny, we need you."

"Usha, my darling. Is that you?"

"Yesss."

"I have missed you and your sister." Renfield sat up and slowly unwound his stiff arms and legs. He could have replied to the little demon in his thoughts, but he spoke out loud just to hear the sounds echoing off the quiet stone walls. "I'm so happy to have you back with me, but I must know if our Master and Mistress Lavanya are well?"

"A Rakshasa has awakened us from a deep spell. We have not seen Mistress Lavanya, but she is in his mind alive. Our Master has a message, Reiny, you must listen."

"I am listening."

"Rejoice! Our Master is awake. He will come soon. Build your fire hot, and a savior will come." The little gargoyle waited for a response and got none. *"Reiny..."*

"Usha…are you certain?" Doubt flooded Renfield's mind. "I cannot feel him."

"Oh yesss. The master is wakening."

"Usha," he coughed. "Usha, I need you to guard Mistress Lavanya until he can get here. Usha and Lilitu, I give you permission to leave your posts and take on your full power for this day and night to guard Lavanya from harm."

"Oh, yesss. You have made Usha happy, and we will not fail."

Renfield felt the gargoyle's excitement as she gathered her magic and rose to her full height of twelve feet with a wing span of twenty. Renfield shuddered as he recalled the sheer strength and power that the gargoyles possessed. In their full size, their claws could rip a human apart as quickly as Lavanya could tear through a tray of cinnamon rolls. A small part of him hoped to see one of the gargoyles find the person responsible for his abduction. A smile played on the edges of his heavily whiskered face as he forced his body into action. He gathered the remaining wood and threw it in the fireplace. Soon he'd be free, and his Master would make their enemies pay a heavy price for threatening them.

Dylan was exhausted by the time he and the boy staggered out of the ancient ruins of the servants wing. Who knew zombies could be so heavy or smelly? If he didn't get a clean breath of air soon, he'd have to vomit.

They dragged the corpse farther up into the mountains and out of easy sight of the guests or regular servants. When they got to a spot that was rocky enough to contain a fire, the two set about gathering kindling for their zombie conflagration. The blaze caught quickly and burned fast.

As he waited for the zombie to burn down to ash so he could be sure that the job was done, Dylan took in the sight of the castle.

"It looks so peaceful from up here, doesn't it?" Joseph asked as he noticed Dylan looking out over the landscape.

"Oh, yeah. The castle is beautiful with its red brick and gray chimney smoke billowing out. Look at the grand turrets on both sides, and its lovely how the smoke puffs out like the chimney stack of a train."

"I'm sorry, sir—I can't see that from here." The boy strained to look where Dylan was pointing. "I just see the mountain and the ruins of the old castle."

"Right down there. You have to see the tall side turret reaching to the sky on the back of the castle." Just then a huge gust of smoke rose from the turret. "See that gust of smoke from the chimney?" Dylan wondered where that room was. He couldn't be sure from where they stood, but he didn't remember ever climbing up that high in the castle.

"I'm sorry. I can't see anything like what you describe." The boy rubbed his head.

"Oh." Dylan remembered Lavanya telling him that the castle was magically invisible to most people, but because some of her blood ran through him, he was immune to the magic. "It's no big deal, kid, don't worry about it. I'll lead us back."

"Thank you, sir." Joseph visibly relaxed, and his hand fell away from where he'd been rubbing his temples.

He should get the kid back to Helgaleena. Dylan checked their zombie pyre. It was almost down to ashes.

"Sir, are you cold?" Joseph asked Dylan.

"No, why? Are you?"

"No, sir, but you're shuffling your feet, sir, as if you're cold. I was going to put another log on the fire for you."

Dylan looked down at his feet and sure enough, he was sort of bouncing on the balls of his feet as if he were getting ready to run the Boston marathon. *What the hell?* He hadn't recognized the feeling, but now that the boy had spoken, he really wanted to get back. Something was wrong. He could feel it.

"Throw the last of the gasoline on the fire and let's go." Dylan headed down the steep, rocky terrain even before the boy was done.

LYNNE STEVIE

CHAPTER TWENTY SEVEN

Calling Dibs

Lavanya pushed herself back, as far away from the knife as the bed would allow. In the process, the black sheet that had covered her slid down to her waist, revealing her breasts. Thank the gods, the boy was still a red-blooded male. When his eyes dropped to take in the sight, Lavanya moved vampire fast and caught his arm.

"Demon!" As the last of the spices fell from the bowl and completed his spell, something shoved Zev against the castle door. The black mist swirled and tightened on him.

"Ahh." Zev didn't struggle with the force holding him. "Soooo glad to have you back, Vlad." *Not.* But this was a thought he kept to himself.

"Lavanya!" Vlad screamed in his head and released him. Zev felt Vlad's fear and then his own joined it. He zeroed in on Lavanya and shifted from the kitchen entrance in a flash of electricity, only to reform in the suite she'd said they'd use tonight.

Lavanya's struggle with Stephen was harder than it should have been. He'd obviously been given a taste of a very powerful vampire, but his heart wasn't in the fight. She could see the sorrow in his eyes even as he tried to hurt her. She gained the upper hand by pinning the boy to the bed with one arm under his chin and the other squeezing the wrist of his knife hand. As the knife fell, Stephen whispered his thanks.

"Grrrraaawr."

Lavanya recognized the growl and turned her head to show Zev that she was all right. "Zev—"

An ear-splitting screech echoed outside her window a spilt second before the window smashed, shooting shards of stained glass, leading, and wooden fragments all around her. Lavanya screamed as something swooped in and jerked her up into the air—

something with huge clawed feet that easily held her around her waist. The sound of its wings beating was the only sound she heard. The creature set her down gently on her butt at the entrance to her suite. Once it released her, it moved in front of her and shielded her with its massive wing span.

"Usha will protect you, Mistress Lavanya," it said. "The human will be appetizer and Usha already know that Rakshasa taste good." Lavanya heard the gargoyle's long tongue tasting the air, and a huge drop of what she hoped was saliva fell from the beast's mouth.

"No! You will not harm them." Lavanya got to her feet. "Usha?"

"Yesss."

"Usha, who sent you here?"

"Reiny send me to protect Mistress." Lavanya couldn't see much around Usha, but occasionally she caught glimpses of Zev as he tried to get to her around Usha's large wings. His head was that of his demon—the wolf head with the panther-like canines and short snout.

"Reiny? Who's—?" Lavanya stopped, floored by the feel of her father's love surrounding her.

Lavanya, my child, please answer me. Are you well? Her father's voice staggered her with relief. She fell back against the door frame, her heart full with the sound of his voice.

"Father, I'm fine, but—" There was no time for joy, because as she peeked around Usha, she saw that Stephen had recovered and was stalking Zev with the knife raised. Of course, neither he nor Usha was paying attention to the human. They were both too fixated on each other.

Lavanya leapt at the young man. Using all her strength she shot into the air. She brushed the top of Usha's large gray wing and caught Stephen unaware, driving him into the ground. Stephen cut her leg, but Zev was unhurt. Both Usha and Zev were on them, pulling them apart, before she could think or even feel the pain. Zev held her while the gargoyle got the young man.

"Give her to me, Rakshasa! She is my ward. Usha cannot fail." Usha's smaller arms reached for Lavanya, while her clawed foot plastered the boy to the floor like an ant under a boot. Zev pushed Lavanya further behind him as Stephen's arms and legs flailed under the gargoyle's weight.

"She's mine!" Zev said. "Take the human and have a feast."

The gargoyle hissed at Zev.

"Know this, Usha—if you touch her again, I will make your sister an only child."

"Enough! Both of you, stop." Lavanya winced as she pulled away from Zev. Her leg would heal, but it still hurt like hell to be cut. Zev tried to cover her behind his large frame, but she wasn't going to let the two of them hurt each other.

"Usha, let the boy up," she said. "I don't want him hurt. But hold onto him so he can't harm anyone else."

"Are you sure, Mistress?" Usha's eyes drooped like a dog begging for table scraps. "Usha could take him away if you prefer not to see her eat?"

"Usha." Lavanya scolded as she stepped around Zev's Rakshasa form. Another wince caught the Rakshasa's attention. When he looked at her leg and back up to her face his eyes turned from demon black to Zev's beautiful hazel color.

"Hey, honey, you can come back now," she said. "Usha won't eat me." The scent of cardamom filled the air as Zev shrank and morphed into his human form. The change seemed slower than last time, but it was still magical.

Renfield felt buoyed by the knowledge that Usha was protecting Lavanya and that soon he would hear from his Master. He had thrown everything he had on the fire and it roared, filling the room with heat. He didn't save a single scrap of wood for later use. He had complete confidence that his Master would come soon.

"Renfield, my old friend, are you safe?"

Renfield dropped to his knees, "Master, Master. I am here. I'm waiting. Please tell me how I can serve you."

"It is I who needs to serve you, my friend. I can feel your hunger and your pain."

"Master, I fear a witch is involved. There was a powerful sleeping spell, and a necromancer. The Rakshasa—Zev—has come and—"

"Sleep, Renfield." Renfield eased down to his side on the stone floor and let the fire warm him as his master lulled him to sleep.

"All will be well, my faithful servant. Let me in now, and I will see what has happened. Rest assured, my friend, that those responsible for attacking you and my daughter will burn."

"Lavanya!" Zev produced a thick, red velvet robe out of the air and wrapped it around Lavanya as she leaned against the wall. Then he gently picked her up and placed her on the big chair across from the entrance and far away from Usha and her pleading captive.

"You've been cut." Zev carefully pulled the robe back from her legs to get a look at the deep cut. The skin was already stitching itself back together, and the blood had formed a nice scab. Although it wasn't pretty, it was healing rapidly.

"I'm fine." Lavanya looked at the wound. "See? It's already stopped bleeding, and in no time at all, you won't even know it was there."

"What were you thinking?" Zev covered her legs with the soft robe and placed his hands over hers in her lap. His big, rough hands swallowed her tiny, porcelain-like fingers, reminding him how small she was compared to him, even in human form.

"Well, I was thinking that he—" she pointed to the boy still struggling with Usha, "—was going to stab you, and I couldn't stand there and do nothing. "Oh…wait." Lavanya remembered hearing from her father just before jumping into the mess of gargoyles and demons. She closed her eyes.

"Lavanya?"

Lavanya raised a finger to Zev, signaling him to wait for a moment as she tried to concentrate on her father. *Father?*

"My child." Lavanya swayed in her seat as relief hit her.

"Father, where's Renfield? I…can't feel him." Lavanya laid her head on Zev's chest as a wave of worry hit her hard.

"He's safe, darling; I'm taking care of him. I'm more worried about you. I felt your fear. Open your eyes and let me see what you see."

"Father, I'm safe." Lavanya didn't open her eyes. She knew what he would see, and she was worried he wouldn't take it well.

"Open your eyes." Lavanya opened her eyes. Zev's worried hazel gaze is what she saw first. He pushed his hands through her

hair so he could catch her attention.

"Are you hurt anywhere else, Lavanya? Talk to me." Zev hands familiarly ran over her shoulders and down her arms, feeling for any other injuries. Behind Zev, Usha was tossing Stephen in the air for fun. His screams echoed off the stone walls.

Zev was thrown back and fell into Usha, knocking her and the boy to the floor.

"Vlad!" he shouted, righting himself quickly as his eyes turned black. He pushed against Vlad's control to get back to Lavanya, but he seemed to be walking against hurricane force winds.

"Father, stop this! He was only looking for injuries. I was cut earlier."

"I know what he was looking for. I don't like the way he was staring at you."

Lavanya wanted to distract her father from thinking about Zev.

"The boy was trying to kill me. He's been feeding my clients, Uki Akiyama and Raziya Afolayan. They must have sent him to kill me after we killed their zombie. Do you know them or why they would want to hurt us?"

As Zev pushed, Vlad's force gradually weakened enough that he could make it back to Lavanya. He smiled down at her, knowing she was in communication with her father.

"No, and I don't care why. But I want you to bring them to me. I'm too weak to leave my crypt now, but they will give me strength."

"But—" How was Lavanya supposed to get them to her father's resting place?

"Bring them to me. Put that Rakshasa to work."

"Yes, Father."

Lavanya pushed her father out of her mind and looked up to Zev. "We have a lot of work to do. Usha, stop throwing the boy around. I need to talk to him."

"Yes, Mistress." Usha dropped the boy on the floor in front of Lavanya. He lay still. All the fight had been tossed out of him, and he seemed resigned to lie there until he died.

"Stephen?" Lavanya knelt down by the young man and bit her wrist.

"No!" Zev said.

"Stay out of this."

"Fine." Zev threw up his arms and began pacing.

Usha's long tongue came out to sample the air. "May I have a taste, Mistress?" Her eyes were dark and glassy, like a deep, cold river at night.

"*No!*" Lavanya and Zev answered together.

"As you wish, Mistress. Usha only wanted to bond with you."

"Oh, I'm sorry, Usha, I—"

"*No!*" Zev roared and stepped in between the gargoyle and Lavanya. Usha rolled her eyes and fluttered to the busted-out windowsill to perch and watch the others.

"Okay, I wasn't planning to give Usha my blood."

"Good, but I don't want you feeding that puny human either."

"Don't be like that, Zev. We need him on our side." Still, Lavanya hesitated about giving the boy her wrist. "He did have a knife to my throat, but—"

Zev's howl cut off her words, and he leaped, tearing her away from Stephen and pushing her up against the stone wall. His hands moved over her body, while he rubbed his mouth and face against her throat.

"Zev, I..." Her mind wanted to tell him to stop this stupid show of male dominance and let her down, but her traitorous body responded by turning to Jell-O and melting against his. She grasped his waist with one hand and buried the other in his thick hair. Her body tingled with need as an excited sigh left her lips.

"Ahek-ahek." Usha made a noise that must have been a gargoyle cough. Whatever it was, it brought Lavanya back to reality.

"Thanks, Usha." Lavanya pushed against Zev's chest. "Watch the boy, Usha."

"Yesss, Mistress, but Usha like watching you and Rakshasa more."

"Usha..." Lavanya pushed at Zev. "Zev?" He answered with a soft purring that vibrated along her collarbone and did nothing to help her control the desire raging through her.

"Zev! Listen to me." When he finally looked at her, one eye was hazel, swirling with the earthy browns and greens that she loved, and the other eye was black.

"I need to feed the boy some of my blood to help him. He didn't want to hurt me, but someone has gotten to him and started to make him their servant. I..."

Zev smelled the air and then looked at her wrist. The wound had closed, but fresh blood from her bite still glistened on her skin. His mismatched eyes met hers, and while she watched, he brought her arm up to his mouth and licked the bite clean. His whole body shuddered, and his muscles tightened against her. His tongue swirled and tickled her skin. He seemed to take pleasure in tasting her, as if she were made of sweet butterscotch. The feel of his breath on her wet skin was delicious, and her core tightened at the sensations. Eyes closed, he continued to nibble at her skin long after he'd cleaned the blood off.

Lavanya cleared her throat. "Zev I..." Zev dug his hips into hers and the hard length of him seared her. She had to get control of the situation. "Enough," she pushed with all her strength and managed to make him step back. As she slid down the wall and settled on her feet, she watched Zev's eyes, both the color of black licorice.

"Rakshasa." She put her hands on his face to focus his eyes on hers. "I need Zev now. Please release him." She needed his calm and wisdom. Zev's head turned in her hands to growl at the human boy.

"Don't worry," she said. "Stephen won't hurt me."

"The Rakshasa not worried about this human *hurting* you, Mistress. He just don't want it to *touch* you." Usha chuckled.

Lavanya pulled Zev's head back to face her. "I will simply break the tie that this human has with another. I will not tie him to me in any way." Zev shook his head and both eyes were an understanding hazel when he looked up again. He released her immediately.

"I'm so sorry, Lavanya." He pulled away and ran his hand through his thick, brown hair. "I—It's—I can't control it. We've never wanted the same thing."

"Zev, it's okay. We can figure that out later. Right now I've got to help Stephen. He's been tied to another vampire, and they sent him here. He could have killed me, but he hesitated. I have to help him and then figure out a way to lead Raz and Uki to my father's crypt tonight."

Zev shook himself like a lion shaking out his mane. "Okay."

Lavanya went to where Stephen lay, bit into her arm again, and passed it in front of him. He greedily grabbed her and began to suckle at her wrist. Zev growled, but crossed to the far side of the room to give Lavanya space.

"Its okay, Stephen. Take of me so that I may be of help to you. My blood will give you strength and courage to serve your true mistress." The young man crawled into Lavanya's lap and sighed as he suckled at her wrist. "That's it. Calm yourself and enjoy the bounty I have to offer."

Lavanya stroked his head as a mother would a child. The boy was greedy. He was already accustomed to the taste of vampire blood and might be addicted. Lavanya let her head fall as a single tear fell. If he truly was addicted, the boy was lost. He would say or do anything to get more vampire blood.

"That's enough." Lavanya pulled her arm away and tilted his head up so he would have to look into her eyes. She used her most soothing voice.

"Now you're at peace," she said. "You don't have to hurt anyone. I would never ask you for such a service." The boy snuggled down and sighed.

"Stephen, who tried to make you their servant?"

"I am only yours."

"Of course, you are. Did Uki and Raz feed from you tonight?

"Yes, Mistress, they feed from me. They love me and want to take me with them. But I'm confused. I want to stay with you now. Please don't send me away."

"Don't worry about that now. Tell me, have you fed from anyone but me tonight?" The young man started crying.

"I just want my freedom. But she said you would never let me go." Trembling, he threw his arms around Lavanya's waist. "I didn't want to hurt you, Mistress. I just want a life of my own, off this mountain. I need to see something more of the world." His tremors vibrated through her. He sniffed her skin and then looked up at her.

"I have to kill you; the only way to freedom is to...kill you." A strange calm took over him and he stopped shaking. "I...still feel it, Mistress. The need, even with your blood coursing through me, I need to—"

Stephen pulled away and crawled toward the broken window as if he wanted to get away from her.

"Kill Lavanya...." He turned with a sharp piece of metal from the window and lunged, but his heart wasn't in it. Zev easily caught him and disarmed him. Stephen sagged in Zev's hold.

"You must kill me, Mistress. I fear I cannot control this compulsion."

"Shh, shh, I understand, Stephen. I'll take care of everything." Lavanya picked her way through the glass to caress his smooth face. "Don't worry. I'll see that you're free of this burden and that you find a way to see the world."

"Oh, thank you, Mistress, you are most forgiving. I do not deserve to live after attacking you."

"You've got that right." Zev chimed in. Lavanya silenced him with a look.

"I told her you were good. She accused you of keeping us as slaves. I tried to explain to her that we serve the Draculesti family by choice, and that it's a great honor."

Uki or Raz, or both, it had to be. Anger at their arrogance flared in her stomach. How could she have been fooled? And why?

"Stephen, do you know why Uki and Raz hate us?"

"They never said they hated you, Mistress." The boy shook his head. When he couldn't get his hands up far enough to rub his forehead, he settled on rubbing his head on Zev's forearm.

"What exactly did Uki and Raz say about my father?"

"It hurts." Stephen struggled to rub his head.

"I know, but I need you to answer me. What did Raz and Uki say about my family?"

"Aaugh!" The boy shrieked in pain. "The control he has over the vampires of the world. They mentioned that..." The boy shook and his head rocked against Zev's chest. Zev looked alarmed.

"Lavanya, it's getting harder to hold him," he said. "Unless you want me to hurt him, you better do something to calm him down."

Lavanya walked toward Stephen, humming a soothing melody. The boy looked up as soon as he heard her.

"Be calm. You feel no pain, and you will sleep until I wake you." She placed her hand over his eyes. The boy slumped in Zev's arms. Lavanya smiled at him.

"You can put him on the bed."

Zev's eyebrows rose. "Hmm, that seemed… nice. I've never seen your father do that."

"It's subtle. He's not into subtle. I learned it because he used it on me when I was being unruly as a child."

The door creaked open and Dylan stuck his head in from the adjoining room with a hand over his eyes.

"Lavanya," he whispered. "I don't even want to know what you're doing in here, but its freezing. I can feel the breeze through the door. Close the windows."

"Dylan."

"Oh, and I need to talk to you as soon as you are, you know, free."

"Dylan, you can open your eyes. We're decent." Lavanya brushed the whimpering boy's hair as Zev laid him on the bed.

"Good, because…" Dylan stopped halfway through the door and looked around the room at the glass and broken window frame that littered the floor. Then his eyes widened and his mouth fell open as he took in the sight of Usha perched on the windowsill.

"Dylan, I can explain." Lavanya worried that the sight of a gargoyle would be too much even for Dylan to take. Dylan barely acknowledged her on his way to the window where Usha sat.

"Dylan, don't get too close," Lavanya warned

"Usha, is that you?" Dylan crooned.

"You know the gargoyle?" Lavanya asked.

"Of course."

"Yesss, Dylan, it is Usha, and the Usha is mad at Dylan for not feeding her." Usha huffed and turned her head away from Dylan.

"Honey, I'm sorry, but with everything going on, I forgot that I'm up to bat if Renfield's busy. Is your sister okay?" Dylan reached up to scratch the big gargoyle's head but couldn't reach her. "How did you get so…big? I thought only Renfield could release your magic."

Usha bent down so Dylan could scratch behind her horns, obviously forgiving him for not feeding her.

"Renfield gave Usha permission so she could guard Mistress Lavanya. Usha so happy to stretch." The gargoyle raised herself up and opened her wings. They were the dark gray of wet concrete, and the skin was so thin that you could see her skeletal structure beneath it. To open them up all the way, she had to turn sideways so that one wing was outside and one inside. Zev and Dylan stepped back to give Usha room.

Lavanya gave Dylan a stern look. "All right. Later we'll discuss why no one introduced *us* before, but right now we have other things to deal with. Usha, when did you see Renfield?"

"Usha not see Renfield." She brought her great wings back in and tucked them behind her, lowering into a crouched position again on the windowsill. Her nails gouged the stone sill as she perched and settled herself. "He talks to Usha in her head."

"When?"

"Usha get okay to be big and protect Mistress just before I bust open window and save you." Usha shuffled from clawed foot to clawed foot, causing little chunks of stone to fall. "Now you talk to him, can Usha eat him? You don't need him anymore." The gargoyle opened her dragon-like mouth, showing off her large, pointy teeth.

"No, Usha, we're not going to kill Stephen." Lavanya pulled away from the sleeping boy. "But we do need to hide him. I don't want them to be able to use him again."

"Lavanya, you are well within your rights to kill him," Zev stated coldly, crossing his arms over his chest. "He attacked you twice. Even after having your blood. He's beyond saving."

"I know my rights. And I also know that if I hadn't brought those bitches into my home, he never would've been violated and manipulated. He's my responsibility." Lavanya touched the sleeping boy's foot. "Usha, can you carry him to the village? I need him away from me and safe either until the effects of this compulsion wears off, or we kill the two controlling him."

"Of course, Mistress. Usha strong."

"Lavanya, the vamps have human servants, just as you do," Dylan piped in. "They may see her."

"True, but in the claws of a gargoyle, with him asleep like this—" Lavanya raised Stephen's foot and let it drop, "—everyone will think we killed him, and I gave the body to Usha to dispose of."

"Not bad, that would work." Zev thought for a moment. "While you're doing that, I'll take care of Uki and Raz," he said on his way to the door. "I'm starving, and their evil souls are just what I need."

"No."

"What?" Zev turned. "Why not?"

"While you were all demony, my father instructed me to bring them to him. Sorry, he's hungry too." Lavanya frowned. "He called dibs."

"Are you kidding me? What are we, five again? And he called dibs?" Zev's eyes darkened.

"Zev." Lavanya walked to him and put her hand on his arm. "I know you're hungry, and I promise we'll take care of that. If you need to feed, I can—"

"Forget it." Zev put his hand back on hers, and his eyes were the hazel she loved.

"Okay, but you've been putting it off for a while. Soon you'll have to feed. I can get you a donor."

"I said, forget it!" Zev pulled away. "How do you plan to lead them to your father?"

"I'm not sure. Any ideas?" She let him change the subject, knowing they didn't have the time right now to talk about his feeding or his aversion to letting her be a part of it. She had to trust that he would take care of himself before he became a danger to anyone.

"Just tell the staff to ready your horse for twilight, and I'll let slip to a few choice servants that you're going to your father because you're worried. Easy." Dylan stopped petting Usha and moved back to the middle of the room.

"That's too easy," Zev stated.

"The best plans usually are," Dylan replied.

"Do you really think they'll follow me?" Lavanya asked them.

"They're desperate," Dylan said. "Please, they sent a kid to kill you. They know Vlad's been sleeping. They all know it, even though they pretend they don't. He'll never be this vulnerable again. They have one shot to catch him before he's fully awake. They'll follow you, they have too. They've come too far to give up now. And Renfield—" He fell to his knees.

"Dylan?" Lavanya rushed to his side.

"I'm all right. I'm all right." Dylan held out his hand and Lavanya pulled him to his feet. "Okay, already, now I get it." He grunted to the ceiling.

"What are you babbling about?" Zev asked.

"I think I know where Renfield is."

"Where?" Lavanya pleaded.

Dylan took a deep breath, as if he was gaining his strength back from the vision that had just knocked him to his knees.

"That's what I wanted to ask you before I saw this mess," he said. "I was out burning the zombie, and I saw smoke coming from the far left turret—the one over the river. I'd never noticed it before, because it's sort of behind the front of the castle. I suddenly had to return to the castle, like a homing pigeon. How do I get up there?"

"Dylan, it's not possible." Lavanya walked to the window. "That turret has been blocked off for centuries. I've never been there. Renfield can't be there."

"Lavanya, I have to go there," Dylan said, shaking his head. "I just feel it. I must."

"It's physically and magically blocked. I can't even get close to the entrance."

"Renfield's there. I know it."

"Wait a minute," Zev broke in. "Who and why is it blocked?" He looked back and forth between the two. Lavanya finally spoke.

"That's *the* tower."

"Pretend I'm *not* obsessed with your father like humans are," Zev said. "Basically, I've spent my whole life trying to pretend he doesn't exist. Now, what is *the* tower?"

"It's the tower his first wife threw herself from to evade capture from the Turks," Lavanya whispered. "I believe her name was Elisabeta, but only my father knows for sure, and I won't be the one to ask him about it. That turret has been sealed since the 1450s."

Lavanya turned back to Dylan. "Are you sure you saw smoke coming from that tower?"

"Yes," Dylan said defiantly.

"Oh, Dylan, that's...how could they have known enough about the castle to use that tower? Even if they did, how did they get up there?"

"Don't know, don't care." Dylan marched toward the door. "Have to go. I *have* to go!"

"Okay, okay." Lavanya thought for a moment. "Zev, go with him. He'll need your muscle and magic."

"Don't think so. I'm not leaving you to those bitches. Your old man would have my hide as a new rug in the library if I left you."

"No. Dad has this under control. He's obviously leading Dylan." They both looked at Dylan. He held onto the door frame with both hands as his feet tried to carry him out the door.

"Come or not, it doesn't matter to me, but make up your mind. I can't hold out much longer." A fine bead of sweat had broken out on his forehead.

"Lavanya, we don't even know for sure if Renfield is there," Zev stressed.

"True. Usha, can you take a little joy ride up to the turret and see if anyone is in that room way at the top of the tower?"

"Yes, Mistress. Anything for Master Renfield."

"Can you do it carrying the boy? That'd kill two birds with one stone." Lavanya smiled.

"Yesss, in full height, Usha very strong."

"Great. Go on ahead and take a look. Then find Zev or Dylan and let them know." She looked at Dylan, now out in the hall, leaning on the wall and gritting his teeth. "They'll be in the tower to the right of the ruins of the old servants quarters. Then take the boy to the caves just above the village."

Zev looked down into Lavanya's violet eyes. "We'll get to Renfield before you have to leave tonight," he said. "Then I can go with you. You will not go alone."

"Zev!" Dylan called from down the hall. "You coming?"

Lavanya squeezed his hand where he held her shoulder.

"Go, I'll be fine. I have plenty to do—I have to rustle up a ride and drum up some gossip before I go so they can follow me. Just find Renfield for me. Please."

"Don't go without me." Zev tilted her head and kissed her fast and hard. Her insides melted and she molded herself to his hard body.

"Zev!" Dylan's bellow broke the mood.

Lavanya forced herself to push away from Zev. "I hear you. Now go!"

"Okay." Zev traced the edge of her cheek with his large, calloused finger and lightly touched her lips with his before he sprinted to catch up with Dylan.

Lavanya ran her fingers over her tingling lips and stared out at the sunshine pouring over the mountains. All the vampires were dead for the day. She realized for the first time how much she would miss seeing the cleansing morning sun burn off the remnants of darkness if she could no longer survive daylight.

"Usha know that look, Mistress."

"What?" Lavanya had forgotten the gargoyle was still sitting by the window.

"Lilitu give me same look."

"What look, Usha?" Lavanya turned from the view to look at Usha.

"You will not wait for the Rakshasa."

Lavanya raised an eye brow, surprised at the perceptive creature. "No, Usha, I need to see my father alone." She planned to ask her father to release Zev—right after she asked him to tell her everything he knew about him.

Usha *tsk-tsked* at Lavanya as she scooped up the boy. Her long tongue whipped out and ran across his cheek.

"No eating him, Usha."

"I know, Mistress, but I can't help the way my mouth waters at the smell of him." Usha swooped out the window with the boy dangling from her claws. She hovered for a moment and then plunged to the earth.

Lavanya rushed to the window, searching for the giant gargoyle. Had Usha been hurt? Had she dropped the boy?

But no. The creature was only playing. Usha opened her wings just as she was about to hit the sharp rocks below. Catching a draft, she playfully sailed high above the castle and then back down to the window.

"Usha will send Lilitu to follow you tonight so you no be alone."

"Usha—" Lavanya's heart was in her throat. "Thank you. Now go and tell Dylan and Zev if you find Renfield, but no one else. Do you understand?"

"Yesss, Mistress." With one flap of her wings, the gargoyle was gone. Lavanya sank back against the window. As the rush of endorphins left her, she felt the cold surround her.

Please find Renfield alive. Shaking and tired, she trudged to her room to change for the long day ahead. At least she'd slept a couple of hours this morning. Zev had had none, and he hadn't fed since coming to the castle days ago. He had to be ravenous.

CHAPTER TWENTY EIGHT

The Wind Beneaht My Feet

Delilah's hooves clopped loudly on the rocks, and her breath misted in the cold night air. She was a bit more willful than her brother, but Lavanya appreciated her unwavering spirit, especially on the steep mountainside. After losing Samson, Lavanya thought it only fair that his twin have a part in bringing their enemies to her father.

The long ride gave Lavanya too much time to think. She was worried about Renfield and wished she could be there when they finally got him out. Usha had seen Renfield sleeping in the tower room, but from her vantage point outside the small window, she couldn't wake him up. Dylan and Zev must have reached him by now. Damn these mountains! Not knowing was killing her. She'd always loved this remote area, but next time she'd make sure to get a satellite phone.

As Lavanya's anxiety flared, the wind shrieked. The huge horse nearly lost her footing on the loose gravel.

"Sorry, Del." Lavanya patted the horse's strong neck and tightened her grip on the reins. "I'm with you, girl."

That had been close. Lavanya took a deep, cleansing breath. The air was so cold it burned her throat on the way down and helped her focus.

As they crossed a peak, both she and the horse rose up in shock. Sitting on a boulder just ahead of them was a gargoyle. Delilah planted her hooves into the dirt and stopped almost before Lavanya could brace herself. The creature fanned its wings around its body and bounced from side to side, its clawed feet scratching the boulder. As it moved, it seemed to…hum.

Dancing? The gargoyle was dancing. Although its shape reminded Lavanya of a small gorilla with bat wings, its movements reminded her of a powerful, predatory bird. When the large creature saw Lavanya and Delilah, it stopped moving and pulled in its long, paper-thin wings. Tilting its head, the gargoyle saluted them with a sharp-clawed hand and smiled slyly, exposing black, block-shaped teeth.

Lavanya had to give Delilah credit—the horse was fearless. She stamped the ground with her hooves; she snorted and plunged, but she never took one step back from the gargoyle. Even Lavanya tried to move as far back as the English saddle allowed.

"Lilitu?" Lavanya asked. *What the hell*. Usha said she'd send her sister, so it was as good a guess as any. Really, how many gargoyles could be flying around the countryside? The coloring of the two creatures was the same, or close. It was hard to be sure in the dark.

"Hello, Mistress. Yes, it is I, Lilitu." The gargoyle pulled her wing away from her face, and Lavanya got a better look at her. She could see differences now. Usha had a large nose, almost like a human, and a large horn in the middle of her head. Lilitu's features were more subtle. Lavanya couldn't see her ears, and her horns were small and spaced evenly like a crown on top of her head. Lilitu's face reminded Lavanya of an English bull dog with a slight under bite and large eyes spaced wide on her big head.

"You are Usha's sister?"

"Yes, Usha my big sister. She cannot be awake in the night, so she send me to help you." The gargoyle rose up on her hind legs, which seemed human shaped, and yet she moved more like a chimpanzee.

"Thank you for being here tonight, but you must leave. If our enemies see you, they won't follow me to my father."

"I am here to report that no one is following you, Mistress." The gargoyle bounced from foot to foot.

"What? Are you sure?"

"Yes, I am sure."

"Maybe they saw you." *Damn it*. How could anyone miss this huge creature?

"Oh, no. No one see me, Mistress. I stay small as a bat for the flight." Lilitu huffed as if outraged that Lavanya would even suggest that she'd been spotted. "I grew only so you would notice me and we could speak."

Lavanya settled back in the saddle and pinched the bridge of her nose. She'd done everything possible to expose the fact that she was going to her father's resting place tonight. Everyone at the stable knew, she'd made sure the kitchen staff knew, and she'd lined up donors and volunteer humans for all the guests, telling them whom they'd be feeding and why she wouldn't be there. Plus, she'd gotten special donors for her father, figuring that he might still be hungry after confronting the two women. Among the Arefu people, feeding the count was a great honor—but that didn't mean they wouldn't talk about it with their friends and neighbors. The rumor mill was going full force by lunch time, and she'd listened in to all the speculation with great hope that tonight would be the end of their enemies.

"Lilitu." The gargoyle had begun to dance around the boulder again. "Are you sure no one followed us? Maybe they saw you and turned around."

"No, no, no. I very sneaky when I want to be. Just ask Usha. I am best at hide and seek. No one can find Lilitu if she wish not to be found."

"Damn it!" She couldn't afford to let her emotions get out of control, but her father would be furious. And Chloe—she worried about the girl. She'd sat with her up until the moment she had to leave tonight. Chloe had been in and out of consciousness the whole day, with Helgaleena hovering over her and applying this and that to her burses. Lavanya had been relieved when Helgaleena finally left them to fetch more herbs.

Lavanya hadn't wanted to spill the beans to Helgaleena about her father's plan, because Helgaleena was a terrible gossip. But Chloe deserved to know that Vlad was involved now. Helgaleena and Chloe's family had been tied to Vlad for centuries, and this attack was personal. Lavanya wasn't surprised that he awoke to handle Uki and Raz himself. Lavanya assured Chloe that he'd stop at nothing to find and punish all the people responsible. Chloe had been so weak that Lavanya wasn't sure she'd even heard her, until Chloe squeezed her hand and smiled a little.

"Now what?" Lavanya asked, but she didn't really have a choice. "Lilitu, stay hidden. I have to continue to Father and hope the women will somehow follow me to him."

What else could she do? Besides, she had a personal request that couldn't wait.

Lavanya watched Lilitu take to the sky. As the gargoyle soared, she shrank until she was no larger than a small owl flying through the night sky. Lavanya felt her own optimism for a good reunion with her father shrinking with Lilitu.

"Let's go, Delilah," she said, urging on the fearless horse.

Zev was irritated that it was taking so long to get to Renfield. "Dylan, help me move this door."

"I am helping you!" Dylan said from behind Zev. "I'm moving these last few rocks so we can pull the door open."

"Sorry, I just finished removing the spell around the opening. I didn't think about the pathway being blocked." Zev leaned against the solid wooden door. He was exhausted, and his head hurt.

"Yeah, I'm starting to get tired of this division of labor, too. These hands aren't used to this kind of work." Dylan threw another rock out the tower window.

"Trust me—if you had any magic ability, I'd be using you even more. My head is killing me. Thank God this is the last door." Zev banged hard on the solid door. "Renfield, can you hear us?"

"Damn!" Dylan exclaimed as he dropped a rock and pulled his hands into his chest. "I make things beautiful. I'm not a ditch digger."

"What happened?"

"Oh, I cut my hand on a sharp stone."

Zev watched a small drop of crimson fall to the floor and felt his tongue stick to the roof of his mouth as the dry stone greedily soaked it up. His nostrils flared, and he strained to breathe in the rich flavor of blood. His head pounded. He took two steps forward and grabbed Dylan's arm.

"Zev. Get control of yourself, I'm not on the *menu!*" Dylan tried to push Zev away with his free hand, but the demon would not be denied..

"Zev! Lavanya wouldn't like it if you ate me!"

Zev held tight to Dylan as a low growl rumbled through him. The Rakshasa wanted fed and it didn't care that Dylan had settled into a fighting stance or that he had palmed the 9mm at his back.

Zev. Let. Go!"

Zev shook himself like a wet dog and shoved Dylan away and against the stone wall. "I'm sorry." Zev's muscles strained as if they could burst through his skin.

"It's okay, buddy." Dylan clicked the safety back on the

Glock. "Just get control of yourself."

"I've got it," Zev said, shaking out his arms.

"Yeah… tell that to someone you didn't almost eat." Dylan pushed off from the wall.

"I've got this!" Zev protested.

"Look, you need to feed or you'll hurt someone, and I'd rather it not be me or Lavanya."

"I know! It's just that I—I'm not like her. Or them."

"And…" Dylan used his hands to motion for Zev to continue. Zev shrugged him off.

"Come on," Zev said, approaching the door again. "Let's get Renfield."

"Will he know what you are and why you won't feed from anyone?" Dylan asked.

Zev shrugged.

"Stop right there," Dylan said. "Explain."

"What?" Zev retreated to the turret window. Dylan waited for Zev to explain. Tired and wanting to be understood he confided in Dylan. "I'm needier than a regular vampire. I'm a Rakshasa demon. I require the total package."

Dylan shook his head. "Huh?"

"Dylan?" Renfield's muffled cry refocused their attention on the mission. Both men rushed to open the heavy stone door. Zev only now noticed the recent scuff marks on the floor as they tried to pull it open.

"Renfield, we're coming!" Dylan shouted.

As cool air rushed through the crack Zev watched a sickening sweat beak out on Dylan's face. Then Dylan's grip on the door weakened.

"Keep pulling, Dylan," Zev grunted.

Dylan fell to his knees and retched.

"It's magic," Zev yelled at Dylan. "Fight it!"

"I…can't."

However, Zev watched as the man fought the spell. In moments Dylan stood, fully recovered, just as Zev pried open the door a few inches. Recovered, Dylan rushed to the opening.

"I can't see inside," Dylan shouted, straining to open the door wider. "It's too dark."

"Shit, its full dark already."

"Yeah—you're just noticing? You must be tired. It's been dark for an hour." Dylan grabbed the door handle.

"What are the odds that Lavanya's waiting for me to go with her?" Zev grabbed the handle, as well, and leaned hard into it. "Pull!"

"No dice," Dylan grunted as he pulled. "She's already halfway to her father by now."

"Damn it, we have to hurry. I need to get to her." Zev gave up when the door wouldn't open. "That's it," he said. "Stand back." The air crackled around them as if lightning had been caged in the stone walls.

Dylan stumbled back to the wall opposite the door. "What are you—?"

"Close your eyes!" Zev yelled.

"Roger that." Dylan crouched low to the ground and waited.

Zev felt the electrical charge of magic raise the hairs on his arms and tickle over his skin. The explosion was small but loud in the tight confines of the round tower stairway. The blast had blown the door into the room, and dust and smoke from the explosion hung in the air, obscuring their vision.

"Zev, you idiot!" Dylan coughed. "What if Renfield was right behind the door?" He waved his arms to clear the smoke. "Renfield!"

"I'm here."

"See? He's fine, ye of little faith." Zev coughed and pushed ahead of Dylan. Together, they found Renfield lying in front of the old stone hearth.

"Okay, so he's not fine, but I didn't hurt him with the door," Zev said as he knelt down to help Renfield sit up.

"Renfield?" Dylan said sounding unsure. The Renfield they knew wasn't the man they saw.

Fear and worry swirled in Lavanya, so the wind lashed the mountainside. Anger threatened to bubble to the surface, but she beat it back by concentrating on her footwear. Dylan would be disappointed in her choice, but she was glad to be wearing her old hiking boots as she climbed the steep, rocky terrain. The wind calmed as she concentrated on planting one foot in front of the other on the treacherous climb to her father's remote crypt.

Vlad would be furious that the women hadn't followed her. But unless Uki and Raz were exceptionally adept at hiding, she was alone. She hadn't even seen Lilitu since she flew off an hour ago. The gargoyle was right: if she didn't want to be seen, she wasn't.

Lavanya's foot slipped again on the rocks, and her anger slid past her defenses.

"Damn it!" she exclaimed.

Then lightening crashed, and the night sky darkened with her fury. She took a deep breath and tried to calm her nerves. Rain would be all she needed to make this climb even more of a pain in the ass.

"Gee thanks, Dad," she mumbled as she dug her feet in and continued the climb. "Why couldn't I inherit the ability to fly or shift into an animal? Oh, no, I had to get the ability to affect the weather."

"Do not take that tone with me, Child." Vlad's voice boomed in her head, and she lost her footing again.

Great. A cranky, hungry Vlad, not someone even she wanted to face.

"I'm almost there," she said.

"Instead of complaining about your newest ability, why not use it to your advantage?"

"Oh!" A gust of wind lifted Lavanya off her feet. Her legs shot out from under her, and she struggled to hang on to the rocky face of the mountain. The wind whipped her hair around her face, and the force of it blew her away from the cliff.

"Child, relax into the power."

Lavanya tried to calm her mind. She closed her eyes, trusting her father's advice. She shivered as the cold wind wrapped around her body, and the sensation of having nothing under her feet sent her stomach on a free fall.

"The ability to affect the elements is a great responsibility and a great gift. However, you must learn to control your emotions. I realize that is a challenge for a woman."

Lavanya landed in a pile of arms and legs as the wind dropped her on the ground. Her eyes flew open to a frightening scene. Lilitu was facing off against two enormous tigers.

"Here kitty, kitty! Hisssss!" the gargoyle urged.

"Roar!" The ferocious beasts stalked the giant creature.

Lavanya scrambled back as Lilitu's black wing narrowly missed hitting her face.

"Ha, ha—you miss the Lilitu," the gargoyle taunted as she jumped and landed behind Lavanya. "You still be it!"

The other shoe dropped. Vlad had lovingly placed her in the middle of a dangerous game of tag between one of his pet gargoyles and his Caspian tigers, Shere and Khan.

"Thanks again, Father," Lavanya said.

The tigers stalked toward Lavanya and the dancing gargoyle, their long bodies stretched out, preparing to pounce on Lilitu. Shere, her head more golden and slightly smaller than that of her mate, opened her enormous jaws as if to taste the air and exposed her sharp, white fangs.

"You are very welcome, Daughter," Vlad answered, his voice sarcastic. *"Lilitu, stop baiting the beasts."*

"Yesssss, Master." Lilitu's voice dripped disappointment. "Game over, kitties. You never catch the Lilitu anyway, phssst!"

Lavanya wasn't sure of the sound, but she knew it pissed off the tigers and she could just imagine Lilitu's face with her long, blue tongue sticking out. Shere narrowed her eyes at the gargoyle, and Lavanya heard a lisping bellow of laughter as the air swirled behind her. She jumped away just in time to miss being caught by Shere's claw, meant for Lilitu—who had lifted off the ground. Lavanya ended up on her side in the gravel and dirt.

"Master," Lilitu drawled as she landed in the shadows at the entrance to Vlad's cave. "Look what those dirty cats have done to my Mistress. Can Lilitu punish them?" Lavanya watched as Lilitu put her wings together like a small child begging for a piece of candy. Lavanya couldn't see Vlad, but she heard him loud and clear.

"Behave, Lilitu. If I let you have them, then who would guard my resting place?" Vlad's pale hand came out of the shadow and scratched the top of Lilitu's head. She bowed and eased into him, closing her eyes and obviously savoring Vlad's touch.

Lavanya began to sit up, but Khan decided to get reacquainted with her. He put his face down and rubbed his rough whiskers and soft fur against her cheek with a force that knocked her over. Then he flopped over on his side next to her, pawing her and begging for a tummy scratch. He'd been greeting her the same way since she was a child, and she giggled at the big cat. Still miffed that she'd missed the gargoyle, Shere roared and circled the cuddling Lavanya and her mate.

"You better get up, Khan." Lavanya ruffled the soft, white fur on his belly. "Shere will kick your ass for fraternizing as it is." Shere strolled to the cave and then looked back at Khan. He stood and stretched. Shere turned back to the cave and Khan took the opportunity to lick Lavanya with his huge sandpaper tongue.

"Oh, yuck! Khan!" Before Shere could turn to see him he bounded off after her.

"Lavanya." Vlad stepped from the shadows. His six-foot, four-inch frame was covered in dust and dirt, and his long, dirty brown hair tangled freely with his full beard. The white fisherman's sweater he wore had been a gift from her mother, and it was full of holes and looked frozen in places. The black slacks were torn and ragged.

"Father?" Lavanya got to her feet and hesitated approaching her father. She hadn't seen him in years and had never seen him after such a prolonged sleep.

"Yes, Child, it is I." He looked down at his appearance. "Not as tidy as you remember? This isn't so bad. You should have seen me after my captivity at the hands of the Ottomans. But that's another story."

"I'm sorry, Father." Lavanya dusted herself off. "I just haven't seen you in so long." She approached the cave entrance, but she paused and scented the air, much like Shere had done, when she detected the sweet aroma of fresh blood.

"Father?" Lavanya lifted her eyebrow. She looked at him more closely. Although his body and clothes looked warn out, his eyes shown with health. "Have you fed?"

"I decided I was rather hungry after sleeping for so many years, and then Renfield needed some help. So..." He stepped aside as Lavanya entered the cave. "An opportunity arose and I decided not to wait."

"Oh, my God." Lavanya covered her mouth with her hands. Sickened with herself because her fangs throbbed with hunger at the sight in front of her. Two young women and a man lay in a mangled heap on the stone floor. Their backpacks lay by a tiny fire in the center of the cave. By the looks of their clothing and shoes, they'd been backpacking for a while. Maybe they'd been lost or out for an extreme adventure. Their clothes were dirty, but not ripped or even disturbed. There was no sign of struggle. Even though she smelled their blood, there wasn't a drop on the hard-packed cave floor.

She immediately started to back out of the cave. Vlad caught her and pulled her forward.

"Oh, dear, you're hungry. I'm sorry. I assumed you'd have eaten before starting the journey."

"Father! *No*! I…the waste of it." Lavanya wrenched her arm free and backed to the entrance of the cave.

"Don't worry, dear, there will be no waste. I would never leave such a mess. Lilitu!"

"Yesss, Master." Instantly, the gargoyle appeared at the cave opening. At the sight on the floor, her eyes widened and her long, blue tongue tasted the air. She walked toward the macabre pile even before Vlad gave her instructions. Lavanya caught a glimpse of the gargoyle's eyes, which were glassy and unfocused with barely restrained excitement.

"Lilitu, there is one for you, and one for Shere and Khan." Vlad caught her by the wing before she dove into the pile. "If I were you, I would pick the bigger male and—are you listening?"

"Yesss, Yesss. Thank you, Master." Lilitu shook her horned head. "It been so long."

"I know, but you will take half to your sister." Vlad grabbed onto her thick chin and held it to get her attention. He had to reach up to do it because the gargoyle towered over him, even at six-foot-four. "She will know if you have tasted human flesh and not shared."

Lilitu's head fell in resignation.

"Go ahead and pick yours. You can have a little taste now and then hide it for after you follow Lavanya home. You and your sister can have a feast together at dawn."

Lilitu tore out of his grasp and grabbed the larger male from the bottom of the pile. The two women fell, replacing him on the ground, reminding Lavanya of the game Jenga. *Pull one from the bottom, and all the little pieces crash to the floor.* She swallowed the saliva and venom that filled her mouth against her will.

"That's not what I meant by waste, Father!" Lavanya moved out of the way as Lilitu pushed past her with the man—really no more than a boy—in her claws. She held him tight to her chest, like a person would hold a lover. "Why did you have to kill them?" Lavanya's anger rose and threatened to choke her. "We don't have to drain humans. We never have to kill!"

"You are your mother's daughter." Vlad folded his arms across his chest and shook his head. Then he inspected his sweater, pulling the sleeves straighter and the torn and dirty collar closer to his face. "I never will understand why I'm drawn to women with delicate sensibilities." His hand brushed the knotted and tangled hair back on his head.

"Well, excuse us for being human!" Lightning lit up the front of the cave, and a cold gust of wind blew around her face.

"Ah, ah, ah, Daughter. Your emotions will cause a storm." Vlad glided closer, shaking his finger in the air. "You must learn control."

Lavanya seethed. A clap of thunder shook the cave walls, and her head felt as if it would burst.

"You—" A thousand curses flashed through her mind, but she held her tongue, gritting her teeth and squeezing her hands into fists. Closing her eyes, she tried to rein in her anger. She would never win a battle with her father if she let herself get emotional. It would just play into his comment about women and emotions. But damn it, he could really be an ass.

"Whoooosh…" She let out the pent-up fury in one long breath. *Time to change the subject.*

She opened her eyes and focused on her father's face, instead of the pile of bodies.

"Father, do you know if Zev and Dylan got to Renfield? Is he all right?"

"Yes." Vlad turned and walked back toward the dead women.

"Yes? Can you elaborate, please?" Lavanya focused on him, even though she knew he was doing his best to force her to look at the bodies again.

"YES! They found Renfield. And YES, he's alive. But only because of this WASTE!" Vlad pointed to the women piled on the floor. "As you call it. I had to bolster their strength to keep Renfield well and to help Zev with the wards on that part of the castle, since I helped put them in place. So tell me, Daughter, are you still disgusted with me? You played a part in all this. If you'd brought me the women as you were supposed to, I might not have had to find my own meal." Vlad smiled then, and it was a terrifying site.

"What!" Then Lavanya remembered a line from her mother's journal: *Life isn't fair. Nor is it good or evil. It just IS and you have to make the best of it.* Arguing with her father wouldn't change a thing.

"What's your plan?" she asked, concentrating on each word to help clear her mind, knowing her father had a plan, he always did. "The women, Uki and Raz, obviously haven't followed me here. So what do you want me to do?" The wind and rain that had started to fall outside settled.

"Very good." Vlad noticed the change in weather and smiled as if he were proud.

That smile made Lavanya's skin crawl, especially as she realized that some small part of her still craved her father's approval. But no matter how far she traveled or what she tried to do, he'd always be her father. As her mother had said, life just is. She didn't trust herself to speak so she just waited.

"Return to the castle. I will join you there."

"But Uki and Raz? They've probably left. They have to know we're on to them."

"Your guests are still there. A sudden *storm* has besieged Castle Poenari and delayed everyone's travel plans."

"But—" If the storm was that bad, how was she supposed to get through?

"Don't worry. Much as the weather cleared here, it will clear enough for your arrival." Vlad went to the cave opening and called for Shere and Khan. "I'll be along after I take care of this *waste*."

Shere skulked into the cave as if she were bored. The muscles of her shoulders rippled across the top of her long back, letting you know just how much strength she had at her disposal. Khan trailed behind, content to let his younger mate lead the way. They both went directly to Vlad and, like big house cats, rubbed their face and bodies along his legs. Khan let out a low growl, like a chuffing sound through his nose.

"I know, my pet. I have missed you, as well." Vlad bent to

give the cat a good scratching and then told them of their supper.

Shere bounded forward first, but Khan blocked her and kept her back with his roar. Shere bellowed back. Both cats rose up on their hind legs to hit each other with their enormous clawed paws. Lavanya stepped back to be well out of the way of the wrestling teeth and paws.

"Khan is just asserting his dominance. If they were truly fighting, their claws would be out." Vlad pointed to Khan, who stood over Shere with his big paw raised to strike her. And as Vlad said, Khan's paw was just a paw—no claws were visible. When Khan roared in Shere's face, all the fight left her. She rolled over, and Khan jumped off his mate and into the pile of bodies.

Lavanya averted her gaze as the hungry tiger latched onto a shoulder. Even though her eyes were closed, she could still hear clothes ripping and the tigers' hungry snarls and roars. Vlad smiled as the first crunch of bone echoed through the narrow cave. Swallowing hard, Lavanya looked at Vlad to see him watching the tigers with delight.

"Father—" Lavanya cleared her throat. "Can I speak to you outside, please?"

"I know what you want to ask, and the answer is no." Vlad looked down at her, daring her to continue.

"You can't possibly know what I want to ask," Lavanya said, letting her anger help her forget for a moment about the tigers munching on humans right behind her.

"You want me to release the Rakshasa demon from my hold. I will not."

"But Father, Zev has done everything you asked. He has protected me. That was your bargain. Now you must release him." Lavanya knew better than to take this tone with her father, but she just couldn't help it.

Vlad lifted his eyebrow as if she confused him. "It's nice that you named him. *Zev,* as you say. He makes a wonderfully dangerous pet, does he not?" He pointed to the tigers now dragging their dinner into the darkness at the back of the cave. "As I named mine."

"He's not a pet, and you made a deal. Now you must release him."

"*I must do no such thing!*" The walls of the cave shook, and the tigers cowered with the bodies still in their mouths. "Your servant Dylan saved you and your maid. Zev did not earn his release, and you would do well to remember that he's a demon and not to be trusted. An animal more dangerous than they—" Vlad pointed at the tigers still chewing on human flesh, "—and infinitely more powerful. That is what you wish me to release on the world."

"He's not an animal, Father, and he's not totally demon, either. What is he?"

Vlad grabbed Lavanya by the arm and forced her to see in his mind exactly what a Rakshasa was. Images assaulted her of an enormous creature, black as soot, with two fangs protruding from the top of its mouth, fingernails as sharp as claws, and the potential to change shape into many animals. The beast used magic to hide its form so it could hunt humans, for which, both body and soul, it had an insatiable hunger.

The last image was of Zev. She recognized his hazel eyes and dark hair matted with blood. He tore furiously into the neck of a blond woman as she lay across his body, while another lay bloody and dead at the bottom of his bed.

"No!" Lavanya yanked her arm away from Vlad's grip. "That's not true."

"Of course it is, Child. But why do you care?" He raised his brow again, and Lavanya turned away. "Ah. You have feelings for this beast. He has charmed you, just like those women you saw lying dead at the foot of his bed."

"It's not like that." But even she heard the doubt in her voice that had taken root.

"Of course, *you* are the exception." Vlad walked out of the cave and into the night. "We shall see." Vlad turned back toward Lavanya.

"Return to the castle. I release my hold on the demon."

"Thank you, Father." Lavanya rushed to him, ready to hug him in gratitude, but stopped. Vlad never did anything without a reason. "Why?"

Vlad took several moments before answering.

"I fear that nothing I do will not cause you pain. If I do not release him, you will be hurt. So I have released him. However, when he realizes I no longer hold him, he will leave. He hates our kind above all else and has fought for his freedom for too long to remain."

Lavanya shook her head in defiance. "I don't believe you."

"You can't trust him, Lavanya. This lesson will be a painful one, but you need to learn it now before you lose yourself to him. He's not worthy of you."

Lavanya shook her head. "You're wrong, Father," she said.

At least she hoped he was.

LYNNE STEVIE

CHAPTER TWENTY NINE

There's Nothing Like The Taste Of Innocence

"Dylan, have you got him?" Another crash of thunder pierced Zev's ears. He held open the door for the other men to get through. Being cold and wet wasn't helping him control his hunger or his temper.

"Yeah, I've got him." Dylan huffed as he manhandled Renfield through the door.

"I'm not an invalid," Renfield wheezed. The cold stone tower had done nothing for his raspy voice.

"Hey, you're back." Dylan smiled at the man leaning on him.

"Where's Lavanya? Do you have a connection to her?" Zev asked in a rush of emotion, grabbing Renfield.

"Did I miss something?" Renfield asked Dylan over Zev's big shoulder.

"Oh, yeah. You better answer him before he goes demon shit again."

"*Do you?*" Zev tightened his grip on Renfield.

"Unhand me, and maybe I'll answer," Renfield replied.

"Renfield—" Dylan cautioned.

"Fine." Zev let Renfield fall back against Dylan. "Just answer me."

"She's with Vlad."

Zev released a breath and felt his muscles relax. "And—"

"I know she's angry, but that's it," Renfield continued. "Vlad can protect her now."

"How? He's been dead for years. How much strength could he have? Tell me where they are so I can get to her."

Renfield smiled. "Give you Vlad's daytime resting place? Not likely, Rakshasa! He's fed, and he can protect her better than you, anyway. His strength is why I'm still alive and why you two could finally reach me."

Lightning lit up the night sky. Renfield tilted his head toward the window in the stairwell. "I'd know that handiwork anywhere.

283

He doesn't want anyone to leave the castle before he arrives." Then he slipped and Dylan caught him.

"Well, he didn't send *you* enough strength," Dylan said, pulling Renfield along. "Let's get you to bed, and then I'll have the kitchen make you something to eat."

Zev was still anxious. Something wasn't right.

"Their plan must have worked—Vlad must have fed on the two vampires Uki and Raz," he said. "Renfield, why is Lavanya angry?"

"I don't know, but truthfully, Vlad doesn't seem much happier." Renfield closed his eyes and let his head fall to Dylan's shoulder. "Get me to my room. Maybe it won't spin as much as this hallway."

"I can feel her, Zev," Dylan said. "She's fine. Seeing her father is stressful. They're not real close or alike."

"Yeah, okay." Zev reached for Renfield's other arm to help carry the old man to his room.

"Maybe you should get cleaned up, Zev," Dylan said. "I can take him. You've been limping for an hour or so."

Zev looked down and realized that his leg was bleeding again. He'd torn open the wound somewhere along the way. And Dylan was right—he needed to get the wound cleaned and dressed again. "You sure you got this?"

"Go ahead. Renfield's rooms are on the main level, so it's not much farther. I'll call for some food as soon as I get him there." Dylan took more of Renfield's weight. "Besides, Lavanya will be back soon, and you don't want to greet her like that."

"Did I miss something?" Renfield asked in a sleepy voice.

"Yeah, I'll fill you in on the love connection after you've eaten."

"Love connection." Renfield stopped and looked at Zev. "Ooh, no wonder Vlad's angry. I'm surprised there's not a hurricane or an avalanche brewing outside. At the very least an earthquake. He's actually being very calm." Lightning lit the sky and thunder echoed through the hall. Renfield laughed.

"Come on, old man." Dylan urged him toward the back hallway and his suite of rooms.

"Thanks. After I get this cleaned, I'll check on you guys."

"We'll be fine," Dylan called over his shoulder.

Zev headed down the hall to the main stairs and their room. Turning the corner, he could just make out Tru's husky laughter over the storm that raged outside. Bypassing the stairs, he crept closer as quietly as he could with a limp. Outside the main parlor, he cracked the door just enough to see inside. Tru sat playing cards with Belle, while Naasir and Arthur watched. Lauren and Phil played backgammon by the fireplace and smiled at each other. *At least someone was enjoying the evening.*

Zev moved to get a better view of the bar at the other end of the room. Uki and Raz weren't there. Had they followed Lavanya, as planned? Dylan had said that Lavanya was fine. He knew that, but he wouldn't feel better until she was back in the castle and he knew for sure that the women were dead.

Climbing the steps was more painful than just walking. If he'd had any strength left, he would have just willed himself to his suite, but he was too tired. The big glass and stone shower was calling his name. All he had to do was get there. He'd feel more in control after a hot shower and some food. His mouth watered in anticipation of a nice, juicy steak.

Dragging himself up the stairs, he caught Lavanya's scent. She didn't always wear the same perfume, but underneath whatever fragrance she wore was the fresh scent of—he stopped to smell again. Yep. Old-fashioned cold crème. The scent made him smile, and it gave him the strength to climb faster.

His head was dizzy and heavy from the exertion, and his sight dimmed as he entered the library. The scent of Lavanya's cold crème and her blood gave him energy. The blood awakened a desperate hunger, but he shouldn't be able to smell her blood. And he and the Rakshasa agreed. They'd never harm Lavanya.

Was she injured? Fear raced through his mind and his vision darkened as he crossed the threshold, ready to kill whatever had caused her to bleed.

The boy. The boy who'd attacked Lavanya earlier. He was covered in blood. Some was his and some was hers. He was breathing hard. He stood over her. He looked down at her lifeless body and his bloody hands and then back to Zev. He stumbled backwards.

"*NO!*"

The Rakshasa, fueled by rage and hunger, didn't give Zev a

chance to question the boy. He had him in his teeth before the young man could speak. As the first taste of blood hit his palate, Zev released the demon. He would relish the taste of evil as the Rakshasa consumed the boy's soul, just as the boy's blood would nourish and heal him.

Zev choked on the taste that should have been familiar, cold, and thirst-quenching. But the Rakshasa took control; he savored the unexpected taste of innocents. The boy was an innocent! Zev had never allowed him to feed on an innocent.

But Lavanya lay dead at his feet: how? He started to release the young man, but at that moment, Zev felt Vlad's band of power snap like a rubber band stretched too far. He was free! Vlad's control was gone, and he was free.

The Rakshasa bellowed and took control as he never had before. He drank deeply of the young man's soul. The beast was free, and Zev was in too much agony over the loss of Lavanya to lament the boy's death. Even if he was innocent, he'd played a part in her death. Zev let his own bloodlust and rage run free.

"Zev! Zev! You must release him. Oh, Gods, what have you done? Zev!"

Zev's eyelids were heavy with sleep and opened only a crack. The scent of rotten flesh and burnt hair made him cough. With the rich taste of a fresh kill still thick in his mouth, he tried to focus on who was speaking. When he couldn't figure it out, he raised his arm to wipe his face and eyes. His hand and face were crusty.

"You've killed them all, demon."

"What? I—" Zev tried to sit up, but he was trapped under something. He pushed it off and only then realized it was a body. He bounded to his feet. "What's happened? I—Lavanya?"

He quickly looked down at himself, then toward the bodies strewn around the room. Blood leaked from their necks. The one he'd pushed off himself had long black hair.

"NO!" he screamed. He turned her over. He couldn't have hurt Lavanya. He wouldn't. He gently pushed the silky black hair from her face. His shoulders slumped in relief, and his head dropped. The dead woman was Uki, Lavanya's Asian guest. He didn't remember killing her. No, he'd found her with the boy standing over her. She'd smelled so much like Lavanya, and with her black hair…. He looked down at Uki again. He should have known then. She was much shorter than his Lavanya, and she smelled nothing like her now.

"Lavanya will kill you—if Vlad doesn't—for what you've done to the innocents."

Zev shook his head. "No, I—" The bloodlust he remembered. He took in the rest of the room. The young man lay a few feet away, his blood covered the tiger skin rug.

"I—" Zev remembered the taste of innocence. He swallowed the hard lump of self-loathing and backed away toward the door, only to trip over Raz. *Shit!*

Soft sobs mixed with the beat of a chant. Across the room, Helgaleena cried over Chloe's limp body.

"No! I couldn't!" he said.

"You did, Rakshasa!" Helgaleena stood, and the air in the room chilled him. "You are evil! When Vlad returns, he will imprison you—as you should be—for an eternity!"

"I could not have hurt Chloe, Lavanya cared for her," he protested. But self-doubt burned his mouth as each word left it. He licked his dry lips, desperate for an answer—any answer—except the one right in front of him. All he remembered was the taste of innocent blood and the Rakshasa bellowing as Vlad released him. "I—"

"They will see you on a spike." The air crackled around the old witch, and Zev inched closer to the door without turning his back to the old woman.

Fear and shame wrapped around Zev as if they were a physical entity. *I am evil. I am evil. I AM EVIL!* A voice inside his head repeated.

"No!" Zev beat at his head with his hands. "I'm not evil!" Sweat broke out over his skin even as he began to shiver. He had to find Lavanya. No—he had to leave, *to protect her*. His whole body quaked in rebellion.

"I have to go!" The voice inside his head was right. He couldn't be around Lavanya. He had to protect her from himself. He backed away from the bodies and the old woman whose hair whipped around her face and vanished.

As Vlad had promised, the storm settled around her as she

hastened back to the castle. She galloped into the stables and threw the reins to the caretakers before running into the castle and right into Dylan.

"How's Renfield?" she asked, breathing hard.

"He's going to be fine. I got him cleaned up, and I am taking him some food." Dylan held out the tray.

"Thank God." Lavanya placed her hand on Dylan's face. "Thank you. Wait, you're just now getting him some food? How long did it take to get him out? And where's Zev?" She looked around expecting to see him.

"It took forever. We just got back maybe an hour ago, and I sent Zev up to take care of his leg." Dylan leaned into her. "I'm guessing the plan worked, and your father took care of it? I haven't seen Uki or Raz, but the others are in the parlor playing games."

"No, the plan didn't work—hence the storm to keep everyone in place for his arrival later tonight."

"Shit. I'll be on the lookout for the women."

"All right. Be careful. Who knows what they'll try next." Lavanya took a deep breath and looked up the stairs.

"Hey, Renfield knows about you and Zev." Dylan smiled.

"Nice to know there's still some privacy here in this huge castle."

"Sarcasm. Funny. I'm thinking it's not just the castle walls that can't hold a secret." He raised his brows. "Nice storm. I'm guessing your father knows about you and Zev, too."

"Yes. Aren't you just the perceptive one? He isn't happy, but he released him, Dylan." Lavanya looked back at the stairs. "I have to find him. Father thinks he'll take off as soon as he gets his freedom."

"I think Zev'll surprise Vlad." Dylan winked at her. "He was pretty upset that you went without him and worried until I told him I could feel you and that you were okay."

"Thanks, sweetie." Lavanya squeezed his arm.

"But he was pretty out of it. He had to do a lot of heavy lifting magically to get Renfield out." Dylan looked back toward the kitchen. "Maybe you should check on him. I thought he would have ordered some food by now, but the kitchen hasn't heard from him."

"Okay. Have you seen Chloe or Helgaleena tonight?"

"No, I've been on Renfield duty. I assume they're sleeping, like normal humans. But I'll check on them as soon as I get him eating."

"Great, but make sure to get something for yourself, too. Promise me." She waited for his answer.

"Yes, mother hen." Dylan shrugged. "I promise to take care of me, too. Now get on up there and check on your man." He started off toward the east wing of the main castle and Renfield's suite.

Lavanya's boots echoed on the stone steps, sounding like hammers hitting a brick wall. A smile grew as she took the steps two at a time. Zev was here, and he'd worried about her.

The smell of cardamom told her she was close. But the smell of fresh blood stopped her three steps from the top. She took a deep breath. It was a lot of very fresh blood. More than one person was bleeding.

"Lavanya?" Tru's husky voice called from the landing at the bottom of the grand staircase. "Hey, I thought I heard you. How's your...father?" Tru took a deep gulp of air. "Is that..."

"Yes, Tru." Lavanya went to the top of the stairs. "Go back into the parlor."

"Not on your life." Tru ran up the stairs and was beside her in an instant. "Let's go see who's bleeding. How many?" She licked her lips.

"Tru, you aren't ready for this. There's more than one human—" Lavanya took another sniff, "—and at least one vampire." And ...magic.

"Zev!" She couldn't mistake the smell of cardamom. Lavanya left Tru and dashed to the doors of the library, throwing them open. The first body she saw was that of the young man she'd sent into the village with Usha. At least she assumed it was he from the clothes he'd been wearing. His neck was torn and ripped, his spine poked through the muscle and ligaments. Blood trickled from his mangled flesh. Lavanya frantically searched for Zev, but he wasn't there.

The scene reminded her of the vision Vlad had shown her, only this was worse. Bloody bodies littered the floor. Uki and Raz lay side by side in an ever-widening pool of blood, their throats neatly cut, their hands still clutching sharp daggers.

No remorseful tears pricked her eyes. She wasn't sorry to see them dead, but she was curious. They weren't healing. Their heads were still mostly attached, and they'd obviously fed recently, by the amount of blood still leaking out of them. There was no sign of a struggle. The room was arranged as it had been for hundreds of years, everything kept according to Vlad's meticulous standards. Not one table was overturned or one chair pushed aside.

Then her eyes fell on Chloe and Helgaleena.

"Helgaleena!"

"Oh, my god." Tru covered her nose and mouth with her hand. "Lavanya, we have to get help." Helgaleena lay atop Chloe, as if she were shielding her granddaughter. Blood had soaked into her clothes and run down to puddle on the floor around Chloe's dead body. The tiger fur rugs were soaking up the blood like they'd been thirsty for a while. Helgaleena sighed as Lavanya gently lifter her.

"Leena..." Lavanya ran her hand over her sister, searching for injuries. "It's me, Lavanya. I've got you."

"Chloe?"

"Oh, Helgaleena." Lavanya was too worried about her sister's health to tell her that Chloe was dead. Lavanya cradled her close and moved them toward the door and away from Chloe's lifeless body. Although Helgaleena felt solid and strong in Lavanya's arms, once she understood her granddaughter was dead, the horror and grief might be too much for the old woman to handle.

Lavanya gently sat Helgaleena against the wall outside the library. "Helgaleena, are you hurt? There's...so much blood." Lavanya fought the urge to lick the thick, syrupy blood from her hands.

"Chloe..." Helgaleena tried to get up.

"No, Helgaleena!" Lavanya pushed her to stay seated.

"I have to protect her from it!" Helgaleena struggled under Lavanya's strong hands. Her strength surprised Lavanya, and she broke free and got to the door before Lavanya could restrain her.

"No!"

The damage was done. Chloe's body was easily seen from the door. Even if you overlooked her blood-soaked clothing, her graying, filmy eyes were a clear sign that she was no longer living. Helgaleena's body swayed in Lavanya's arms.

"Helgaleena, I am so sorry."

Moving with a speed and balance that defied her age, Helgaleena broke out of Lavanya's hold and rushed to her granddaughter's side. Kneeling beside her, she carefully placed the young woman's hands on her chest and lowered her eyelids.

"Rest in peace, Child," she said. "Your life has not been in vain, and you've given me more than I can ever repay."

"Helgaleena, I'm sorry. I loved her, too." Lavanya felt the rush of adrenaline subside; the wave of fatigue that followed left her trembling. But she had to find Zev. Lavanya pointed to Uki and Raz.

"Who killed them?" she asked Helgaleena. "Zev was here, I know it. Did he follow the killer? And who attacked Chloe? I don't understand any of this."

Helgaleena didn't move.

"Helgaleena?" Lavanya shook her by the shoulders. "What happened here? Where's Zev?" She knew now that Helgaleena wasn't injured, and she needed answers. Her fear and anxiety were eating away at her control.

"The Rakshasa." Helgaleena turned her cold stare up to Lavanya. "You are worried for the demon!" Lavanya took a step back as she stared into hate-filled eyes rimmed in red. Helgaleena's hatred wasn't the fresh anger of a new offense, but a fire that glowed behind her eyes, showing a lifetime of resentment. Lavanya shivered as a small slice of fear trickled up her spine.

"Sister?" Lavanya shook off Helgaleena's malice. After all, the woman had suffered a terrible loss. That would account for the outburst—and the threat she saw in her eyes.

"If not for the demon, my Chloe would still be alive! She would never have died, but for that worthless beast."

"Zev's not responsible for this." What was Helgaleena talking about? Zev would never have hurt Chloe. Uki and Raz, yes, he could have easily killed them, but she couldn't believe that he could have hurt Chloe.

"Vlad!!" Helgaleena screamed. "I blame your father for releasing that beast upon us here and hiding in his crypt like a coward. That Rakshasa killed them all! I found him feeding on their souls. I wasn't in time to save Chloe, and I wasn't strong enough to kill him. But he's a cowardly demon. He ran off and disappeared when I explained what Vlad would do to him for killing what was Vlad's to kill or let live.

"No, Helgaleena, you must be mistaken. Zev would not have killed Chloe and he would never have run off."

"He did, Lavanya. How else do you explain the vampires Uki and Raz? Their wounds would not be enough to finish them. They should have been able to heal. And yet, you can see they are gone by the demon's magic."

"I don't believe you, Helgaleena. Why would he do this?"

"He's a demon!"

Lavanya ran down the hall to her suite, a mere blur to those below. Zev was her only thought. She had to find him. Helgaleena was wrong. He couldn't have killed Chloe. The images from Vlad's vision of Zev tearing at the woman's neck looped continually in her mind, playing over and over with the image of Helgaleena closing Chloe's eyes.

She refused to believe Zev had killed anyone. There had to be some other explanation. But if she didn't find him and figure it out fast, Vlad would kill him for this.

A breeze wafted under the door of Zev's suite and hit her legs. Lavanya paused, apprehensive about finding him now. She didn't want to find that the Rakshasa was in complete control without her father's leash. What would she do? How could she love someone who killed so viciously?

Hold on. Was she a monster too? She took little drinks from willing donors—was she any better?

But she'd never killed a human. Renfield had taught her to take only a little from them. *Them.* She wasn't human as much as she tried to believe she was. *They* were her food. As much as she tried to be civilized, she was a monster, and she had to stop being as *delicate* as her father had shown her tonight.

If Zev had killed Chloe, she couldn't forgive that. Chloe was hers. *You want me to release something that evil on the world?* Vlad's words rang in her memory, as did the image of Chloe's gray eyes. But Zev wouldn't have killed her. His control was better than that.

With her resolve set, she burst into the room. "Zev!" The staff had covered the broken window with wood, but the room was still cold and drafty. She searched the dark with all her senses to see if Zev was here. Nothing but cold mountain air and the lingering scent of rain from the storm.

She crossed the room and pushed back the rug that someone had shoved under the door to keep the drafts out of her suite. She opened the door to find…another cold, dark room.

Dread trickled up her spine like a cold shiver. The room was beautiful. Everything was back to normal, like the zombie attack had never happened. All her things were back on her night stand, broken glass was swept up, and all signs of a struggle had been repaired. Light from the fire that burned in the grate danced along the black stone floor.

She entered her dressing room out of habit. All her cosmetics were arranged exactly as they should be on the mirrored vanity. She picked up the jar of Noxzema and opened it. The astringent scent burned her nose. *Almost gone*, she noticed.

He wasn't here. He had left. She hurled the jar across the room. It sailed from her hands like a bullet and exploded against the rainforest granite, shattering and splattering the antique, cobalt blue glass and white crème all over the bathroom.

Buttercup barked and dashed out from under the bed, scampering over to her. Lavanya scooped up the dog and hugged her tight.

"Oh, baby," she said. The little dog tried to look around Lavanya and yelped. "I miss him too." Lavanya sank to the floor and held Buttercup tightly.

"Lavanya?" Her father's voice startled her. How long had she been sitting on the stone floor? Long enough. Her legs had fallen asleep.

Her vision blurred with unshed tears, but she reined it all in before answering. "Yes, Father." She cleared her throat and dragged herself back into her suite, still holding Buttercup. The little dog barked ferociously at Vlad, but before he could complain, Lavanya put Buttercup down and shooed her back under the bed.

"I checked in on Renfield before coming upstairs," Vlad said. "He's doing well under Dylan's care."

"Thank heaven. Dylan is a godsend." Lavanya moved to the center of the room so Vlad wouldn't have reason to look into the bath suite and see the broken glass. His eyebrows shot up, letting her know he already knew about her tantrum. However, proving that he did know a thing or two about women, he didn't say anything about the broken jar.

"Of course, I've been to the library, too," he purred.

"How is Helgaleena? She was hysterical when I left her." Lavanya dropped down into the chaise. They were both just delaying the inevitable fight. "Did she say who she thought killed them?" Lavanya couldn't look at her father. She was too afraid of what his answer would be.

"You already know the answer to that question. And you also know that she doesn't *think* but *knows* who killed her granddaughter and the others." Vlad looked around the room. "I assume that the cowardly demon is already gone, since he's not here hiding behind your skirt."

"He's not here. But I don't think…"

"*What!* You don't believe he killed part of our family? Lavanya, Helgaleena, and Chloe were ours to protect, Child! Plus, those two deceitful women were mine to punish. Now Chloe is dead, and I have no gratification in the deaths of my enemies."

Vlad grabbed her arms, forcing her to stand and look at him. "I should have never released him," he said. "I knew he would leave, but I never imagined that he would dare take what was mine. I'm grateful that you weren't here when he lost control." Vlad rubbed her arms, looking at her with a sorrow she'd never seen before. "You imprudent girl. I couldn't stand to lose you, too." Vlad acted as if he wanted to hold her, but couldn't. He released her and walked to the fire.

"Father, he would never hurt me." Lavanya felt that truth in her bones.

"Did you know that he almost attacked Dylan while they were freeing Renfield?" Vlad placed one foot on the hearth and stared into the fire.

"Almost. You said *almost*. He didn't go through with it. Even after allowing me to feed from him twice and being injured and using up magic like it was free. He had to be ravenous, but he still didn't attack Dylan." Lavanya dusted off her pants and stood her ground, pretending to check her nails. They were terribly chipped from the climb up the mountain.

"You fed from that demon?" Lavanya froze as she watched Vlad's muscles tighten and his temple pulse as if his body were convulsing with anger. Moving lightning fast, he held Lavanya in a bruising grip. "You will not protect that thing. You will not see that thing again, and if I find it, I will destroy it. Do you understand?"

"Father—"

"*Do you understand?*"

"I don't believe he did this. I—" Lavanya squirmed in his hold. She wasn't a child anymore, and she wouldn't bow to his orders. "You're hurting me!"

Vlad tossed her into the chaise and left, leaving a cold breeze in his wake.

"Always nice speaking to you, too, Father." Lavanya rubbed her arms and lay back on the chair. All her energy and fight just vanished.

Run, Zev.

CHAPTER THIRTY

The Choice

The freezing wind rushed through his black fur and the rocks felt cold to his paws, but in his wolf form he hardly felt it. The wolf didn't think in terms of past or future. He felt no guilt or regret. However, the Rakshasa could feel longing, and they both hungered for the touch of the one woman they could never have.

The beast howled a long, sorrow-filled wail that echoed off the mountains. Zev used all his will to control the demon and keep them moving farther away from Lavanya. He had to get farther away to protect her. *He had to get away. He had to get away.* The same thought had been all he could concentrate on since he'd woken up covered in the blood of the innocent boy.

Zev slowed and skidded to a halt on top of a mountain peak. It was always winter up here. His big claws dug into the frozen gravel and icy snow, and his breath fogged the air as it left his nostrils. He'd been running fast, worried about getting away more than what direction he was heading. Where was he?

He looked at the surrounding forest and realized he'd traveled the same path he'd traveled earlier in the week to get to the castle. His cabin was close, and he was grateful to be so near his home. He needed a place to rest. He didn't want to relive the killing, yet he wondered why the memories hadn't assaulted him yet. It was bad enough that he could still taste the innocent human boy, but why could he taste only him?

He shook his big head and snorted in the cold. He should be happy he didn't have to remember all the details. Maybe it would save his sanity. His beast let out another pining howl as he shook off his emotions. *Get away, run.* The thought spurred him onward, and he bolted toward his cabin and some sort of sanctuary.

"How is she, Dylan?" Renfield asked his comrade and friend as he pulled himself into a sitting position. Dylan tried to help him, but Renfield brushed him off. A full twenty-four hours in bed and some good food and he was feeling almost normal. His strength was returning and his head finally felt clear. Although brief, his incarceration had taken a toll on him physically and mentally.

"I'm worried about her," Dylan admitted. "She's in denial." Dylan took the tray of empty dishes from Renfield's hands. "I got this, you just rest. Remember, the little magic jail cell took a lot out of you."

"Yes, Dylan. And I'll never forget as long as you keep babying me and bringing it up." Renfield brushed down the heavy covers, folding them at the top to form a perfect rectangle.

"It's her eyes, Renfield." Dylan stood at the foot of Renfield's bed, holding the heaping tray. "They're all glassy, and they shimmer as if they're full, but the tears are too afraid to fall." He put the tray on the stand by the door. "On the outside, she acts as if everything's fine. I know she didn't sleep all day, and now she's up there working on profiles for another round of matchmaking."

"She is a Draculesti." Renfield sighed. "They're not good at showing emotion. It's why her father sleeps when confronted by any emotion other than anger." Renfield shifted against the headboard. "He's not her first lover, and she's a smart woman. She'll be fine."

Dylan leaned against the door. "I know he wasn't her first, Renfield, but I've never seen her like this with a man. Hell, I trusted him." Dylan fisted his hands. "Is there any way that he's not responsible for Chloe's death? I mean, any way it could have been someone else who killed her and the others? Vlad spoke to Helgaleena, so you have to know what was said."

"Dylan, you have to prepare her. The demon will be dead by the break of day tomorrow." Renfield leaned back against the massive headboard of the old bed and closed his eyes. "Helgaleena's family has been tied to Vlad for centuries. She and Chloe are family, and as you can see by the chef's magical resurrection due to Helgaleena's spell, she is a very powerful ally. Vlad will never let this stand. Let alone the fact that Lavanya is still in danger. Vlad knows she cares for Zev, so he won't let him live. He won't take the chance that Zev could hurt her."

"I just—hell, Renfield, I'm a good judge of character, and I had no idea. I should have known. I'm here to protect her. I'll admit I've never failed before, and I don't like the feeling."

"Don't be too hard on yourself, Dylan," Renfield chuckled. "He may have been a decent guy, but when Vlad released his hold on the demon, Zev lost control."

"All right. I'm going to head up and help her prepare to send the guests home tonight. Do you need anything else?"

Renfield surveyed the room. "Ah, can you hand me that book that's on the little table by the fire?"

Dylan retrieved the battered hardback book and looked at the cover as he handed it to Renfield. "*Macbeth?* Well, that ought to put you right to sleep."

"It's one of my favorites, and it'll comfort me. Thank you." Renfield cradled the beat-up book in his hands as if it were a precious jewel.

"To each his own, I guess. I'll check on you later. Call down to the kitchen if you need anything."

"I'll be fine. Take care of Lavanya."

Renfield had told Dylan the truth. Normally reading his worn copy of Shakespeare's play settled his nerves. However, this evening the book made him feel anxious. He flipped through the pages, searching for a place to start or something to catch his eye or jog his memory. He wasn't sure why he was searching through the book like a treasure hunter, but from the moment he touched it, he knew it contained some answer he needed to find.

"Hi, doll!" Dylan yelled from the door to Lavanya's suite.

"I'm in here, Dylan." Lavanya sighed in relief and dropped the brush and bobby pins on the vanity. They bounced around the jars and debris, evidence of her failed attempt to get herself ready to see off her guests.

"I just came up to see if I could help—"Lavanya knew he was taken by surprise at her clumsy attempt to fix her own hair and makeup. "Well, now, that's not your best look."

Her hair hung in crazy wisps around her face, and makeup caked under her red and swollen eyes where she'd tried to hide the dark circles.

"Just think of it as job security," she said. "I don't seem to be able to focus."

"Wonderful, because I was worried I'd be replaced as soon as you mastered the ponytail." Dylan stood back and Lavanya watched him assess her in the mirror.

"You've done a great job. We just need to put a few finishing touches on the look." He began pulling out the bobby pins and ponytail holder that secured her long black hair. "I love the outfit, and I never would have thought to put that tiny black sweater with the tea-length pink chiffon skirt." He stroked a brush through her hair. "But with some simple strappy heels and a simple up do, you'll be all set."

"Thanks, Dylan."

"What is this?" Dylan pulled at the leather strap at the back of Lavanya's neck.

"Oh, the necklace." Lavanya played with the worn pendent Helgaleena had given her. "Whoever cleaned up the mess after the attack on Chloe found it with Helgaleena's reading." Lavanya pointed to the vanity top and the crumpled paper. "With Chloe gone and Helgaleena..." Lavanya ran her fingers over the cold medallion. "I just wanted to wear it."

"That's fine. We'll just tuck it into the little turtleneck, and you can wear it next to your heart." Dylan pushed the leather strap under the soft cashmere neck of the sweater. "Let's see about that makeup next."

As Dylan worked on Lavanya's eyes with a charcoal liner, he smiled and a little chuckle slipped out.

"What could possibly be funny right now?" Lavanya asked.

"I don't know how you're doin' on the inside, honey, but your hair sure is holdin' up beautiful." Dylan chuckled under his breath.

"Did you just quote *Steel Magnolias?*" Lavanya asked in a stern voice.

"Yeah, I guess I did."

"I—" Lavanya looked at Dylan as he squirmed, trying to hold back his laughter. After a moment she burst out laughing herself.

"Laughter through tears is my favorite emotion," she said, wiping her eyes. They both laughed until they held their sides.

"Okay, okay, stand up and let me look at you." Dylan smiled at her. "It's almost full dark, and your guests will be anxious to leave."

Lavanya wiped under her eyes again and stood for inspection. Dylan tucked in a few stray hairs that had fallen during their outburst and dabbed under her eyes for any stray liner.

"You look lovely. Now go wish everyone good-bye, and I'll check on Helgaleena and Renfield."

Lavanya reached for Dylan and tucked herself under his chin and clung to him as he embraced her. "Thank you…for everything. I—" Dylan pulled away.

"Now don't start that. I'll just have to fix your makeup again." He gave Lavanya a tender smile that she rarely saw. "Get going. When you get back, we'll start packing up. I'm ready for some sun, a big mojito, and a Cuban cigar." He released her and began cleaning up the makeup and brushes they'd used.

"That sounds wonderful. I can't wait to be warm again." Lavanya had turned away, but stopped at the sound of crumpling paper. "Wait!"

Dylan had wadded up the notes she'd taken on Helgaleena's rune reading. "Don't throw that away. Just… leave it. I may want to look through it again." Dylan straightened out the paper on the vanity.

"Okay, if you really want it," he said. "But get going. I bet they're waiting for you downstairs." He shooed her out of the room.

Zev picked up his pace when his cabin came into view. His huge breaths fogged the air as he pounded along. Relief filled him, even as the beast struggled to break free. He wasn't a danger to anyone here in this remote space.

In one breath, the fog turned to black mist and he hit a wall so hard he bounced backward. Before he could move, he was surrounded and pined to the cold ground.

"I'm going to enjoy your death, demon."

Vlad. Sparks circled Zev's vision as his brain rang in his own head. The Rakshasa in him sprang forward in his consciousness to confront their enemy. His hind legs elongated and his spine straightened, bringing him to a standing position as half beast, half man. The demon gave Zev the extra strength he needed to push out of Vlad's hold. His roar shook the mountain.

"I should have killed you the day your grandmother brought you to the castle." Vlad snarled, his own fangs long and sharp. His face stretched into something inhuman.

"Why didn't you?" Zev bellowed, recalling his lonely

existence and realizing what lay ahead for him since he could no longer be with Lavanya.

Vlad circled. "Because Inez begged me to save you. Her daughter had foreseen that you would protect my heart. Your mother was the most powerful enchantress and psychic I've ever known. I believed her vision and your grandmother's words." Spit flew as Vlad snarled. "I don't know how Inez managed to lie to me, but after I finish with you, I'll take care of her, too."

"*No!*" The thought enraged Zev and the demon answered his call, lashing out at Vlad and managing to cut deeply into Vlad's chest with his long, extended claws.

Vlad didn't take time to check his wounds, but spun with the impact and came down with his fists on Zev's shoulder.

Pain exploded along Zev's shoulder blade, and he hissed.

The two snarled and ran at each other. The crash as their bodies hit loosened rocks from their resting place at the top of the mountain, and pebbles rained down on their heads.

"*Enough!*" Inez appeared in their path. Her frail body stood between the two huge monsters. Her long, gray hair cloaked her tiny shoulders; her voice echoed off the stone.

Vlad's eyes were the color of garnet as he charged them. Inez backed into Zev, and he felt her calloused hands on his wrists just before the velvet hands of her magic encircled them. Vlad struck out at Inez with his long, sharp nails. The air shimmered like heat coming off blacktop and absorbed Vlad's strike.

"I'll love the taste of you, old woman." Vlad struggled to break through the protective bubble that encircled Inez and Zev. Inez leaned heavily on Zev and put her hand to her temple as if she were in pain.

"Damn it, Inez." Zev cradled his grandmother and watched Vlad with hatred. "Let me kill him so we can finally be free."

"You won't be able to hold me off for long, old woman." Vlad spat and struck at the field around them.

"I'm very aware of my abilities. I only hope I can hold you off long enough for you both to come to your senses. Now hush, both of you, and let me think." Inez continued to rub her temples, but shook off Zev's attempt to hold her. Zev pushed at the magic with his own, looking for some weakness he could exploit to free himself, but it was useless.

"Grandmother, release me so I can kill him. If you don't, he'll kill us both. He knows you lied to him about my mother's prophecy. Our only choice is to kill him before he kills us."

"*Lie?* I could no more lie to him than any human could. I wouldn't even try." Inez fluttered her hands in the air as if waving away a fly.

"Liar! You told me that the beast would protect my heart when he was grown. It's the only reason I protected him from the villagers who would have killed him as a babe." Vlad struggled in vain against the magic that cocooned the demon and witch.

"Hmmm, did I say that?" Inez seemed to ponder the wording. "That was the truth behind my daughter's prophecy, which she told to me on her death bed." Inez wrinkled her eyes and shrugged her shoulders. "Her actual words... no. But that was the gist of it. I did not lie."

Inez looked into Zev's hazel eyes. The beast had retreated when it realized there'd be no more fighting for a while. "*Protect him mother, take him to The Prince.* That's what she said. I knew she meant the Prince of Darkness. *Zev will be most valuable to him. Zev will take the Prince's heart after a great battle.* Those were her words."

Zev's eyes returned to the demon's midnight black.

"I will kill you, old woman." Vlad bellowed.

"*Yet the Prince will be relieved to release it to him.* Her assurance. My dying child said that he would be happy to release his heart to you, Zev, for protection." Inez paced inside the tight confines of her magic. Vlad mirrored her movements, no doubt looking for a weakness to exploit for his own gain.

"Riddles! You speak in riddles!"

"Inez, let me out of here." Zev grabbed her thin arms and looked down into the gray eyes. "I'm strong enough, he's released me. I can kill him." Zev looked over her shoulder into the red eyes of his enemy, feeling the truth of his words.

Inez pulled away. "He released the small hold he had over you, but it is my hold that, when released, will open your full strength. But this is not the question for now. For now we must try to understand Nya's words."

"The time for words is over." Vlad ran his finger down the edges of the clear, protective bubble of magic, causing sparks to flare a trail down the side. "The demon took what was mine to protect, Inez. Chloe was a decedent of your original tribe and part of a family that chose to serve me rather than seek your destruction. That alone is cause for his death. But he has harmed my Lavanya. Had he not tainted her body with his blood and his hands, I might have let him live." Vlad roared and ripped at the magic barrier.

Zev burst through the magic membrane. "I would never harm Lavanya." His anger and his beast crashed against Vlad's and the two battled again. "I would do anything to protect her. I don't remember attacking Chloe, but I ran from the castle to protect Lavanya. I couldn't trust my demon." The demon let out a soulful howl of loneliness as Vlad landed a strong blow to Zev's side.

"I will protect her from your demon. I will kill you and spread your ashes over the mountain." Vlad pushed Zev up against the jagged rock wall. "Lavanya is my only reason for living, all that I have left of her mother. My heart beats for her alone."

"Stop!" The shrill scream of a bell rang in Vlad's ears, and the ground shook under his feet. Both beasts gripped their heads and keened in pain, stumbling and scratching at their ears.

"Stop," Inez said again. She gripped Zev's face in her hands. Blood dripped from his forehead and nose. "What did you say about Chloe? How could you not remember killing her?"

"Fucking witch! I'll kill you!" Vlad raged against the sound tearing his head apart.

"Hush. You are both fools." Inez bent and sniffed Zev's hair deeply, then moved on to his clothing.

"What are you doing, Inez?" Zev tried to bat her hands away. "Get out of the way."

Inez held on with unnatural strength. "Look at me. Did you kill Chloe?"

"I—" Zev couldn't finish the sentence, but a snarl of rage came from his demon.

"Why ask him? He'll just lie to you, as you lied to me," Vlad snarled.

"Have you been away from us for so long that you can't smell the magic on him?" Inez stepped away and very intently smelled the air around Vlad. "On you?"

"What!" Vlad stopped pacing and faced the deceptively frail

woman. "I haven't been tainted by magic, unless it's your own."
Rage colored his eyes a dark shade of red.

"Are you so blinded by fear and hate that you can't think?"
Inez yelled. "Zev, tell me what you remember."

His expression was bewildered. "Why does it matter?" he
asked, keeping an eye on Vlad.

"It matters greatly. The Rakshasa is immune to the magic, let
me speak with it."

"Never. I have to keep it under control. No one's safe." Zev
shot to his feet. "I have to leave." He swished his head from side to
side, looking for a way to escape. Inez blocked his retreat. With
each move he made, she countered it with her own. And Vlad
stood between him and the path to the cottage.

"I don't remember killing. The boy—he killed Lavanya." Zev
rubbed his head. "No, I just thought that. When I woke, it was Uki
lying on the floor, but I'd been so sure he'd done it." Zev paced
faster.

Vlad sniffed the air. "What is that smell old woman? And why
is he acting like that?"

"The boy, he tasted too good. I was so hungry, but he was
innocent and his blood so sweet. I couldn't stop..." Zev moved
faster.

"It's a powerful compulsion." Inez spoke softly to Vlad as
they both moved in on Zev.

"It's not safe for Lavanya to be around the Rakshasa." A
bellow of sorrow bubbled up from Zev. "I must leave. I must
control it. I must make Lavanya safe. I must leave. I must leave."
Zev fell to his knees as the fear for Lavanya crushed his mind.

"Zev, you must let the Rakshasa out. The demon can't be held
by this compulsion."

"No!"

"Zev, while you were with Lavanya, did the Rakshasa ever
take control?"

"Yes."

Vlad snarled and lunged at Zev. Inez blocked him with the
help of her magic.

Zev remembered the surge of jealousy and possessiveness
when the beast took control. "After the boy hurt Lavanya. It broke
free."

"Did it hurt her, Zev?"

"No. It wanted her, but it didn't harm her." Zev spoke softly now, remembering Lavanya's touch. "She spoke to it and calmed it."

Vlad snarled again, but Inez hushed him with a gesture.

"Zev. Let the Rakshasa out. It can fight the magic that's holding you."

"I must …leave…?" Zev doubled over, as if in pain. Then the Rakshasa burst out, completely taking over Zev. It stayed on its knees, but turned its black eyes to Inez and winked. The animal cunning behind his black eyes was as easily seen as his clawed hands. A long bellow rose from his chest and thundered through his black lips as the Rakshasa pulled his head back to stare at the moon. Then just as quickly as it took control, it was gone. Just like that the spell was broken and Zev returned. He swayed, but didn't fall all the way to the ground.

"Zev?"

"Inez." He shook himself off. "Thanks. I needed that." Zev kissed her on the cheek, and she was so short that he didn't even have to stand to reach her face. Then he stood.

"I killed the boy—or started to—and that's all I remember until I woke and found Helgaleena leaning over Chloe," he said. "The women vampires were there among the dead. I felt guilty and ashamed for killing Chloe and the boy so powerfully. Helgaleena was grieving for Chloe, certain that I'd killed her since I was covered in blood. But I don't remember anything except that I felt so evil. To protect Lavanya I had to leave. I didn't have a rational thought, just felt the need to get as far away as possible."

"I was too late to see the dead. By the time I arrived, they were cleaning up the library." Vlad gazed to the heavens. "What did the scene look like?"

"I was covered in blood. What do you think it looked like?"

"I've seen you feed the demon. It's not a neat thing." Vlad raised an eye brow. "I was surprised that they could have cleaned it up before my arrival, and I'm curious as to what you remember."

"I…" Zev looked at his grandmother.

"You've no cause for modesty or shame on account of me." Inez gently touched his hard, whiskered jaw.

"The boy's throat was gone, and his blood soaked the fur, but

306

the others—there was no sign of struggle. The women—their throats were cut neatly. I hadn't thought of it before." Zev took a tentative step toward Vlad, all the rage gone. "No way I could've killed everyone without a fight or fed that neatly. That room would've been torn to shreds, and blood would have been everywhere."

"Ah." Vlad rubbed his face and then his head shot up. "No!"

"What?" Zev grabbed Vlad by his coat lapels.

"We've got to hurry. She's in grave danger." Vlad turned back the way they had come.

"What are you talking about?" Zev held him tight.

"I've got to get back to the castle." Vlad pulled Zev along. "Renfield's memories. *Double, double toil and trouble.* That's what he said. I didn't understand. I couldn't see it. I wouldn't let myself see it."

"Very powerful magic, indeed," Inez added.

"When he was held captive." Vlad pulled away from Zev. "The girl Giselle. She tried to tell him who was attacking us. We just couldn't believe it. Ah, and the tower, of course. Who else could it have been?" He took flight as the wind changed directions.

"Inez?" Zev watched him go with anxiety and fear tearing through him.

"Go child. Save Lavanya."

Zev charged down the mountain, changing from his human form to the beast with four paws as he ran. If he could just get closer, within sight of the castle, he could use his magic to will himself to her.

Double, double toil and trouble. The quote was from *Macbeth*, the three witches. He thought they were prophets in the play, but that was all he could remember. To the Rakshasa, it didn't matter who posed the danger, he just knew he'd kill anything that threatened Lavanya. For once Zev and the Rakshasa were in total agreement.

"Lavanya." Tru waited to approach until the others had left. Lavanya had seen the way her friend had hung back, waiting to ambush her and get the news on the murders and where Zev might be. Tru's concerned face should have warmed her. She was a good friend, but Lavanya had no interest in putting her heart out on display for Tru and her new lover.

"Are you heading back to Miami, or to Naasir's home?" Lavanya formed a perfect smile that somehow managed to hurt her face.

"Naasir, can you leave us alone for a minute?" Tru asked.

"Of course, dear." Naasir kissed Tru's hands before turning to Lavanya. "It was a pleasure and an honor to be invited here and to meet you. I am forever in your debt for introducing me to Tru." Naasir kissed Tru lightly on the head. "I will be waiting out front. Please take as long as you need."

"Thanks, babe." Tru slapped him on the ass as he turned to go. Lavanya watched Naasir shake his head as he left the castle.

"I'm so happy for you both." The words burned her tongue as she spoke, but she kept her smile in place, even though she knew it didn't reach her eyes.

"Whatever." Tru put her hands on Lavanya's face and massaged her cheeks.

Lavanya pulled away. "What are you doing?"

"I thought your face might crack if you held that shit-stupid grin any longer." Tru put her hand on Lavanya's forearm. "We're heading to Miami. I've already spoken to Dylan, so I know that's where you'll be too. Frankly, that's why we're going there. I'll be there for you, no matter what. Finish all this bullshit and then come home. I'll be waiting to help you heal or just to kick your ass if you wallow for too long."

"I—" Lavanya began to crack, but she knew she couldn't. If she let herself, she'd be a puddle on the floor, and no one needed to see that. "Thanks. We're going home, but just for a short stopover. I've already booked a ship for the next group of couples. I leave in a little over a week."

"Lavanya, I know how much you cared for Zev, whether you want to admit that now or not."

"I barely knew him. Obviously."

Tru held up her hand. "Save it. I'm not buying it. Just call me when you get in."

"Oh. My. God." Lavanya held Tru's arms to the sides, taking in the black leather and tattoos. "You're a mother hen type. I never would have guessed it."

"I keep it very well hidden. Thank you very much." Tru

hugged Lavanya one last time. "Promise you'll call."

"Yes, yes, I'll call you. Now get going. That gorgeous man is waiting." Lavanya pushed her toward the doors.

"See ya soon." Tru looked back over her shoulder before slipping through the huge doors to the courtyard and the waiting Humvee.

Lavanya put her hands to her face. She felt as if her smile was cracked. But the moment she started to feel, she cut it off. This was all so insane. She really had known Zev only for a few days. Why was she so surprised that he'd let her down? He was a demon. Wasn't that in the job description?

"Lavanya?" She'd been so deep in self-pity that she hadn't heard Helgaleena come into the entry hall.

"Helgaleena." Lavanya straightened and ran her hands down her full skirt. "How are you feeling? Better, I hope." She tucked a stray hair back into place as she turned to the frail-looking woman.

"Yes, I'm regaining my strength. How are you?"

"Me?" Lavanya looked toward the stairs, anxious to get back to her suite and pack. Her hands fisted at her sides without her noticing. "I'm *fine*. Let me apologize again for your loss, Helgaleena. Chloe will be greatly missed, and I hope that Vlad will find the guilty party and put them to death." She couldn't bring herself to say Zev's name. She couldn't accept that he could have killed Chloe.

"Vlad will find the guilty party? But we know it was—" Helgaleena stopped at Lavanya's cold stare before she spoke of Zev. "Of course he'll put him to death. Are you tired, dear? You keep inching closer to the stairs."

"No, but I need to pack. Dylan and I are leaving shortly for the States. I have work to attend to."

"So, you're not planning to be here when your father punishes the demon?"

"No."

"Oh, I'm sorry—the guilty party—when he brings in the murderer." Helgaleena's eyes were rimmed in red and both women tensed for a fight.

Lavanya dropped her shoulders. "I don't have the strength to argue with you right now, Helgaleena. I just want to go home." Lavanya turned away and headed for the stairs.

"Wait." Helgaleena followed her. "I'm hurting, and—" Helgaleena's spirits seemed to lift. "Why don't you let me help you pack? Dylan is attending to Renfield right now, and I'd be happy to help. It will give me something to do with my hands and quiet my mind." Helgaleena reached out and touched Lavanya's arm.

"All right. Are you sure you're up to this?" Lavanya took in the frail woman's stooped shoulders and darkened eyes.

"Yes. I don't know if I'll see you again, and I don't want us to part with these feelings between us. No matter what happened, you will always be my sister."

"Oh, Helgaleena. I'll miss her so much, but she was your blood. I'm so sorry." Lavanya embraced Helgaleena. "I just can't accept it. I can't believe that he could have done that to Chloe." Lavanya broke down then.

"Now, now, there's no need for tears. She had purpose in life, and I'll see that her spirit lives on." Helgaleena seemed to grow taller under the weight of Lavanya's arms; her conviction seemed to boost her frail frame.

"Good." Lavanya pulled away. "I would love for you to help me pack, although I doubt very seriously that this is the last time we'll see each other. You're too stubborn to die. You'll probably outlive us all." Lavanya squeezed the older woman's arm and was surprised to feel the muscle tighten under her hand.

"Come. I'm anxious to spend some time with you," Helgaleena said, pulling Lavanya up the stairs.

"Dylan, I can feel Vlad," Renfield said. "He's trying to reach me, but I can't make a connection. It's just like when I was trapped in that damn tower." Renfield paced his room, holding the worn copy of *Macbeth* in his hands.

"Renfield, Renfield! Calm down." Dylan reached out to the trembling Renfield, and the volume slipped from his shaking hands. Renfield gasped and fell on the book.

"What is with you and that book?" Dylan hoisted him into a chair by the fire. "Give it to me."

"No." Renfield rubbed the old binding. "I…there's something important about it. I just can't remember."

"Shit, old man, you're losing it."

"I know, I know." Renfield looked down at the old cover and the pages that were uneven in the binding. He flipped open the cover and ran his hands over the first page.

"Why this book? I mean, do you always read it when you're upset? Or is it just now?" Renfield's paranoia was rubbing off on him.

"I haven't seen it for a long time." Renfield looked at the bookcases lining one side of his suite. "I remember how it calmed me when I was young, and I got it out for Giselle when she was going through her change into vampirism...Oh, holy hell!"

"*What?*"

"Giselle." Renfield thumbed through the pages to a dog-eared section close to the front of the book.

"What? *What?*"

"Wait." Renfield finally stopped. "Giselle kept repeating a passage from the book. I just thought she was nuts from the change and the kidnapper was basically using her, but...yes, here it is." Renfield held the book out to Dylan. "Read it."

"Okay. *Witch 1: Thrice the brinded cat.*"

"No, no. Farther down. Start where it says *all*."

Dylan rolled his eyes, but looked for the spot, giving Renfield the benefit of the doubt. "*Double, double toil and trouble*," he read, adding his own eerie voice to the second part of the quote. "*Fire burn and cauldron bubble.*"

"That's it! She just kept repeating that. But why?" Renfield asked.

"How should I know?" Dylan plopped down on the sofa with the book. "It's a famous quote, though. Even if you know nothing about *Macbeth* or the prophecy or the three sisters, everyone has heard some form of that quote. Really, even Willy Wonka references it in the movie."

"That's it! Dylan—" Renfield ran to the door and yanked hard on the glass knob.

"Willy Wonka?"

"No! The sisters!" Renfield fought with the door, struggling and twisting until his face was red.

"Renfield?" Dylan went over to help. "Here, let me. You must be weak or something." He turned the knob and pulled, but the door didn't budge.

"Is it locked?" he asked as he struggled. "Do you have a key?"

"We have to get to Lavanya." Renfield walked around the room as if looking for another way out.

"Stop." Dylan turned away from the useless struggle with the door. "What are you thinking? What does the quote mean?"

"Dylan, don't you get it? The *sisters*." Renfield held up his hand, checking points off on his fingers. "They're *prophets*. And *witches*."

"But…*NO!*" Dylan turned back to the door with renewed strength and purpose.

"Dylan, it's no use. I told you it felt just like the spell in the tower. That's why I can't hear Vlad. Can you feel Lavanya?"

Dylan stilled, holding his breath. "I can feel her." He exhaled. "She's calm, but it's like she's far away. I—she's okay right now."

"We have to figure out a way to get the door open. Lavanya's a sitting duck. She won't even think of protecting herself."

"That should be the last of the clothes," Helgaleena called from the closet.

"Thanks. I'll tackle the cosmetics next." Lavanya left the walk-in and headed for the vanity. "I appreciate your help, Helgaleena, although I'm starting to get a little worried about Dylan and Renfield. Dylan said he'd meet me here to pack when the guests were all gone." She picked up a few makeup brushes. "He has to know everyone's gone."

She turned to Helgaleena. "You don't think Renfield is worse, do you?" She put the brushes down and headed out of her suite, but Helgaleena caught her arm in a tight grip that surprised Lavanya with its strength.

"Lavanya, everything is fine. Calm down. You're just restless because of everything that's been happenin'." Helgaleena released her and swiveled the vanity chair toward Lavanya.

"Come, sit here, and I'll take your hair down. It'll calm you as it did when we were both young. You always loved being pampered, and my family—really, the whole village—just loved to fawn all over you. Sit."

"All right." Lavanya thought Helgaleena was acting odd, but she didn't feel like facing anything tonight. Truthfully, she wanted to forget everything about this weekend.

"I just feel adrift," she said. "I don't know. I can't even feel Vlad right now. It's strange." She sat down and took a deep breath to calm her nerves.

"Didn't the two of you fight about the Rakshasa before he left?" Helgaleena placed her hands heavily on Lavanya's shoulders, anchoring her in the chair.

"Yes. I should talk to him before I leave. I don't want him tracking Zev." Lavanya dipped her head, remembering the fight with Vlad and what Helgaleena thought of Zev, too. "I'm sorry, Helgaleena, I know you're convinced he killed Chloe, but I just know he couldn't have done it. I can't explain why. I just know that even if the Rakshasa had been in control, it wouldn't have hurt me that way."

"Of course," Helgaleena said, pulling bobby pins from Lavanya's hair. "You've always been delusional where your charms are concerned. I'm not surprised that you'd think you could tame a Rakshasa demon. You're sooo very special...*Lavanya*."

Helgaleena said her name as if her mouth was full of dirt and she had to force out the word.

"Helga—" Lavanya tried to turn around to see if the venom in her sister's voice matched the look on her face, but Helgaleena held her in place.

"You're wrong! The Rakshasa cost my Chloe her life!" Helgaleena's hands stilled and she took a deep breath as if she could inhale calm from the air around her. "Oh, everything has gone wrong this weekend, you're right about that! Not one thing has happened the way I planned. I'm sure you feel the same way, Lavanya."

Lavanya looked at Helgaleena's reflection in the mirror. Her sister's eyes were wide, and the whites were too bright for a woman of her age. Helgaleena picked up the bristled brush that Lavanya loved and began to brush her long, black hair.

"I'm sorry." Lavanya chalked up the small outburst to grief. She was having trouble following Helgaleena's mood swings, but decided not to look too deeply into Helgaleena emotions.

Lavanya felt Helgaleena's hand rubbing her neck. "That feels so heavenly," she said. She closed her eyes and enjoyed the simple pleasure. "Thank you, Helgaleena."

"It just proves that if you want something done right, you have to do it yourself," Helgaleena said with an odd chuckle.

"Ah…" Then Lavanya felt a tug on her neck and opened her eyes. Helgaleena's stare was hard as she held the family medallion that she'd given Lavanya earlier in the week.

"Why are you wearing this *now?*" Helgaleena roughly snapped the leather cord, leaving a burn mark on Lavanya's neck.

"Ow!" Lavanya rubbed her neck. "I wanted to be closer to your mother, I guess." Lavanya watched Helgaleena rub her thumb over the worn etching on the medallion.

"If only you'd worn it when I asked you to, Chloe would still be alive."

"How could it have hurt Chloe? You said it was for my protection."

"Yes, The Helm of Awe is for protection and… *irresistibility.*" Helgaleena tossed the necklace down on the vanity and ran her hands through Lavanya's hair. "You always had such beautiful hair. Didn't you?" She tugged harder.

"Helgaleena, stop it. You're hurting me!" Lavanya reached up to settle Helgaleena's hands, but now the hands she held felt smooth and soft—and not only smoother, the skin was thick and plump. The reflection showed Helgaleena's face was wrinkle-free, and the dark age spots that used to dot her jawline had disappeared.

"What—" Lavanya was mesmerized by the display in the mirror. Helgaleena's gray and brittle hair was transforming into thick, wavy, chestnut brown locks beginning at the roots and flowing like a waterfall over her straight shoulders.

It had to be a trick in the mirror. Lavanya tried to stand and turn to see for herself.

"Sit." Helgaleena rested her hands on Lavanya's shoulders, restraining her in the chair. "I need to explain something to you."

"What's happening to you?" Lavanya looked at Helgaleena's reflection in the mirror, amazed at the miraculous changes taking place to her sister. "You're getting younger. It's marvelous, Helgaleena. How?"

"It is amazing, isn't it?" Helgaleena spun the chair around and laughed as Lavanya watched the years reverse with each turn. Her sister's age reversal was incredible to watch, but something on the vanity caught Lavanya's attention. Next to the medallion was the scrap of paper with Lavanya's notes on the rune reading

Helgaleena had done for her days before. The symbols stood out starkly— bold and easily seen—against the white paper.

ᛊ **Sowilo: energy, health, life—wolf**

ᛁ **Isa: blindness, treachery, betrayal—(feminine)**

ᛇ **Eihwaz: immortality, transformation—thirteenth card, DEATH**

For the first time she saw what she should have noticed long before. Lavanya put her feet on the floor to stop spinning. She stood and snatched the scrap of paper, but fell back, dizzy, against the vanity.

"What's wrong, Sisterrr?"

Lavanya heard her, but Helgaleena sounded as if she were speaking from the end of a long tunnel. Lavanya hung on to the vanity and waited for the room to stop spinning. Helgaleena reached out a smooth, long-fingered hand. The moment she made contact, a jolt of pain went through Lavanya's body and her knees went out from under her. She almost knocked over the vanity, and bottles and brushes fell and littered the floor. She backed herself into a corner.

"Helgaleena! Stop this!"

"But I'm finally having some *fun*." Helgaleena straightened the mirror and then admired herself, smoothing her hair and pinching her plump cheeks.

"How are you young again?" Lavanya held her head. The pain was less now that Helgaleena wasn't touching her, but she gained nothing by announcing that fact.

"You had to wear that stupid necklace tonight. I was just going to kill you quickly, but noooo." Helgaleena rolled her eyes as she righted the vanity cushion and sat down gently. "Oh, well, there's no hurry, I guess."

She pulled the old skirt up to her hip and kicked off her arch support shoes to examine her new, shapely legs. She twirled around in front of the mirror and ran her hands over her new body like a lover. "You can't imagine how good this feels after being so broken and old. Do you like the new me, Lavanya?"

"What have you done, Helgaleena?"

"I'm done being a slave to your father. And you." She spat on Lavanya.

Lavanya flinched and turned her head, reaching up to wipe her face. Helgaleena's eyes brightened.

"What's this now?" she asked, reaching for the slip of paper Lavanya had crumpled in her hand. Helgaleena smoothed out the paper, read it, and then roared with laughter.

"Oh, my Goddess, I didn't realize the rune symbols spelled SIS when written out! That's priceless." She threw the paper at Lavanya. "And you never took the readings seriously. Huh, *SIS.*" Helgaleena laughed until her laughter sounded like the giggle of a young girl, and her body matched the sound.

"But Uki and Raz? …Chloe?"

"Don't even think about my poor Chloe." Helgaleena bent and wrapped her hands around Lavanya's neck, squeezing it. Helgaleena's touch was cold, and Lavanya could feel black magic creep across her skin—deceiving to the eye, yet deadly, like black ice on a mountain pass.

Lavanya felt something stir inside her, something that understood Helgaleena's black magic and wanted to meet it with its own. It was alien to her, and it frightened her more than the black witch she used to call sister.

She didn't put up a fight. Helgaleena felt unnaturally strong, and Lavanya wanted to wait for the right moment. She hoped that would come before Dylan or Renfield arrived to check on her. All she had to do was keep Helgaleena talking.

"It's your fault she's dead!" Helgaleena raged, kicking Lavanya. "Uki and Raz were pawns. Easily excited about the opportunity to rid themselves of Vlad's rules and perfect distractions. When their usefulness was through, I killed them to consume their strength. Really a win-win situation."

"But what about Chloe?" Lavanya asked, breathing through her pain.

"My Chloe should never have died. "That zombie attacked her because she was holding the medallion when he came for you. When she awoke last night she confronted me. Being of my blood, she recognized my *touch* in the spell."

"What?"

"You poisoned her against me. She loved you, as my mother did and all the others. No one could see you and your father for the ruthless slave owners you are. We've served at your beck and call for centuries, with nothing of our own to show for it. No one but me could see the truth!"

Helgaleena stood then, yanking Lavanya to her feet, and backhanded her with unexpected force. Lavanya staggered back, falling again to the floor, knocking over the vanity and all its contents. Pain shot through her face and jaw.

Helgaleena possessed more power than a simple woman should have, even a young woman as Helgaleena was now. Her magic infused every movement she made. She sizzled with it. She threw off black sparks like a black diamond under a jeweler's lamp. Lavanya had never seen an aura before or really even understood what that meant, but something inside her now was enabling her to see the darkness around Helgaleena. It was foul and had consumed what used to be her sister. Nothing was left of Helgaleena, the girl she had known.

"Why not just leave if you felt so used?" Lavanya pushed herself up and wiped at her bloody lip. It was the wrong question to ask. Lavanya knew that, and yet, as she felt her jaw swell, she enjoyed Helgaleena's reaction.

"Leave! Why should *I* leave? My family has been here since this valley was formed! Vlad is the cancer who needs to be destroyed." She sat on the vanity as if weary.

"This should have been so easy. But as you can see from our little rune reading—" she waved the scrap of paper in the air, "— prophecy is never a simple matter. It seems that even if I live to be two centuries, I'll never fully understand the art of interpretation. These prophesies can never be understood until you have time to reflect on the events that have come to pass and see their true meanings."

"What prophecy?" Lavanya's head was clearing, and the strength she felt she now recognized as that of the Rakshasa. It recognized the evil in Helgaleena and wanted to consume it. When Zev allowed her to feed from him, he somehow infused her with the Rakshasa's strength and appetite. She just needed to keep Helgaleena talking until she saw an opportunity to overpower her.

"Old prophecies I found in my great-grandmother's things.

Along with a wonderful collection of black spells." Helgaleena seemed lost in thought as she gazed at her reflection. "She documented so many wonderful magic incantations and curses, like the one that I used to give me back my youthful appearance." Helgaleena smiled at Lavanya, but it didn't reach her eyes.

"Mother thought the price for black magic was too high, but I believe the price is definitely worth it." Helgaleena was drawn back to her reflection in the mirror and smiled again as she turned to take in her whole appearance.

"But I digress. Back to the prophecies." She pulled her attention back to where Lavanya lay. "They described a powerful witch who bore a demon destined to take the heart of Vlad. Zev fit that description to a T. I was so sure. But I waited decades for him to act." Helgaleena threw the scrap of paper on the floor.

"When I couldn't wait any longer for fear I'd waste away, I put in motion a simple plan to speed things along. Those stupid women Uki and Raz were easy to manipulate and frame. I knew Vlad would sense a threat once they started plotting against him. I simply gave them a little magic nudge to get them riled. I also knew he'd send the demon to protect you because, he'd be too lazy to wake from his slumber. I got rid of Renfield and the zombie I conjured should have been enough to kill you. Easy. Vlad would be forced to rise. He'd blame Zev for not protecting you, they would fight, etcetera, etcetera. The demon would kill Vlad, and all would be right with my world." Helgaleena spun around like a child in the vanity chair.

"Everything was so simple. The village would be rid of you both, and we could return to our own lives, free from servitude. Obviously, looking back, I underestimated your *allure*." Helgaleena bent to tilt up Lavanya's face. "But who could have guessed you could tame a Rakshasa demon, or that your pretty boy stylist could kill a zombie? No prophecy could have predicted that."

Lavanya—or the Rakshasa's blood flowing through her—had had enough. She pushed Helgaleena's soft hand away.

"Don't touch me." She stood and felt the demon's blood hot in her veins. "I'm not surprised you underestimated me or Dylan. You never could see past your own childish, selfish, vain, evil needs. Your mother Velka loved you, but she knew your true

318

nature. That's why she didn't want you to have those old spells. She begged me to watch over you when we were young and help keep you in line."

Lavanya adjusted her sweater. "You're right, it is my fault that Chloe died. I never should have let you out of my sight. You turned out just as your mother feared: evil, alone, and turning on the only family you have."

A red flush ran up Helgaleena's neck until her face was almost swollen with anger. "How dare you speak of my mother!" She pushed her hands out, and Lavanya saw sickly black veins throb on her forearms.

Lavanya was pushed back by an unseen electrical force. Her own anger was strong enough to withstand it, but she could see that this power was just a touch of what Helgaleena was capable of now. She needed to finish this quickly if she was going to survive it.

"Vlad! Stop!" Zev caught Vlad's arm as the wind pushed them forward.

"Let go!" A loud crack of thunder joined the wind. "I can't feel them, Lavanya or Renfield." Vlad pulled away.

"We've got to work together!" Zev turned so his hair was out of his face.

"It may be too late already."

"It isn't!" Zev grabbed Vlad's arm again.

"What?!" Vlad stared at the brash demon.

"I know she's alive. I—" Zev released Vlad. "Somehow she's pulling my Rakshasa. It doesn't matter how. I just know that we won't make it like this, but if you can help me get within sight of the castle, I can will myself to her. You fed me strength when we rescued Renfield. Do it again, and I can reach her faster."

"I will save her."

"We don't have time for this, Vlad! I can feel her. She's fighting and she's pulling on me...the Rakshasa for strength. Frankly, I don't know how much longer I can hold him back to talk this over."

"Why would I trust you, Rakshasa?"

"Because my Rakshasa is the only thing that the black witch can't control! She's cut off your connections to your servant and to your daughter again. Help us save her!"

"Your demon is just as likely to kill her as save her."

The Rakshasa burst out, bending Zev's spine and taking over his shape, stretching him to the beast's seven-foot height and three-hundred-pound frame.

"She is mine," he thundered. Then the beast raced toward the castle, moving faster than animal or man.

"Rahhh!" Vlad screamed his frustrations to the heavens. How could he have missed the signs? Helgaleena was lost to the black arts and more powerful than any witch he'd ever seen.

He sent the winds to help the beast reach the castle faster. It was a gamble, but it was his daughter's only chance.

"Helgaleena, you're my sister. There's still time. Please don't let this blackness take you." Lavanya pushed back at the wall of magic that was scooting her toward the toppled vanity.

"I was never your sister! We were all your servants, second class, lowly slaves to you and Vlad." Helgaleena's hand twisted and Lavanya felt the air around her thin as the witch squeezed the oxygen out of her lungs. "We were worse than slaves. We were nothing more than trained food."

"Helgaleena!" Lavanya fell against the vanity. She saw the deadly calm in Helgaleena's eyes and knew it would be the last thing she ever saw if she didn't think of something fast. Desperately she searched the wreckage of the vanity for a weapon as Helgaleena squeezed her diaphragm as tightly as an old-fashioned corset on steroids. She threw perfume bottles and jars of face cream at Helgaleena with no effect. Everything just bounced off the sparkly black aura that surrounded her.

She collapsed to the floor, clutching her chest. Lack of air wouldn't kill a vampire, but it could kill her, and Helgaleena was well aware of that.

"Good-bye, dear sister. I hope you'll understand if I do not mourn your passing." Helgaleena kicked Lavanya so hard her body flipped over. Stars circled her vision. But then she felt the sharp edge of Dylan's Kenchii Dragon shears against her fingers. If only she could draw one more breath.

Helgaleena twisted her hands together as if she were wringing out a towel, forcing every last bit of air from Lavanya's body. As her body stilled, Helgaleena dusted her hands.

"Good riddance," Helgaleena murmured. Then she spread her arms wide. "I am ready to accept your strength."

Lightning flashed in the dark sky, lighting the room as the Rakshasa demon began to form in the middle of the suite. It could see a young woman standing over Lavanya's body. She looked nothing like Helgaleena, but the demon recognized the black aura surrounding her. He didn't hesitate to move her away from Lavanya. Almost before he was fully formed he charged Helgaleena and shoved her back. She flew through the air and smashed into the standing mirror in Lavanya's bathroom.

The Rakshasa roared at the woman, his displeasure and pain making the sound horrible to hear. He saw Lavanya lying unconscious on the floor. He bent to smell her and then howled with grief before tuning to dispose of the witch. He panted with anger, waiting and hoping that she'd move and he'd have something to attack.

The beast needed something to punish. When the witch didn't move on her own, he lost patience. He pulled her body from the broken glass and threw her across the bedroom sitting area. Then he kicked her as hard as he could. The witch hit the wall across the room and blood bubbled from her mouth, further exciting the beast.

The Rakshasa wanted to devour her body and soul. She would taste bitter, and her soul would feed the demon. Zev was aware enough to let the Rakshasa run wild. His grief combined with the Rakshasa's anger and consumed them both. Later he would burn the witch's remains to prevent the black magic from tempting another. But for now he let the demon rage with his claws and fists.

Vlad's connection to Renfield was returning, and he could feel his anxiety. But Lavanya was his only concern, and he couldn't allow his panic and stress to combine with Renfield's. The emotions would hurt his servant, maybe beyond repair, so Vlad closed him off. The Rakshasa seemed to be busy tenderizing his witch dinner by kicking the woman. The beast barely noticed Vlad's entrance, and Vlad gave the Rakshasa a wide berth as he made his way to his daughter.

Lavanya lay in a crumpled heap. He concentrated on his connection with her. He closed his eyes as he picked up her limp body, holding her gently against his chest. He rocked his daughter and patted her as if she were a child again. The total grief he'd felt when his beautiful wives passed away was nothing compared to the grief he felt at this moment. A parent should never outlive a child. He'd heard the humans say that, but he'd never understood it until this moment.

"Please, Lavanya" he murmured. "I need you, my baby girl. I may never wake again."

Lavanya's head lay on Vlad's shoulder as he whispered tenderly to her. So much love he contained. Why hadn't he told her this before now?

As if in a dream she saw the wreckage around her and watched the Rakshasa beat Helgaleena from above the action—at once a part of the room, but separated. The demon had pushed Helgaleena against the fireplace while he tore into her neck. As Lavanya let her life fade away, she felt some satisfaction that Helgaleena would not gain power from her death.

One last look at Zev. That's all she wanted. As she gathered her strength, she opened to the sight again. The Rakshasa still attacked Helgaleena. But the witch wasn't lifeless, as before. Helgaleena was drawing symbols in the air between her body and the Rakshasa.

No! Lavanya thought.

Lavanya fought against the darkness that wanted to swallow her. Vlad patted her back and rocked her. Between one beat and the next, she pulled strength from him. Her body jerked as she pulled in a huge gust of air. Pushing away from her father's chest, she aimed and threw the sterling silver dragon shears in one quick movement.

Helgaleena was impaled right between the eyes. Her hand fell limp just before she could push the spell she was casting into the Rakshasa's heart. The force of the scissors drove Helgaleena's head into the big, open fireplace. The Rakshasa jerked back and released the witch's neck in time to be out of the way of the flames that engulfed her body. The Rakshasa growled in rage that his dinner was denied.

"Lavanya, get behind me." Vlad's voice was whisper quiet, but his tone was no-nonsense. He never expected anyone to disobey him.

"No. Father, get out of the way." Lavanya tried to push him back from where she still sat in the broken glass. The Rakshasa lost interest in Vlad as soon as she spoke. The beast had eyes only for Lavanya and looked as if he'd go through a mountain to get to her. Her father was basically indestructible and yet she doubted he could stop the demon. She pushed around his legs and spoke to the advancing demon. "Zev."

"The Rakshasa is in control! Stay behind me!" Vlad pushed her hands back and stayed in front of her.

A crash and shower of glass erupted from the large windows that overlooked the mountains. Glass rained down on all of them. Lavanya covered her eyes against the flying debris. Before she could see what caused the explosion, someone—or something—picked her up, carried her into the suite's bathroom, and dropped her with a thud on the marble floor.

All she could see when she came to rest on her ass was the black, marble-covered back of the Rakshasa demon. His growl echoed off the inner walls of the room, hurting her ears. Lavanya peeked between the beast's strong, muscled legs. First she saw clawed, black feet, and then a graceful black wing whooshed through the room, taking up most of the space.

"Ooh, Lilitu see the Rakshasa! Renfield, please make the Rakshasa give the Lilitu a small taste. Usha had more than Lilitu. It not fair." The gargoyle stomped her foot like a toddler who wanted extra dessert. Lavanya giggled at the simple, childlike innocence of the gargoyle.

"Lavanya!" Dylan rushed to the door that the angry Rakshasa demon had blocked and pulled up short. "Zev! Get that thing under control! I need to see her and make sure she's not hurt!"

Dylan moved forward, and the Rakshasa growled a warning from deep in his throat.

"Zev." Lavanya stood and placed her hand on the back of the Rakshasa. The beast's muscled back rippled, and he purred at her touch. "Thank you." She wrapped her arms around the beast and held tight. The Rakshasa howled, and the vibrations went through Lavanya, tickling her and warming her inside and out. The clawed arm wrapped around Lavanya's back and held her in place.

"Lavanya, step away from the demon." Vlad's deep voiced echoed in the room. "Lilitu, come along, my darling. I'll give you more than a taste of that Rakshasa."

"Stop it, Vlad!" Lavanya rubbed her face against the demon's back, trying to keep him calm.

"Lilitu, if you come near him, I won't let Renfield make you big anymore." Lavanya slowly wound her way around to the front of the demon, never leaving his arms, and looked up into his black eyes.

"Thank you for coming for me, Rakshasa. I could feel you, and your blood allowed me to see the evil in the witch and kept me alive."

Lavanya put her arms against the beast's shoulders. "I need Zev now. I'm safe." The Rakshasa looked over her head and growled a warning to Vlad and everyone else before he released her. With a loud roar, he shifted back into Zev.

"Lavanya!" Zev wrapped his arms around her and pulled her into his embrace. "I was crazy when I saw you there beneath the witch. I couldn't—I thought you were dead."

"Nope. Well, almost. But I saw Helgaleena twist a spell directed at you, and I couldn't let go."

"Nice toss, by the way. I owe you one." Zev smiled down at her. And then began brushing glass and plaster out of her hair.

"Humm. Are you okay?" Dylan rushed over to look at her now that Zev was back in control.

"I'm fine now." Lavanya and Zev moved out into the main room and took in the mess. "Well, Lilitu, you and your sister are even." She took Zev's hand, not wanting to stop their connection. "You both certainly know how to make an entrance."

"I sorry, Mistress, but Renfield said I had to break the window and get him and Dylan to you. He was mighty worried about you." Lilitu shuffled her clawed feet and pulled her wings back. It reminded Lavanya of a child who'd just broken their mother's favorite vase.

"Ahhh, Lilitu, it's only fair. Your sister got to bust in and save me last time, it was your turn. Thank you."

Lilitu seemed to get taller from the praise and thanks. "You are most welcome, Mistress." The gargoyle bowed to her and perched at the smashed window so she could open her wings.

"Actually, Lilitu is one up on Usha," Renfield said with a smile. "She had to break my window to get us out before we could come rescue you."

"It was a stroke of genius, Renfield," Dylan said. "I would have never thought of the gargoyles." He gestured, laughing. "So I'm guessing that the pile of smoking ash over by the fireplace is Helgaleena?"

"Yes." Vlad stepped into the middle of the group. "Lilitu, I thank you for your service to Mr. Renfield. You will be rewarded. Please return to your position with your sister." Vlad motioned to the window.

"Yes, Master. Always happy to serve you." Lilitu's great wings opened and caught a draft. She hovered and nodded at Renfield before she dipped below the window.

"Master Renfield, I'm glad to see you up and about. Please see that the servants clean up this mess and replace the windows as soon as possible."

"Yes, Master." Renfield bowed and headed to the phone by the bed.

"Dylan, I trust that you will see to getting your Mistress's things in order and packed for your journey."

"Yeah. Of course." Dylan looked at Lavanya to see if Vlad was being an ass on purpose or if he truly was just a bastard. Lavanya mouthed *sorry* to Dylan behind Vlad's back. Dylan gave her a hug. "Are you really okay?"

"I am now. Thanks for coming to my rescue. Very noble. You'll have to fill me in later about why you had to fly a gargoyle into my suite." Dylan broke out laughing.

"Double, double toil and trouble! I see the luggage, I'll finish up." Then he whispered, winking in Zev's direction, "You'll need to fill me in later."

It was Lavanya's turn to laugh. "You'll be the first to know as soon as I do." As she looked into Zev's hazel eyes, he drew her in closer to his side. She melted against him.

"Lavanya, I'd like to speak with you, if I may." Vlad held out his hand, motioning her to the door. Lavanya looked down to where her hand entwined with Zev's.

"Go ahead," he said. "I'll help Dylan find your stuff."

"I—"

"Go ahead. I won't go anywhere without you." When Lavanya seemed like she wouldn't let go, he leaned down and whispered in her ear. "The wicked witch is dead, and I don't think anyone could force the Rakshasa to leave again. I don't have that much control over him now that you've charmed him." Zev kissed her lightly.

"Lavanya." Vlad's stern voice broke the magic of the kiss. Lavanya sighed against Zev's lips.

"Yes, Father." She pulled away and left the room.

"Your services are no longer needed, Rakshasa," Vlad said when she'd gone. "Go back to your shack and do not dare to bother my daughter again."

Lavanya marched right back into the room in time to see Zev move into Vlad's face. She pushed her way between the two men.

"Father, I am not a child, and I haven't been one for more than fifty years. I won't let you treat him this way. Or me, for that matter. We—" she looked for Zev's reaction and got strength from his smile. "We'll be leaving tonight as soon as we can gather a few things. I'm not sure where we're going." Zev pulled her into his arms. "But I'll contact Renfield and let him know where we are and how I can be reached."

She caught Dylan's raised brow. "And Dylan's going on a vacation, a much needed vacation." She smiled at her best friend. "For as long as he'd like, but I hope not too long, because I'll miss him. But that's up to him."

"Sweet! Beaches, babes, and booze! I'm sooo happy!" Dylan winked at her.

"Lavanya." Vlad's face was like stone. "You cannot go away with this animal. He is a demon!"

Lavanya leaned back against Zev. "Funny. I'm reminded of an old friend and the great advice she always used when making a tough decision. She always said, *between two evils, I'll always choose the one I haven't tried before*. I'm choosing him, Father."

"He's a monster, an animal—a demon! I will not allow it!"

"And you're Vlad the Impaler!" Lavanya took a deep, calming breath and softened her tone. "My mother found something to love in you. I may never understand the relationship she had with you, but I've found something to love in Zev. We're both unique, and I love him and his Rakshasa." A low hum of a growl rippled through

Zev and into Lavanya, tickling her.

Lavanya, I forbid it. If you disobey me I will disown you.

"We're leaving tonight. I'll let Renfield know where I am and how we can be reached if you change your mind." She started to reach out to him, remembering the loving words he'd said as she'd almost died in his arms. But he turned and left the room. She buried her face in Zev's embrace.

"Don't worry, dear." Renfield came over to where Lavanya and Zev huddled together against Vlad's anger. "I'll keep him updated on where you are. It'll take time. The master never likes change—and even less when it's not his idea."

"No shit, Sherlock!" Dylan piped in as he stooped to pick up Lavanya's brush. "So, do I really get a vacation? Is it paid?"

"Yes, you get a vacation, and of course, it's paid," Lavanya said. "Oh, right after you reschedule the cruise for the couples that was supposed to sail next week." She looked up into Zev's face. "I think I'll be busy for a while."

"You'll be very busy." Zev pulled her into his arms. "Where would you like to go?"

"Anywhere with you." Lavanya stood on her tippy toes and kissed Zev.

"Uggh, Renfield, save me from this lovey-dovey stuff." Dylan hurried out into the hall with two Louis Vuitton chests.

LYNNE STEVIE

EPILOGUE

The Prophecy Fullfilled

Vlad sat in the shadows of a small café in Prague. He pretended to read. But as his tea cooled, he eyed the young woman working on a computer a few tables away. His cheeks held a light flush that said he'd fed recently, but he still felt hungry as he watched the woman chat with the barista.

Part of his restlessness was caused by anger, and since he couldn't go back to sleep, he decided that a few years of reckless behavior with a few thousand women might help change his attitude. Four months had passed, and he still couldn't bring himself to ask Renfield about Lavanya. He knew logically that Zev was a good match for her—strong enough to protect her and unusually suited to her because she was a child of the night and day, as he was. But he couldn't forgive her blatant disobedience. He still fumed. Lost in his thoughts, he didn't hear the old woman sit down behind him.

"So, are you gonna drink that tea?" she asked.

"What?" Vlad turned to find Inez sitting at a small table tucked among the bookshelves lining the wall. She looked old and feeble, yet she had the confidence of a woman who could handle anything. He leaned back in his chair, legs out, his feet crossed at the ankle, and his hands behind his head. Looking to everyone like a young man without a care in the world.

"How did you find me, old woman?" Vlad spoke to her without turning or giving her his full attention.

"Well, dear me, I didn't realize you were lost." Inez left her seat, kicking at his legs as she passed, forcing him to move. Once he acknowledged her and sat up properly, she sat down opposite him at his small table. "Are you planning to drink that, or can I have it?" She tapped the delicate china cup that sat untouched in front of him and a crease wrinkled her brow. "It may be too cold already."

"What do you want?" Vlad pushed the cup across the table

toward her.

"How old are you, Vlad?" Inez took the cup in her shaking hands to test its warmth.

"What? I'm old—you know that. Did you track me down just to ask my age?"

"When was the last time you were surprised?" The old woman's eyes lit up with delight. She held the cup as if it were precious.

"What. Do. You. Want!" Vlad's small outburst, though not loud, disturbed a few of the scattered diners, who stirred in their seats and looked at the exit.

"It's ironic," Inez said. "The number of years a man lives doesn't correlate to how mature he is. I'll never understand how you all remain spoiled little boys under all that muscle and hair." She set the cup gently on the table.

"Don't you have something better to do than irritate me?"

"Aye, I do, actually, but here I am anyway." Inez leaned over and softly blew into the cup as if it needed to be cooled. "Do you doubt my grandson's love for your daughter?"

"What?" Vlad feigned ignorance about the abrupt topic change, but he knew why she'd sought him out. The only reason had to be Lavanya and the demon. "I don't wish to discuss this with you, Inez. The matter is closed. Nothing you can say will change my mind. She disobeyed me. She is not my daughter."

"Do you believe Zev isn't strong enough to protect her? Or that his Rakshasa wouldn't protect her, as well? Or maybe you believe she doesn't really love him." Inez put her pinky into the china cup and swirled the cold tea.

"None of that matters," Vlad insisted, and it was all true. He wouldn't forgive her willfulness and blatant disregard for his word.

"So your mind is set. Nothing I could say, or nothing that could occur, would sway your hardened resolve." Inez peeked into the cup as if looking for something.

"You know the answer to that question. My mind is set. I'm surprised Lavanya would stoop to sending you out on her behalf." Vlad pushed his chair out to leave. His appetite was gone.

"Oh, she didn't send me." Inez pulled her finger from the tea and flipped the dripping digit at Vlad, splattering his face and shirt with cold tea. "I just wanted to share this moment with family."

"Inez, go home." All the anger left him. She must have finally gone crazy, and he knew that killing the insane old woman wouldn't make him feel any better. "We've known each other a long time, but we'll never be family."

"You heard me correctly." She held up her hand as he started to speak. "See for yourself."

She pushed the tea cup toward him. Vlad hesitated, but couldn't stop from looking down into the cup. Where there was once cold tea the shade of clear amber, now he saw a picture of Lavanya and Zev embracing. Lavanya's face was without makeup, and her hair was pulled high on her head in a messy knot. It somehow reminded him of her beautiful mother and how much he longed to see her smiling face again.

"Did you want to anger me, old woman? Do you want to die? Is that it? I'd be happy to—" His eye caught on the scene as Zev pulled away from Lavanya and put his hand on her belly. Vlad watched mesmerized as Zev bent so that his head rested on Lavanya's... *Was her stomach bigger?* Then Zev looked up at *his daughter* with love so strong that Vlad had to close his eyes because the sight threatened to double him over.

"No, it can't be," he whispered.

"Do you want to know the rest of Nya's prophecy?" Vlad was too stunned to answer, but the old witch didn't need any encouragement to continue.

"Nya foretold that you'd give your heart to Zev, and that you'd be relieved, almost happy, to give it to him. You know that part, but she also said that Zev would continue our blood line!"

Vlad stared into the old woman's bright eyes, and all the feedings didn't keep any color in his cheeks. He was pasty white when she delivered her final words.

"We're gonna be grandparents! Well technically, I'm gonna to be a great-grandma, but you get the idea. Welcome to the family, Vlad."

The End

LYNNE STEVIE

Hello Reader! I hope you enjoyed reading Between Two Evils as much as I enjoyed writing it! I have to say that one of the best parts was learning about Runes and the art of Divination. The Runes Workbook by Leon D. Wild is a great source of information as well as the site Rune Meanings, if you'd like to read a little more about them. As always I took the information and embellished a bit for my own purposes to create this novel, but I tried to stick close to the original meanings of the staves.

I hate to impose, but if you liked Between Two Evils, please tell a friend or leave a review. As an independent Author I need all the word of mouth marketing I can get. If you like Immortals, Dark Angels, and Magical Ancient Weapons read on for an excerpt of my novel Angel's Kiss. To connect with me in the social media world visit my Author's page on Facebook at Author Lynne Stevie, or I can be found on Goodreads, Twitter and Pinterest. Thanks again for reading Between Two Evils!

Alexandria Hayes-Lewis was blessed with the perfect life. By day she managed her family's detective agency. By night she made love to her devilishly handsome husband.

Lexie never knew she'd been marked at birth by an Angel's Kiss—until one ordinary case turned deadly.

A brutal attack awakens a deeply hidden family legacy: a superhuman strength and vitality. Not only is she stronger—her gift also increases the power of immortal beings. With the secrets of her heritage unlocked, and her legacy revealed, Lexie becomes the prey.

Terrified by changes she doesn't understand and sensual

nightmares she can't control, Lexie desperately searches for ways to harness the power flowing through her veins. But when people die and her family is threatened, she takes the ultimate step against those who want to shield her, those who want to possess her, and those who want to kill her. In a frantic bid for freedom, she enlists the help of an unusual guardian and an ancient weapon.

Will it be enough to save her?

For a taste of a Dark Angel's Kiss click here Excerpt from Angel's Kiss or visit my web site at www.lynnestevie.com

www.ingramcontent.com/pod-product-compliance
Lightning Source LLC
Chambersburg PA
CBHW030401030726
47497CB00002B/436